"Please..."

"Please what?" She should resent his teasing, but even through the mad tumult of her heartbeat, she heard the edge in his voice.

"Please touch me," she whispered. "You're tormenting me."

"I like to see you desperate," he said softly.

"Aren't you desperate too?" Where did she find the courage to ask the question?

"Oh yes."

"Then why not touch me?"

He laughed and the sound fizzed through her blood, heating it to boiling point. "Because your desperation builds my anticipation."

"Do you always play games?"

"Only when I enjoy them."

By Anna Campbell

MY RECKLESS SURRENDER
CAPTIVE OF SIN
TEMPT THE DEVIL
UNTOUCHED
CLAIMING THE COURTESAN

Anna Campbell

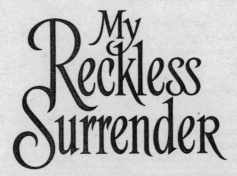

My Reckless Surrender

AVON

An Imprint of HarperCollinsPublishers

AVON BOOKS
An Imprint of HarperCollins*Publishers*
10 East 53rd Street
New York, New York 10022-5299

Copyright © 2010 by Anna Campbell
Excerpts from *Captive of Sin, Tempt the Devil, Untouched, Claiming the Courtesan* copyright © 2009, 2007 by Anna Campbell
Excerpt from *Sugar Creek* copyright © 2010 by Toni Herzog
ISBN 978-0-06-168431-9
www.avonromance.com

First Avon Books paperback printing: June 2010

Avon Trademark Reg. U.S. Pat. Off. and in Other Countries, Marca Registrada, Hecho en U.S.A.
HarperCollins® is a registered trademark of HarperCollins Publishers.

Printed in the U.S.A.

10 9 8 7 6 5 4 3 2 1

To my very dear friend Amanda Bell,
who has listened to me talk about writing
for the last thirty years!

Acknowledgments

As always, I have a lot of people to thank!

Firstly a big thank you to the wonderful people at Avon Books. My great editor May Chen. Her tireless assistant, Amanda Bergeron. The art department who designed this beautiful cover. Everyone in marketing, particularly Pamela Spengler-Jaffe and Christine Maddalena. I'd also like to thank the people at the Australian Avon office, including Shona Martyn, Linda Funnell, Karen-Maree Griffiths, Christine Farmer, and Jordan Weaver. And I'm adding a really heartfelt thank you to my agent, Nancy Yost.

There are two people to whom I owe more gratitude than I can express when it comes to this book. Thank you to Annie West and Christine Wells who are the best critique partners a writer could ask for.

Thank you to all my writing friends, particularly Helen Bianchin, Sophia Nash, Pamela Palmer, the fabulous Romance Bandits, Kandy Shepherd, Cathleen Ross, Nicola Cornick, Kathryn Smith, Keira Soleore, Louisa Cornell, Stephanie Laurens, and Lorraine Heath. Gratitude also goes to Michelle Buonfiglio, Kim Castillo, Marisa O'Neill, and Maria Lokken. You girls always brighten the day for me! Two fellow writers who deserve a special mention are Sharon Archer and Vanessa Barneveld.

I'd also like to thank the many readers who have contacted me to say how much you love the books. I can't express to you how much your wonderful messages mean to me.

Chapter One

London
July 1827

I want to be your lover."

Diana was shocked to hear herself issue the invitation. Even more shocked that she didn't stumble over the bald words.

She'd never been sure she'd summon courage to speak them aloud. Yet they emerged clearly, firmly, without hesitation.

The statement sounded confident, as if she spent her life asking strangers into her bed.

Silence descended. Lengthened. Drew out to become uncomfortable.

She curbed the urge to twine her gloved hands together in her lap. Even though she was sick with nerves, she needed to appear strong, in control. Her heart battered the walls of her chest. She prayed its frantic gallop wasn't audible in the quiet room.

You can do this, Diana.

On such a sultry summer afternoon, the veiling over her

face was suffocating. Her teal dress clung more tightly than her usual clothing. Part of the plan, of course, but uncomfortable. She realized she gritted her teeth, and even though he couldn't see her face, she relaxed her jaw.

The veils obscured her view. Nonetheless, her attention fixed unwaveringly on her target, sitting across the mahogany desk from her. Through the filmy barrier, she discerned little, apart from his height and dark hair.

Tarquin Vale. The Earl of Ashcroft.

Plutocrat. Collector. Devotee of reformist politics.

Rake. Debauchee. Hellspawn.

Unwitting key to a future greater than she'd dared dream was possible.

An instant before the electric pause became unbearable, the earl leaned back. She couldn't see his expression in detail, but tension snapped in the heavy air, scented with the tang of old books, leather, and ink. He braced his elbows on the arms of his chair and steepled his elegant hands in front of him. An incongruously scholarly pose for a man she knew to be shallow and worldly.

"I . . . see," he said slowly.

He had a deep voice, pleasant, musical. She imagined he employed it to devastating effect when he set out to seduce. Even sitting here, despising him, despising what she must do, that dark honey baritone rippled down her spine like a caress.

Taut with anticipation, she waited for him to say more, to agree. Reputation indicated he was an undiscriminating and profligate lover. No chance he'd refuse her. She was easy game.

Still, he sat in silence. Still, that strange tension crackled and sizzled. Like summer lightning trapped inside this opulent library with its beautifully bound books lining the walls, its gleaming celestial and terrestrial globes, its elaborately carved furniture.

Her lurid imagination had conjured many settings for her ruin. Bowers of sin draped in scarlet satin. Cabinets decorated with murals of fleshy nudes. A dark cellar crammed with instruments of gothic torture. A library wasn't on the list.

So far, nothing had gone as she'd expected.

For a minute upon her arrival, she hadn't even been sure Lord Ashcroft would see her. His butler looked surprised when she asked for his lordship. Although a libertine like Ashcroft must be used to unaccompanied, unidentified women turning up on his doorstep.

But the tall, austere old man, more like St. Peter than a family retainer, had stared down his nose in disapproval as he admitted her into the black-and-white-tiled hall. And he'd taken a discouragingly long time to return with news that his lordship awaited her.

She hadn't given her name, just said she was "a lady" calling on business with the master. She supposed "business" described her mission as well as any other word.

Surreptitiously, Diana straightened a backbone already stiffer than a ramrod and forced herself to breathe the hot fug that substituted for air. She felt light-headed with the heat, with trepidation, with suspense. Everything she wanted hinged on the next few seconds. She couldn't let Lord Ashcroft guess how badly she needed him.

Through her veils, she watched him tilt his head as if acknowledging a point in a debate. Or first blood in a fencing match.

"An interesting proposition."

She licked dry lips, thanking heaven he wouldn't detect yet another sign she wasn't as composed as she struggled to appear. "I see no point in coy games."

"Clearly." Was that a hint of irony?

She braced herself against a crippling mixture of shame and embarrassment. She'd sworn to do this. Nothing would stop her. Nothing. When she weighed this moment and the moments inevitably to come against the promised reward, her present discomfort didn't signify.

"Are you a bawd?"

He asked the question casually, as if it made little difference. She was sure it didn't. She'd heard he bedded anything in skirts, lady, professional, milkmaid. Still, heat prickled her face. Once again, she was grateful for the gauzy gray veiling.

"No."

In spite of her efforts, the denial frayed with resentment. She couldn't read his reactions with great accuracy, but something told her the sharp response piqued his curiosity in a way nothing else had.

"And yet . . ." His quiet voice held a trace of derision that, illogically, angered her.

Of course, he suspected she was a professional touting for trade. What else could he think when she arrived uninvited and proposed herself as a candidate for his squalid attentions?

Get used to it, she told herself grimly. She'd just set out on this particular path to perdition. Before she reached her destination, she had mountains and chasms and deserts to negotiate. It was too late to turn missish, even if humiliation curdled like sour milk in her belly.

When she didn't reply, he went on, still studying her over his braced hands. "Why choose me for this honor? I hesitate to say singular."

She registered the insult. It puzzled more than angered. He was a legendary voluptuary. Women must accost him constantly. He certainly accosted them. What right had he to claim the high moral ground?

She raised her chin and shot him a glare he wouldn't see. In her bedchamber, when she'd dressed for this encounter, she'd recognized her mission would be difficult. Here, faced with a polite, recalcitrant gentleman who wasn't acting at all like the rapacious rake of renown, it began to seem impossible.

Anger had one useful effect. It lent her spirit to continue, to launch into the story she'd prepared should this roué bother to ask why she offered herself. "I am a country widow."

He gave another of those terse nods. "My commiserations."

Her gloved fists clenched on the arms of her chair before she realized the gesture contradicted her spurious calm. She straightened her fingers and sucked in a deep but inaudible breath.

Already she didn't like this man.

No matter. All that mattered was what she gained if she persisted. One short descent into sin, and in return, she'd win everything she desired.

It seemed a fair bargain. Or at least it had until she sat in front of this surprisingly formidable man and offered to become his mistress.

She was annoyed and uncomfortable and at a disadvantage. Strangely, for all her uncertainty, she wasn't frightened. Before she'd arrived, she expected fear to be paramount. After all, Lord Ashcroft would soon have her at his mercy.

Or at least that was what she wanted him to think.

She forced herself to speak. "I'm in Town for . . . experience."

"How edifying. And am I now included in the sights of the capital, a human version of the Tower of London?"

He spoke evenly, but his question held a bite. She was disconcerted to realize he was a proud man. The perception sat incongruously with everything she knew about his prodigal appetites.

She still didn't feel any fear. Something else. The heady awareness she taunted a tiger, perhaps.

Confused by his reaction, she didn't answer directly. "As I

said, my lord, what purpose beating around the bush? I want a lover. I've chosen you."

His low laugh shivered over her skin. "Why? Have we met?"

"No."

"So my question remains. Why me?"

"I've . . . I've seen you." She cursed the betraying stammer.

Last week she'd arrived in London and glimpsed him at a distance, driving a terrifyingly fragile phaeton down Bond Street. She'd received an impression of a gentleman of fashion, one who imposed perfect discipline on his high-bred horses. Perfect discipline at odds with his unruly life. A stylishly angled hat had shaded his features although she'd noted a determined jaw and a firm, expressive mouth. Her experience with rakes was nonexistent, but she'd imagined someone less compelling, someone whose face immediately revealed his moral weakness.

"The fleeting sight of me ignited a fiery passion?" He sounded cynical, as well he might.

"No."

Before she'd arrived, she'd decided to stick to truth as much as possible. Anyway, she doubted she could carry off an appearance of being love-struck. Not to mention she guessed any mention of love was likely to send her quarry hurtling in the opposite direction.

She swallowed, her throat tight. "Even in the country, your feats as a lover are famous."

Another soft laugh. Another frisson of awareness down her backbone. "How . . . flattering."

She knew he meant absolutely the opposite.

Damn him, why didn't he just leap on her and have done with it? This dance of question and answer was torture. She steeled herself to continue. "I want a man to show me the pleasures of the flesh without making further claim. I want a man of reliable discretion."

Strangely, this rogue had a reputation for keeping his mouth shut about his exploits. Most of the gossip emanated from women who had either shared his bed or knew women who did.

"So one encounter?"

Once? Good Lord, no. She didn't endure this humiliation, sacrifice her honor for a single chance at the prize.

"I thought the summer until the ton return to Town, and scandal becomes a risk."

"So a shabby little affair to while away a few uneventful weeks?"

"I don't understand, my lord." She frowned, although she knew he couldn't see her face. Her instincts screamed that, contrary to everything she'd been led to believe, this was no simple transaction with a lusty male animal. "You seem almost . . . hostile."

"Do I indeed?" This time the bite in his voice was unconcealed. "I can't imagine why. After all, a stud bull should be delighted that his services are in demand."

Before she could stop herself, a horrified sound emerged from her throat. He couldn't know how close to the truth he ventured with this sarcastic response.

Thank goodness, he misunderstood her reaction. "Your pardon if plain speaking offends, madam."

She dragged scattered thoughts together. With every moment in Lord Ashcroft's company, the unhampered progression of her plan to its fulfillment seemed less and less likely.

When she'd planned confronting the earl in his lair, she'd asked herself how she could intrigue a man jaded with the easy availability of any woman. She'd hit upon the veils as likely to tickle his curiosity, arouse his interest. A man tired of the usual amusements would surely find mystery alluring. Mystery combined with complete willingness. She'd assumed a stranger offering a few weeks' entertainment, a stranger who asked nothing more than the use of his body, would elicit immediate cooperation.

But then, before she'd met him, she'd imagined a slavering debaucher. This self-possessed man was a million miles away from those imaginings.

Now she wondered if perhaps she should have tried some more subtle approach than a direct invitation. But it was too late to back out.

Her jaw ached with tension. "Surely you don't respond to all women who . . . invite you this way?"

"Only strangers who remain anonymous and shrouded from my sight." The snap was still there, astonishing her. Anger was the last reaction she'd expected. "Do you intend to wear your veils when you fuck me, madam?"

His language jarred her, reminded her she teetered closer to the gutter than she wanted to contemplate. Or acknowledge.

Foolish woman she was, in the privacy of her bedroom, she hadn't imagined he'd care what she looked like. Not when her body was his for the taking, and she promised to do anything he wanted.

But of course he cared what she looked like. He was famous for only choosing the most beautiful of paramours.

Yet again, she felt completely outmatched in this wicked game.

Her heart accelerated to a crazy gallop. She licked her lips again and told herself, compared to what else Lord Ashcroft and she would do before they finished, uncovering her face scarcely counted.

Still, it was almost impossible to lift the veils. Her hands trembled, revealing her real feelings. She gathered faltering courage like a shield. To fail at the first fence? Over something as trivial as showing her face? God give her strength.

With a suddenly defiant gesture, she flung back her veils.

A chaos of impressions slammed into her. The day was humid, no breeze entered the room, but even so, the air felt cool against her cheeks after the stifling concealment. The library came into focus, its rich colors glowing in the afternoon sunlight.

And at last she saw Lord Ashcroft without a distorting filter.

Her heart crashed to a halt and her throat squeezed shut, trapping her breath.

Lucifer, the most beautiful. Prince of angels. Bearer of light.

The great tempter.

The Earl of Ashcroft was dark, almost swarthy. With an angular, strong-boned, ascetic face. A scholar's face. If one ignored the full, sensual mouth.

If one ignored his eyes.

Jade green and appraising her with unsettling intelligence and a palpable cynicism. "Very pretty."

Heat rose in Diana's cheeks. She wasn't vain enough to expect swoons of delight at the merest sight of her, but surely she warranted more reaction than those two flat words.

"Thank you," she said, equally flatly.

Perhaps Lord Ashcroft was so used to rutting with diamonds of the first water that her charms paled in comparison. For the first time, the prospect of failure—and all that meant—loomed.

When she'd contemplated this scheme, she'd wondered if she possessed the audacity to carry it off. Naively, she'd never considered that this notorious rake might consider her beneath his touch.

His lips twitched with sardonic humor. "And your name?"

"Diana."

She'd toyed with using a pseudonym and abandoned the idea. It was hard enough playing the strumpet's part, however temporary. Lord Ashcroft addressing her by another woman's name when he took her would shatter her.

"Just Diana?"

"Yes."

He wouldn't recognize her family name even if she had any intention of providing it. Once this was over, she planned to disappear without possibility of discovery. Although a man like Lord Ashcroft had no need to pursue a reluctant lover. He'd quickly find another warm body to fill any vacancy in his bed.

Now she sat before him, it was more difficult to treat him as the cipher he'd become in her mind. The jade eyes were beautiful, startling in his saturnine face. His nose was long and haughty. His brows were straight and black as sin, like the thick hair tumbling over his high forehead.

Like his heart, something in her whispered.

He was handsome. She'd known that. She'd seen sketches of him in the papers. But nothing readied her for the magnetic attraction of those intense, masculine features. Or the vibrant sexuality emanating from him like a low incessant hum.

She'd prepared to deal with a weakling, a victim to his vices. If that was true about Tarquin Vale, it didn't show in his face. For a terrifying moment, she doubted all she'd heard about this rapscallion.

He looked a man of experience. He looked, to her astonishment, a man of judgment. He looked, curse him, anything but bowled over by either her brazen offer or her rustic attractions. Her unformed, hopelessly optimistic ideas about bringing the Earl of Ashcroft under her spell and keeping him there faded like mist under hot summer sun.

This man, she could already tell, did nobody's bidding. Unless it fitted precisely with his own inclinations.

"So we're to be strangers in every sense except the carnal?"

She forced herself to maintain her role. "I seek pleasure. Experience. I seek knowledge from a man who knows his way around a woman's body. Memories to warm a cold, lonely night."

"Quite a responsibility."

To her surprise, she found herself releasing a breath of laughter. "I'm sure you'll rise to the occasion."

His arched eyebrows acknowledged the unintentional double entendre. She blushed and hated herself for it. She needed to appear sophisticated and confident.

"So what's in it for me?"

She bit back an urge to tell him in the bluntest terms. She hadn't expected to have to plead her case. In her wilder imaginings, she'd expected him to drag her off to a bedroom the moment he saw her. Or shove her down onto the carpet.

So far, her imaginings had caused nothing but trouble.

So what was in it for him? "A cooperative, undemanding lover."

A superior smile curved that expressive mouth. "Cooperation I've already got. And believe me, I insist upon a demanding lover."

Curse him and his word games. She tried to sound seductive. Even in her own ears, she didn't succeed. "I offer you an adventure. I offer you something outside your usual pastimes."

The smile didn't waver. "And of course you're completely familiar with my usual pastimes."

How did a lady convince a reluctant gentleman that she belonged in his bed? With every moment, Diana edged further and further away from what she knew.

"I've heard the gossip. A chaste female has the advantage of novelty. Especially a chaste female who makes no call upon you apart from sexual congress."

He released a short laugh. "I've had the best. What makes you think a chaste female will hold my interest?"

She quashed a twinge of pique that she had to draw in this buyer like a costermonger selling apples by the roadside. "Then take up the challenge of transforming a chaste female into a wanton."

His bright green gaze turned speculative. "Ah, now that could be interesting."

Diana's shoulders tightened as she made herself ask the one question that mattered. "Do you accept my terms?"

Another of those electric silences fell. Bristled. Extended.

Lord Ashcroft tapped his fingers together in a considering gesture and surveyed her with glinting jade eyes. She couldn't tell what he was thinking. Automatically her hands curled around the pearled reticule in her lap. She tensed as she awaited his answer.

His gaze left her face to sweep her body. Long black lashes shadowed his cheeks. They should look feminine. They didn't.

Astonishingly, in spite of her nervousness and her irritation with this dissipated scoundrel who refused to fulfill her expectations, her skin tightened in arousal. As the cool gaze studied her breasts, her nipples hardened.

Surely it was fear that stirred her reaction. Her suddenly damp palms. The frantic tattoo of her pulse.

She never lied to herself. Something in her responded to this dismissive, arrogant, spectacular man. Something long denied, crushed, unfamiliar, perturbing. Planning this reckless gamble, she'd never factored in cravings of her own.

"Lord Ashcroft?" she asked sharply when his attention didn't shift from her bosom.

The eyes he raised were opaque, like cloudy green ice. "My dear lady, flattered as I am, I must decline your generous offer."

Chapter Two

❦❦❦❦❦❦❦❦❦❦❦❦

$\mathcal{T}$he earl's voice was wintry. He sounded as if he turned away an importuning tradesman. To Diana's chagrin, her color rose higher. Anger stirred. Anger and shock.

Wildly, she cast around for some inducement to convince him he wanted her in his bed. She looked into that handsome, implacable face and saw not a spark of attraction. Not even a spark of interest.

Mortification knotted her belly. She wanted to be proud and disdainful. Treat him with the contempt he obviously felt for her. Instead, one shaky word emerged from her lips. "Why?"

Annoyance darkened his striking features. "Madam, there is no point in . . ."

As she rose, her legs were unsteady. She had no idea what to do, she was lost, bewildered, embarrassed. She couldn't countenance defeat even though defeat stared her in the face. And so early in the game. "Your pardon."

He stood as she did and rounded the desk in two or three powerful strides. Blindly she turned toward the door. She should stay, fight him. All she wanted right now was to leave.

The glittering, magnificent reward that lured her to pros-

titute herself sailed completely out of reach. She couldn't
bear it.

"Madam. Diana . . ."

She made a gesture of denial although the sound of her
Christian name in that deep, vibrant voice made every nerve
buzz with awareness. Her trembling hand closed around the
doorknob and turned it.

The door didn't budge.

A large masculine hand flattened on the mahogany panel
in front of her. A large masculine hand attached to a long
masculine arm.

Panic joined her whirling maelstrom of emotions.

They were alone. It was his house. She'd placed herself
outside the protections society offered chaste women.

The breath jammed in her lungs. Slowly, she turned and
looked up at him. Surprising really, how far up. She hadn't
realized quite how tall he was. His body was so beautifully
proportioned, his height hadn't seemed unusual when he'd
stood for her entrance and exit.

Except she clearly wasn't making an exit anytime soon.

"What do you want?" she asked in a thready whisper, her
eyes fastening on that remarkable face, with its intelligence
and wickedness.

"Perhaps I want you," Ashcroft murmured. And watched her
gray eyes darken with fear and a fascination she couldn't
hide, much as he knew she tried to.

Which made no sense when she'd boldly offered herself,
cool as a drink of springwater on a summer's day.

She had beautiful eyes. Large, clear, and brilliant, shadowed by thick dark gold lashes that matched her elegant
brows but not her bright gold hair, just visible under the
bonnet.

Ashcroft frowned down at the woman, the pores of his
skin tightening with unwelcome arousal. And warning.

Nothing about her added up. He didn't trust her. Instinct

urged him to throw her out on her stylish rump and pray he never encountered her again.

Yet he wasn't entirely ready to let her go.

This close, his senses filled with her scent. Green apples. Disconcertingly innocent. And beneath that fresh perfume, a subtle female warmth.

Since she'd raised her veils with that absurdly dramatic gesture, he hadn't been able to look away. She was exquisite. Slender and graceful, with a purity of feature he'd never seen before. She looked like a Madonna, yet hawked herself like a streetwalker.

Any man would pay a fortune for her favors. If she was a courtesan. He already knew she wasn't.

Perhaps she was the country widow she claimed. His intuition insisted she wasn't completely honest. If not about everything, about most of what she'd said.

His intuition, unlike the women he'd known, never lied.

"You don't want me." Resentment beaded her low voice. "You just said . . ."

A pulse fluttered under the delicate skin of her bare throat. He told himself he should take pity on her. Except she didn't cringe away, and her face held stubbornness as well as fear.

He didn't know what she wanted of him. Not what she asked, although he recognized the signs that she found him attractive. She'd needed courage to come here, and she needed courage to continue staring into his eyes.

He'd always admired courage. Unwilling interest wove its way through anger and doubt. "Perhaps I'd like a taste of what's on offer before I decide whether I want more."

Her white throat moved as she swallowed. "You play with me."

His response was curt. "You come here unbidden and insult me. I deserve some fleeting entertainment as recompense."

"In . . . insult you? I meant no . . ."

He leaned closer and bent his head to the crook of her neck and shoulder. With every second, the urge to taste her burgeoned, but he reined it in. Instead, he drew in a lungful of her sweet fragrance.

"That only added to the insult," he murmured. "You appear from nowhere, proposition me as if I were a whore, then you're surprised I'm less than overwhelmed at your generosity."

He heard the ragged saw of her breath, but she didn't pull away. He was astonished he had to struggle to resist kissing the smooth flesh so close to his lips.

"I can't be the first woman who's wanted to . . . sleep with you." Her voice strengthened. "You've invited plenty of women into your bed. What's sauce for the goose is sauce for the gander."

He laughed softly and watched her tremble as his breath brushed her skin. "This gander likes to do his own chasing, Madam Goose."

"So . . ." She paused, and he knew she scrambled after her scattered courage. "Are you chasing?"

He lifted his head and studied her. Except for two hectic flags of color high on her cheekbones, she was pale. Her pupils dilated, the black threatening to swallow the gray. A pink tongue flickered out to moisten her lips.

Hunger slammed through Ashcroft.

Before this he'd toyed with her. In that second, the game became serious.

He wanted her.

By God, he could take her. She'd offered herself. He only needed to hike up her skirts, part her thighs, and ease the aching hardness of his cock in her wet heat.

The idea filled his head with fire.

The onset of such powerful desire made him pause. His instincts still shrieked danger.

Very slowly, he edged away, although his hand remained splayed next to her head on the door. Each inch he removed himself felt like an excruciating mile. That in itself was admonition to banish this puzzling visitor.

"Lord Ashcroft?"

Her low voice played along his veins like music. In spite of his best efforts, he couldn't help but imagine that voice whispering salacious wishes in the privacy of his bed.

As she spoke, her lips parted. All he saw was that lush, glistening mouth. The hint of darkness within. While the rest of her features could be carved for a cathedral sanctuary, her mouth was pure sin. He already knew she'd be delicious.

Against every dictate of self-preservation, he leaned down. One taste. One taste only . . .

He loomed close enough for her breath to warm his face. The sweetness made him close his eyes in sensuous appreciation. When he opened his eyes, her lids drooped, and her body curved toward him in unmistakable surrender.

Kiss her, his physical self insisted.

Don't kiss her, his brain frantically demanded over the rising clamor of his senses.

He stood motionless, caught between the two contradictory impulses. While his heart thumped like a drum, and his blood surged hot and turbulent.

A tiny moan escaped her, and she angled her chin higher in appeal.

The sound snapped his strange paralysis.

Abruptly he stepped away. Another step to ensure temptation remained out of reach. He straightened and folded his arms over his chest. Only he knew the gesture was to stop him from grabbing her. Whatever magic she exerted, it was devilish powerful.

Her return to actuality was slower. She lifted heavy eyelids and sagged against the door. One gloved hand rested on the wood as if she needed support.

He knew how she felt. His own knees weren't completely solid. And he hadn't even touched the jade.

Good God, what did she do to him?

"My original decision stands, madam."

She frowned in puzzlement. Either she was a superb actress or she really was hopeless at concealing her thoughts and feelings. "I don't understand."

He took another step away and grabbed the ledge of his desk behind him to keep himself from lunging for her. "While I find you charming, that's as far as my interest extends."

Her skin was so fine and clear, he saw the color drain from it. The eyes she leveled on him were dark with an anguish completely out of kilter with his rejection.

"Lord Ashcroft . . ."

He had to get her out of this room, out of his house, before he did something foolish. Like touch her. "Our interview is at an end."

Trembling, undecided, she remained poised before him. He braced for some embarrassing scene, begging or tears.

She surprised him as she'd already surprised him so often. She drew herself to her full height. She was tall for a woman. An Amazon, firm-muscled and full-breasted. He had a sudden dizzying vision of how her long legs would wrap around him in coitus. He stifled a groan.

Her chin rose, her mouth hardened, although nothing hid its generosity. The voice that emerged was crisp. "I wish you good day, then, my lord."

Even her hands were steady as she tugged those damned veils down. Only a few minutes in her company, and already he regretted the concealment of her features.

Oh, she was good, whoever she was.

With a snap of her skirts, she turned and strolled from the room as if those searing seconds of sexual awareness had never existed.

"Stupid little bitch!"

Diana braced but didn't flinch as Lord Burnley raised his hand. She'd long ago learned the only way to hold her own with the marquess was to pretend to a courage she didn't possess.

As she stood before him, she kept her voice steady and she planted her feet firmly on the carpet. "If you bruise my face, you'll delay our scheme until the marks fade, my lord."

"I don't have to hit your face," he snarled. Nonetheless, he lowered his fist and began to pace the tiny library of the house he'd rented for Diana in Chelsea. The area wasn't fashionable, but it was close enough to Mayfair for their purposes. "What possessed you to beard him in his den? I told you how to snare him. A chance meeting. A sprained ankle in the park. A lost dog."

His impulse to violence seemed to have subsided. She bent her head to hide her relief. "I decided a direct approach would intrigue him."

"Now he's rejected you out of hand."

She shrugged with completely artificial nonchalance. "He's a man who can have any woman in the world. Why should he be interested in me?"

Burnley stopped, and his cold green eyes ran over her with an assessing glance she'd become used to in recent weeks. "Don't be a fool, girl. You'll prove utterly irresistible."

"Well, that certainly wasn't the case today," she said with asperity.

His thin mouth lengthened in displeasure, whether at her failure or her defiance, she didn't know. "Try again. I've fought this bastard in Parliament for ten years. For all his numbskull ideas, he's damned clever. But I know his weaknesses. You're just the woman to appeal to those weaknesses."

Even she, who didn't follow politics closely, was aware of the long-standing enmity between the draconian Edgar Fanshawe, Marquess of Burnley, and the reformist champion, Tarquin Vale, Earl of Ashcroft. The two men clashed over and over, with the marquess usually emerging victorious because his cruel, eye-for-an-eye principles received general support from the upper classes. Burnley viewed Ashcroft's unreliable politics as a sign of his unreliability as a man.

The tall old man leaned back against the desk and folded his arms over a chest that had once been broad and powerful and was now thin and hollow. Diana hid a shiver. In spite of the obvious differences between the two men in age and vigor, the stance was exactly like Lord Ashcroft's when he'd sent her packing.

Today had been painful and frightening. Her brief was clear—seduce the Earl of Ashcroft. So simple at a distance. So complicated now she'd met her quarry. Already events teetered out of her control, and Ashcroft hadn't even touched her yet.

For one dizzying moment, longing to be safely back at Cranston Abbey made her heart clench. She didn't belong here in London. She belonged in that beloved place, the house and estate she'd devoted her life to as much as any mother devoted herself to her offspring.

She reminded herself that if she held fast to her purpose, Cranston Abbey would be hers. This was one case where ends really did justify means. She did no harm to Lord Ashcroft if she persisted, and in return, all her dreams would come true.

She forced herself to sound stalwart. "I haven't finished with Ashcroft."

A smile twisted the old man's thin lips. He was still handsome, but illness took its inevitable toll. Deep lines scored his cheeks and drew down the corners of his mouth. His eyes sank into their sockets. "You always had spirit, I'll give you that. Even when you were a brat."

Wearily, Diana brushed at the stray tendrils of hair that tickled her forehead. After her stymied attempt to engage Lord Ashcroft's interest, she was tired and humiliated. Keyed up in a way she didn't dare examine too closely. She felt like someone had rubbed her skin with glass paper, excising a layer or two, leaving her too exposed to the world. The sensation was unfamiliar, unwelcome, uncomfortable.

She'd give her right arm for a cup of tea and five quiet

minutes in a chair to enjoy it. But such prosaic luxuries were out of reach. When she'd returned from the debacle at Lord Ashcroft's, Burnley had been waiting.

Burnley frowned thoughtfully. "I can't stay. If we're seen together, the scheme will unravel. Remember what's at stake."

Oh, she remembered. She thought of little else.

Had she always coveted the magnificent house and its rich acres? She didn't think so. But when Lord Burnley offered her a chance to guide the estate's destiny into the next generation, it was as though she suddenly lifted her head and saw to the horizon instead of just the patch of ground at her feet. Ambition and determination had filled her with purpose. Her love for Cranston Abbey would find its true expression at last. She discovered a task fit for her intelligence and abilities.

The reminder of that revelatory moment steadied her nerve, reminded her why she was in London. Her voice rang with certainty. "I'll write with my progress."

"Daily."

"I hope you'll leave me time to accomplish my charge," she responded with a trace of sarcasm.

He laughed, the sound scratching like dry sticks in a winter wind. "You've become insolent since I raised you in the world, Mrs. Carrick. Don't think I'll forget if you fail."

She rubbed at her temples where a headache gnawed. In spite of the fortifying memory of what she set to gain, anxiety made her belly cramp with nausea. Burnley had chosen her because he thought she was strong. After meeting Lord Ashcroft, she didn't feel strong.

"I won't fail," she muttered, even as her heart quailed to recall the finality of Lord Ashcroft's dismissal. Surrendering her virtue promised to prove more difficult than she'd originally thought.

"You'd better not. For your father's sake as well as yours." The old man straightened from the desk and stepped nearer, using his height to intimidate. "Don't think to fob me off with false coin. I'll know whether you've seen Vale naked. He's the only man you'll take into your bed."

Dear God, as if she'd toss another person into this poisonous mix. The old man must be going mad. "I gave my word, my lord. If I promise something, I carry it out."

The smile crooking his lips sent fear oozing down Diana's spine. With one desiccated finger, he tapped her cheek. "I know that, child. It's one reason I chose you for this honor."

She bit back a bitter laugh. "No honor. Dishonor."

"Cranston Abbey and my fortune, not to mention becoming a marchioness, will compensate for any spots on your soul. You'll find after you lose it, that a soul is a completely unnecessary encumbrance."

She shivered, although it was a decision she'd already made. She'd long ago decided Edgar Fanshawe was Beelzebub incarnate. Was she wise to deal with the devil? She was merely human, and he'd used both threat and reward to lure her. Too late now to renege.

"I won't play you false," she said stonily.

"You have too much to lose if you do," he said in an equally unrelenting voice. "I hope your wrong step today doesn't spoil my plans. I shall be most . . . displeased if it has."

When the Marquess of Burnley expressed displeasure, people got hurt. Nonetheless, she still had to make him see reason. "There's a possibility Ashcroft won't want me. There's a possibility his no today means no forever."

Burnley traced her cheek again. She struggled not to flinch. His touch was cold, as if death already sank its claws into him. "That will be unfortunate for you."

The threat was barely hidden. Helplessness surged in her heart. "He's not a puppet."

The marquess's lips narrowed. "His cock leads him. His cock is unquestionably interested in you."

She ignored his profanity. If she'd become freer in her speech since they'd become coconspirators, so had he. He used strong language to remind her she prostituted herself in this endeavor.

She needed no reminder.

Again, she made herself think of Cranston Abbey and how much she loved it. Such a prize was worth brief degradation.

Her surge of determination quailed under a sudden recollection of Lord Ashcroft as she'd last seen him. He'd looked frighteningly acute, not like a man at the mercy of his base appetites. He'd scared her. He'd attracted her, and that had stoked her fear.

Until now, her fear had been focused purely on the marquess. A fear founded in twenty-eight years of acquaintance. After today, she wasn't sure who was the more formidable, her pimp or her prospective client.

Burnley paused, as if expecting argument. What could she say? She nodded.

"Good girl. I await developments." He tilted her chin. She wished he wouldn't touch her. She hated it. "I have every confidence you won't fail me. Or your father."

"My father's the only good man in this whole mess," she said sourly.

Contempt edged Burnley's laugh as he released her. "Your father is good because he lives in ignorance."

It was true. She'd give anything to maintain her father's contentment. That was why she was here now. Or at least one reason. She'd never deluded herself her purposes were altruistic. She sought advancement the way so many women had before her, with her body. Her heart was as black as Lord Burnley's. And would turn blacker before she was done.

"I'll leave you to contemplate your mistakes and assess how to avoid them in future," Burnley said silkily.

He shuffled toward the door. Soon, he'd need a cane. Shortly after that, he wouldn't be able to walk at all. They both knew what awaited Lord Burnley. That was what prompted this mad gamble.

"Good evening, my lord." Habit made her sink into a curtsy. He turned and arched an ironic eyebrow. He must guess her acid thoughts. He'd always delighted in the rebellious soul of his bailiff's daughter.

Once he'd gone, she slumped into a chair and stared sightlessly at the unlit grate. What was she to do? How was she to seduce a man who expressed no interest in her? Did she have the nerve to try again?

Given what she gained if she succeeded, she couldn't let cowardice deter her. Even though cowardice prompted her to pack up this luxurious little house right now and return to the familiar comforts of home and honest toil.

She was so lost in her troubled thoughts, she didn't hear the door open. The first she knew of anyone else in the room was Laura's touch on her shoulder.

"He's gone." Her friend's words were a statement, not a question.

"Yes."

Her friend sank into the chair opposite Diana. "He's a bad man. You should run a thousand miles."

Laura loathed Lord Burnley. As well she should. He'd hanged her father and transported her mother. All that had been left of the Gypsy family was a small dark-eyed girl. For once Diana's father had stood up to his employer, who wanted to cast the eight-year-old child out to beg on the highway. Instead, John Dean had raised the orphan as his adopted daughter. Now while Diana and her father ran Burnley's estate between them, Laura managed their home.

Burnley had insisted that Laura join her foster sister in London. Diana still wasn't sure why. Perhaps for appearance's sake, although this house would remain a secret from everyone apart from the few trusted servants necessarily involved.

"You know what I stand to gain." Diana had continued this argument with herself since Lord Burnley's offer several weeks ago.

Laura's face didn't lighten. "Yes, you become chatelaine of Cranston Abbey. Once your husband meets his Maker."

Or goes to the hell he deserves.

Laura had never approved of Diana's involvement in this scheme. Diana had tried again and again to make her see that whatever price she paid now, the reward was worth it. Cranston Abbey was a generous return for a few uncomfortable weeks in a rake's bed.

Diana itched to take over the reins of the estate, to institute the improvements that had frustrated her all the years she'd played Burnley's right hand. She'd be a fool to turn her back on what fate offered.

She prayed fate was kind.

Her possession of Cranston Abbey and her father's comfortable old age relied on one incalculable factor. Whether she could get Tarquin Vale to plant a child in her empty womb.

Chapter Three

Ashcroft sipped his champagne, the cold bubbles bursting against his palate. It was the only coolness in the theater turned ballroom for the night. The oppressive heat that had hung heavy over London all day hadn't eased with evening. Around him, the crowd heaved in sweaty, forced gaiety. Discordant laughter and chatter overwhelmed the orchestra scratching out the latest waltz.

What was he doing here? He hadn't meant to come, although his presence at the courtesans' ball was as much an institution as the ball itself.

He glanced around, deliberately avoiding avid feminine eyes. He never left the ball without a companion, sometimes more than one. What had seemed exciting decadence to a man in his twenties now palled.

Damn it, he was thirty-two. Was he really the same fribble he'd been a dozen years ago? Were his amusements as banal? Would he stand here, leaning against the orchestra rail, searching for a warm body to relieve his solitude when he was forty? Fifty?

Bleak, disturbing thoughts.

He took another sip, grimaced at the wine's cheap bite, and wondered if he should go home.

His self-reflective mood wasn't completely the fault of his evening entertainment. Since ordering his visitor from his library yesterday, he'd been restive, discontented.

No woman had made a lasting impression in years. But something about the mysterious intruder lodged in his memory and wouldn't shift.

Breaking his habit, he'd stayed in last night. So he'd woken unusually early, before noon, and with a clear head. And immediately remembered Diana—if that was her real name, which he took leave to doubt. That automatic recollection made him sorry he hadn't sought oblivion in the fleshpots.

He'd forget the jade quickly enough. He wasn't even sure he remembered what she looked like. Half an hour in a wench's company, however intriguing she and her proposition might be, wasn't likely to linger in his mind when so many pleasures offered distraction.

Except pleasures lost their charm through sheer repetition. Here he was surrounded by the most spectacular light-skirts in London. And he couldn't generate energy to crook a finger in any particular woman's direction.

You're a hopeless case, Vale.

He ignored yet another lure from a masked woman. Perhaps a courtesan. Perhaps not. The ball was open to the public, which made it such an illicit thrill for members of the ton who attended. One never knew if one danced with a duchess or a Covent Garden drab. All one needed was the price of a ticket. A lot of women didn't even have that, but hung around outside in hope some sap scratched up the blunt to get them in.

"Have you chosen a companion yet, my lord?"

The sultry voice penetrated his brown study, and he found himself looking down into a pair of big blue eyes under a silver mask so flimsy as hardly to justify the name. Familiar big blue eyes.

"Hello, Katie," he said without enthusiasm. Although the courtesan was as much friend as occasional lover, their association harking back to when he first came down from Oxford.

"My escort for the evening proved disappointing." She sipped her wine and sent him a meaningful glance under her artfully darkened lashes. "Young men can be so . . . young."

Ashcroft laughed softly. "But sadly old ones can be so old."

"There's a stage in between that's just right." Her lips, reddened to ruby with a glistening salve, curved upward in unmistakable invitation, and she placed one hand on his arm. "Would you like to remind me?"

Normally, Ashcroft would accept her overtures. She was a luscious armful with the deftest hands in the business. And he was grimly aware he had nothing better to do tonight.

He didn't know why, but tonight Katie, for all her obvious allure, didn't answer his strange mood. Perhaps "obvious" was the problem. Although God forbid he tired of beautiful women who knew just what they wanted from him.

Regretfully, he shook his head. "Not tonight, sweeting."

As he'd expected, she took her rejection with good grace, pressing his arm and smiling. "I can see you're blue deviled. Perhaps a friend of mine will lighten your humor. She's new to Town. A true redhead. A Long Meg, tall as a Grenadier Guard, legs like a Thoroughbred."

Great Jehovah, what was wrong with him? Even the idea of bedding an Amazon fresh to the capital didn't appeal. "Maybe later."

Katie cast him a searching look, but she knew not to pry. A few remarks on the latest scandals, and she sauntered off with a sway of her voluptuous hips.

After half an hour more of pretending to enjoy himself and unaccountably failing, Ashcroft handed his glass to a passing footman—probably an out-of-work actor. The urge to escape, to seek fresh air, was overwhelming.

He nearly always stayed in Town through summer. He caught up on his parliamentary work when the city was quiet, and the social whirl temporarily slowed. This year, he wondered if he should retreat to the gloomy magnificence of Vesey Hall, his country seat. He hated the house, but London didn't seem to answer his current, inexplicable frame of mind.

In the distance, he caught a glimpse of a Titian-haired cyprian towering over short, plump, and obviously bedazzled Lord Ferris. Katie, as usual, was right. The wench was spectacular enough to take Ashcroft's fancy. But somehow tonight he couldn't summon a jot of interest.

Time he went home and shook himself out of this unwelcome humor. He nodded to two acquaintances, both like him unmasked, both married, and began to clear a path toward the entrance. Difficult when traffic flowed into the cavernous room rather than out. He tried not to admit that it was embarrassingly early to seek his bed. Especially as he went alone.

For all his height, strength, and sheer bloody arrogance, he became trapped in an eddy, unable to proceed or retreat. His attention dipped to the woman facing him.

Tall. Graceful. Hauntingly familiar.

"Lord Ashcroft."

Her voice slid over his skin like perfumed oil. How she achieved this effect over the hubbub was a puzzle. Every cell in his body went on instant alert. The nagging dissatisfaction that had dogged him all night vanished.

His heart pounded out a single word. *Mine. Mine. Mine.* The reaction was as elemental as a hungry lion scenting an antelope.

Except this particular antelope smelled of freshly harvested apples.

"Diana." He, famous for his eloquence, was lost for words.

His eyes devoured her. He retained enough self-awareness to wonder how he recognized her among hundreds of women. Her black-and-gold mask was large and gaudy and hid her face to the jaw. Her eyes were mysterious, concealed, but he could see her mouth, pink, moist, full. He'd know that mouth if he were dying.

He wanted that mouth on him.

"You know who I am?" The cool jade didn't sound surprised.

"Yes." Hell, he needed to untangle his tongue before she discovered just how she bamboozled him. If only he untangled his tongue ready to use it on her. The carnal images rocketing through his mind made him rigid as iron. "What are you doing here?"

She was suddenly still, even as the crowd flowed around her.

Was she afraid? Previous acquaintance indicated little frightened her, even when it should. Then, to his amazement—and reluctant admiration—that luscious mouth curved into a confident smile.

He caught a flash of defiance in the eyes she leveled on him. "Looking for you, of course."

Her boldness scattered what little sangfroid he retained. "I believe our dealings came to an end two days ago, madam."

"I lost a preliminary skirmish, my lord, not the war."

His instincts still screamed danger. But nothing could make him retreat, even when the crowd divided, and a path opened to the door. "What if the enemy is invincible?"

Her smile broadened, developed a mocking edge. "Are you my enemy?"

"I'm not your friend."

"What a pity. You'd make a good . . . *friend*."

The euphemism for "lover" in that suggestive tone roared through his blood like fire. He hadn't touched her, and already he wanted her more than any woman he remembered.

He ached to tear off her mask. Her eyes glinted behind their covering, but he couldn't read her expression. All he had to go on was that sinful curl of her lips and the warm, laughing voice. Warm, laughing, sensual, *knowing*.

She sounded considerably more self-assured than the woman who had accosted him two days ago. He shouldn't like it—he'd thought her overweeningly confident then, and she was more brazen now—but somehow his body didn't heed his criticism.

"I told you I like to do my own hunting."

Presumptuous baggage. His rakish attitude didn't cow her. He wished he didn't find her nerve so appealing. He wished he didn't find *her* so appealing. He battered back a wild impulse to kiss that smile from her mouth until she joined him in the turbulent storm.

"If you insist, I'm willing to run away from you, my lord. Not too fast."

He laughed again. He couldn't help it. She was so damned impudent. "Are you implying I'm in my dotage?" At most, he was only a few years older than the chit.

"I don't like to waste time. We both know I'm perfectly willing to be caught. Can we take the headlong pursuit as read?"

His heart leaped. She was out of the usual run of women. The searing curiosity to see whether she carried that daring into bed intoxicated him. Still, he tried to pretend she didn't captivate him utterly.

"I need to be interested in pursuing."

Even without seeing her face, he knew she stared back in blatant disbelief. Who could blame her? Attraction sparked between them like electricity. "Aren't you?"

The crowd shifted again. The illusion that he and this gorgeous, troublesome woman were alone in a glass bubble shattered. A man dressed like Henry VIII jostled Diana, propelled her into Ashcroft's chest.

As her head jerked up, her gasp of surprise feathered his jaw. Automatically, he reached to catch her, circling her slender arms with his hands. His heart slammed against his ribs, then began to gallop. Desire flared, hotter than Hades.

"Are you all right?" he asked in a strangled voice.

That damnable smile was back. The urge to kiss it from her full lips became nigh irresistible. "Yes."

He waited for her to straighten. Instead, she trailed one gloved hand down his jaw. "You're not as invincible as you claim, my lord."

The noisy, whirling world careened to a standstill as she nestled her hips into his. His cock throbbed against her skirts. Any show of indifference was futile. He realized the glitter in her eyes was excitement. He wasn't the only one responding to the building awareness.

Some survival instinct made him fight back although nothing could make him draw away. "It's mere human reaction."

She laughed, the sound low and alluring, and stretched up on her toes. The sensation of her body lengthening against his almost blew the top of his head off.

"Oh, you're human, my lord."

Her lips came closer. He should avoid her, but an attraction beyond anything he'd known in years, perhaps ever, held him transfixed.

He braced himself for the touch of her mouth but at the last, she hesitated. The scent of apples swam in his head. Her warmth seeped through his clothing to his skin. Briefly, he recalled the impression of innocence she'd left after their first meeting. An impression at odds with everything else about her.

Her fleeting uncertainty passed, and she pressed her mouth to his.

Shock held him still. Through the riot in his head, he knew he should have expected this. She'd hardly been shy at their first meeting, even if she hadn't assaulted him.

Not that this was exactly assault . . .

Her kiss was astonishingly sweet. Barely sexual. The tentative cling of her lips. The honey taste of her mouth. The glorious closeness of her body.

The scent of apples left him tipsy as if he'd downed a bottle of brandy.

His arms curled around her, drew her into his heat, so he felt the wild hammer of her heart. To his surprise, she stiffened before abruptly melting. With that softening, her mouth opened, and her tongue flickered out to trace the seam of his lips. His daze faded, and his hold tightened. He answered her foray with an exploratory sweep of his tongue. She moaned, and the muffled sound hurled his excitement to the sky.

She kissed him back, but something made him pause. Her reaction puzzled him, forced him to fight through the fog in his brain. For a woman so outspoken about what she wanted, her response seemed unsure. As if it was a long time since she'd kissed anyone.

Given her lavish beauty, this was so unbelievable, he lifted his head and stared at her. Holy God, what he'd give to see her face right now.

This wasn't the place. Already, the ball whirled out of control. Drunken whooping echoed off the walls, and he wasn't the only fellow taking liberties with his companion.

If Diana was indeed a respectable widow, mindful of her reputation, he couldn't shame her before the dregs of society. And his intentions toward her rapidly became a private matter.

Her lips were damp from his, red and swollen. A delicate flush marked what he could see of her pale skin.

He slid one hand down her arm to seize her gloved hand. For a woman with seduction in mind, she liked to cover herself. Her dark red dress might cause comment at a county assembly. Here, among the demimonde, it seemed as modest as a nun's habit.

His glance dipped to her bodice, which offered teasing glimpses of her magnificent breasts. His groin tightened. She might display her charms with more subtlety than he was accustomed to, but that didn't mean they lacked appeal.

"What's wrong?"

Part of him, the part capable of thought, noted she no

longer sounded like a worldly siren but like a woman dazzled by unexpected pleasure. She hadn't kissed like a siren either. She'd kissed him like she meant it.

The ultimate lie.

Even through his pounding excitement, his misgivings howled. Everything about her contradicted everything else. Unfortunately, he'd reached such a pitch of need, he hardly cared.

"Nothing." He bared his teeth in a smile that conveyed his wolfish thoughts. "Come with me."

"My lord . . ."

He overrode her protest, if protest was her intention, and dragged her toward the doorway, mercifully empty of crowds at last. "You started this. It's time to pay the piper, my girl."

To his surprise, she laughed. "Are you asking me to blow you a tune, Lord Ashcroft?"

The hussy's reawakening summoned a burst of genuine laughter. "We'll definitely make beautiful music, madam."

Chapter Four

$\mathcal{D}$iana was aware of nothing else apart from the powerful man hauling her unceremoniously through the disorderly crowd. Feverish desire made her head spin. How had she become this mindless wanton?

Everything was Ashcroft. His salty flavor was on her lips. His hand curled tight around hers. His long legs ate up the distance between them and freedom with such speed, she stumbled to keep up.

It wasn't just her own surrender that bewildered her. The swiftness of his capitulation left her reeling. Although she had a chary feeling he hadn't capitulated at all, and he remained in complete control of her and circumstances. She'd baited the tiger, and the tiger had pounced.

Now she must wait to see if he intended to devour her whole or leave only a few scratches to show for the encounter.

He'd kissed her as if he meant to devour her.

She licked her lips, savoring the rich taste that lingered. She'd never been kissed like that in her life. She didn't know anyone *could* kiss like that.

Still, Lord Ashcroft tugged her through the milling hordes with the hard certainty of a clipper plowing through the sea in a high wind. Still she bobbed in his wake like a pinnace.

Diana didn't know where he took her on this mad dive. The unfettered, heedless part of her hardly cared as long as he soon swept her into his arms and kissed her again.

More than kissed her . . .

On this close night, the air outside the theater was no fresher than the miasma inside. Still without speaking, Ashcroft swerved into a dark side street away from the line of coaches. She staggered as the acrid stink of decaying rubbish assaulted her.

He shoved her against the cold, dank brick of the alley walls. The tiny fraction of her brain that still worked insisted she should resent his proprietary attitude. Instead, she experienced a deep feminine thrill at his strength and steely determination to have her. Her heart crashed against her ribs in uncontrollable excitement.

Dear God, she was hopeless. She hardly knew this man, yet already she fell under his spell. And she didn't know how to stop herself.

With sudden purpose, she raised her head to object to his cavalier handling. He read the tilt of her chin as invitation and pressed his mouth to hers.

Heat blasted down to her toes. His kiss at the ball had been rapacious. Now she realized he'd reined himself in amidst the seething crowd. His utter ruthlessness astonished her. He ravished her lips, using tongue and teeth to subjugate resistance.

Not that, to her shame, she mustered any resistance.

She gasped, sinking into the kiss like a drowning woman sank into a dark ocean. Every bone in her body dissolved, leaving only glorious sensation.

Nobody had touched her like this for years. She'd forgotten the power of a man's hands on her in desire. All thought flew from her head, replaced by a thick, drugging syrup of pleasure.

Ashcroft tasted of night and sin and devilry. The dish was so delicious, she'd never get her fill.

To her mortification, she whimpered in disappointment when he finally drew away. A roué like him would know that with one touch, she yielded. Her chest heaved as she struggled to drag air into starved lungs.

She didn't want air. She wanted more dazzling kisses.

Dazed, Diana stared up into his face, a pale blur in the darkness. His breath was a soft, uneven susurration. Although she knew better than to imagine he could be as overcome as she, when she placed one hand on his chest, he was shaking.

He felt something.

She didn't know why this confirmation that he was vulnerable to sexual longing mattered. After all, the man who held her was undeniably flesh and blood. She'd tasted need on his lips and felt desperation in his embrace.

"Damn you, I have to see you." His hoarse baritone soaked into her skin and made her bones melt once again. When he released her, she swayed back against the bricks. Her legs felt like custard.

How had her coldhearted seduction come to this?

Without awaiting permission, he tugged at the strings holding the mask. He caught it in one elegant hand and flung it into the mud at her feet. His hands framed her face.

"What if I want to go back into the ballroom?" she asked on a spurt of defiance, feeling the attention he focused on her features like a physical touch.

"Why should you?" His chuckle was soft and knowing. "You caught the quarry you set out to snare."

This time his kiss was rougher, his mouth more predatory, his grip tighter. The pressure of his mouth made her blood beat hot and fierce in a way it hadn't beat in eight years. Her senses thawed after a long winter under ice.

In the dim recesses of her mind, disquiet stirred. There was danger in what they did. She wasn't a highborn lady, but until now, she'd been a respectable, virtuous woman. Lord Ashcroft treated her like a trull he'd picked up in a gutter.

Hauling her into an alley to take his pleasure and kissing her as though he had the right to command her.

There were other, more insidious dangers. She'd embarked on this plan intending to stay in control, uninvolved. At this torrid moment, it was laughable how far she strayed from either description.

If she remained cold in his arms, she could justify what she did. Losing herself to heady rapture made her a whore indeed. And she'd never be able to live with herself afterward.

It made no sense, but pleasure seemed the ultimate betrayal of her principles.

Too late . . .

The warnings were dim and far away. Much more immediate was the magic of Ashcroft's touch. She met his passion with rising passion of her own.

When his tongue thrust into her mouth, she sucked hard on it. He groaned and pressed into her. Even through the layers of skirts, she felt his erection. She was so lost to hunger, she thrust her hips forward to meet that raw male power.

Foolish, naïve Diana. She'd never expected to want Lord Ashcroft. Now, with astounding swiftness, she was so aroused that if he didn't fill the aching emptiness inside her, she thought she'd die.

With a complete absence of tenderness that only built her excitement, he ran his hands up and down her sides. He must know she burned for him to touch her breasts, but his exploration remained almost innocent. Apart from the blazing pressure of his mouth. And the throb of his rod against her belly.

She made a protesting sound. She'd never known kisses like this. Kisses that stole her soul, changed her into an unabashed sensualist.

A terrifying thought invaded her mind. If he could turn her into his willing creature with just his mouth, what would happen when he took her body? Because it was as inevitable as sunrise that he'd take her body. Also inevitable, she now realized, was that she'd long for his possession more than a saint longed for a glimpse of heaven.

He kissed her neck and shoulders, roughly pushing the dress aside. She shivered, wild response rippling through her. "Stop teasing me," she gasped, as he bit down on a sensitive nerve, and heat blasted her.

He laughed and bit again, more gently. The rasp of his teeth made light explode behind her eyes. "You've never been shy before about telling me what you want."

"One meeting doesn't count as before," she objected, rubbing herself shamelessly against him, frantic to ease the painful ache in her breasts, the even more painful ache between her legs.

"It was enough." He trailed his lips up to her ear, where he nipped the lobe. Another arrow of need pierced her. Her knees wobbled so badly that only his hands around her waist held her upright.

She wanted those hands to touch her properly.

She wanted those hands on her breasts. Oh, shocking admission, she wanted those hands on her sex.

Trembling, she grabbed his wrist. Clumsily, she pressed his palm into her breast. Even through her bodice, the sizzle of contact made her gasp.

"Please . . ." she begged, hating her open need.

Her seduction of Lord Ashcroft wasn't supposed to be this heated encounter. She had intended to remain in charge.

Desire turned her into a pleading slave. Too late to create a distance. Too late from the first moment she'd seen him, she acknowledged in hazy bewilderment.

Automatically, his fingers curled around her breast. Fiery pleasure streaked through her. Breathing unsteadily, she leaned into that touch, but it wasn't enough. She yearned for him to explore her naked body. She was dizzy with the heady scents of soap and warm, aroused male. She'd forgotten what an evocative fragrance that was.

She'd forgotten so much in the last eight years.

His other hand slid up to hold her face, turning it toward his. His features remained in deep shadow while torchlight from the main thoroughfare revealed her every reaction.

The contrast should frighten her, underline that this man was a stranger. She was too trapped in craving to do more than strain toward him. She wanted him to kiss her. She wanted him to hitch up her skirts and plunge deep. She wanted him to make her his in a way no other man had.

"Please . . ." she said again.

Who was this impassioned woman with her untrammeled reactions? Surely not staid Diana Carrick whose idea of excitement was a new book for her small library or the chance to try out one of her agricultural theories on a field at the Abbey.

"Please what?"

She should resent his teasing. But even through the mad tumult of her heartbeat, she heard the edge in his voice.

"Please touch my . . . my breast," she whispered. The shock of hearing the words penetrated the fog of arousal like light breaking through a heavy cloud cover.

What was she doing?

She wasn't here to submerge herself in hedonistic delight. All she'd heard about the Earl of Ashcroft had led her to expect a contemptible, slobbering seducer from a cheap novel. Instead, he drew her like a magnet drew iron filings. And she needed to resist. This visit to London didn't launch her on a courtesan's career. Her purpose was clear, and once she achieved it, she meant to do her best to forget her brief fall from grace.

She couldn't risk letting Ashcroft become more than just a means to an end.

The chilling instant of clarity dissolved as the hand curving around her breast drifted upward in a caress. He dipped beneath her neckline, tightening the lace edging. Then he paused.

Her skin tautened in aching suspense. What the devil was wrong with the man?

"You're tormenting me." Her choppy breathing lifted her breast under his hand and made her aware how close he ventured to her nipple.

"I like to see you desperate," he said softly.

"Aren't you desperate too?" Where did she find the courage to ask the question?

His hand flexed but, curse him, slid no lower. "Oh, yes."

"Then why not touch me?"

He laughed, and the sound fizzed through her blood, heating it to boiling point. "Because your desperation builds my anticipation."

"Do you always play games?"

"Only when I enjoy them."

"My lord . . ."

"Ashcroft." The undertone of amusement lingered. She wished she didn't find it so compellingly attractive. "My hand is halfway down your dress. It's absurd to stand on ceremony."

Fighting back nerves, she slipped her hand between them and cupped him. She couldn't contain her astonished gasp at his raw heat and power.

The only other man she'd touched so intimately was William. That felt like a lifetime ago.

Lord Ashcroft was bigger and heavier than her husband. A shudder, partly fear, partly excitement, quivered through her as she imagined that strength pounding into her. It would be like living through an earthquake.

He groaned. "Dear God, woman."

Tentatively, she curled her fingers, testing his size. When he kissed her this time, his mouth was ravenous, burning. At last—*at last*—his hand shifted. Time staggered to a stop until his fingers brushed her pebbled nipple.

She jerked. The sensation was beyond anything she remembered—or had imagined in the long lonely nights since William's death. Her belly clenched, and moisture welled between her legs. A red-hot wire extended between her nipple and her womb, and it tightened with every flick of his fingers.

She ripped her mouth from his and hid her face in his neck, trying to muffle the lascivious sounds escaping her. Vaguely through her approaching storm, she felt him shove up her skirts. Then a blinding pleasure as his hand thrust between her thighs.

He wasn't gentle. He wasn't kind. His fingers pierced the slit in her drawers and found her. She shuddered in reaction.

She suffocated. She trembled close to bursting into endless flame. She was adrift and disoriented.

He pressed up into her, and every muscle convulsed. The world exploded, replaced by a hot, dark place lit with showers of fiery sparks. She bit down hard on his neck to stifle her scream.

Ripples still flowed through her when his hand slid free and curved around her thigh. His touch was pitiless. She welcomed that. She didn't deserve the pretense of tenderness after what he'd just done. And something deep inside her responded to his mastery.

She tried to remind herself that she played a part, but the knowledge made no impact against the waves of satisfaction. Ashcroft pulled her leg higher and hooked it around his hip.

She gasped for air, scrabbling for some shred of control, of reason. But both floated out of reach like cinders in a draft.

With one shaking hand, he tore at the front of his trousers. She should help, but she could barely stand after that astounding release. Clinging to his shoulders, she leaned against him, pliant as a reed. Pleasure bubbled in her blood, left her aware only of Ashcroft's big powerful body and what he was about to do to her.

The burst of salacious laughter belonged to a different

world. Terrified, she lowered her leg and flung her head up to meet Ashcroft's eyes. He looked tense and angry. And frustrated. His hardness against her belly testified to his incendiary readiness.

Trembling with fear and the quaking remnants of her climax, Diana pressed closer to Ashcroft. Stupid to seek his protection even if it felt so natural. But he seemed the only solid object in a world that had become alien.

"By Jove, Ashcroft, take the trollop somewhere private." The voice was loud, slurred with drink, and unmistakably upper-class. "She must be a treat. You're not usually so eager for Covent Garden wares that you poke them in the street."

Diana cringed, and a distressed murmur escaped her. Shame tasted rusty in her mouth. Her stomach knotted with nausea.

Dear heaven, had she gone mad? She'd been ready to let Ashcroft take her in an alley.

"Bugger off, Belton," Ashcroft growled without turning.

Diana's heart beat out a wild demand to run. She was desperate to leave, but she couldn't go while there was a chance the interloper might see her face and remember it.

"Who's the jade?" Belton, whoever he was, didn't heed the threat implicit in Ashcroft's snarl. He continued with a tipsy good humor that lifted gooseflesh on Diana's skin. "If it's a fresh wench, I'll take my turn when you're done. I've got nothing against a buttered bun, and you always have the pick of the doxies. Never rogered one of your leftovers who wasn't pure gold. You surely know how to warm up a slut."

Behind Diana, the brick wall was clammy and the stink of her surroundings was rank in her nostrils. She couldn't blame the unknown Belton for assuming she was a tart.

She acted like a tart.

By all that was holy, what had Ashcroft done to her mind? Except she couldn't blame him. She'd fallen into his arms like a leaf tumbled from a tree when winter gales blew.

No wonder he was such a devil with the women.

Ashcroft's hand settled hard behind her head and he pressed her face into his coat. Black filled her vision even as humiliation choked her. She tried to struggle, but she couldn't shift that implacable hand.

"Belton," Ashcroft said pleasantly, "you have two choices."

"Jolly good, old cheese." Belton's laugh was thick with anticipation as he shuffled closer. "Her and me? Or you, her, and me?"

"No." Even through her churning misery, Diana listened to the snap in Ashcroft's voice.

Belton however was too far in his cups to notice. "Something better?"

"Belton, you can leave now and continue your pathetic life untroubled, or you can meet me tomorrow morning over the barrel of a pistol."

Shocked disbelief held Diana rigid against Lord Ashcroft. Had he just challenged a friend over her honor? An honor that after tonight she could no longer claim? Her hands clenched in his coat.

"Steady on, old man. Not worth losing a chum over a bit of muslin."

"So you choose the second option?"

Belton sounded considerably shakier—and more sober. "Good gad, no. I've seen you shoot the club out of an ace at Manton's."

"Then I suggest you choose the first option."

"First option?"

"Leave. Now."

"Oh. Right. Assuredly." Diana heard bootheels scrape across cobblestones as Belton beat a hurried retreat. "No offense meant to you or your lady, old man. No offense."

Over the noise from the street, Diana listened to the drunkard's stumbling departure. She assumed it was safe to look up, but still she kept her head buried against Ashcroft. Beneath her cheek, his heart thumped steadily.

She was all kinds of a fool to trust this embrace. His arms

promised safety and security. Lying promises. Those were the last things Ashcroft could give her. Those were the last things she wanted from him.

But she couldn't forget how quickly he'd shielded her. When she deserved no such consideration.

Her heart contracted in miserable denial of everything she'd learned about Ashcroft tonight. She desperately wanted him to be a pig of a man. She wanted him to treat her badly. She didn't want to like or respect Tarquin Vale.

Because then she might need to feel guilty about what she did to him.

Chapter Five

*H*e's gone." Lord Ashcroft's whisper was a breath across the top of Diana's head.

"I won't . . ." Her unsteady response was muffled against his shoulder. A woman who had just shuddered to completion in public shouldn't be backward about voicing her wishes, but forcing the words out was impossible.

Shame crushed her in a grip of steel. Her belly cramped with a vile mixture of fear and self-disgust.

After tonight, there was a stain on her soul. One could wash a soul clean, surely? Good works, prayer, repentance. But with every minute in Ashcroft's disconcerting company, her certainty of eventual salvation faded.

I'm not a whore.

The emphatic declaration lacked conviction when she remembered how she'd yielded to his caresses.

"It's all right. He didn't see your face." Ashcroft's voice was a deep rumble under her ear, and his arms tightened around her. She fought unsuccessfully against deriving comfort from his embrace.

"I won't . . ." She jerked her head up and gulped in a lungful of air. She felt like she hadn't taken a breath in an hour. "I won't let you have me against a wall."

She read reluctance in the way he withdrew, as if he derived strength from their embrace just as she did. Oh, how she deluded herself. She stood trembling while he removed his coat and slung it over one broad shoulder.

"Contrary to what that blundering fool indicated, I usually restrain myself from rutting in backstreets."

"He said . . ." She flinched to put Belton's assumptions into words. That any trull would do for Lord Ashcroft, and tonight the trull was Diana Carrick. Although the Lord Ashcroft she'd imagined was just such a profligate lover.

When had she started to think of him as more?

No, he was a man who treated women as casually as the scythe sliced a blade of wheat. One moment of thoughtless kindness didn't compensate for a lifetime of sin.

With unsteady hands, she tugged her bodice up. She must appear an utter slattern. Humiliation prickled her cheeks, and she fumbled.

With an efficiency that irked because such coolness was completely beyond her, Ashcroft tweaked her dress into decorum. His hands were adept, and little trace remained of the desperate, shaking man of a few minutes ago.

His control made her feel even more of a trollop. Satisfaction still swirled through her veins. His taste was rich in her mouth. Her breasts ached from his touch.

His voice was clipped. "Belton and I were young idiots together at Oxford. Good God, that was half a lifetime ago. I've learned a little about finesse since. Difficult as you'll find that to believe."

She did find it difficult to believe. A strange, compelling madness had overcome her. She didn't flatter herself he'd been similarly affected. His aplomb now indicated his desire was easily conquered. "Then why . . ."

"Let's get out of this alley." He sighed and ran his hand through his hair, ruffling it. Even in the dim light, the gesture was endearing.

Diana, be careful.

"Keep your head down. I was precipitate in discarding your mask." He wrapped his coat around her, lifting the collar so it shadowed her face.

Again he guarded her honor. He left her completely befuddled. What sort of debaucher demonstrated such care for a lady's reputation? Especially when the lady behaved so unwisely.

"My carriage isn't far away."

He'd drawn her halfway down toward the street when she came to enough to register what he said. "No."

He stopped and glanced down. The unsteady light revealed puzzlement instead of annoyance in his expression. She couldn't blame him for taking her consent for granted. Shame tightened her belly.

"I still have the right to say that," she said in a low, throbbing voice. "Or did I relinquish that along with my honor?"

"I have no call on you beyond your willingness, madam."

He'd used the same cold tone when he sent her from his house. She shivered. She'd hoped never to hear that tone again. After his unexpected kindness, the abrupt change cut like a whip across her face.

She jerked back and tried to free her hand, but his hold turned firm just before she attempted escape. He looked at her fully for the first time since he'd wrapped her in his coat. She stifled the traitorous softness the memory of that tender, protective action evoked.

He drew in a jagged breath, and his broad shoulders relaxed. "Diana, I'm sorry." A soft, self-derisive laugh. "I'm usually not such a bear. Blame it on frustration."

Understanding descended like a dousing bucket of cold water. She'd left him hungry. His calmness formed a thin veneer over a seething volcano of arousal. Now they were close to the light, she noticed a muscle flickered erratically in his cheek.

It couldn't have been easy for him to stop when he did.

Without Belton's interruption, they'd be lovers now. In a

sordid encounter in an alleyway. She should be grateful the clodpole had burst upon them and dragged her out of her daze of sensual joy. Except the sensual joy had felt more real than anything since William's death.

Her voice was subdued, and she huddled into his coat. "I'm sorry too."

"Come home with me."

The soft demand's potent lure was warning in itself. She stiffened against the request, as if his will alone could make her relent. Her body demanded she go with him, test the limits of desire. Her mind remained in control—barely. Her mind insisted she had to reinforce her defenses before she saw Ashcroft again, before he placed those skillful hands on her yearning flesh once more.

She'd undoubtedly gained his interest. Although there had been little calculation in her success. So little calculation that every nerve tightened against going with him now. Her surrender when she was so vulnerable would be too complete, too honest.

I am not a whore.

A couple paused at the mouth of the alley, arms around each other, and peered into the darkness. As quick as sound, Lord Ashcroft stepped before Diana, shrouding her in shadow.

Her heart clenched in anguished response. Why did he act like a knight in shining armor when she needed him to be a heartless devil?

The longing to cede to blazing passion tugged at her. He was close enough for her to feel his warmth. That radiating heat was its own invitation. She'd been cold for eight long years.

Once, she'd basked in a husband's love and care. Then death had ripped William from her arms, and she'd been lonely ever since.

The reminder of her husband propelled her back to reality. For her sanity's sake, she couldn't afford to lose herself in passion. "I want an affair, not a quick tumble then good-bye."

"You do yourself an injustice, Diana," he said slowly. "And me."

"So you accept my proposal?"

The word hung between them, with its connotations of permanence, virtue, wedded bliss. Eventually, he lowered his head in a sharp nod. "I accept."

She waited for hallelujahs of triumph to ring inside her. But instead her heart beat a preternatural warning that she should end everything now. She should flee London and return to the woman she'd been last week, yesterday, an hour ago.

The woman she was before she'd succumbed to a rake's touch.

"Thank you." What else could a woman say when she consented to surrender her honor?

He reached for her hand. Even through her glove, his touch scorched. "Now for pity's sake, come with me before I lose my mind."

He jerked her against him and slipped one hand behind her head. He kissed her thoroughly. Her toes curled in her brocade slippers, and pleasure flooded her veins.

When sensation threatened to overwhelm her, she wrenched her head back. In the darkness, she couldn't read his expression. His breathing was tattered, and his heart raced under the hand she rested on his chest.

How she wanted him. Desire should ease her way. Instead, it made everything fiendishly difficult. She hadn't expected to navigate the rapids and ravines of emotional involvement.

Untold danger lay ahead unless she controlled her responses and remembered she did this monstrous thing for purely selfish reasons. She wanted something from Lord Ashcroft, and once she got it, he was no more use to her.

He groaned and leaned his forehead against hers. Their breath mingled in the space between, almost more intimate than his kiss. "You torture me. Damn it, Diana, I must have you."

"Not tonight," she forced out, even as the urge to yield, to run away with him and never look back made her shake with longing.

For all her harsh reminders of why she was here, it was impossible to forget what they'd shared tonight.

She wanted one last memory to carry home. Her kiss was soft, tentative, unlike the earlier passionate ravishing. His lips were soft, too, like warm satin. She clung for a sweet moment that whispered innocence. She glanced swift kisses at the corners of his mouth and along the hard line of his jaw.

His scent filled her head. Musk and clean skin and some essence that was Ashcroft himself.

Temptation drew her on. She feathered her mouth across his commanding blade of a nose, hearing his sharply indrawn breath. Almost as if she were blind, she glided her mouth over his cheeks, felt a hint of bristle. This evidence of masculinity made her toes curl again.

She cupped his face between her hands and returned her attention to his lips. His hold tightened at her waist, and he opened his mouth. Any hope of restraint evaporated in incinerating heat. He took control, lit the kiss to flame.

She was lost to the world before something, the whicker of a horse or the rattle of a carriage, pierced her flaring madness.

He speared his hands through her hair in a rough gesture that scattered bright shards of desire through her veins. His voice was rough too. "My house. Tomorrow."

Diana struggled to muster her thoughts, difficult when his kiss still tingled on her lips. She couldn't mistake his urgency. His urgency fed hers.

"No. Someone might see me." Whatever tonight's excesses, she couldn't compromise her reputation.

"You came to me before."

A wry smile crooked her lips. "The risks were equal to the rewards."

"Your house?"

"No. Someone might see *you*."

The greater danger was he'd learn where she lived. When she abandoned him, as she would once she'd conceived, she didn't want him tracing her in London or even worse, back to Marsham.

"Hell, Diana . . ." A thoughtful expression crossed his dark face. "There's somewhere. Where do you live? I'll collect you in my carriage."

"I'll meet you," she said hurriedly, noticing the way his eyes narrowed with suspicion. "The Serpentine in Hyde Park at four."

"Three."

Poor fool she was to find his eagerness flattering. Poor fool she was to capitulate so readily. She wanted to say it was because her scheme promised to reach fruition all the sooner. But in her heart, she admitted it was because she ached to see Ashcroft again.

She needed time apart from this rake before she forgot what was at stake.

"Three then." He leaned forward and kissed her. A brief, uncompromising salute expressing frustration and desire. "Are you sure you want to go home alone?"

"Yes."

She wasn't sure at all, part of the reason she must leave. Her mind was topsy-turvy. Her blood still thundered with the echo of pleasure. She needed to remind herself she hadn't embarked on this cause to become a whore in her soul as well as her actions.

"I'll take you home."

A trip through dark streets offering Ashcroft opportunity to demonstrate his disreputable skills? Far too appealing. And she still had to keep her address a secret.

Hurriedly she shook her head. "I brought my carriage."

"You mean to leave me unsatisfied?"

She remembered his inflammatory comment earlier and teased him with repeating it. "I mean to build the anticipation."

She wondered if he meant to drag her up for another kiss, but instead he drew her head into his shoulder. "Tomorrow at three."

"Tomorrow at three." She wondered if the words augured heaven or hell.

"And naturally you'll host dear Charlotte's coming out at Ashcroft House, Tarquin. It will be the event of the season."

Ashcroft frowned. His aunt Mary, Countess of Birchgrove, was as encroaching as ever. He surveyed the family gathered for the christening of another Vale offspring and tried to think of one relative who wasn't encroaching.

He couldn't come up with a candidate.

"That's impossible, Aunt Mary," he said in a clipped voice.

He'd learned long ago that unless he scotched his father's sister's schemes at the outset, life became a nightmare. He shuddered to remember her imposing upon him to host a country house party years ago, when he'd been too young and naïve to refuse. He'd still been tripping over strangers three months later. It had been like having the place infested with cockroaches.

The countess drew herself up to her full six feet and produced a delicate lace handkerchief that looked completely ridiculous in her platelike hand. "You have no gratitude, Ashcroft." She always used his title as a mark of displeasure. She dabbed at her eyes. "I've given succor to a reptile."

It wasn't the first time she'd called him cold-blooded, and it wouldn't be the last. "Snake or not, Aunt Mary, my home isn't at your disposal," he said crisply. "Birchgrove House has a perfectly adequate ballroom."

She patted again at dry eyes that now glinted with annoyance. "Your ballroom is twice the size of ours, and you never use it."

"Nonetheless, my decision stands."

He let her vociferous complaints fade into the background. Instead, he sipped his champagne and considered the family gathering with the cynicism born of a lifetime's acquaintance with the Vales.

Fortunately, the unfashionable time of year meant only fifty or so Vale leeches and toadies were present. If his new second cousin Josephine had arrived a month later, the crowd would have been considerably larger. His purse appreciated the baby's timing. As head of the family, he'd been inveigled into paying for the celebration.

"Ashcroft, are you listening?" his aunt snapped. "You owe your uncle and me more respect after all we did for you."

Ashcroft bared his teeth. "Any obligation was repaid years ago, Aunt. And if you wish me to contribute to Charlotte's season, you should accept discretion is the better part of valor."

She looked angry but chastened. He'd silenced her for the moment, if not forever. The problem was he couldn't ignore his obligation to his father's relations. Although there had never been the slightest pretense of love for him, his family had taken him in when he was a child.

Of course, the income from the Ashcroft estates sweetened his relatives' duty. They'd treated their hounds and horses with more affection, but nonetheless, they'd given him a home, food, clothing, an education.

Since he'd reached adulthood, he'd juggled his responsibilities with the undoubted fact that his relations conspired to suck every penny they could from him. Most of the time, he struck a balance that suited him if not their endless avarice.

Perhaps his unhappy, displaced childhood was what gave him impetus to champion the poor and dispossessed. He'd never been hungry or homeless, but he profoundly understood deprivation.

He strolled toward the open windows. The heat was still oppressive. The champagne in his glass was flat and lukewarm although of much better quality than the swill he'd drunk at the ball last night. Just before he saw Diana, and his night took fire.

Worryingly, his thoughts constantly turned to the mysterious temptress and her contradictory behavior. A drive to be with one woman over another hadn't bothered him for years. Which was exactly how he liked it.

Diana shattered his barriers.

Since last night, she'd haunted him. He was still far from sure pursuing her was wise, but desire gripped him, and not even the gravest suspicions of her motives could keep him away.

She'd only offered the merest glimpse of the heights they could climb together. He wanted to scale those mountain peaks and lose himself in wild passion. Because whatever else was false about her, her passion was real.

Dear God, the prospect of her shuddering her release while he was actually inside her made him break into a sweat. A sweat that had nothing to do with the sultry weather.

As the buzz of conversation rose, and Josephine gave a loud wail—probably the only honest expression of feeling here—he lost himself in pleasurable contemplation of his plans for his new lover.

Beside the Serpentine's dark green water, Ashcroft sat in a closed carriage and wondered if the enigmatic Diana had destroyed his sanity during their short association. Here he was, waiting for the woman. He never waited for a woman.

For the tenth time in half an hour, he checked his engraved gold pocket watch. The hands hadn't moved much since last time he looked.

Ten to three.

He'd arrived before two, knowing he was ridiculously, mortifyingly early, knowing she wouldn't be here.

His rational self loathed these games, this mystery. He didn't trust Diana. There were too many questions and not enough answers.

His rational self loathed the way he behaved in her vicinity. He was unaccustomed to playing the supplicant when it came to sex. He was unaccustomed to feeling out of control, however much he relished the delicious pull of desire.

But it was always a desire he could walk away from.

Could he walk away from Diana? He didn't know. That was the hell of it.

Self-preservation insisted he leave right now. Unfortunately, his cock didn't care about self-preservation. His cock just wanted to bury itself between those slender thighs.

He checked his watch again.

Blast it. Only three minutes had passed.

If he had half a brain, he'd tell his coachman to return to Ashcroft House. If he had half a brain, he'd call on one of the many willing women he knew and work off the painful frustration Madam Diana had left behind last night.

God knew why he didn't.

Except he'd caught her taste and scent, and no substitute would do. He couldn't say he enjoyed the sensation. Life was so much simpler when any dish on the menu could appease his hunger.

Back in his formative years as the Birchgroves' unwelcome ward, he'd learned wanting things was the sure route to misery. Better just to take what the world offered, then move on swiftly before the flavor cloyed.

Would the mysterious Diana cloy? Surely, inevitably she would.

He checked his watch. Just before three. Even if she meant to honor the appointment, he suspected she'd delay. She'd want to torment him.

He'd quickly discerned a layer of hostility in her reaction

that should repel but somehow proved part of her fascination. She'd treated him like a whore when she presented herself at his house. Last night, she'd been too carried away to allow her disdain free rein, but it was still present.

That was the most worrying aspect of all. Her derision for his character cut him to the quick. He was the Earl of Ashcroft, careless, notorious, infinitely seductive. He had no illusions about what he was and what he'd done in his unruly life. Where women were concerned, he was a scoundrel through and through. His only genuine virtue was honesty, with himself and his paramours.

Yet he wanted Diana to stare into his eyes with the same melting expression she'd revealed when he'd wrapped his coat around her in the alley.

As if his chivalry caught her unawares, curse her.

Growling softly with frustration, he stretched his cramped legs until his heels bumped the back of the carriage. It was bloody hot. Thick air lay over London like a steamy blanket.

Tobias, his coachman, knocked twice on the roof. It was the signal they'd arranged if a woman approached.

His wayward heart beat a rapid tattoo as he opened the door and stepped out. He tried to tell himself the relief tightening his chest was merely anticipation of passion. Automatically he swept his hat off in a bow. "Madam."

"My lord." Diana didn't curtsy, and she was veiled again.

The park was empty, a far cry from how crowded it would become later when the fashionable hour began. Nobody was there to see him take Diana's hand and usher her into the carriage. He realized he'd never seen her naked hands. She always wore gloves.

Always? They'd only met twice before this.

He slammed the door and closed the curtains so dimness surrounded them. Gently he drew her down to sit next to him. Her hip brushed his, and the contact blasted him with heat.

As quickly as that, his cock rose hard and ready.

"Take off your bonnet," he demanded harshly.

Wordlessly, she obeyed. Her hands were steady as she lifted the gauzy draperies, untied her bonnet, and laid it on the facing seat.

She raised a troubled gray gaze to his. Marks of sleeplessness stood out beneath her eyes. She clearly shared his disquiet about their attraction. Although God knew why. She'd asked for this.

The air was baking, weighted with unspoken feeling and building lust. Delicate color lined her cheekbones, and her tongue flickered out to moisten her lips. Arousal jolted him, made a mockery of his attempts to maintain the upper hand.

Without shifting his stare from her face, he reached up and knocked sharply on the ceiling. His driver had orders to cover the park until Ashcroft indicated otherwise. The carriage rolled into motion, and Diana lurched as she briefly lost balance. He caught a drift of her scent. Something floral and under it all that damnably evocative perfume of apples.

"Sit across my lap," he snapped. His hunger reached such a level, he lost capacity for sweet persuasion.

Silence extended. Silence marked by the clop of horses' hooves and the creaking of the carriage. Silence vibrating with a thousand possibilities.

She licked her lips again. Slowly this time. He bit back a groan. Her gaze dropped to the bulge in the front of his trousers.

When she looked up, the gray depths held curiosity and desire. And, inevitably, secrets.

Without shifting her attention, she rose onto her knees, hitched up her skirts and straddled him.

Chapter Six

❧❧❧❧❧❧❧❧❧❧❧❧

*A*s she spread her thighs across Ashcroft's lap, Diana forced air into her starving lungs. She felt like she hadn't breathed since she'd entered the stuffy carriage. She drowned in Lord Ashcroft's evocative scent. Her heart slammed against her chest as if it wanted to break free.

The carriage jolted again, and she grabbed Ashcroft's powerful shoulders. He vibrated with urgency. She knew he wanted her. The impressive erection straining toward her was indication enough, even if she didn't read his drawn, unfixing concentration as desire.

The time had arrived.

If she proceeded, she set Lord Burnley's scheme into motion. It would be too late to retreat. She sold herself for worldly reward. Her honor would be irretrievably lost.

If she balked, she'd miss this incredible chance to change her life. Her talents would remain forever unfulfilled. She'd have to deal with Burnley's anger and her own knowledge that at the crucial juncture, her courage had failed.

She steeled herself to go on.

She'd created this moment. She couldn't shirk from seizing it. The opportunity to place her imprint on Cranston Abbey was worth it.

Right now she was grateful Ashcroft didn't treat her with consideration. Tenderness would break her. Meaningless copulation was all she wanted. Nothing to hint at last night's fleeting, unwelcome intimacy.

The exchange was clear in her mind.

He wanted her body. She wanted his seed. A fair exchange, surely? This unemotional encounter saved her from despising herself as a complete hypocrite.

If heaven had mercy, she wouldn't enjoy what happened. She didn't want pleasure, even as the memory stirred of last night's stunning climax. With unnecessary violence, she ripped her gloves off before returning her hands to his shoulders.

He leaned forward to kiss her.

Dear God, no. None of those bewitching kisses. That was how she'd run into trouble before, letting him gull her into believing more happened than a joining of bodies.

Abruptly she turned. His lips glanced across her cheek.

Even that much contact exploded heat through her, but she battled her arousal. Her hands fisted in the fine black material of his coat. Although whether she pushed him away or pulled him closer, she couldn't say.

For one broken instant, she recalled the last time she'd accepted a man into her body. It had been with love and sweetness and trust. A thousand miles distant from what she did now.

Remembering William while she poised to take another man was the ultimate heresy.

Ashcroft sucked in a hissing breath. "Damn you, Diana, I want to kiss you," he snarled, and grabbed her face, forcing her to meet his blazing green eyes. He was pale under his tan, and a muscle flickered in his cheek. His dark, intense face reflected her own conflicted emotions.

She'd arrived intending to play the seductress. But now, when finally there was no escape, that particular masquerade became impossible.

Instead, she was just Diana Carrick, vulnerable and lost in this new world ambition forced her to enter.

She'd never lied with her body before. She hated to lie now.

Some lies were beyond her. "No," she said in a cracked whisper. "No kissing the first time."

Suspicion struggled with hunger in the glittering jade gaze. She'd adjusted to the carriage's rocking, so she easily kept her balance while she reached down. She gasped to feel his hard length. He jerked as her fingers made glancing contact. Desire glazed his eyes, erased the brief wariness.

Urgently, his hands stroked up her legs, lifting her skirts. She shivered with response as his palms skimmed fragile silk stockings, up to garters, to bare skin above.

"Sweet Christ, Diana," he breathed in satisfaction.

He'd just discovered she wore no drawers. His hands framed her hips.

At last, her fumbling fingers found the trick of undoing his trousers. A couple of hurried movements, and he sprang free against her thigh. His hands slid around to grip her buttocks.

"Now," she groaned.

His hold tightened. "You're not ready."

"I'm ready."

To her shame, it was true. Just those few rough touches and hot moisture bloomed between her thighs. In spite of her resolution to remain uninvolved, her heart raced with excitement as much as trepidation.

His fingers slipped to her center, stroked, spiked pleasure. "By God, you are."

She grabbed his hand. She didn't want him satisfying her with his hands. She wanted his body in hers. And not, heaven forgive her, so she stole his seed.

No, she just wanted him.

The wild release in his arms last night should have warned her she was helpless against him. She brought his hand to her mouth and bit down hard on the heel of his palm. He shuddered beneath her as she lowered herself.

She felt the smooth pressure of the head of his penis, blunt and larger than William's. She waited for him to surge up and take control, but he seemed content to leave her in charge. Only the tight skin of his face indicated what his restraint cost.

Her thigh muscles strained with discomfort. She spread her legs more widely and pressed down.

Her body hadn't known a man in eight years. She hadn't expected that to cause difficulties. In truth, she'd never thought of the practical details of becoming Lord Ashcroft's lover.

Now practical details became paramount. Time crawled by, every second extending into an eon. Ashcroft's eyes stared into hers with a ferocity that only stoked her arousal. Their ragged breathing filled the creaking coach. His hands were bruisingly tight as he supported her above him.

She shifted to ease the discomfort and he closed his eyes as though she tortured him. He was so tense, she thought he might shatter. The slide of his penis against her thigh clenched her belly, sent rushing moisture to bathe the head.

All this should make it easier to take him. It didn't.

She pressed down again and felt herself stretch over his thickness. She sobbed for breath. Could a man be too big for a woman? Surely that was anatomically impossible.

"Diana, you're driving me mad," he gritted out.

He used one hand to guide himself inside. She cried out at the painful stretching, and her hands formed claws on his shoulders. If he were naked, she'd have drawn blood.

Gingerly, she sank lower, feeling the burn. She found no pleasure in what they did. This was like being impaled.

"Relax your muscles," he said roughly, surging up and making her whimper as she accommodated the thrust.

His fingers stroked between her legs. Electric reaction jolted through her. Her muscles clamped around him, the sensation excruciating. Moisture flowed even as her passage closed against further incursions.

Squeezing her eyes shut, she prayed for strength. Her mind

told her she'd accommodate him. Her body contradicted that idea.

She drew a jagged breath. She couldn't bear the waiting, whatever pain lay in store. She pulled his hand from between her thighs and plunged down.

As she took him full length, she screamed. He was so big, she felt he invaded her right to the womb. Blind, trembling, fighting the urge to cry, she buried her face in his shoulder.

"Diana, Diana," he murmured, brushing her hair back from her damp face with one shaking hand. "It's all right."

She didn't want his tenderness, but she couldn't summon the will to reject it. She panted, praying for the agony to fade. Perhaps in the years since William had died, she'd become malformed. Sex had never hurt like this.

His fingers, tormenting against the sticky skin of her face, slid around the back of her head. "Don't cry."

"I'm not crying," she said thickly before she realized tears streaked her cheeks.

He kissed the side of her face. Sweet kisses from a different universe to that pulsing presence between her legs. His big, lean body vibrated with tension, and she guessed what effort he exerted to maintain the stillness.

Gradually, the pain receded and her mind scraped into rusty function. Lord Ashcroft became more than just the bearer of a greedy and hurtful masculinity.

What must he make of this?

He couldn't mistake her discomfort, her lack of enjoyment. She'd enticed him into taking her, then derived no pleasure from the act.

Yet desire still lurked beneath her clumsiness. The admission that, at the end, she wanted Lord Ashcroft was the cruelest cut of all.

Again, she had cause to be grateful for his patience and consideration. Again, she had cause to resent his care. She didn't want to think of him as anything more than a body that invaded hers.

She knew how aroused he'd been. Still was. Yet he gave her time to adjust to his size. He didn't thrust and seek his own pleasure. He kissed her as if he extended comfort. As if he understood the devastation that blighted her soul.

Inevitably, the rain of kisses ended at her lips. She tried to evade him, but he held her captive.

The kiss was gentle, brief, undemanding. Her lips tingled from that tantalizing touch. He skated another kiss across her nose and on her chin. Before she could stop herself, she tilted her face.

"You said you didn't want kisses," he whispered, tracing lines of kisses along her neck.

She made a disgruntled sound. Her interior muscles loosened a fraction, settling him deeper. This time, thank heavens, there was no pain.

"I don't," she whispered back.

"Well, that's good." The undercurrent of laughter in his voice bubbled through her blood like champagne.

When his mouth met hers, passion flared. For the first time since the disaster of taking him, she forgot herself and surrendered to feeling. His tongue flickered to tease hers. Last night, he'd tasted of wine and decadence. Today, he tasted of desire and heat.

Delicious.

She shifted to pursue that tormenting, skillful mouth. As she moved, he slid more fully inside her and she felt the first twinge of pleasure. She released a soft, surprised murmur.

He laughed again and kissed her, ravishing her mouth. His hands shifted to her waist and he lifted her slowly so she felt the glide of his body. Her passage clenched to hold him. Friction buzzed through her like lightning.

"No," she whimpered. She didn't do this for pleasure. This was nothing more than a union of bodies. Nothing more.

He bit down on the side of her neck, even while he poised at her entrance. "Do you want me to stop?"

She shivered under the nip. "Don't stop." Terrifying as it

was to admit, his presence made her feel complete, his absence made her feel empty and alone.

He answered with a smooth thrust of his hips. She braced for pain. Instead, after a brief teasing resistance, she took him. Hot pleasure streaked through her, burning away the last hesitation. Her body opened as if it had waited for his possession forever.

A dark flush marked his high, slanted cheekbones. The green gaze was fierce as it roved her features.

Every second, the selfish lover she expected, wanted for her own selfish reasons, moved further out of reach. Instead, here was a man who took care with her, who let her find her own path to paradise with his help.

She closed her eyes, refusing the unwelcome revelations. Immediately in the velvet darkness, sensation cloaked her.

The rasp of Ashcroft's breath as he leaned forward to bury his face in her shoulder. The heat of his embrace, even through her clothing. The sharp, evocative scent of his arousal. Sweat. Healthy male. Soap.

Before she could stop herself, she tightened her arms around him. She trembled too. She'd forgotten how a strong man's vulnerability in the throes of passion twisted her heart.

She rose, relishing the slide of his flesh. With an ease completely beyond her a few seconds ago, she lowered. She settled into a glorious rhythm, working in concert with the carriage's gentle sway.

It was like last night except the crescendo was slower, more powerful. It built every second. Never quite taking her over the edge. Pitching her higher and higher.

Ashcroft's hands shifted, and she found herself on her back against the cushions. She sank onto the velvet and gripped his shoulders as she fought to catch her breath.

She opened dazed eyes. Ashcroft crouched over her, filling her vision. His black hair was ruffled and damp, and a single lock fell over his high forehead. He was breathtakingly beautiful.

Ruthlessly, he dragged her hips up so his hardness probed higher. A long moan escaped her, and she arched to maintain the exquisite pressure. She sighed with regret when he withdrew, only to bask in pleasure when he thrust again.

The wool of his trousers created soft friction against her thighs. Her fingers dug into the fine weave of his coat as if they meant to tear through to his skin.

Everything, the rocking carriage, Ashcroft's whispered encouragement, her misgivings about how this physical possession invaded her emotions, receded. All she knew was a headlong drive toward completion. Her starved senses craved release.

He kept going, long, slow strokes that tormented as much as assuaged. A continuous low keening rang in her ears. Eventually, she realized the sound emerged from her throat.

Ashcroft's superhuman control faded. His breathing became choppy. His shoulders turned as unrelenting as rock under her hands. His thrusts became wilder, harder, deeper.

Her mighty climax peaked on a blast of heat. Every muscle in her body caught fire. Burning darkness possessed her, rushed in searing rivulets through her veins, compressed her heart. Her world turned to raging scarlet flame.

Her interior passage clenched, clutching him hard as she quivered in blazing delight. This was beyond anything she'd ever felt before. Anything she'd ever imagined.

She still trembled with shocked reaction when Ashcroft began to move again. Without breaking rhythm, his shaking hands shoved up her skirts to reveal her belly under her short stays.

A few swift caresses before he wrenched free of her body. He released a massive, choked groan. He tensed, then jerked uncontrollably.

Hot slippery wetness flooded onto her bare skin.

Chapter Seven

She'd failed. She'd failed. She'd failed.

Lord Ashcroft rolled to lie against the back of the seat and slid his arms around Diana's waist, holding her secure. His breathing was unsteady, and the scents of sex and sweat filled the carriage. The bench was narrow, so she had no room to push him away without risking a tumble. Even if she could summon energy for such definite action.

A noxious combination of self-disgust and sexual repletion swirled in her belly. Her legs splayed awkwardly, and Ashcroft's seed dried on her exposed stomach.

Amidst her soul's bitter chaos, one thing was clear. She'd whored herself for nothing.

She was too heartsick to acknowledge the pleasure that contradicted her claim. She blinked back stinging tears. What point crying? Weeping like a woman betrayed would be the final humiliation. In the heat, Ashcroft's embrace should be an irritant. Yet she was so bereft and alone, his touch felt like a benediction.

Slowly, she drew her legs together, noting the pull and ache of well-used muscles. She should clean herself up, pull down her skirts, salvage something from this disaster.

Thank heaven Lord Ashcroft wasn't talkative after sex. She felt like she'd never speak again. She stared up at the richly brocaded ceiling with its twining blue-and-gold pattern and wondered what she should do now.

The landscape of her life extended ahead like a bleak, never-ending steppe. She was trapped between a past she couldn't revisit and a future she couldn't imagine.

She'd been so lonely since William died. But nothing cut as deeply as her loneliness in this moment after the greatest pleasure she'd ever known.

Lord Ashcroft was first to move. Briefly, his arms tightened, he placed a kiss on her nape and sat up.

She tried not to miss his embrace. Some remaining shred of pride had her grabbing her tumble of skirts and pushing them down to a decorous level.

"No. Wait," he said softly, catching her trembling hand.

She stilled immediately and closed her eyes. In spite of her desolation, her wanton blood surged with the memory of other ways and other places he'd touched her.

He released her when it became apparent she offered no resistance. Over the carriage's steady creak, she heard his clothes rustle. Presumably, he ordered his appearance. She heard a faint clink.

Then a blessed coolness on her belly.

Her inertia vanished. She opened her eyes and struggled up on her elbows.

Ashcroft washed her with a damp, snowy white handkerchief. His eyes downcast, he stared at his hand moving upon her pale skin. Thick lashes shadowed his high cheekbones, and concentration marked his striking features. He looked like he considered this the most important task in the world.

She must have made some sound of protest because he glanced up. His green eyes were dark and soft like moss beside a woodland brook. She had a sudden memory of how

fierce and driven he'd looked when he plunged into her body.
He seemed a different man now.

God help her, both men tugged at her senses like nobody
else. Even her beloved husband William.

"Are you all right?" he asked, still in that same soft voice.

"What are you doing?" She didn't want him to be kind.
She didn't deserve his kindness.

A faint smile lifted Ashcroft's lips as he uncapped a silver
flask and poured some of its contents onto the handkerchief.
"Making you more comfortable."

"What's that?" she asked suspiciously, hardly heeding his
answer.

"Water."

Of course it was. If it had been anything else, perfume or
a spirit, she'd smell it.

"I suppose you need supplies on hand for encounters like
this." Guilt and a sick awareness of her devastating failure
prickled at her, prompted a sarcastic response. She felt tired
and sticky and furious with herself. She wished she was anywhere but here. Odd, in all her planning for becoming Lord
Ashcroft's lover, she'd never considered how she'd fill the
awkward moments once the deed was done. "I'm surprised
you don't travel with a hip bath."

The smile deepened. "Are you always this bad-tempered
after sex?"

"I can't remember," she sniped back before she questioned
if it was wise to reveal so much of her history. The last thing
she wanted was to arouse his curiosity. She didn't want him
tracing her to Lord Burnley and Marsham. More, she didn't
want him developing a knowledge of the real woman and not
just the falsely willing lover.

Except they were both aware that, at the end, there had
been nothing false about her response.

Returning his gaze to her body, he wiped the handkerchief
across her belly. He parted her thighs to continue his min-

istrations. The coolness felt marvelous on her aching flesh, and she gave a muffled sigh of pleasure.

His lips turned down. "I should have taken more care. I'll do better next time."

Next time? Heaven help her, could she go through this again? For no purpose?

Right now, she yearned to say good-bye to Lord Ashcroft and never see his handsome face again.

Already her soul quailed at what further contact with Ashcroft meant. She had trouble recognizing herself in the woman who had reached shuddering completion not once, but twice. Only moments in the earl's company, and she turned into a round-heeled trollop.

What would she be like in a week? A month?

She'd wanted to keep her essential self separate. That intention had burned to ashes in the conflagration of their lovemaking.

One stark fact was undeniable. Cranston Abbey threatened to cost her more than she'd ever thought to pay.

Abruptly, she registered the intimacy of his actions. Quickly she closed her legs and scrambled to sit against the side of the carriage. The movement shot a twinge of discomfort through her, sharply reminded her of his painful and ultimately rapturous possession.

"Thank you. I feel much better," she said breathlessly, pushing his hand away, bundling her skirts down with more haste than grace.

Amusement lit his green eyes. She wished it didn't make him even more attractive. "I'll order you a bath when we reach our destination."

Astonishment made her straighten. "Haven't we . . . ?"

He laughed and slid the flask into a pocket on the coach door. He drew out another silver flask and unscrewed its top. "Haven't we what? Finished? I hope not. I haven't begun to plumb the delights you offer."

"I don't feel very delightful," she mumbled. She wasn't sure she had it in her to continue the seduction. What she wanted was to go home to Marsham and curl up in the dark safety of her bedroom.

Oh, poor-spirited, Diana.

Ashcroft frowned in concern and caressed her cheek. One touch conveying more tenderness than anything yet this afternoon. Fleetingly, something pure and joyous bloomed in her heart. Like the first snowdrop in February after a harsh winter.

Brutally, she crushed the feeling.

She didn't want tenderness. She wanted a baby. And unless she could entice Ashcroft to continue the liaison and lose himself inside her, a baby was beyond her reach.

When his eyes met hers, she read no trace of guile in the jade depths. Unlike her heart, which was black with deception.

Next time, she had to ensure he didn't waste his seed.

How on earth was she to manage that? Her path became more tangled and difficult the further she went.

"I know you won't believe me, but I didn't mean to tumble you in this carriage," he said steadily.

Flaring cynicism tolled the death knell to what remained of that brief, fragile emotion. "You're right. I don't believe you. You seem remarkably prepared for . . . accidents."

He didn't immediately understand, then comprehension dawned, and he laughed again. "Diana, a little water in a flask hardly constitutes a familiarity with endless sin."

He reached up and knocked sharply on the roof. Diana felt the carriage change direction.

He poured wine into the top of the flask. She accepted the cup with a word of thanks. His gaze was opaque, unreadable, a stranger's. She found this urbane companion hard to reconcile with the shaking, desperate man who had spilled himself on her belly.

They'd known each other physically, but with every second, she became more aware she didn't know him any other way.

She tried to tell herself that was what she wanted. But as she sipped her wine—the highest quality, Lord Ashcroft seemed only to have the best of everything—she couldn't convince herself that was true.

Everything became so horrifically complicated. She was painfully aware she didn't belong here. Only the beckoning promise of guiding Cranston Abbey's destiny kept her in this carriage. Otherwise, she'd run like a scared rabbit.

"Where are we going?" She shifted on the seat. Her body still smarted from his ruthless lovemaking, even as unwelcome tides of satisfaction still ebbed and flowed in her blood.

"Lord Peregrine Montjoy's house."

Ashcroft spoke as if she should know the name. She didn't keep track of London gossip. She only knew about Ashcroft because Lord Burnley had told her. Gradually, reluctantly, she came to the realization that prejudice had informed that description. The man with her now didn't equate to the clumsy brute featured in employer's tales.

"Is Lord Peregrine in residence?"

"No. He left for France this morning. He's visiting the Earl and Countess of Erith outside Rouen. While he's gone, he's turning his library into a music room, and I'm taking some of the books."

"Does he know you use his house for assignations?"

He arched his black eyebrows in mockery. "Very elegantly put."

She blushed but tilted her chin at a challenging angle. "Would you rather I use the name it justifies?"

He frowned, and his tone deepened into seriousness. "What happened was the result of mutual desire, Diana. There's no need to be ashamed of it—or yourself."

She resented how easily he read her. "Spoken like a man at the mercy of his appetites."

He laughed softly. She couldn't blame him. She was being absurd. He hadn't forced her to anything. This affair started at her invitation. If anyone had been cajoled against his better judgment, it was he. "You sound prim as a Methodist preacher."

She sighed, loathing herself, loathing what she did, and brushed back the strands of hair clinging to her damp neck. After her recent exertions, the tight braids Laura had arranged it in threatened to tumble around her face. "I'm sorry. I'm not accustomed to this."

He lifted her left hand. Immediate warmth flooded her, made her feel muddled, uncomfortable, awkward. She hated to be so susceptible to his most casual touch. But so far, she'd discovered no defenses.

She drifted into very deep waters with Ashcroft. Pray heaven they didn't close over her head and drown her.

"I know you're not." He sounded thoughtful as he absently fiddled with her wedding ring. "What puzzles me is what drives you to these actions."

Her voice dropped to a husky murmur. "I told you—I seek experience with a man whose discretion I can count on."

Back in Marsham, that explanation had seemed perfectly credible. Here it sounded threadbare, unconvincing. Especially after what had happened when she'd taken his body into hers. She couldn't blame him for doubting her.

She wasn't a very good liar—an issue Lord Burnley had brushed aside as he'd brushed aside all her misgivings. He should have listened. With every minute, she felt less adequate to this task.

His hand tightened, and the absent, almost tender stroking ceased. "You're married, aren't you?" he said flatly.

She tried not to mind that he believed her an adulteress. After all, she was definitely a liar and a cheat and now, a whore.

But still chagrin edged her reply. "No."

"Don't lie, Diana."

She ripped her hand away. "I told you—I'm a widow."

He went on as though she hadn't spoken. "If you're married, it explains a great deal. Your reluctance to let me take you home last night, your guilt over what we've done."

She shook her head, while she wondered if inventing a mythical husband might be a smart tactic. "Ashcroft, I'm not married. Even if I were, what do you care? You've had married lovers."

His lips flattened in displeasure. "Somewhere you've listened to a lot of nasty tattle, madam."

"You're world-famous," she said, although she couldn't help feeling shabby. In their short, event-filled acquaintance, she'd learned he was far from an indiscriminate debaucher.

"Apparently," he responded sourly. "But my mistresses have all been a damn sight more worldly than you, Diana."

Truly, she had no idea why he tolerated her questions. She had no right to demand an accounting of his life. "You needn't excuse yourself."

That mocking eyebrow rose again. "I wasn't."

"And I'm not married." She took a gulp of her wine, hoping to bolster flagging courage. "My husband . . ."

She paused and fought for calmness. Talking about William always swept her back to those months of hollow misery after his death. How could a man who was perfectly healthy one day perish of fever the next? Any faith she'd held in a benevolent universe had died that day with her husband. He should still be alive. He should still be with her.

She'd wandered around in a gray miasma for months. Neither her father nor Laura had been able to reach her. All that had kept her going was her duty to Cranston Abbey. Eventually, running the estate had become the purpose that sustained her.

Was that when the seeds of her ambition were sown? The idea of becoming the Abbey's mistress was so outlandish, it would never have occurred to her until Burnley presented his scheme. But when he did, she felt like she'd been preparing for the role all her life.

She forced herself to answer Ashcroft's question. "My husband died eight years ago."

This was something else she hadn't expected, that she'd have to explain herself to an intelligent, perceptive lover. That he'd invade more than just her bed. The Lord Ashcroft of her imaginings had been happy to use her body and leave her secrets intact.

His eyes narrowed. "You're an anomaly, Diana. I don't like anomalies."

She stiffened, and her hand tightened on the cup. "Don't like?"

His brief laugh indicated he was amused despite himself. "Don't trust, then. You know how much I like you. You've known from the first, even when I threw you out of my house."

Had she? Some bond had immediately linked them. Something strong enough to send her stumbling out of that ballroom last night and into the alley. Strong enough to make her unhesitatingly obey his command to take him today.

He raised the silver flask in an ironic toast, then drank. She tried not to stare in fascination at the working of his strong throat.

Back in Marsham, she'd pictured a rake as wan and etiolated from never seeing daylight. Lord Ashcroft looked like he could take on a team of wrestlers and win.

"Perhaps you like a challenge," she said with a lightness she didn't feel. "Although my resistance hasn't been noticeable."

"Amen to that and praise the Lord."

"You must be used to women flinging themselves at your head."

He shrugged. "Modesty forbids a reply."

In spite of her disgust with herself, she couldn't resist smiling. She took another sip of wine, letting the rich flavors fill her mouth and slide down her throat. Curiosity about him was a fever inside her. Something else she hadn't prepared for. "Do you always say yes?"

The carriage slowed and stopped. A deep shiver ran through her as she realized they'd reached Lord Peregrine Montjoy's house. Which meant Lord Ashcroft would touch her again.

She shouldn't want him to. But she did, oh, how she did.

In the last eight years, she'd forgotten passion's power. Except even in the first dazzling rapture of marriage, she couldn't remember being so focused on physical pleasure and the man who provided it. Perhaps it was because that was all she and Ashcroft shared.

His gaze remained cryptic. "Not always."

"So availability isn't your only requirement in a lover?" Nerves made her voice quake. Nerves and a simmering need.

Oh, she was a sad, sad case. He wasn't touching her, and still she burned. In his company, her body became something alien, beyond her control.

He burst out laughing. "Diana, do you have any idea how insulting your questions are?"

Her color rose again. "I'm trying to understand."

He shrugged. "Attraction is always mysterious."

Ashcroft watched as Diana digested his remark.

For all her beauty, he didn't completely fathom what drew him to this particular woman. She wasn't his usual style. His lovers were polished and sophisticated and accustomed to society's sexual games.

Diana wasn't like that. Diana was an intriguing mixture of passion and reticence. Diana fought to keep him at a distance even while she surrendered her delectable body. And succumbed to pleasure with wholehearted delight.

During his restless night—alone, damn her—he'd told himself her fascination would fade. It was just another symptom of this strange mood that gripped him this hot summer. Once he had her, she'd lose her allure.

How wrong he'd been.

He took her cup. She looked uncertain and absurdly young, although he recognized that she was past first youth. Her skin was clear and unlined, but her gray eyes held a knowledge of sorrow that indicated this was no green girl.

To his relief, she no longer appeared utterly devastated. When he'd pulled out of her, she'd looked as though he crushed her heart. Was it some lingering grief for her dead husband? It was clear she'd loved him dearly, and taking a lover must prompt poignant memories. She wasn't comfortable with what she did with Ashcroft. He'd known that even before he'd invaded her painfully tight body.

Ashcroft watched her cover her disheveled hair with the bonnet and lower the veiling. He knocked on the ceiling and pushed up the blinds. They were in the mews behind Perry's mansion. He tipped out the rest of Diana's wine—she hadn't drunk much, he noticed—and recapped the flask, slipping it back into its pocket.

Tobias opened the door. Ashcroft stepped out and reached in for Diana's hand. It trembled in his, and he fought the urge to gather her up and carry her into the house away from prying eyes.

Hell, what was this continual urge to protect her?

She bent her head and walked docilely by his side as they entered the garden. She looked neither right nor left.

"Take off your bonnet," Ashcroft said, remembering he'd used exactly the same words before they'd come together in his carriage. The echo fed his stirring arousal.

If he didn't get her into a bedroom soon, he wouldn't be able to walk. As if to confirm that thought, they passed a Herm with a massive erect phallus. Assorted ancient statuary punctuated the garden. All male, all intact, all unadorned with fig leaves.

"Goodness gracious!" Diana paused to remove her bonnet.

Her face flooded with pink as she stared at the lewd statue.

In spite of the desire eddying through his veins, Ashcroft couldn't help laughing. He was surprised he found her provincialism charming. Naïveté wasn't a quality that usually appealed. "He's a fertility god."

She released a breath, half amusement, half shock. "Believe me, I can see that."

She reached out and slowly stroked the stone projection from base to tip. Heat blasted Ashcroft. Sight faded to black.

When he returned to reality, she wandered ahead as if she hadn't done anything out of the ordinary. Her audacity intrigued him. It proved such a contrast to her diffidence after they'd made love.

Now they were alone, she seemed more at ease.

More at ease? Great Jehovah, she'd just done one of the most provocative things he'd ever seen. Any more at ease, and she'd be tupping him in the bushes.

She glanced back and, for the first time, sent him a genuine smile. Just a slight lift of those lush red lips, but enough to propel his heart into a drunken gallop.

Good God, but she was exquisite.

Tall, deep-breasted, long-legged. She was created for his pleasure. Once she'd taken him and adjusted to his size, they'd fit together perfectly.

He gritted his teeth and battled for control. He was thirty-two years old, an experienced man. How lowering that a country bumpkin turned him into this slavering, desperate supplicant.

He was desperate for no woman, damn it.

His eyes fixed on the subtle sway of her dark green skirts as she sauntered along the gravel path. Now he looked more closely, she couldn't quite carry off the careless confidence. Her gait was slightly uneven, reminder of how he'd ravished her in the carriage.

Delicious memory.

How he loved her desire. It was honest and real.

He hadn't realized until these last days how he'd itched for something deeper than superficial flirtation. What happened with Diana held a rawness he hadn't experienced in years.

If ever.

"Ashcroft, are you all right?" She tilted her head in inquiry. The late-afternoon sun caught her, transforming her to pure gold.

Ashcroft's breath snagged. The moment seemed to hold a significance beyond the present.

Then a cloud covered the sun. The strange preternatural feeling vanished.

A bewigged footman appeared at the doors leading from the garden. Like all Lord Peregrine's staff, he was young and handsome. Diana spared him hardly a glance. Instead, her gaze clung to Ashcroft. He knew she had no idea she betrayed her attraction with every breath. And she had no idea how her unfettered hunger fed his.

He strode after her. It suddenly seemed a sin not to touch her. He caught her hand and drew it around his arm.

"Lord Peregrine has unusual taste in statuary." She fell into step beside him.

Ashcroft gave a grunt of laughter as they passed naked Hercules wrestling a well-endowed lion. "Wait until you see inside. Spare my blushes and promise you won't measure every appendage."

Another delicious wash of color marked her cheeks. "My father says curiosity is my besetting fault."

"Curiosity has its uses."

This time her glance held no shyness. The gray was deep and dark, and excitement stirred to life in her face. "Oh, I look forward to satisfying my curiosity, my lord."

Her purring response raised the hairs on his skin. Ashcroft stumbled, scuffing his soles on the gravel path. The wench had the nerve to laugh. She swept into the luxurious mansion as though she marched into lavish town houses as a matter of course. Again, she proved an enigma.

Ashcroft burned with such desire, he scarcely cared.

She paused just inside the room and stiffened with surprise. He couldn't blame her. Lord Peregrine, the younger son of the Marquess of Farnsworth, did much of his entertaining in the long salon. Even to Ashcroft, who knew the room well, the gold on every surface was blinding.

"You're right." Her breathless undertone of amusement threw coal on his flaming need. For the moment, the shy, almost hesitant woman from the carriage had vanished. "It is rather . . . spectacular."

Behind them, he heard the footman close the door. "This way, my lord."

Diana and Ashcroft crossed the polished marble floor, avoiding the shrouded furniture. Ashcroft had been to so many parties in this salon, it was disconcerting to see it empty. As if disapproving of his lustful intentions, the sulky faces in the huge painting of Zeus and Ganymede frowned down from the far wall.

Ashcroft and Diana approached the impressive staircase with its gilt railings. He noted that she looked around with interest but no awe. Even members of the ton were rendered speechless when confronted with the spectacle that was Perry's home. Diana treated her expensive and luxurious surroundings like a diverting trifle.

He couldn't quite place her in the social scale, which was intriguing as he'd learned in leading strings how to assess people's stations. She spoke with cultured accents and had practiced manners. Yet something hinted at fancy dress, as if playing the fine lady wasn't her normal occupation.

Devil take her, she was nothing but shadows and secrets.

And temptation.

Her warmth curled out to lure him as he escorted her up the staircase, past the floor with the huge ballroom. Finally, they stopped outside a closed door.

"Lord Peregrine made these rooms available for your use, my lord." The footman opened the door as calmly as if host-

ing his employer's friends and their lovers was a normal part
of his duties. Perhaps it was. Perry had a huge number of disreputable acquaintances, with notable names and without.
"He also requested we keep the library ready."

Unlike the rest of the house, the room spoke of charming,
almost feminine, simplicity. A small dining table perched
under the large window, and on the sideboard, an elaborate
supper waited, including champagne in melting ice.

"Thank you." Reluctantly, Ashcroft released Diana and
moved inside. She remained poised on the threshold, as if
unsure whether she stayed.

Stay . . .

"What is your name?" Diana asked their guide.

"Robert, madam." He bowed with a respect that seemed
incongruous, considering he must know why she was here.

Or perhaps he, like Ashcroft, noticed her natural distinc-
tion. Could she come from a great family? Somehow that
didn't fit. Neither did his original assumption that she was a
tradesman's wife out to spend her husband's copious blunt.

"Shall I show you through the apartment? Beyond this sitting room, there's a bedroom, a dressing room, and a bathroom."

Diana's eyes settled on Ashcroft and something in the
gray depths told him she read his burgeoning hunger. "No,
thank you, Robert. We have all we require."

"Madam. My lord." He bowed again. "The staff are at
your disposal."

Ashcroft hardly noticed him leave. Instead, his eyes followed Diana, who strolled across to drop her bonnet on a
low mahogany chair. The air swirled with unspoken desire.

She sent him a faint smile, and while her color was higher
than usual, her eyes didn't waver. She knew as well as he
what would happen in this elegant room.

She flicked back her untidy tumble of hair. "Alone at
last."

Chapter Eight

~~~~~~

$\mathcal{D}$iana felt like a cat on top of a stove. She wanted Ashcroft to touch her again. She wanted it more than she wanted to live to see the sun rise tomorrow.

How quickly she'd adopted a mistress's role. The change would have terrified her, if she hadn't been so edgy with need. Her heart battered her chest, and craving pricked her skin.

He pushed the bedroom door open. "Come with me."

Diana trailed after him as he prowled across to lean against one bedpost. Behind him the huge four-poster bed loomed large and ornate, like everything else in this house. In contrast, even Cranston Abbey's baroque excesses seemed restrained.

The room must overlook a rose garden. Sweet fragrance lay heavy on the air. The perfume was heady, almost as heady as the desire flowing through her veins.

His green eyes settled unwaveringly on her. There was something predatory about Lord Ashcroft. She shivered with anticipation as she imagined him seizing her and devouring her.

Oh, yes, please.

She licked parched lips. His eyes glinted as they dropped

to her mouth before returning to meet hers. It was as if he'd kissed her. Her heart, already galloping, kicked up a notch.

He untied his neckcloth, his tanned hand dark against the snowy white linen. What had happened in the carriage had been wild, fiery, overwhelming. What happened now promised to hurl her into a new world.

She wasn't sure she was ready. With every second, it became clear she was no longer in charge of the ship of her life. The winds of passion pushed her far from harbor. Now she drifted, lost in turbulent seas of desire.

Ashcroft dropped his neckcloth to the rich red-and-blue Turkey carpet. His shirt gaped, allowing glimpses of his throat and the crisp dark hair on his upper chest.

He'd brought her to climax twice, and she was yet to see more of his body than she would in a ballroom. Her eyes fastened feverishly on that revealing vee. Her lips parted as if she already tasted him there. The prickly sensation on her skin heightened. Air pressed against her.

Still with that casual air—an air the banked fires in his eyes contradicted—he tugged his coat from his shoulders and tossed it on the chair behind him.

Diana swallowed to ease the dryness of her mouth. She wished he'd say something. Anything to snap the building tension.

He unfastened the beautiful gray waistcoat with its delicate embroidery of vines and fruit. With the pull and release of each button, her heart crashed against her ribs. He shrugged off the waistcoat and dropped it to lie next to the unraveled neckcloth.

Her fists clenched in her skirts as she fought for control. What was happening to her? When she'd invited Ashcroft to be her lover, she hadn't wanted it to be like this. This threatened to take over her entire existence.

He stood before her wearing only his fine white shirt and dark trousers. Fully dressed, he was a magnificent figure of a man. In shirtsleeves, he took her breath away. Feverishly, her eyes traced the straight shoulders, the broad chest, and narrow hips, down to his strong horseman's thighs.

Out of his elegant garb, he should appear more approachable. Instead, he looked hard and male and overpowering.

Her belly turned hot and liquid, and she shifted to relieve the pressure between her legs. Then blushed when he noticed her discomfort.

"Take off that dress," he growled.

She shivered. In eight years, she hadn't been naked for a man. Now she'd reveal her body to an acknowledged connoisseur. She was no longer a lissome girl, and this man was used to diamonds of the first water.

She shot him a defiant glare. "Are you always this imperious with your lovers?"

He laughed. "Only when they drive me as mad as you do."

The humor cut through her fleeting insecurity like a hot knife through butter. With surprisingly steady fingers, she began to undo her bodice. She'd chosen a dress fastening in front as she hadn't been sure she'd have the services of a maid.

The first few buttons loosened easily before Ashcroft's fixed regard made her falter. When she glanced down, her bosom swelled over the top of her short stays. She'd always been a regrettably overendowed woman although William had appreciated her assets. One look at Ashcroft's face, and she guessed he was another man who liked more than a handful.

"Don't stop," he said hoarsely. His hands opened and closed at his sides as if he restrained the urge to grab her.

Three more buttons, and she wriggled out of the gown. Carefully, she laid it upon the mahogany chair.

Her hair fell about her face in a disheveled, heavy mass. She tossed it behind her shoulders. Lifting her chin in a proud gesture, she confronted Ashcroft. She forced words from her tight throat. "You'll have to help with my corset."

"With pleasure."

She presented her back and bunched her hair out of the way with one hand. A man of his experience must have undressed thousands of women. The thought stung, although she told herself she had no right to resent his former lovers.

Within seconds, he had her corset unlaced. No maid had performed the mundane task as deftly. He slid it from her shoulders and flung it across her dress. Without invitation, he untied the tapes holding her petticoats. Rustling softly, they dropped to the floor.

She stepped out of them, then slowly turned. Her shift was made of silk so fine, it was transparent. Fleetingly, perilously, she forgot the role she played, of eager, rapacious, heartless lover. Instead, she was just plainspoken Diana Carrick. Bookish. Lonely. Driven. Selling herself to gain a magnificent dream.

Her shaking hands rose to cover her breasts. Her nipples pearled so tight, they ached. The onslaught of desire left her floundering.

"Diana, don't be shy," he said softly. He gently uncrossed her wrists. "You're glorious."

"This is . . . this is more difficult than I expected," she said in a shaky voice. Then bit her lip as she realized what she admitted.

Would he guess she seduced him for her own purposes? Although who was the seducer and who the seduced had become blurred since last night.

To her relief, he took her words at face value, and a smile of surprising tenderness curved his mouth. It made him look younger, less cynical, more vulnerable. She struggled to close the rift that opened in her heart.

"Don't do anything you don't want to, sweetheart," he said softly, and raised her hands to his lips, placing a kiss in the center of each palm.

The brush of his mouth was warm and sweet and set a

long slow pulse beating low in her belly. The problem wasn't whether she wanted to make love to him, the problem was how very much she wanted it.

But she was too rapt in enchantment to wrench free.

He released her and tugged his shirt over his head, ruffling his dark hair. The shirt drifted down to lie in a crumpled heap next to his other clothing.

"Oh, my heavens," she whispered, any more eloquent expression eluding her. Almost in a daze, she drank in the smooth golden skin of arms and chest, the scatter of dark hair across his pectoral muscles, hair arrowing down to his waistband.

He was utterly irresistible.

Hesitantly, she placed a trembling hand in the center of his chest. He was like sun-warmed rock under her palm. Her lips parted in sensual delight as she stroked downward, stopping just short of where she knew he wanted her.

With brief amusement, she recalled how she'd assumed a rogue of his decadent reputation would be pale and weak from too many late nights, too much brandy, and too many women. If that regimen resulted in this superb specimen, every doctor in the country should recommend it.

He surveyed her out of lazy dark green eyes. "You look like the cat who got the cream."

"The cream is still waiting." Distantly, she wondered where the confident woman came from. This siren couldn't be busy, clever Diana Carrick, virtuous widow from Marsham.

"Does that mean you'll lick away every morsel?" The hint of laughter didn't hide the gruffness in his voice.

Diana's heart slammed against her ribs. The prospect of licking him all over intensified the throbbing between her legs. "Only if you beg."

His laugh trickled down her backbone like fine wine would slip down her throat. "You're suddenly very cocksure."

"So are you." Her attention focused on where he pressed against his trousers. No mistaking his heavy, seeking arousal.

His impressive chest rose on a deep breath. "I'll make the pleasure last this time."

Reluctantly she stopped ogling him and met eyes that held a rueful light. "An admirable ambition," she said, with a coolness she was far from feeling.

"If you look at me like that, it's an ambition fated for failure."

How she enjoyed this subtle push and pull of wits between them. She ran a questing finger down his chest. "You're stronger than you think."

"Every man has his breaking point."

"Hmm, I'd like to see that."

His muscles bunched and firmed beneath her touch. "I guarantee you'll see it."

A few weeks ago, she wouldn't have understood what he meant. But in preparation for her trip to London, Burnley had lent her some naughty French books. The detailed illustrations had kept her and Laura giggling and horrified for a week.

"Not yet," he said in a rough voice. "Later."

Startled, she glanced up, catching the excitement in his eyes as he obviously read the wicked direction of her thoughts. The way he followed her reactions so closely was thrilling. Her nipples beaded with longing as she imagined him devoting that attention to her pleasure.

"I . . ." She lost track of what she meant to say when he tangled his hand in her hair and tipped her face toward his.

"You're a very beautiful woman," he said hoarsely.

Before she could respond, his mouth descended. He hadn't kissed her for what felt like an eon. Terrifying, really, how quickly she'd become addicted to his kisses. She sighed and gave herself up to his skillful mouth.

His tongue invaded her mouth, and her bones melted. She'd missed kissing more than she'd missed marital relations. Odd to realize it.

She closed her eyes and sank into velvety darkness. Her

knees buckled, and her head swam with pleasure and lack of breath. He shifted his attention from her lips to the sensitive skin of her neck. She moaned and rocked her hips, testing his hard masculinity.

He groaned and drew apart from her. She made a wordless protest before she realized he'd only moved to tug her chemise over her head. As the silk slid away, reality intruded on her sensual dream.

She was naked. At his mercy. This encounter promised to be deeper, purer, more dangerous than what had happened in his carriage. Ruthlessly she reminded herself why she was here. It wasn't to lose herself in Ashcroft's attractions.

She couldn't yield to her desperate craving. She could cope with a coldhearted seduction where both of them took what they wanted. There was nothing coldhearted in how she felt right now.

But how could she keep herself apart from him?

His eyes blazed as they ran over her body. The tips of her breasts tingled as his gaze lingered. His attention slipped lower to the damp triangle of dark blond curls. The insistent throbbing built, and she felt another liquid surge. She moved restlessly. The awareness between them was animal-like in its intensity.

"What's wrong?" he asked softly, tilting her chin to see her eyes.

Dear heaven, she needed to be careful. She bit her lip before she realized how that too betrayed her nervousness. With sudden recklessness, she risked honesty. "This is more . . . powerful than I expected."

He arched a sleek black eyebrow, and his voice was steadier than she'd imagine possible, given the need sparking in his eyes. "You're full of preconceptions, Diana. You speak as if you and I are machines. Wind us up, put us into motion, pack us away when the performance is over."

Her color rose, not because she was naked, although that was discomfiting enough. He made her feel so tawdry.

"Diana?"

She still stared helplessly into his face. Like a besotted chit mooning over her first love. She quashed the thought as soon as it arose. Love had nothing to do with this. "I've lived a quiet life since my husband's death."

That much was true. Tragically true, she realized. How many years she'd devoted to her duties as her father's diligent assistant and Burnley's loyal servant. The woman Diana had disappeared in the efficient, hardworking, endlessly reliable Mrs. Carrick.

The woman had awoken tonight. In a rake's arms.

Ashcroft's warm hand cupped her jaw. She tilted her head in a subtle movement that rubbed her cheek against his palm. "This is my chance to take a share in life. I wanted . . . I *want* some excitement."

The curve of his lips and the white glint of his teeth sent another jolt of arousal through her. She was so hot, she'd ignite any second.

"I can definitely give you that."

She took the step that brought her flush against his powerful body. As she'd guessed, his calmness was deceptive. Her senses filled with the scent of aroused man. His heart pounded in a furious gallop.

"Prove it."

Ashcroft's heart soared in admiration as Diana reached out to snatch what she wanted. Especially as what she wanted seemed to be him.

Unclothed, she took his breath away. Juno. Venus. An Amazon. All woman.

Grabbing her naked hips, he drew her hard against him and kissed her. He couldn't get enough of the taste of her mouth. Like wine. Like honey. He could hardly wait to taste the rest of her.

In a smooth step like a waltz, he turned her toward the bed. He flung back the blue brocade bedspread to reveal snowy white sheets and plump pillows. Another step, and he slid her onto the mattress.

Bless Perry. For all the woeful decorating, everything here was the latest word in comfort. Tumbling Diana in this bed would be like floating to paradise on a cloud. Although to speak true, Ashcroft was so rampant, he'd take her on the bare floor if he had to. "Patience" entered his lexicon as a synonym for "torture."

"Don't stop kissing me." Her sigh breathed passion.

Sainted heavens . . .

He closed his eyes, gritted his teeth, and prayed for control. When he opened his eyes, his heart skipped a beat at how she looked, all ruffled and frantic. Her rich blond hair spread around her like a golden veil.

"Oh, I intend to kiss you," he growled, kneeling over her.

How simple to take her now. She was close to ready. It wasn't enough. He wanted her so needy that she cried out for him. He wanted her dripping with desire.

He refused to suffer this incendiary craving alone. Some instinct told him she offered the right lover a depth of passion unlike any he'd experienced.

He intended to be that right lover.

Listening to the uneven tenor of her breath, he set his hands on her ribs and bent to kiss her. She opened immediately, dancing her tongue across his lips and into his mouth. Very slowly, knowing he tormented both of them, he slid his hands up.

Until his fingers cupped her lush breasts.

Hunger slammed through him. She made a mewling sound of pleasure against his mouth. Ashcroft raised his head to see where his tanned fingers splayed over her curves. A perfect picture. Her nipples stood out proudly, dark pink, tantalizing.

He struggled for control against his raging need. He brushed his lips across one rosy peak. Her breath hitched. Delicately, he took her into his mouth, savoring her flavor. Salt. Apples. Diana.

She gave a long guttural moan and arched. He drew harder until she started to shake.

He'd made love to hundreds of women, seeking enjoyment, brief forgetfulness, mutual pleasure. He always treated his affairs lightly, like a game.

As he tongued the sweet tip of Diana's breast and felt her tremble with delight, he recognized this time, he mightn't be lucky enough to escape with a shrug and a farewell kiss. Something about this woman penetrated more profoundly than mere appetite.

Her beauty stole his breath. Her wild responsiveness excited him. Her secrets intrigued him.

None of that explained why his heart rose in her presence. His life had been devoid of joy, but joy was the closest he could come to describing this feeling.

The niggling problem drifted away as she squirmed under his mouth. She tasted sweeter than sin. She was so sensitive, he suspected he could make her come just by touching her breasts.

He was more selfish than that, at least this time.

Still kissing her breast, he trailed one hand down the silky plain of her stomach and tangled his fingers in the soft curls. She bucked and smothered a shocked sound.

She vibrated to his touch like a bell.

He dipped between her legs. She was gloriously wet. He stroked her center, feeling the swollen flesh. A deeper pressure and she cried out and tautened. Her fingers clenched in his hair. The sting added to the other dizzying sensations rocketing through him.

Anticipation. Enjoyment of her enjoyment. Need.

He slipped his drenched fingers from between her thighs and gripped her hips. If he didn't taste her there, he'd go mad.

With nipping kisses, he worked his way over her quivering belly to the top of her thighs. "Open for me, Diana."

Her legs remained chastely closed. She lowered a shaking hand to hide her mound.

He lifted his head and looked up her lavish body to where she stared at him in dark consternation. A consternation that contrasted sharply with the full, red dampness of her mouth and the flush of passion on her cheeks.

She'd lifted herself on her elbows and he felt her bristling tension. Only seconds ago, she'd been all melting surrender.

"You can't want to do that." Her voice quivered with horror.

He couldn't help himself. He laughed. And was rewarded when her eyes flashed brilliant silver annoyance.

"Do what?" he asked with faux innocence. He loved teasing her.

"You know." She tried to wriggle free until he tightened his grip. "*That*."

"Has someone kissed your . . ." With most of his lovers, jaded, sophisticated creatures all, he'd use the Anglo-Saxon profanity. Something about Diana curbed his tongue. "Have you been kissed like this before?"

She shook her head with an emphasis that made him hide a smile. "Of course not. It's bizarre. I can't imagine you enjoy it."

"Perhaps the purpose is for *you* to enjoy it."

Her color rose, and she tried again to escape. Foolish woman. Didn't she know she might have cast the lures, but he'd shut the trap? He had no intention of letting her go anywhere.

"I wouldn't enjoy it," she said with complete certainty. "Don't put yourself to any trouble on my behalf."

He laughed again. She was delightful. And challenging. He'd have her screaming her release with his head between her legs before too much longer.

"Believe me, Diana, it's no trouble."

She reached down to cup his jaw. Strange that the simple gesture contained more significance than anything else they'd yet done together.

Passion had long been part of his life. Tenderness was notably absent.

Yet he felt tenderness in the way her fingers touched his skin, the warmth of her hand, even the vulnerable light in her eyes.

"Make love to me, Ashcroft." He watched her swallow, the movement of her slender throat ineffably affecting. "I . . . I want you."

When he placed a kiss on her damp curls, the musky female scent drove him mad with desire. "I want you too."

She must have read his surrender because the nervousness leached from her expression, and her luscious mouth crooked in a faint smile. "Then for heaven's sake, Ashcroft, take me."

Diana watched Ashcroft's striking features change, harden as he rose over her. The angular jaw under her hand became adamantine.

Relief flooded her that he wasn't going to put his mouth between her legs. She remembered her astonishment when she'd seen that particular act depicted in Burnley's books. It seemed disgusting, animal, something no civilized man would do to a woman. Something no civilized woman would want a man to do.

Even as she told herself nothing would make her submit to a man kissing her sex, wanton curiosity jabbed her. Ashcroft hadn't been repulsed by his suggestion. He'd seemed excited and eager. And disappointed when she refused.

Her fingers drifted across his face in an almost absent exploration, feeling the faint roughness of stubble. She came to rest on his mouth, and his lips parted as his breath caught. There was a strange, poignant intimacy in feeling the warm air brush her fingers. His lips were firm, satiny, sleek with her kisses. She brushed her fingers side to side, tracing the defined line of his upper lip with its sharp dip in the center, the cushiony fullness of his lower lip.

"You're a strange libertine."

"You know many libertines, madam?"

His lips moved beneath her fingers. The sensation spiraled heat through her. "Perhaps one or two."

"Hardly enough to reach a conclusion."

"Ouch!"

She didn't believe it. He'd bitten her. A sharp nip on her finger. Glaring at him, she snatched her hand away.

He laughed and slid up her body in a smooth movement that was a caress in itself. Very deliberately he rubbed his chest against her breasts, and she smothered a moan at the friction of crisp hair on her nipples.

"I'll bite you again before I'm done." His voice was rich with humor, the sound as dark and beautiful as a low note on a cello.

He settled between her thighs, so close to where she wanted him. She frowned in puzzlement. "You're still wearing trousers."

"They're part of my strategy to drive you wild with passion without losing control myself."

"I'm wild with passion," she said dryly, although it was true. If he didn't take her soon, she'd leap on him like a bacchante at an orgy. She'd surrendered any pretense to caution long ago. "If that's their only purpose, you can safely remove them."

He arched an eyebrow with his characteristic wry amusement. "Safely? What a flat description."

"Do I insult your masculine pride?"

With luxurious thoroughness, he rubbed himself between her legs. She shuddered with reaction. "I'm still very proud indeed."

"Easy to boast. I'd like to see for sure," she said unsteadily. Odd how bantering with Ashcroft built arousal inch by inch until it threatened to immolate her.

"I live to serve," the man who would prove her ruin said, and placed a quick, hard kiss on her lips. She stretched to continue the contact, but he rolled away. In a surge of movement, he stood.

Diana lay where he'd left her and watched as with a couple of adept movements, he shucked his shoes and trousers. She couldn't look away if the house were on fire. Every drop of moisture in her mouth evaporated, and demand throbbed between her thighs. Her heart danced a crazy tarantella.

Behind him, late-afternoon sun flooded through the sash windows. The light illuminated a man more like Apollo than a mortal. Her avid gaze swept down to where his rod thrust forward. A preternatural shiver ripped through her, and she edged up against the pillows.

He was huge. Large and thick beyond anything she'd imagined. No wonder she'd felt split in two when he took her. Without volition, her hands closed in the sheets as if they ached to explore that hard masculine flesh. William had been a boy, full of youth's promise. Ashcroft was unquestionably a mature man.

She forced words past a throat tight with nerves and excitement. "Come to me."

Chapter Nine

*A*shcroft launched himself into the bed, tangling his bare legs with Diana's and pressing her deep into the mattress. Desire trumpeted a tumbling fanfare in his blood.

He'd promised himself he'd linger, tease, make up for his roughness in the carriage, but his hunger was too sharp. The frantic clutch of her hands on his back, the quick rattle of her breathing, the yielding curve of her body told him she didn't want him to delay.

He slipped his hand between her thighs and stroked the hot, wet folds. Her legs fell open, and she made a low, yearning sound.

Carefully, he pushed one finger inside, feeling resistance, the swift clasp of interior muscles.

Another finger.

Devil take it, she was snug. Even after last time. The prospect of hurting her again made his gut cramp in denial. She moaned and lifted her knees, giving him greater access. He bent to tongue her pebbled nipple and felt her tighten. He sucked hard on the peak and slid his hand free.

Let him hold back long enough to give her pleasure. Raising his head, he stared into her face. She looked nervous, afraid, needy. Her lips parted over small white teeth.

She threaded an unsteady hand through his hair. More tenderness. "Take me, Ashcroft." Her low voice made his blood thunder.

He dragged in a deep breath, paused at the entrance to her body, then slowly, relentlessly pushed into her. Her hips rose, and her fingers curled into his naked back, her nails digging in. She inhaled on a broken sob. He paused, struggling for breath.

"Don't stop." Her nails scored deeper, the sting feeding his arousal.

He inched farther. Pressure set off vermilion fireworks behind his eyes. Every muscle in her body denied him. If she didn't relax, he'd hurt her again.

He set his jaw and told himself he could stop.

And wasn't sure he spoke the truth.

"For God's sake, Diana, breathe," he gritted, as the tight passage pulsed around him.

She didn't seem to hear. Her eyes were glazed. The heavy lids fell as if their weight made it impossible to keep them open. She released the air in her lungs on a long, shuddering sigh. The clenching pressure relaxed. He took advantage of the reprieve to thrust.

She fit as if made for him.

Although it killed him not to push to fulfillment, he remained unmoving, letting her adjust to his size. After brief bliss edging close to torture, she shifted infinitesimally.

The movement shot sparks through him. He ground his teeth, the need to possess her deafening thunder in his ears.

Only when her hips tilted in unmistakable encouragement did he slowly, luxuriously withdraw. With a smoothness he could hardly credit, he plunged back inside.

She opened as sweetly as a flower in morning light. Her hands feverishly stroked his back, then slid down to clasp his buttocks, kneading in a silent invitation to continue.

"Yes," she hissed in surrender.

For a glorious interval, they moved together. His aware-

ness shrank to the searing hold of her body, tension and release, the way her breathing echoed what he did.

Even so, he knew the exact moment she edged toward her
peak. With clumsy haste, his hand sought her center. He
stroked hard as he thrust.

"Ashcroft!" Her muscles tightened, milking him, insisting
he cede to the darkness.

He resisted the flooding pleasure. His jaw ached as he
struggled to hold back. Blackness came and went behind his
eyes. He remained hard and still as she quivered under him
for an eternity.

Gradually the waves receded. He braced himself to pull
out, to spill himself on the sheets. The urge to stay where he
was threatened to master him. He battled it like an enemy.

"Don't," she muttered, eyes closed, fingers digging into
his back. Her face was pale and sheened with dampness.

"I must." His throat was so tight, it hurt to reply.

"Don't leave me." She opened eyes misty with satisfaction
and stared at him. "I want you to finish inside me."

He'd traveled beyond thinking clearly. All he knew was
he couldn't lose himself within her. The rule, always unbro-
ken, pounded insistently at what few shreds of awareness he
retained.

"Let me go," he growled, as her fingers tightened into
talons.

She cried out as he hauled free and flung himself against
the mattress. In a fierce, gasping release that left him trembling and exhausted, he pumped his seed onto the sheets

He collapsed beside her and closed his eyes, panting for
breath. Struggling to return from the brink.

Diana lay silently, fighting to calm her racing pulses. Familiar bitterness flooded her even as she trembled with rapture.

Twice, she'd failed.

She forced her mind into creaking movement. Staring up
at the room's ceiling, she gathered her courage.

"My nurse was a Gypsy." Her voice rasped with nerves and the aftereffects of pleasure. Oddly, talking about what they'd done was more difficult than participating.

She turned her head on the pillows and met Ashcroft's unblinking jade gaze. He looked tired but relaxed, and lazy satisfaction glinted in his eyes.

When he didn't offer encouragement, she forced herself to continue. "She had ways of preventing pregnancy."

The ease leached from his expression, and he rose onto one elbow to study her. Part of her wished he'd kiss her. Another part knew if he did, her already failing ability to pursue this subject would evaporate completely.

And she had to pursue this subject.

If he didn't mean to give her his seed, she couldn't justify her presence in his bed. She'd have to end this affair. Against her will, her heart contracted at the idea of never seeing him again.

And the prospect of informing Lord Burnley of failure was terrifying.

Ashcroft frowned. "What's wrong?"

She tried to make her expression neutral as she cast around desperately for a reason why she wanted him to climax in her body. How did a woman ask for such a thing?

She licked her lips. His gaze flickered to the betraying movement. "I feel . . . I feel cheated when you don't . . . when you don't finish . . ."

"I do finish." His voice was even, as if they discussed the weather or a promenade in Hyde Park.

"Not inside me." The words were a whisper.

"You're blushing."

"I'm sure I am," she said with an abrupt return of spirit. "I hate it when you withdraw. I feel you're . . . you're robbing me of the full experience."

He tapped her cheekbone in gentle reproof. "I'm robbing you of the disaster of a bastard."

"I told you . . ."

"Yes, you have some mysterious Gypsy potion." She winced at his tone's dryness. "You'll forgive me if I express skepticism."

Damn him for not believing her. Although she couldn't blame him. "Even if you got me with child, I wouldn't expect . . ."

Hauteur replaced the smile. He became the worldly, supercilious Lord Ashcroft. The tender, affectionate man might never have existed.

"I don't bring unwanted children into the world." His strong white teeth bit off each word.

She could almost have laughed. How wrong he was. This child was wanted beyond anything he imagined. "Surely with all your women . . ."

Releasing a frustrated breath, he rolled away and left the bed. She tried not to miss his nearness. How easy to let herself drift into a voluptuous dream. What was terrifying was she suspected it was too late to save herself. Because she wanted him lying next to her. She didn't want him glowering at her from several feet away.

"Madam, it is extremely bad form to mention a man's previous lovers."

He should have sounded absurd, rating her like a general with a raw recruit, while he stood there without a stitch on. But his body was so magnificent, he looked daunting and powerful.

Nonetheless, she didn't back down. "How do you know you've never left a bastard behind?"

"I've been careful." He drew in another breath, clearly searching for patience. "We can, if you wish, use a sheath."

Thanks to her educational if uncomfortable discussions with Burnley, she knew what he meant. A whole world had opened since she'd entered into this scheme. A world she wasn't entirely sure she liked.

The idea of Ashcroft covering himself with sewn sheep's gut seemed outlandish. Anyway, a sheath would stop her conceiving. "This Gypsy remedy is safe."

He frowned. "Nothing's safe."

"I never conceived when I was married."

He folded his arms over his impressive chest. "Forgive me for saying this, but I've gathered that your husband wasn't the most passionate of men."

She lurched up against the pillows, dragging the rumpled sheet across to hide her nakedness. "He . . . he was. We were." She strove for calmness and her next words emerged more evenly. "We weren't married long."

"Which is why you didn't fall pregnant. Mysterious magical charms had nothing to do with it."

"We were married a year. Long enough to have a baby."

Heaven help her, it had been. When William died and left her alone, she'd thought her heart would shatter. Without her work at Cranston Abbey, she'd have found nothing to live for.

Perhaps bringing up William's child would have made the years since then less lonely. Perhaps a child would have saved her from sacrificing her soul to other, less holy gods.

If she'd had a child, she wouldn't be here now, deceiving a good man so she could lay claim to a house she knew in her heart she had no right to own.

How tragically wrong she'd been about Lord Ashcroft. If she'd known the truth about him when Burnley broached this scheme, she would never have agreed to participate.

She wasn't stupid. She'd read signs since the affair started that Ashcroft wasn't the brutish, blundering debaucher of Burnley's description. But blindly, she'd continued, convinced her lover wouldn't care what happened to her after their liaison, as long as he obtained his selfish pleasure.

The simple transaction of her willingness in return for a baby was a wicked lie she'd used to justify unjustifiable actions.

This conversation made her feel vile, disgusting, dirty. It shone a stark, unforgiving light on everything she did. But even as she cursed herself for deceiving Ashcroft, Cranston Abbey lured her. All her dreams. And a single chance to turn them into reality.

Surely recognizing that Ashcroft was essentially a good man didn't alter her quest. If Ashcroft never knew what she did, if he never knew she sought a child from him, her ambition would cost him nothing.

Or was that another lie she told herself?

Too late to succumb to wrenching guilt. She was in Ashcroft's bed and committed to obeying Burnley. Still she heard the falsehood in her voice as she spoke. Could Ashcroft hear it too?

"My nurse's daughter Laura has had a string of lovers, and she's never fallen pregnant either." How Laura would hate to hear Diana malign her. To her knowledge, her friend was a virgin.

Ashcroft looked annoyed and suspicious. Difficult to believe not long ago he'd shuddered with desire in her arms. She wondered nervously if she tried him to a point where he'd decide she wasn't worth the trouble, and he'd prefer easier, less demanding prey.

Chagrin stabbed her as she imagined Ashcroft doing what he'd just done with her to someone else. Chagrin with no connection to her mission for Lord Burnley and far too much connection to Diana Carrick and her longing heart.

Diana, grow up. He's been in hundreds of beds, and he'll be in hundreds more. You're nothing special, and you're asking for trouble if you imagine you are.

"No woman wants the burden of a fatherless child."

He spoke with a depth of feeling that attracted her attention. It indicated something greater than just a wish to shield a lover, something touching his heart.

The secret knowledge she possessed coiled in her gut like an adder. Bile rose to sour her mouth as she thought of the layers of deceit she practiced on this man.

He won't care, she assured herself, fisting her hands in the sheets until they ached. Every time she said those words, she believed them less. This discussion indicated he *did* care.

"Lord Ashcroft." She tried to match his coolness but spoiled the effect when her voice trembled. "I've looked after the possibility of conception. I came to you for sexual experience. So far, you've proven a disappointment."

She'd hoped to needle him. Instead, he arched those knowing brows. "Oh, harsh words."

Betraying color flooded her face. Damn him. He knew she'd attained her peak each time he'd taken her. How could he not? "You don't know what I hoped for," she snapped.

"Believe me, pumping my juice into you won't improve the fuck."

Her eyes rounded at his coarse language, although she knew she'd asked for it. As perfect as a Greek god from a statuary, he strolled forward to lean against the bedpost. Naked, he should be at a disadvantage, but he unquestionably remained in control.

Helplessly, her attention flickered downward, over the defined musculature of his chest to where his penis jutted from a nest of curling black hair. To her surprise the organ began to swell and stiffen.

If her face became any hotter, she'd go up in flames. Nervously she shifted her focus to the left. A small dark patch on his hip captured her attention. She hadn't noticed it before. Hardly surprising, considering how overwhelmed she'd been when she saw him unclothed.

Was it a scar? A birthmark? A tattoo?

"I shock you."

She dragged her gaze from the interesting mark to meet his. A phantom smile hovered around his mouth.

"Yes." She risked an honest answer. She'd tried to play the sophisticate, but he must know she was hopelessly outclassed in these games. "I'm a complete country mouse. That's why I'm here. I'm sure I'll become used to your ways."

She hoped to heaven he wouldn't toss her out before she

had the chance to become used to him. Back in Marsham, she'd told herself she'd play the perfect lover, biddable, co-operative, responsive. In the throes of passion, it was impossible to hide her real self. How deluded she'd been to imagine she'd keep some distance from the man who took her. The intimacy of sex inevitably meant intimacy of other, unwelcome kinds.

The tension drained from his long body, and his rueful smile made her heart lurch with reluctant warmth. "You're such a goddess in my arms, I forget your inexperience."

Astonishment had her recoiling against the carved headboard. The sheet slipped unconsidered from her bare breasts. "You . . ."

Words deserted her. A goddess? Her? He couldn't mean it. He was a man practiced at wooing. His arsenal must include quivers full of sweet compliments.

Even as she chastised herself for believing he meant what he said, her eyes searched his dark face. His gaze was steady and glowed with unconstrained admiration.

His attention dropped to her breasts, and interest sparked in the green eyes. She blushed again and hitched the sheet up, even though she knew her behavior was ridiculous. He'd already seen all of her. Touched all of her.

Ashcroft laughed at her continued silence. "Now I really have shocked you."

"No." She blinked, trying to understand this new world, where women like Diana Carrick were called goddesses. A world where superb examples of masculinity like Tarquin Vale considered her irresistible. "Yes."

He distracted her with his flattery. She clutched the sheet tighter and almost wailed her frustration. A frustration not only with him but with herself and her wayward responses. And the fact that she couldn't stanch the pricks of a guilty conscience, no matter how she struggled to ignore them. "Surely it can't be enjoyable to pull out at the . . . ultimate moment."

The fugitive lightness faded. "I won't inflict my bastards upon the world."

She extended a hand toward him palm upward. Because beneath the denial, she read a longing that made her heart cramp. He burned to spill his seed inside her. She should have seen that from the first time, when he'd withdrawn with almost painful violence.

Her task was clear, distasteful as it was. She must break down his will.

Which, against all expectations, was prodigious.

Lord Burnley, the world, the respectable Mrs. Carrick from Marsham, all had underestimated this man.

She cringed at how she twisted her words to mislead. "I promise on my soul there will be no unwanted children because of what happens between us, Ashcroft."

He took her hand, moving closer to the bed. Her other hand automatically rested on his hip. Had she won the battle? She didn't know, and she couldn't ask. If she pushed the issue further, he'd become suspicious.

What if he never gave in? Where did that leave her?

"What's this?" she asked absently, stroking the small dark patch she'd noticed earlier. Up close the mark formed a familiar shape. She traced it with her fingers.

He looked down and shrugged. "A birthmark."

"It's like a tree." With her index finger, knowing she teased him, she followed the almost perfect circle of the foliage, the short, thick trunk below.

"Why are you smiling?"

She looked up. The idea that she knew this intimate secret about him seemed special. Which was absurd. He'd had so many lovers. All must have seen this brand on his hard hip.

He'd run a hundred miles if he knew she nursed such sentimental notions about him. Nonsensical, untenable, dangerous notions. Instead, she let her smile widen. Her eyes focused on the part of him she found enormously interesting.

Enormously.

"I'm looking forward to what happens next."

"Saucy wench," he murmured, leaning forward and landing a swift kiss on her lips. As he drew away, she licked her lips, relishing the flavor.

Bringing his hand to her face, she kissed his palm. He tasted salty, delicious. With a shock, she realized the musky flavor of his skin must be her, lingering from when he'd touched her center.

Instinct was her only guide. Very deliberately, she licked between his fingers and thrilled to hear his breathing change. Very slowly she took his long middle finger between her lips and sucked.

"Diana . . ." he groaned, and shifted closer.

She could smell his skin. Fresh sweat, sex, some essence she'd recognize in a crowded room as Ashcroft's. The scent was heady, seductive.

Her confidence edged higher at his immediate response to her tentative attempts to please. She slid the hand resting on his hip around to cup the heavy sac between his legs.

"Good God . . ." He held himself quiveringly still as she sucked harder on his finger and stroked him from base to tip. He was hard as steel, hot as fire. Like satin over living oak.

Very gently she circled the head. A drop of pearly liquid oozed out to lubricate her finger's tantalizing journey.

He pushed his hips forward, demanding more. His eyes blazed like fiery emeralds in a face pale with strain. A muscle jerked in one lean cheek, and his jaw set hard as granite.

Carefully, she ran her hand up then down the heavy length. He groaned and grabbed her hand, demonstrating the movement. She quickly caught the rhythm that incited him to madness.

His eyes closed and his nostrils flared wide. His unabashed need sent hot shivers through her to coalesce into molten desire. The urge to replace her hand with her mouth became overpowering. How odd to be so eager to taste him when the thought had once repulsed her.

Groaning he grabbed her hand, pulling it away. His chest heaved as he fought for breath. With shaking urgency, he pushed her onto the mattress, following her down. His mouth opened over hers in a devouring kiss. She countered his passion with passion of her own, drowning in crimson darkness.

He slid between her legs, and she tightened her thighs around his narrow hips, anchoring him. He tilted her toward him. Breathlessly, she waited for him to plunge inside. He paused and stroked his hardness along her cleft until she shook and gasped with need.

She became the aggressor in the endless kiss. Silently insisting he stop teasing. "Do it. Do it now," she moaned, hardly aware of what she said.

"Oh, yes." With a long, low growl deep in his throat, he surged inside her.

She was so wet and ready, all she felt was a ravishing fullness. She drew a long, juddering breath and crossed her ankles behind his buttocks, changing the angle of penetration. Fresh sensations made her moan with delight.

He shifted in and out, wild and relentless as a stormy sea. She opened her eyes to see him rising above her. The image burned into her brain. His face was stark with ferocious passion. His lips drew back from his teeth as if he was in pain. The tendons of his neck were distended, and sweat dampened his skin.

He looked like a man crossing the extreme edges of control.

She closed her eyes and arched as he thrust hard. Over and over he plunged into her, lost to his hunger.

Flames filled her vision, dazzling and golden. It was like falling headfirst into the sun. She twisted as lightning battered her from every direction. Vaguely, through her shuddering crisis, she heard him release a deep, heartrending groan.

Liquid heat flooded her womb.

Chapter Ten

Blind to everything but his volcanic release, Ashcroft pumped into the woman beneath him.

The act's unprecedented freedom fractured all restraint. He unleashed himself as if he dived into a deep blue ocean. Helpless to resist, he closed his eyes and let the waves wash him far out toward the horizon, where he saw only brilliant light and sky.

On the last of the breakers, he coasted into shore to find himself beached in a large, luxurious bed in a darkening room. He lay spread-eagled across Diana. His face was buried in a soft mass of golden hair, which smelled gloriously of apples.

He stayed where he was, utterly exhausted, utterly replete for the first time in his life.

He felt her breathe, softly, unevenly. The scent of her satisfaction filled his senses. Her arms wound tightly around his back, her bent legs framed his hips. Call him every kind of fool, but he read tenderness in her soft caresses.

Hell. Hell. Hell. He hadn't pulled out.

The reality of what he'd done seeped through his torpor like a trickle of ice water. Dear God, let her not be pregnant. Let this bliss not lead them to disaster.

Too late to do anything about that. And for all his turmoil now, nothing could make him repent those heedless, blazing moments in her arms.

He'd meant to withdraw as he always did. But somewhere in the wild heights, his body had taken over. He'd never lost control with a woman before. With every moment in her presence, Diana launched him into new levels of experience. Ironic to think this virtuous widow opened whole worlds of sensual pleasure to a jaded rake.

He'd desperately wanted to spill himself inside her. And, heaven forgive him, he had. Heedlessly. Endlessly. Powerfully. He'd flooded her with his essence, claiming her as his with a primitive fervor he'd never imagined he'd feel with a lover.

He should regret what he'd done. But he was such a barbarian that, deep in his heart, he couldn't.

The sensation of filling her had been extraordinary. At the peak, no barrier had existed between them. Male and female united to create a whole. Tarquin and Diana. Together.

He'd never felt as close to another lover as he felt to this woman stretched naked beneath him.

Naked and crushed.

"I'm flattening you." Even muffled in her silky hair, he heard the betraying huskiness of his voice.

He couldn't shake the impression that what had just happened marked him for life. That it would linger in his memory like few other encounters. That Diana would leave her brand on his soul, a brand countless future encounters wouldn't erase, no matter how he'd wish they would.

How long since sex had impinged on his emotions? What they'd done this afternoon bypassed his defenses. He'd spent his life resisting vulnerability. Yet even after such a short time with her, he knew this sweet, passionate woman would devastate him with her departure.

Just let heaven be merciful and spare them a bastard as the result of today's rapture.

"I . . ." She had to clear her throat before she managed a whole sentence. "I don't mind."

He roused himself enough to mention what had just happened. "I didn't withdraw."

With an unsteady hand, she brushed his unruly hair back from his forehead. "I know."

The fool woman didn't sound perturbed. He closed his eyes, reveling in her touch, trying to summon horror adequate to the occasion. He could have created an unwanted child. He'd sworn he never would.

Yet any consequences of his carelessness seemed far away, unreal. What was real was the beautiful woman who lay under him. The woman whose face was glowing and gentle in the aftermath of that astounding communion.

"The Gypsy remedy is safe, I promise you," she said softly. "Don't worry, Ashcroft. And . . ." She released a sigh that seemed a soft echo of ecstasy. "And what we just did was . . . wonderful."

Yes. *Wonderful.* And worthy of a thousand other superlatives as well. Too good to spoil with stewing over something that mightn't ever happen.

He let himself drift. His body still joined hers. Heat and intimacy enfolded him, made him feel he existed inside a magical golden cocoon, where grim reality couldn't impinge.

Oh, that conclusion definitely resulted from too much good sex.

He angled up on his elbows to stare at Diana. She looked well loved. As she should after what they'd done. Her thick blond hair tangled around her face, and her lips were cherry red from his kisses. He noticed a graze on her neck where he'd kissed her too hard.

Savage he was, he was pleased that she wore his mark.

Hell, he couldn't feel possessive. He was never possessive. Yet the idea of anyone else touching Diana made him seethe with denial.

She shifted, and he felt a surge of arousal. He was such a beast, he was ready for her again.

She still floated in postcoital languor, but when she moved, she'd be sore. He was a large man, and he'd used her relentlessly.

He could wait before he had her again.

At least until he'd fed her and given her a glass of wine. Except it meant withdrawing from her and shattering this strangely comfortable silence.

The room was shadowy with twilight. Last week, he'd made plans to meet his cronies at the opera tonight. He wasn't going anywhere. All the music he needed was right here. "I hope the champagne's cold."

With a satisfied sigh, he pulled away and turned onto his back, staring up at the ceiling, while his mind sifted the various delights of the afternoon.

The mattress dipped as she slid up in the bed, her breasts jiggling deliciously. They truly were magnificent. White and firm and voluptuous. He hadn't paid them nearly enough attention. Something to remedy next time. His cock stirred in agreement.

"I . . . I have to go," she said unsteadily.

Ashcroft's uncharacteristically amiable mood evaporated. Sharply, he turned his head and stared at her, trying to read her expression.

She looked uncomfortable. More than at any other time during the whole passionate afternoon. His curiosity awoke. And his wariness. She met his eyes, then glanced quickly away to where her fingers plucked at the crushed white sheets.

He couldn't mistake her nervousness. And she looked guilty.

Why?

"Must you?" he asked neutrally even as his brain picked and fretted at the barriers she erected.

She nodded with a jerkiness that indicated she lied. "Yes. Yes, I must."

"Don't go." He reached to still her fidgeting. "We'll have supper. Conversation. And I promised you a bath."

He didn't mention how the evening would end. She knew as well as he that they'd make love again. Probably several times. He was insatiable. He'd never wanted a woman so much.

Her hands trembled, and the gaze she directed at him was dark with misery. Good God, she looked on the verge of tears. What had happened here?

Suspicion slithered like a snake through his gut and warned him he should never have fallen for her lures. But it was too late to break away. If she promised destruction, it was destruction laced with a pleasure as addicting and deadly as opium.

"No, I . . . I must go." She shook her head and lowered her eyes. A wave of golden hair slid across one bare shoulder and dipped over the sheet she clutched with incongruous modesty.

Except he knew at heart she was a modest woman. Her wildness resulted from passion. Which made her surrender all the more gratifying. He was barbarian enough to relish the contrast between her essential reticence and her overpowering desire.

She quickly glanced at him then away. "I . . . I wish you'd put some clothes on."

How did she hope to pass herself as a worldly woman when her color revealed her feelings so immediately? He made no move to obey. Her attention drifted to his nakedness, and he hid a smug smile. She wanted him. She might try to create a distance between them, but she failed miserably.

He sat up and slipped a hand behind her head, the warm softness of her hair tickling his fingers. "Stay."

"Ashcroft, not now . . ." she faltered although she made no attempt to evade him.

Her words might deny him but her body definitely said

yes. He dropped kisses on the corners of her mouth. Her lips parted in silent invitation.

He slid his other hand down and, after a soft tug, pulled the sheet from her hold. With one finger, he circled her hardening nipple.

He lowered his head to kiss her properly. His lips glanced across hers, he caught a hint of heat and moisture before she wrenched away.

Another jarring warning clanged in his brain. Why was she so devilish skittish?

In a flurry of movement that offered a breathtaking glimpse of full breasts and long, slender legs, she rolled off the bed. To his regret, she dragged the sheet with her. She wrapped the white linen around herself and raised her chin with a defiance he recognized.

"I must go, Ashcroft. It's been . . ." She paused and swallowed. Her traitorous color rose again. Her voice was thick as she continued. "It's been a revelation."

He liked the word. He liked it very much indeed. He also liked that he clearly wasn't the only person swept away in turbulent emotional currents. "I'll see you tomorrow."

"I'll send you a message."

He frowned as he rose from the bed. Reticence was all very well. Her answer hinted at delay before he touched her. "Don't make me wait. I want you again. Good God, I want you now."

That almost sounded like a plea. Hell, he didn't need to importune female companionship. He spent his life tripping over women slavering for his attentions.

Except none of those women was Diana.

Until he'd worked off his inconvenient obsession, no other bedmate would do.

Her eyes flickered to his cock, then up again. His rebellious flesh hardened. Just so simple an act, and he needed her under him. "Believe me, I want . . . I want to do this again."

"Good," he snapped. He fought back the craven urge to beg her to stay, never to leave. Instead, he turned on his heel and stalked toward the door leading into the bathroom. "Just don't wait too long."

Diana returned to Chelsea in a daze. Like a coward, she'd avoided Lord Ashcroft when she fled Lord Peregrine's mansion. No angry naked man appeared on the landing to demand what she thought she was doing, sneaking away like a criminal.

She wondered if he sulked because she refused his invitation to stay. But after the last intense hours, she knew whatever lay between them garnered a stronger reaction than pique.

She felt shabby creeping off without a farewell. Shabby and used, like a prostitute slinking away from an uncongenial client.

Except it was she who'd used Lord Ashcroft.

And the client was far from uncongenial.

Which was why she was so frantic to escape before her teetering world crashed in and destroyed her. Lying didn't come naturally to her. Lying to a man who carried her to heaven in his arms became more impossible with every second.

She was utterly ruined. Any pretension to virtue fled. She'd given herself to a man who wasn't her husband. Worse, she'd thoroughly reveled in the act. Her body ached in places she'd forgotten. Even at the height of their passion, William hadn't taken her with such urgency.

She needed time to herself, time to remind herself why she did what she did.

Fate had presented her with the chance to become mistress of Cranston Abbey. A chance to achieve every dream she'd ever had, dreams she'd never dared have.

But even the Abbey faded into insignificance when she

recalled the dazzling hours of pleasure in Ashcroft's arms. The man she'd prepared to despise proved more fascinating with every moment.

Like a thief, she crept home through the back garden. She had become used to entering houses by hidden entrances. Deception fed upon itself and infected everything she touched.

She knew Laura would be waiting with questions and endless disapproval. Laura had never wanted Diana to participate in this scheme. She'd always insisted that the price was too high, whatever the rewards.

After today, Diana wondered if her friend's misgivings were prescience.

Diana Carrick wasn't made for secrets and lies. She couldn't offer her body without enlisting her emotions. She couldn't trample a good man's rights without feeling like the lowest creature born.

As a conspirator, she was a rank failure.

"It's all a lie," she muttered, pushing the door open.

"Talking to yourself now?" Laura asked from the shadows near the entrance.

Diana gasped and pulled back. She hadn't noticed her friend although she was visible in the light from inside the house. "What are you doing out here?" she asked sharply.

Laura stepped into the empty back hall. "Lord Burnley wants to see you."

Diana frowned, following her. "He's in London?"

"No. In Surrey."

"It's so late."

"You know his lordship. When he wants something, he doesn't wait." Laura stepped back as Diana passed her. The shock on her face was vivid. "You look . . ."

Diana's color rose, and she crossed trembling arms over her breasts. Although nothing hid her lack of corset or that her gown was barely fastened.

As she had for so many years, she took refuge in practicalities. "I can't go down to Marsham like this. Who did Burnley send?"

"Fredericks."

The most superior of the footmen. Unfailingly loyal and obedient. A brawny thug who did Burnley's dirty work. "How long has he been here?"

Laura, thank goodness, took the hint and didn't pursue the subject of Diana's disheveled appearance. "An hour. Maybe more."

"Where is he now?" Diana removed her bonnet, and her hair tumbled around her face, another silent testimony to how she'd spent her afternoon.

"Downstairs in the kitchen. I sent him for supper."

Diana picked up her creased skirts and hurried toward the back staircase. "I'll change."

"Do you need help?"

What she needed was a long soak in a bath and a night's sleep. What she needed was a few hours without a howling conscience. What she needed was the chance to go back in time to a month ago. Before the devil offered her everything she coveted if she committed just one small sin that did no harm to anyone else.

One small sin that now threatened to destroy her.

"No, I'll manage," she said huskily.

Absurd to feel so close to tears. What she'd done today finally put her dreams within reach. That's what she needed to think about, not the piercing sweetness of Ashcroft's possession.

Laura touched her arm as Diana started climbing the stairs. She lowered her voice. "Did he hurt you?"

"No."

From the time Burnley first broached his plan, Laura had listed pitfalls, including the possibility that Lord Ashcroft was violent. Diana wished Ashcroft had been less careful with her, less willing to rein in his desire to ensure her pleasure. She desperately needed to find something about him to dislike.

I do him no harm.

The rote insistence didn't even register against the shriek of her conscience. It had been easy believing him immune before she met him. Harder when she'd breathed his musky scent, touched his sleek skin, listened to his hoarse praise while he took her to the stars.

Laura didn't immediately release her, although they both knew Lord Burnley hated to wait. "Are you sure? You don't seem yourself."

Diana shook herself free, and a humorless smile twisted her lips. "I just whored myself in return for life as a marchioness. Of course I'm not myself."

A frown drew Laura's fine dark brows together. "You slept with him, then?"

Diana made a derisive gesture toward her disorderly clothing. "Isn't it obvious?"

Laura looked pale and distraught. "I wondered if, when the moment came, you'd change your mind."

Diana knew what her friend really meant was she'd hoped some shred of ethical behavior would surface from the murk in Diana's soul.

She couldn't retreat now. She'd gone too far down Lord Burnley's luxurious path to hell. And she couldn't tell Laura that her desire for Ashcroft was so powerful, she'd barely recalled her wicked plans once he'd touched her.

She could hardly countenance that reality. The honesty of her passion made her scheme all the more tawdry.

And made her feel a whore indeed.

"No, I did it," Diana said curtly. She turned and purposefully marched up the stairs. "Please tell Fredericks I'll be ready in twenty minutes."

"As you wish." Laura's voice was flat with all the things she resisted saying. Thank the Lord, she did resist.

Chapter Eleven

*L*ord Burnley's carriage rolled through the impressive stone gates marking the boundary of the Cranston Abbey estate.

After several tumultuous hours of reminding herself why she'd gone to London, Diana had a firmer grip on her unruly emotions. Every mile she traveled away from Lord Ashcroft helped.

When she embarked on this plan, she'd known she needed to be strong. That she needed more strength than she'd ever imagined was difficult but not a disaster.

She'd be careful. Ashcroft need never find out what she was up to. The affair would reach its natural end as all his affairs did, and he'd move on to his next conquest. She'd become a marchioness and create a fulfilling future here with her child.

Simple.

Nothing changed her original arrangement with Lord Burnley. Ashcroft might prove more complex, more compelling, more . . . *everything* than she'd expected. But that didn't alter her mission. Or the rewards that awaited her if she held her nerve.

The moon was at three-quarters, sailing in a clear sky

above the thick woods that covered the hills behind the Abbey. Not that she needed light to see where she was. She knew this place better than any other in the world. The estate encompassed the geography of her heart.

Joy surging, she leaned out the window and drew a deep, steadying breath of fresh country air. The fragrances of Cranston Abbey filled her senses. Rich earth. Dankness from the lake, low because of the hot weather. Newly cut grass.

But her happiness at her homecoming was for once tarnished. Under the familiar essences, another scent lingered. A scent reminding her she was no longer the woman who had departed through these gates for London. Although she'd washed before leaving Chelsea, traces of Ashcroft's passion clung to her skin and hair. It was like he was still with her.

The deceit she practiced in London seeped down to poison the place that had always been her personal heaven. Would that be the case from now on? Or would the potent magic of Cranston Abbey keep her transgressions at bay?

No matter. Cranston Abbey was worth it.

She repeated the words over and over like a silent prayer as the carriage followed the lime-tree-lined driveway. They rounded the bend in the road, and just as the genius who designed house and grounds had intended, the Abbey sprang into view like a perfect miracle.

However many times she witnessed this marvel, wonder still transfixed her. Down in the valley, the magnificent baroque façade seemed to call a welcome, telling her it missed her, that it wanted to enfold her inside its elegance forever. That she and only she could ensure its well-being.

She'd adored Cranston Abbey all her life, first ignorantly as the bailiff's motherless daughter, cosseted by the denizens of this enchanted kingdom. Only later had she comprehended how lucky she was to be part of this splendor.

When she married William at nineteen, she'd loved him. But if he hadn't been Lord Burnley's secretary and librarian, tied to the estate, she wondered if she'd have accepted his offer. She'd received several marriage proposals before William's and always refused, claiming her father needed her. Her love for the Abbey was strong, infinite, self-sacrificing, and it had only grown stronger over the years.

But her love had always contained a bitter core.

However she dedicated her life to this beloved place, she could never lay claim to it beyond what her employer allowed. Until Lord Burnley offered a satanic bargain that would give her all she coveted if she compromised every principle.

She'd hardly hesitated.

As she watched the long, symmetrical façade of the house loom closer, she couldn't help thinking she'd made the right choice. She would become the custodian of Cranston Abbey. Her blood would continue forever in this place, her footstep would echo in its corridors, her ghost would haunt its galleries.

Nothing would stop her.

Not lying to a man who showed her only consideration. Not the fermenting guilt that weighted her belly even now as she surveyed the treasure that awaited if she persisted with her quest.

Could she already be pregnant? The idea was impossible to encompass. Yet it was as real as the ebony window frame under her gloved hands.

In agonized tumult, she closed her eyes and relived again the liquid surge of Ashcroft's seed into her womb. *Dear God, let a baby form. Let the child be a boy. Let him grow to be a worthy custodian of the Abbey.*

Fredericks ushered Diana into the house and down the elaborately painted and gilded halls toward the library. Diana hardly glanced at the images surrounding her. Although she knew every panel. She knew every inch of this estate like a mother knew every feature on her child's face.

It was late, well past midnight. Burnley had summoned her, he'd be waiting. Even old and ill, he exercised despotic power over his domain.

The marquess sat at his desk, a Boulle monstrosity that reputedly had once belonged to Louis XIV. Diana suspected the French king's arrogance hadn't matched Lord Burnley's.

He ignored Diana and studiously completed reading the document before him with eyes that needed no help from spectacles. As she regarded him, she noted the toll of a lifetime of lovelessness, scheming, and acrimony. Lord Burnley had always been considered handsome. No longer. Now the evil in his soul was written on the harshly carved features.

Lamplight was kinder than day, but nothing hid the ravages of disease. Not long ago, he'd been a strong, terrifying figure, a monolithic presence in the lives of his tenants and servants. That was before last year, when fire killed his two sons and their families.

Diana recalled the day when news arrived of the Christmas celebrations that ended so calamitously. The fire had started overnight and engulfed the old manor at Deshayes before the residents could save themselves.

The loss of life had been appalling. Not just Lord Burnley's heirs, but servants and family friends and relatives passing the festive season with the Fanshawes.

That winter, Lord Burnley had conducted one of his periodic feuds with his oldest son. He'd brooded in Cranston Abbey instead of attending the family Christmas.

His absence had saved him.

In spite of the all-encompassing horror of the tragedy, Diana had never seen grief in the old man. She knew the fire had proven a blow to his ambitions. The Fanshawes had held high office since the reign of Henry VII. Suddenly, at the age of seventy-five, Edgar Fanshawe was the last of the direct line. One day, the succession was secure unto the second generation. The next, a distant American cousin, descended from an obscure junior branch, was the closest male heir.

Diana hadn't needed to hear the marquess's derisive dismissal of this fellow to know how that knowledge chafed.

Lord Burnley was proud and amoral and accustomed to shaping obedient destiny. For several months, he'd become a hermit, stewing on his misfortunes. He'd emerged changed, still purposeful and focused, but death had laid its bony hand on him.

Before he departed this world, he intended to make one last desperate attempt to control the future.

Which sparked this Machiavellian plan Diana helped bring to fruition.

Finally, he laid aside the paper. He steepled his long thin fingers and surveyed her out of sharp green eyes that conveyed a complete lack of pleasure.

She straightened and returned his stare. She was always bold with him—strangely, she suspected he respected that quality. It was certainly among the reasons he'd chosen her for this task. That and her fatal longing for Cranston Abbey.

"What do you have to report?" he barked.

So typical he didn't waste time on social niceties. But then, they both knew time was one luxury he no longer had.

She hesitated although she knew what she had to tell him would gain his approval.

Her shyness was absurd. They both knew why she'd gone to London. After what she'd done, she had no right to claim modesty. Still, the words stuck in her tight throat.

She found herself challenging him instead of announcing her triumph. Which felt like no triumph at all. "If you're going to drag me away from London whenever the mood takes you, you risk everything."

His lips thinned until they almost disappeared. She hid a frisson of fear. He was a devil, Mephistopheles to her Faust. He wouldn't care if he destroyed her in his bid to control Cranston Abbey beyond the grave. This scorpion might be old, but he was still poisonous.

His voice emerged as a growl. "Where did you go this afternoon? My man lost you after you left Chelsea."

Dismay flooded her although she should have expected this. "You're having me watched?"

He didn't even blink, his eyes lizardlike in the flickering light. "Of course."

Drawing herself to her full height, she fought the urge to cling to the elaborately carved chair in front of her. It had been a long day, exhausting, emotional, wrenching. Her head felt like it was stuffed full of wool.

He had a right to know where she'd been. It was painful to force the words. "I was with Lord Ashcroft."

She awaited some expression of approbation. Instead, the old man's eyes sharpened and his rake-thin body braced with quivering tension. "How can I be sure?"

She summoned her courage. Like all predators, if he sensed weakness, he'd attack. "It's too late to decide you don't trust me, my lord."

"I don't trust anyone." He tapped his fingers together in front of him without shifting his gaze. "Tell me."

Betraying color flooded her cheeks, and she stiffened. Surely, this foul old man couldn't expect a detailed description of Ashcroft's technique in bed. "We made love."

He made a disgusted sound. "He fucked you. Don't pretty up what happened. Did he leave his seed?"

Quivering with humiliation, she swallowed to clear the obstruction in her throat. She should have realized Burnley would subject her to an inquisition. "Yes."

"Tell me about him."

Her spirit revived and she snapped a reply. "He's a man. We copulated. What else do you need to know?"

"Did you see him unclothed?"

The question was odd, although at least Burnley wasn't asking her to relate each moment of Ashcroft's possession. "Yes."

A taut silence descended. After a few bristling seconds,

Burnley made another of those impatient sounds. "Well? Speak, girl!"

She spread her hands in confusion. What did Burnley want her to say? "I didn't notice anything unusual. He wasn't deformed." Perhaps that was behind these questions. The concern some defect would pass to the heir. "But my husband is the only other man I've seen naked. I don't have too many grounds for comparison."

He scowled and his hands tightened so his bony knuckles shone white. "Most unsatisfactory. Is that all you have to say?"

Helplessly, she stared at the marquess. Lord Burnley's wrath was a terrifying force. She had no wish to provoke it. Especially as she didn't know how she'd incurred his displeasure. She thought he'd be delighted.

Clearly, she'd been wrong.

Her mind scrabbled for a description of Lord Ashcroft's body. The picture was vivid in her mind, as if painted in oils. Her voice faltered as she began. "He's tall, strong, lean. Broad shoulders. Dark hair on his chest but not too much. No scars that I saw." Then she remembered. "And he has a birthmark on his hip shaped like an oak tree."

It was as though something sucked the tension from Burnley. He collapsed back in his huge, high-backed chair, and his breath rattled in his dry throat. His talonlike hands relaxed and spread on the green leather blotter before him.

Satisfaction smoothed the deep lines on his face. "Ah."

Nothing more. Bewilderment filled Diana. "Is the birthmark important?"

"Damned important, you fool girl." The old man's lips curved in a ghost of a smile.

When she didn't respond, he went on. "It's the Fanshawe mark. Tarquin Vale is indeed my son. And you carry his seed."

Chapter Twelve

~~~~~~

$\mathcal{D}$esperately, Diana searched the old man's face for some resemblance to the son who'd proven such a generous and passionate lover. As always, she found no likeness, apart from perhaps the green eyes. Eyes that right now sparked with something approximating joy, if Satan could feel such a positive emotion.

Perhaps Ashcroft instead resembled his wayward mother. The lady who had presented another man's child to her husband as heir to the Vale estates and titles.

When Burnley had told her about Ashcroft's parentage, he'd been remarkably close-lipped about the countess. He'd snapped Diana down when she'd asked about the woman who had given birth to his bastard son.

The marquess lifted a bell on the desk and rang it sharply. Immediately, Fredericks entered, officious as ever. "Yes, my lord?"

Burnley made a sweeping gesture. "Wine." He returned his attention to Diana. "Sit, girl."

Blinking with astonishment at this acknowledgment she was human, she subsided into a chair. In truth, her legs were close to giving out. She felt so tired, she could hardly speak. "Thank you."

She accepted a glass of claret from Fredericks and sipped, but the fine vintage tasted acrid on her tongue. Everything tasted acrid right now. She knowingly deceived Lord Ashcroft, so she couldn't claim any particular morality, but she loathed Burnley's crowing triumph.

The man she used was worth a million of her coconspirator.

Her coconspirator had what she wanted, God help her.

Burnley took a gulp of wine as Fredericks left with a discreet bow. The liquor couldn't be good for the marquess's health, but she forbore commenting. He was old and sick. He was welcome to what pleasures remained. She just wished those pleasures didn't include his gloating satisfaction.

"I take my hat off to you. I didn't believe you'd do it."

She didn't find his admiration gladdening. After tasting her wine, she set it down on the desk. She felt sick and lightheaded. Tiredness, she told herself, although she knew most of her malaise stemmed from self-disgust and a long, hard sexual session after many chaste years.

When she didn't speak, Burnley's tone became aggrieved. "I would think you'd be happy. If your womb quickens, you're set for life. Don't tell me you're having second thoughts. Not when you finally faced the fence and jumped it."

Second thoughts. And third and fourth thoughts into the thousands. She couldn't reveal her conscience's writhing discomfort. It would be like speaking the King's English to a Mongolian nomad. Burnley had no acquaintance with scruples.

"If I get with child, I'll become your wife," she said dully.

He slammed his hand on the desk in a brief return to the vigorous man she remembered. "Damn you, chit. If our plan works, you'll be a marchioness with guardianship of the heir and control of this estate until the boy reaches his majority."

"It mightn't be a boy," she said for what felt like the hundredth time since he'd broached this scheme.

However he chose to ride roughshod over her uncertainties, Lord Burnley's ambitions faced enormous stumbling blocks. "If it's a girl, you'll still be rich beyond your wildest dreams. And the girl gets all my property that's not entailed."

"I mightn't get pregnant."

He glowered. "You're damned gloomy for a woman with a fortune in her sights. Don't forget, it's not just you in the lap of luxury, but your father and that Gypsy slut as well."

She liked to tell herself her father's future had weighed heavily in her decision to cooperate with Lord Burnley. But in her heart, she knew it was the lure of this house that made her betray everything she believed in.

She still remembered her astonished elation when Burnley suggested the scheme. The interview had been awkward, difficult. A man who never admitted weakness had to explain he was riddled with cancer, and one irreversible effect of the disease was impotence.

At last, she'd comprehended Burnley's deep anger since the fire. It wasn't sadness for so many lives lost. It was frustration that he was in no position to spawn a new heir.

To secure the succession with a child of his blood, he needed a woman willing to whore herself to his bastard son. The bastard son Burnley despised and who remained ignorant of his heritage. The woman had to be of otherwise unimpeachable virtue and discretion because once she fell pregnant, she'd become Lady Burnley.

His bailiff's widowed daughter was perfect on all counts.

God help her, she'd agreed within a day. Presented with the promise of taking over the running of Cranston Abbey, she couldn't say no.

Weak, greedy Diana.

But the risks had seemed so minor and the rewards so princely. As marchioness, Diana had no ambitions to cut a figure in society. Instead, she intended to live quietly, raising her son to love the estate as she did. After all, the Abbey would be his when he turned twenty-one.

The chances of running into Lord Ashcroft once the affair ended were minimal. He'd have no reason to assume the child she gave Lord Burnley was his.

Unless he calculated the months . . .

Unless he was suspicious . . .

Unless the child looked like him . . .

Before she'd met him, she'd assumed Lord Ashcroft wouldn't care about eventual consequences. She'd since discovered he cared deeply. After today, one thing was starkly clear. If he ever found out she'd deceived him and stolen his child, he'd be furious.

Burnley watched her with his reptilian regard. "Does he want to see you again?"

"Yes."

"The ruffian is a connoisseur of the petticoat brigade. You have hidden talents, Mrs. Carrick." He spoke the last words with a sarcastic edge as if reminding her she'd lost any claim to virtue.

She hardly noticed. He couldn't castigate her more than she castigated herself. Her honor was gone. She could never claim it back.

"Don't wait long." Burnley shifted in his chair and fleeting pain contorted his face. "The more he uses you, the more likely his seed takes. We can't assume once is enough."

She cringed at his frankness although she should be accustomed to it. His plan wasn't that different to mating a prize sow to get a litter of fat piglets.

With every moment, the old man looked more drained as his elation faded. His assertion that she didn't have long to achieve her aim wasn't his usual bullying. It was true.

If she was any judge, Edgar Fanshawe would claim his seat in hell well before winter.

Timing was everything.

In a little over three weeks, she should know if she was pregnant. Otherwise, she'd have to wait into September. After that, the fashionable hordes returned to London. Her

chances of concealing her scandalous liaison would dimin-
ish. She also acknowledged the undeniable risk that Lord
Ashcroft would tire of her. She might have decided he
possessed unexpected qualities, but facts spoke for themselves—he never stayed with a woman long.

"I'll return to London in the morning," she said, rising.
"I'd like to see my father before I go."

"If you must." Burnley paused to catch his failing breath.

She didn't like this man, she feared him, she knew how
cold and manipulative he was. But simple humanity made
her protest that he sat up working when he needed his bed.
"My lord, why don't you rest?"

He scowled, his eyes filmy. "We're not damn well married yet, girl. Save your nagging until there's a ring on your
finger."

She should have known she wasted her concern. "Your
pardon, my lord."

He nodded in acknowledgment. "And when you get back
to London, wring Ashcroft dry."

The next morning, Diana appeared at the door of the study
in the neat little house where she'd grown up. Familiar scents
overwhelmed her. Paper. Ink. Her father's old spaniel Rex.
The dog raised his head from the rug before the unlit hearth
and banged his tail in welcome.

John Dean dictated a letter to Ezra Brown, the young man
from the Abbey staff whom Burnley supplied as assistant
in Diana's absence. Sun poured through the open casement
window behind her father, lighting him like a saint in a de-
votional painting.

The young man had his back to the door and didn't realize he was under observation. Her father, however, tilted his
grizzled head and directed his gaze to exactly where she
stood. She was used to this immediate awareness of what
went on around him although she knew it disconcerted
strangers.

"Diana?" His soft voice was warm with pleasure, and his face lit with expectation.

"Yes, Papa." She stepped into the room as the secretary turned in surprise. He was a shy young man who reminded her of William before she'd married him. "You look well."

It wasn't completely true. Her father looked tired and harried. And the stacks of paper on his desk were considerably higher than they'd been before she left. She'd already noticed the air of neglect the house wore in Laura's absence. The knowledge only added another layer to the suppurating guilt that had become Diana's constant companion.

Her father stood and stepped unerringly around the desk, opening his arms wide. "Daughter, I'm glad you're back."

She'd sneaked into the house and slept in her room for the few remaining hours of the night. After the decadent splendor of Lord Peregrine's house or even the more modest luxuries of Chelsea, the narrow cot had seemed incongruously innocent.

For all her exhaustion, she'd tossed and turned, and disturbing, difficult dreams shattered what scraps of slumber she snatched. Most involved Lord Ashcroft banishing her from his life, contempt darkening his lean face.

Eventually, she'd lain awake listening to the familiar sounds of home. The faint creak of the house as it settled. The chirp of a night bird. The distant bustle of their two servants starting work before dawn.

Every sound insisted she no longer belonged in this haven of safety.

She'd risen early to alert the staff to her presence. She'd told them not to let her father know she was here. They'd been puzzled, but they'd obeyed. While her father might be titular head of the household, Diana had been mistress since long before her marriage.

She'd eaten in her room, then dressed in one of her old gowns. It too felt unfamiliar, and her eyes, freshly accustomed to fashionable clothes, immediately recognized that the dress was cheap and worn.

Now she rushed into her father's embrace. His arms closed around her with the unconditional love she'd known since she was a little girl.

If he learned of the evil she did, would he greet her with affection? She buried the troubling thought as she buried her head in his shoulder. Hot tears stung her eyes, but she blinked them back. The arms she snaked around his waist returned his hug with unusual fervor. She tried to draw on his strength as she had so often.

Awareness of her sins prevented her taking comfort from her father's presence.

He was the one who broke away. Diana straightened her spine and battled for composure. She summoned every acting skill. He'd immediately divine the slightest hint of distress or falsehood.

She'd considered not seeing him. But the gossip mills at the big house would soon alert him to her visit. If she didn't look in on him, he'd worry.

He worried anyway. As was clear from the frowning, fond glance he leveled on her. "I've missed you, child."

"I'm so glad to see you, Papa."

Most days they worked closely. She might be bailiff in all but name, but he was still a source of advice and wisdom and experience. She suffered a pang of nostalgia for the busy, worthwhile, honest life that had been hers until she left for London. She also missed her father, his integrity and his sweetness and his endless trust in her.

A trust she no longer deserved, she was grimly aware.

John Dean directed a glance toward his secretary. "Ezra here is a worthy substitute, but you and I are such a team."

"I hope he isn't working you too hard, Mr. Brown." She made herself smile at the young man.

Brown blushed and stood with an eager expression. She'd

long ago realized Ezra Brown harbored a tendre for her. She'd thought he'd grow out of it, but he never had.

"He's taught me a great deal, Mrs. Carrick, even in this short time. I'll be sorry to return to my work at the Abbey."

She deliberately made her tone light, as if she spoke of unimportant matters. "You won't be going back just yet, Mr. Brown. I'm only here to collect a few belongings. I'm for London this morning."

In a few minutes if his lordship's carriage arrived on time. She'd delayed this meeting until the last possible moment so her father couldn't quiz her.

Her belly clenched with anguish as she watched disappointment shadow her father's expression. "Must you? There's work here. Work only you can do."

How typical he wouldn't mention that her absence left him lonely and lost, rattling around this house like a pea inside a box. She'd even taken Laura away.

Mr. Brown ducked his head, his prominent Adam's apple bobbing as if he scented an argument in the offing. "If you'll excuse me, Mr. Dean. I'll find Mr. Parker and ask about the lumber for the west wing."

"Yes, yes," her father agreed with a hint of impatience.

John Dean was the kindest of men. The edge in his tone indicated that his assistant wasn't everything he'd hoped.

When they were alone, Diana forced herself to persevere with the story she and the marquess had agreed upon what felt like so long ago, although it was only a matter of weeks. Disconcerting to think subterfuge had completely altered her life in that short time.

"Lady Kelso is most insistent I return." She hoped her father wouldn't hear the lie. "Lord Burnley wrote to say he appreciated my efforts."

Her father looked unconvinced. "Why should Lady Kelso care whether a stranger does her bidding? What are you and Laura to Lady Kelso? You waste your time in London, Diana. And I . . . need you."

Regret gnawed at her. She knew what the admission cost him. "Lord Burnley is most insistent I stay with Lady Kelso for the summer, Papa. You know what we owe him."

They did in fact owe Burnley more than she wanted to acknowledge. He'd allowed her father to continue in his position even while Diana took over the reins of the estate. Most employers would have pensioned her father off, but for some reason, Burnley showed a loyalty to his bailiff he'd shown nobody else in his self-indulgent life. And Burnley had given her a chance to prove her mettle when the majority of men would have dismissed her as a useless female.

Her father grumbled under his breath and fumbled for his stick. It was a sign of his distress that he missed it and knocked it clattering to the floor. Rex whined and struggled onto his arthritic legs, shuffling over to nose at his master's leg in canine comfort.

Swallowing more stinging tears, Diana bent to pick up the stick and pass it to her father. She wished to heaven she hadn't waited to see him. She'd thought their interview before she left was bad enough, but this was worse.

Perhaps because after what she'd done with Ashcroft yesterday, she could no longer claim to be his pure daughter. The woman he'd raised to be a credit to him. The realization of how she'd changed made her feel sick.

Her clarity of purpose sank into a mire of conflicting emotions.

Before she'd left for London, everything had seemed straightforward. She'd sleep with a man who would care only that she offered a willing body. She'd get pregnant. She'd take over Cranston Abbey as its custodian until her son reached his majority.

That tidy, inevitable progression of events now seemed almost laughably implausible. She hadn't considered the subtle influence of personalities. Hers. Burnley's. Her father's. Laura's. Above all, Ashcroft's.

You are such a naïve little fool, Diana.

She'd entered into Lord Burnley's plot too lightly, without considering final costs. Excitement at the promise of becoming mistress of Cranston Abbey had blinded her.

Surreptitiously, her hand flattened across her belly, knowing her father wouldn't see. Could a child be growing there? It still seemed unbelievable, but after yesterday she might indeed be pregnant. She hoped her baby grew up to be a better person than its mother.

When Burnley broached the scheme, six weeks playing another woman with another life had appeared easy. After experiencing Ashcroft's passion, she knew if she didn't bring this affair to a swift end, it would destroy her. Already she felt torn in two with what she did.

"So when will you be home?" her father asked sharply. "I don't like this. I don't like it at all."

Clearly, her daily letters reporting completely mythical activities with Lady Kelso, Lord Burnley's cousin, hadn't soothed his displeasure. She laid her hand on top of the fist that clutched the head of his stick. "Papa, I told you, I may have to stay until September. If I change my mind now, I'll displease Lord Burnley."

Her father's anger evaporated, but to her dismay, concern replaced it. "There's something you're not telling me, child. I fear you'll find yourself beyond your depth with people not of our class. I'd hate you to be hurt."

She stiffened, then forced herself to relax before her father sensed her discomfort. Wildly, she cast about for something to allay his fears. "Papa, I do Lord Burnley's bidding."

"While I'm always grateful for his favor, Lord Burnley's schemes are usually to the advantage of Lord Burnley, Diana."

That was true, but this scheme worked not just to Burnley's advantage, but to hers too.

She tried to sound lighthearted even as remorse weighed down her heart. "Papa, I'm too smart to let anyone take advantage of me."

Her father's lips twitched in reluctant amusement. "I know you think you are. You're far away and among strangers. I worry when I can't watch over you."

She wondered if he realized the irony of what he said. "Papa, don't worry. Please. I'm enjoying the city and wearing nice clothes and sampling some high life."

His smile sliced at her heart. "I don't want your head turned."

"Don't worry, it's screwed on tight." If only that were true. She'd felt ridiculously giddy when she made love to Ashcroft, and she wasn't sure her balance had returned yet.

Her father continued as if she hadn't spoken. "Perhaps you'll meet a nice young man. You bury yourself at Marsham, and you never see anyone new. You deserve a life of your own, not to spend your years chasing after your decrepit old father. Is that what this is about, Diana? Is that what you can't bear to tell me?"

Oh, Papa . . .

She leaned forward and hugged him with a mixture of guilt and love. "No, no, no. I told you—Lady Kelso needs someone to run her errands while her companion visits her sick mother in the north. I'm not husband hunting."

No, she already had a husband lined up. A great catch indeed. At least in the world's eyes.

Her father wouldn't support the match. He wouldn't like his daughter stepping outside her class, however rich the bridegroom. Nor would he want her to marry an old, sick man for his fortune. Her father's principles were immovable, probably one of the reasons Lord Burnley kept him on despite the drawbacks.

Men of scrupulous honesty were rare. Her father, unlike his daughter, was incorruptible.

A discreet knock announced Mr. Brown's return. "Lord Burnley's carriage is outside, Mrs. Carrick."

Her father frowned, his displeasure reviving. "This visit hardly merits the name, Diana."

How she wished Burnley had left her in London, trusted her to follow her own strategy. This short conversation would do nothing to allay her father's fears for her in the big, bad city.

She hugged him again, wretched to feel how stiffly he accepted her embrace. She was distinctly out of favor. As she deserved to be.

Would this plot drive a permanent wedge between her and her father? Dear heaven, pray not. She loved her father more than anyone else. She couldn't bear if he turned away. Worse, she couldn't bear to hurt him.

Everything hinged on falling pregnant quickly.

"I'm sorry, Papa. It's only for a few weeks." The words were as much for her reassurance as his. Her sight glazed with distress, she drew away and turned for the door. "Don't come out. I know you're busy."

"Of course I'll see you off and wish you Godspeed," he snapped.

She took his arm although he knew the house so well, he was unlikely to have difficulty. The contact was for her benefit. She wanted to confirm the love that had sustained them for so many years.

He was tense under her hand, indication he was still annoyed with her. She hated knowing that nothing she said, apart from an immediate and impossible agreement to return, would content him.

Hot air blasted her as soon as she stepped out of the house. London would be sweltering. She should be grateful for the uncomfortably close weather. It meant the capital was emptier than usual at this time of year. But she couldn't help wishing circumstances wouldn't conspire to further her affair with Ashcroft. Like a coward, she'd dearly love an excuse to come home.

She climbed into the coach and, when Fredericks shut the door, she leaned out the window to catch a last glimpse of her father. He looked unhappy and irritated and bewildered.

She could hardly blame him. His daughter ran wild, and even if he didn't know what she did, he knew she acted to her detriment.

He stepped forward and patted the wood until he found her hand. He squeezed hard and with a love she felt to her bones. Again her heart lurched with guilt and pain for what she did. "Take care, Diana. And remember, whatever happens, I'm your father and I love you."

As the coach rolled out of the neat little village, Diana subsided trembling against the upholstery. Her father's blind eyes always saw more than she realized.

Chapter Thirteen

*O*ne *hundred and fifteen hours.*

So long since Ashcroft had seen the mysterious Diana. He loathed that he counted the time like a moony adolescent. Every second passed like an hour. The days were perpetual torment.

Had she finished with him? After what they'd shared?

It didn't make sense. But as day followed day, and the promised message didn't arrive, he couldn't avoid the inevitable conclusion she'd sampled what he had to offer and decided she wanted no more.

For a man of his sophistication and experience, it shouldn't smart. But it did. It smarted like hell.

He had no idea where she lived. He had no idea of her last name. Tracking her down would prove nigh impossible. Hell, she'd kept him completely at a distance. He, blockhead that he was, had let her.

He'd heard her leave Perry's house, but some vestige of pride prevented his protesting. Since that afternoon, he'd consigned his pride to the deepest circle of hell. He'd been reduced to asking the servants if they noticed where she'd gone. According to Robert, she'd left by the back gate and taken a hackney cab at the corner. Now Ashcroft's only chance of finding his elusive mistress was endlessly walking the streets of London.

By now he was just desperate enough to consider the crack-brained idea.

He told himself there were plenty of other candidates for his attentions. He'd trawled his usual haunts last night to prove that any woman would scratch his itch.

He'd trudged home an hour later, aware that for once, only one woman would do. And that woman had disappeared into thin air.

It was bloody frustrating.

His mood wasn't improved by the niggling awareness that it was usually he who treated his lovers in this casual fashion. It was usually he who played elusive, who refused to make firm arrangements.

His mind plagued by the wench, he glanced around the empty British Museum. Empty of all but fusty Egyptian relics and his annoying Aunt Mary and his even more annoying cousin Charlotte. The museum generally swarmed with people, but the sweltering summer chased the patrons as it chased people from London as a whole.

He wished to God it would shift his relatives, who hadn't yet returned home. His aunt was still set on using his house for Charlotte's ball, and it seemed she wasn't abandoning the capital until she gained his agreement.

Which was a pity, both for him and for her, because he had no intention of granting her request.

"Tarquin, I don't know how you can look at those horrid dusty things," she complained, when he paused before a mummy in a glass case.

As if to prove his aunt right about the dust, Charlotte released a violent sneeze. His cousin suffered a virulent summer cold. "They're old and dirty," the girl said in a whiny voice not improved by blocked sinuses. "I want to go home."

"We'll go home soon, Charlotte," his aunt said reprovingly.

"I mean home to Roselands," she said sulkily, tugging at her handkerchief. "Nobody comes to Town at this time of year."

Ashcroft quashed a sigh and tried to concentrate on his relatives rather than on where the hell Diana had run off to. "Your mother believes you'll benefit from educational excursions."

Her mother was misguided, Ashcroft suspected. Charlotte was a bloodless nonentity, interested only in escaping notice. Not that he blamed her. He knew from harsh experience how smothering the countess's personality was. The prospect of his aunt taking over his house for the Season made him break out in a cold sweat.

"Charlotte, stop fidgeting," the countess snapped. "You have no consideration for my nerves."

Charlotte ignored the command. Instead, she spoke to Ashcroft with a rare show of spirit. "Cousin, I believe Bond Street is educational."

Ashcroft gave a short laugh. "It is at that."

"Don't encourage the child." Aunt Mary still treated him as though he were twelve. It was a sign of her remarkable stupidity that she didn't register how, these days, the power was all his.

"She's not interested in Ancient Egypt, Aunt," he said wearily. At this rate, soon he wouldn't be either.

He owned a famous collection of antiquities, mostly amassed when he was young and eager to escape England. He'd returned home to the realization that no exotic setting altered his essential solitude. The travel he'd done since only confirmed that bleak fact.

"Very well. Let us pass by these foul cadavers," his aunt said in a voice that would shred leather. "There must be heathen jewelry somewhere."

"What about Lord Elgin's marbles?" Charlotte asked with sudden interest, then sneezed again.

Ashcroft smothered another sardonic laugh as his aunt reddened. "Absolutely not, Charlotte Jane Alice Goudge."

The girl sighed with disappointment and subsided into her usual obedience. "Yes, Mama."

The two women drifted off, his aunt still haranguing his unfortunate cousin. Ashcroft hung back until they entered the next room.

His male relations had decamped to Kent for a wrestling match. Stultifying as the masculine half of his family was, he heartily wished he'd gone with them instead of agreeing to escort his aunt and cousin.

For the thousandth time, he told himself he should break with the Vales. All were leeches and parasites. Or ciphers like Charlotte. Not one would have a feather to fly with if he hadn't taken control of the family finances upon his majority. That was after he'd discovered what chaos his uncle, the Earl of Birchgrove, had made of the Ashcroft fortune while he'd been guardian both of the estates and the heir.

So many times Ashcroft had been on the verge of cutting ties with his unappealing family. He didn't pretend the link continued because of affection. They'd resented being saddled with him when he was a child—even though the money they'd wrung from his estate had kept them afloat. Now they resented his hold on the purse strings and the way he curtailed their worst excesses.

If only he could shake the irritating but persistent tug of obligation.

He stopped to admire a basalt carving of a First Dynasty official, briefly dismissing his family from his mind. His thoughts returned immediately to Diana and how to locate her. He tried to focus on the fine sculpture, noting the monumentality and the way the artist conveyed character. As with everything since Diana had left—since he'd met her in fact—he couldn't concentrate. Her face intruded between him and all else.

Out of the corner of his eye, he noticed two modishly dressed women wander into the room. He hardly paid them any attention. Only one woman interested him.

He paused.

Something indefinable sizzled in the air.

He raised his head from his contemplation of the statue and looked more closely at the women. His skin tightened, and his pulses started to race.

He was going mad. He saw Diana everywhere.

Their backs to him, the women stopped beside the mummy. Both wore bonnets that concealed their hair. Their quiet murmur was a low, melodious hum in his ears.

Nothing distinguished these women from a thousand others. He swiftly dismissed the one on the right as a stranger. The one on the left, taller, bending over the glass case, she, she seemed familiar.

Could it be?

His heart set up a frenetic pounding. His hands clenched at his sides.

Hell, he wasn't even sure it was Diana.

Except he knew to his bones it was.

Turn to me.

As if he'd said the words aloud, the woman stiffened and straightened, although her attention remained fixed on the mummy.

Turn to me.

Slowly, almost reluctantly, but inevitably, as if drawn by forces stronger than herself, she turned.

Diana . . .

He watched gray eyes widen and darken to the color of a stormy sky. He watched the pink seep from her cheeks. He watched her lips part as they did when she waited in breathless suspense for his kiss.

His chest constricted. He'd taken a pace toward her before he realized this was neither time nor place to seize her.

"Tarquin, what is keeping you?"

His aunt's braying voice harked from a different world. As if waking from a dream, he ripped his gaze from Diana and focused on the countess's stout figure in the doorway.

"Tarquin!" she barked impatiently. "Charlotte wishes to go to Gunter's for ices. There's nothing here of interest."

He caught the fleeting amusement that replaced the dazed shock in Diana's face and found himself smiling back at her. How like Mary Goudge to dismiss the treasures of thousands of years as completely below her notice.

His brain clicked into working order. He struggled to convince himself that his breathless wonder when he saw Diana was perfectly natural. Although his heightened awareness of colors and light and textures indicated the world had miraculously transformed in the last few seconds.

He'd found her.

With an aplomb beyond him seconds ago, he strolled up to the woman who had troubled his every moment since she'd disappeared. He swept off his hat and bowed.

"I'll introduce you to my aunt," he said under his breath.

At her side, her companion, for whom he'd hardly spared a glance, gasped with shock and drew away. His concentration remained fixed on the tall woman in the striking dark blue ensemble.

He expected her to become less mysterious, now she eschewed her veils. But the contradictions seemed even more marked. The clear-cut bone structure, the character and will in her face with its strong jaw and straight nose. The mouth that promised sensual paradise. The eyes that surrendered and resisted.

She was as much an enigma as ever.

Trembling, Diana retreated against the glass case. "Don't be absurd, Ashcroft," she whispered. "I'm your . . . mistress."

The last word was so low, he had to lean close to hear. He caught a whiff of scent, sweet, erotic, unforgettable. Apples. Diana. For one forbidden second, he drew the evocative fragrance deep into his lungs.

"What's your last name?"

"Tarquin! What are you doing?" Aunt Mary bellowed from the doorway. "Didn't you hear me?"

"What's your last name?" he repeated in a murmur.

"You can't do this. I won't let you," Diana muttered through tight lips. The vulnerable expression faded, and he recognized a return of defiance. His smile broadened. He loved that she stood up to him.

"How will you stop me? Give me your last name."

Her eyes narrowed. "I could lie."

"Then lie."

He grabbed her slender arm, his heart leaping at even such innocent contact, and hauled her toward his aunt. He expected Diana to resist, although she must know he was prepared to use strength if he must. To his surprise, though, she yielded without a fight. Under his fingers, he felt her quaking anger. He glanced across to where her friend watched from the far side of the room. Her eyes were sharp with interest.

"Carrick," Diana said on a snap.

Carrick.

She'd never escape him so easily again. Immediately, he accepted that it was her real name although he couldn't say why. Perhaps the way she spat the two syllables. As if daring him to do his worst. Satisfaction coiled in his belly, along with the hunger that had been his constant companion since she'd left.

For five days he'd been utterly miserable. A misery intensified because he refused to search his heart and admit what a blow Diana dealt when she absconded. Now bright enjoyment burgeoned. He felt alive for the first time since she'd deserted him.

"Aunt Mary, allow me to introduce a lady of my acquaintance, Mrs. Carrick." He turned to Diana, who studiously refused to look at him. "Mrs. Carrick, may I present my aunt, Lady Birchgrove?"

"Mrs. Carrick," his aunt said with a distinct lack of enthusiasm, nodding at Diana.

"Your ladyship." Diana curtsied, as etiquette dictated, waiting for the countess to indicate whether she desired conversation.

Yet again, he found himself puzzling over exactly where his paramour fitted into society. Once she'd accepted that an introduction was inevitable, her manners were impeccable. One would assume she met countesses every day.

"Are you a Londoner, Mrs. Carrick?" his aunt asked, when it became clear Ashcroft had no intention of removing Diana.

Diana shot him an annoyed glance under her lashes, but her voice remained steady. "I'm from a village in Surrey, your ladyship. I'm sure you wouldn't know it."

Briefly, Ashcroft imagined his investigations would be easy. He'd find out everything he wanted to know without exercising further guile. His aunt would inquire, and Diana would answer.

Clearly he'd been mistaken.

The countess arched her thick eyebrows. "I know Surrey well. I've visited a number of houses in the county."

"It's a very beautiful part of England," Diana said neutrally.

Charlotte chose that moment to return from whatever exhibit occupied her. A cavalcade of sneezes accompanied her arrival. "Mama, I just saw Susannah Meredith in Greek vases. She says there's a . . ." She paused and stared at Diana through watery eyes. "Oh, my, that's a beautiful dress."

"Charlotte, you haven't been introduced to this lady. I swear you are the most rag-mannered hoyden. Goodness knows how we'll get vouchers for Almack's if you don't mend your ways."

"Your pardon, Mama." Charlotte bowed her head, her brief vivacity draining away.

Diana sent the crestfallen, obviously ill girl a smile. Ashcroft's heart set off on its wayward gallop again. She really was the most beautiful woman. Now his dizzying relief that he'd found her receded, he noticed her gown was indeed extremely becoming. A rich blue with gold trimming the bodice. A bodice up to the throat. He couldn't help approving that she hid herself from every scoundrel who wished to ogle her bosom.

He was the only scoundrel allowed to ogle Diana Carrick.

Diana's voice was warm. "No need to apologize, Lady Charlotte. The ensemble is a favorite of mine too."

The countess gave a humph of disapproval, and her voice was icy. "Mrs. Carrick, may I present my daughter Lady Charlotte Goudge?"

Diana dipped into another of those intriguingly self-possessed curtsies. "Lady Charlotte."

"We have an appointment, Tarquin," his aunt said. "Mrs. Carrick."

Another curtsy. "Your ladyship." Her voice remained firm and polite.

As his aunt marched away, Charlotte lingered and smiled at Diana with a shy pleasure that made him wonder if he'd underestimated her. "I hope we meet again, Mrs. Carrick."

"I'd like that," Diana said. "But I'm in Town only a short while."

Charlotte spared Ashcroft a nervous glance. He could guess the terrifying tales she'd heard about him from the family. He wouldn't be surprised if his relations featured him as the monster in their bedtime stories. "Mama holds a musicale next Thursday. I'm sure she'd be delighted if you attended."

The fleeting wryness in Diana's expression indicated she knew the countess would be anything but delighted to have a woman of unknown pedigree infiltrating her house. To her credit, she responded calmly. "I'm already engaged Thursday next. Thank you for your kind invitation."

"Charlotte!" His aunt paused in the doorway and shot a gimlet glance in their direction. Charlotte blushed, curtsied to Diana, and hurried after her mother.

"That performance was completely unnecessary," Diana hissed, at last looking at him. Her face was pale, apart from a flush of color high on her slanted cheekbones. "What if she fathomed I was your mistress?"

"I wouldn't introduce my mistress to her," he said with an equanimity born of his drunken pleasure in being with her.

Oh, he was in sad straits. Poor Ashcroft, slain by a pair of brilliant gray eyes. And who would think gray eyes could scorch? Yet unquestionably they did as they leveled on him.

"Yet you did," she said implacably.

She didn't budge. He'd be disappointed if she had. So far, she'd never disappointed him. He couldn't imagine that continuing—experience indicated she would sooner or later.

"Tarquin!" His aunt still stared at them.

He ignored the summons of family authority. The countess should be used to that. Beatings had made minimal difference to his younger self. A sharp word to the man would have no more effect.

He bent closer to Diana, inhaling more of her delicious fragrance. "Does one encounter make you my mistress?"

"Clearly under your definition, not." She made an angry sound deep in her throat, not that different from the sounds of pleasure she made when he took her. A molten surge of desire turned him blind to his surroundings.

"*Tarquin!*"

"I have to see you tonight," he said urgently, desperate to continue the argument but knowing it was impossible. How tragic he found squabbling with Diana more rewarding than any other conversation he remembered.

"I said I'd send you word."

"You didn't." Vaguely, he was aware of her friend stepping closer, but his attention was all for Diana.

"No."

"Wait here."

Her lips tightened with displeasure. "I'm not a hound, Ashcroft. I don't do your bidding without question."

He broke his rule about never begging. "Please."

"You have to go. The countess is waiting." She started to wheel away, but he grabbed her arm, using his body to shield her from his aunt's curiosity.

"One minute. That's all I ask."

She sent him a straight look under her marked brows. They were dark for a woman of her blondness, adding an intriguing severity to her face. "But that isn't all you ask, is it?"

"Diana . . ."

She released an impatient sigh. "I want to see the antiquities. I'm not going home yet."

With that, he must be content. He gave a sharp nod and snatched her hand. He pressed a brief kiss like a brand of possession on the back of her glove. For one tantalizing instant, he felt the living heat of her flesh through the thin kid. He watched with satisfaction as her pupils dilated in helpless response, in spite of her defiant words.

She tried to play games with him. That was fine. He could play games with the best of them. Nothing could make him doubt the genuine attraction drawing them together.

He let a confident smile curve his lips, partly because he knew it would make her seethe. Without another word, he turned on his heel and followed his aunt into the next room.

Chapter Fourteen

$\mathcal{D}$iana sucked in a shuddering breath and collapsed against the case behind her. The edge of the glass dug into her back, but she wasn't sure her knees would hold her if she tried to stand unsupported. One shaking hand lifted to press against her breast as she tried to quiet her heart's wild race.

"So that's Ashcroft," Laura said softly, coming forward.

"Yes." Anything further was beyond her.

Only five days since she'd seen him. How had she forgotten his physical impact? The way her senses flared in response to his voice or the touch of his hand. The spark in the air when he was with her.

"He's . . . impressive." Laura's voice was neutral. Which was odd, given how strongly she opposed Burnley's scheme.

Diana fought to regain her equilibrium. She was a mature woman of twenty-eight. She was a widow. She'd run the Cranston Abbey estate for the last ten years. She wasn't a silly green girl in a flap after her first encounter with an attractive man.

"I'm sorry I didn't introduce you." Her voice was unsteady.

Her friend's lips curled in a wry smile, and her dark eyes were alight with curiosity. "You were otherwise occupied."

Diana straightened, drew another shaky breath—she kept forgetting to breathe—and flexed her tingling fingers. He'd kissed her hand. Given what else he'd done, that should hardly register. Something about the gesture's possessive gallantry pierced right to her heart. Nor could she forget the brief heat of his mouth, burning even through her glove.

Laura paused thoughtfully. "He isn't what I expected."

Diana released a short, unamused laugh. Gradually, the world stopped wobbling and returned to its normal orbit. "He isn't what I expected either."

"I thought he'd be cold, vain, self-obsessed. I thought he'd treat you with contempt. That's far from the truth." Again she paused, as though considering whether to continue. Her voice lowered. "He's besotted with you."

Dizziness returned with a vengeance. For a second, the room revolved before Diana remembered to gulp a breath. "Don't . . . don't be ridiculous."

Laura shrugged. "I know what I saw."

Diana tried to adopt a careless tone. "He's a rake. He's had more women than I've had hot breakfasts. I'm just one more."

"If you say so. After all, you know him better than I." Laura's eyes focused on a spot over her shoulder. "He's back."

Diana whirled, her heart hammering wildly. Ashcroft stood in the doorway, watching her. He was dressed in the height of fashion in a dark blue coat and biscuit-colored trousers. He carried his stylish high-crowned hat in one hand, and his hair was disarmingly ruffled. As there wasn't a hint of breeze inside or out, she guessed he'd run his hand through it in frustration at dealing with that fearsome aunt. That shouldn't strike her as endearing, but somehow it did.

"Besotted," Laura murmured *sotto voce* at her side.

"You waited," he said softly, striding toward her and stopping a few paces away.

"Yes."

"Good."

The words they spoke belonged to a different world from the silent communication flowing between them. She resisted the overpowering urge to step forward and fold her arms around him, rest her head on his shoulder.

It seemed beyond belief that their sexual encounters, however torrid, created this intensity. It was like her heart beat at his command. Her head swam, and she forced air into her lungs.

Still, the silent conversation continued, incessant as waves against the seashore.

I want you.

Touch me.

Take me to your bed.

Never let me go.

She gasped in distress and faltered back as if she'd spoken the last words aloud.

What was wrong with her? She used Ashcroft for her own ends. She lied and cheated and treated him little better than a stud bull. Nothing existed between them except sex.

Although that wasn't how it felt right now.

If she was honest, that wasn't how it had felt when he held her in his arms through a long, hot afternoon either.

She did him enough injury without risking an emotional connection. What she'd planned had always been predicated on his feeling nothing beyond passing sexual interest.

Laura's certainty plagued her, set up an ominous drone in her head. One word.

Besotted.

No, he couldn't be. It was outside the realms of possibility. He was a man of the world, and she was a country bluestocking. He was just caught up in the excitement of a new affair.

She blinked and forced herself into the present. Laura stood silently at her side, avidly watching the interaction. Her friend, so perceptive, would divine something of what ran through Diana's head.

Pray God she didn't divine everything.

Another quivering breath, and Diana made herself speak, act as if nothing out of the ordinary occurred. "Lord Ashcroft, allow me to introduce my friend, Miss Laura Smith."

She found little satisfaction in noticing Ashcroft took a fraction too long to return to reality as well. He bowed low to Laura just as he'd done to her, as if he addressed women of rank. "Miss Smith."

Laura curtsied. "My lord."

"Are you enjoying your visit to Town?"

"I must admit I prefer the countryside." Laura made no attempt to mask her inspection of him.

Nor did he conceal his interest in her. Perhaps he subjected every female to this detailed appraisal. Perhaps he sized Laura up as a bed partner. The man Burnley had described wouldn't hesitate to seduce another woman while in a current mistress's presence.

Diana didn't think that was what Ashcroft was doing.

There wasn't a hint of the sensual assessment she'd read in his eyes from their first meeting. Laura and Ashcroft weighed each other up as adversaries before a fight.

"Has your aunt gone?" Diana asked, forcing a steady tone even as her heart dipped and leaped with excitement.

He shook his head. "They're a few rooms ahead. I told them I forgot my gloves."

"Did you?"

"No, they're in my pocket." A faint smile slanted his lips. She wished she didn't find it utterly beguiling.

"If you delay too long, she'll suspect something."

He grabbed her arm, his hold unshakable. "Give me five minutes alone with you."

He couldn't mean what she thought he did. Not here. And not in five minutes.

"We're in a public place," she protested, although the thrill of his touch through her silk sleeve surged across her skin like flame.

"Well, let's find somewhere less public."

"I'm not going to . . ." She cast a frantic glance at Laura, who watched as if observing a theatrical performance.

He laughed softly, and said under his breath, "Wait until you're asked."

She might take his dismissive response seriously if she couldn't smell his desperation. He was fired with lust and frustration. She'd recognized that from the second she'd seen him today.

She wasn't in a much better state.

"I'll go into the next room." Laura sent them a surprisingly conspiratorial smile.

Ashcroft chuckled. "You're an angel, Laura Smith."

"I'm unfailingly loyal to my friends, my lord." Even through rising excitement, Diana heard the warning in the words.

"I admire that," Ashcroft replied without a trace of mockery.

Even more surprisingly, Laura graced him with one of her lovely smiles. She was a pretty girl and would be considered a local beauty if she wasn't so self-effacing outside her immediate circle. "Just remember it, my lord. Five minutes."

Without sparing them another glance, she walked toward the second door. Diana's attention immediately focused on the man towering over her. She fought back a foolish feminine feeling of safety.

He was about as safe as a cobra.

"What do you want, Lord Ashcroft?" she asked with completely manufactured bravado.

"Don't be a fool, Diana. You know what I want." His voice lowered to a purr. "I want you." His fingers tightened, and he dragged her toward a large alabaster sarcophagus propped against the wall.

"Ashcroft!" She tried and failed to summon any real resistance. He was mad to consider seducing her in the hallowed halls of the British Museum. "You will not do this!"

"Oh, I will damn well do this," he muttered, shoving

her into the corner behind the monolith. The stone coffin shielded them from the doorway, although if anyone came into the room, they'd immediately notice the couple embracing in the shadows.

"Your aunt . . ."

"Bugger my aunt." Roughly, he pressed her against the wall, gripping her arms above the elbow.

She was such an idiot. She should scream for help. She should kick him in the shins until he let her go. Instead, a torrent of anticipation crashed through her veins, making her heart dance and her breath catch.

She forced a calmness she didn't feel into her voice. "Laura said five minutes. She'll return even if your aunt doesn't find us. Someone else could come in. There's enough scandal in the two of us being seen together in a crowd, let alone caught *in flagrante delicto* behind some pharaoh's coffin."

He growled low in his throat. "Diana?"

Something in the way he said her name halted her tirade. She sucked in a breath and gazed into his face. He was pale, and a muscle flickered in his cheek, a sign of extreme emotion. His green eyes were brilliant and focused unwaveringly on her. He shifted one hand to hold her face, his thumb beneath her chin, his fingers warm against her jaw.

"Y . . . yes?"

"Shut up."

"Wha . . ."

Her outraged question died on a muffled moan as he bent his dark head and placed his mouth on hers.

Her anger, her confusion, her guilt, her piercing loneliness, all coalesced into white heat. She closed her eyes and parted her lips, inviting him in. It no longer mattered where she was or who might discover them. What mattered was that Ashcroft touched her.

For the first time in five days, she felt whole.

His tongue tangled with hers as she sagged against the wall. He made a sound of unmistakable satisfaction and swept her up against him, devouring her with rapacious concentration. She countered his blazing passion with her own, no longer pretending she didn't want him as much as he wanted her. Her arms circled his back, drawing him closer.

She wanted him closer. She wanted him inside her. Primitive need was like a mallet pounding on her heart.

Just as she thought her legs would fold under her, he raised his mouth. He sighed and pressed his cheek against hers.

She gasped for air, lost in the wild memory of the kiss. She felt the faint roughness of his beard. She smelled the fresh warmth of his skin, the heat of his desire.

"Why didn't you send me a message?" His voice grated like stones across gravel, his breath brushed her ear, stirring tendrils of hair. "Why did you make both of us wait?"

She swallowed and opened her eyes and strove to put two words together. He was hot and hard against her skirts. She stroked his back in a rhythm that soon developed suggestive momentum.

She closed her eyes again and basked in the quiet, glorious communion. So stupid to feel she belonged here, in Ashcroft's arms.

"Diana, tell me why," he whispered.

Why hadn't she contacted him? She should have. Lord Burnley insisted she go to Ashcroft's bed as soon as she returned to London. The marquess would be furious to know what little use she'd made of the last days. Given he had her watched, he probably did know.

She'd left Cranston Abbey determined to bring this snarled scheme to an end. That meant spending every hour with Lord Ashcroft in the hope his seed took root.

With a man like Ashcroft, out of sight meant out of mind. If she didn't entertain him while he expressed interest, he'd likely look elsewhere. She was an idiot if she expected him to wait in chaste expectation like Sir Galahad praying for the appearance of the Grail.

Yet still she hadn't pursued her conquest.

On the first day, she'd claimed a headache and retired to her room. Not completely a lie. Guilt and emotion had tormented her all the way back from Surrey.

Then at her suggestion, she and Laura had set out to sample the delights of the capital. She knew it was childish to avoid her task, but she couldn't bear to fling herself back into the sea of deceit.

Desperately, she searched for some lie to explain her tardiness in contacting Ashcroft. Instead, she found herself answering honestly.

"I can't tell you," she replied, hating the sadness in her voice. She settled more closely against him. He was so big and strong, he made her feel no harm could befall her while he held her. "Don't ask me."

How could she admit that sheer terror stopped her contacting him? Terror of this overwhelming joy she felt holding him, touching him, kissing him. Terror of how helpless she was against her unwelcome fascination. When she'd made her devil's deal with Lord Burnley, this wasn't what she'd bargained for.

Five minutes, Laura had promised. If not Laura, the countess would appear with her stentorian voice and cold eyes.

He'd been careful of her reputation with his aunt. Now her brain functioned again, she knew he wouldn't compromise her here where discovery was so likely. She smothered the insidious warmth that filled her at the knowledge.

Slowly he drew away. Only far enough to look into her face. He framed her cheeks in his palms and stared into her eyes. *Dear heaven, let him not see the falsehood there.*

"Were you torturing me?"

"No!" she said before she thought that the role she played, of a woman learning worldly games, supported such a claim. Her hands dropped to his hips. She yearned to feel his bare skin under her palms, test his heat and power.

"Are you going to torture me tonight?"

She'd regained enough of herself to react with amusement.

Where had she learned that low, sensual chuckle? "Only if you ask."

He laughed and pressed his mouth to hers in another intoxicating kiss. "It's torture having you here and not being able to do more," he said, confirming her assessment of his intentions.

His reputation indicated he was a man without honor, he might even believe that was true. But she came to the realization that Lord Ashcroft followed a code of ethics as immovable as any biblical morality that guided a fire-and-brimstone preacher.

A sardonic smile twisted his beautiful mouth. "Is there something you're not telling me?"

The question surprised a startled cough of laughter from her. "I'm sure there's a lot I'm not telling you."

He didn't smile. "Something I need to know. Are you sure you're not married?"

"I'm not married." At least this far, she could be truthful.

"God help me, I don't think I care."

He speared his hands in her hair and tilted her head. She waited for his kiss, but instead his eyes ravished her features.

"Don't look at me like that," she whispered, distress constricting her throat.

He groaned and rested his forehead against hers. Briefly, their breaths mingled before he straightened without releasing her.

Heaven help her, she never wanted him to release her.

"Diana, will you come to me tonight?"

She panted as if she'd run a mile. Her heart thundered in her ears. There was only one answer. She gave it because she needed him, not because of any collusion.

"Yes."

She felt his deep sigh of relief. Tension drained out of him. Only now did she realize how on edge he'd been. "Thank you."

Her hands formed talons in his coat. "Where?"

Suddenly she was aware how relentlessly time passed. They didn't have long to make arrangements. If she could, she'd run off with him now and snatch at pleasure like a child snatched at a new toy.

"Your house?"

"No." She had to stop him learning where she lived. As it was, he'd discovered her name and that she came from Surrey. Small concessions, but a clever man like Ashcroft could use them to expose her whole life.

And she couldn't bear to lose him yet.

Not yet.

Although a grim voice in her heart reminded her that losing him was inevitable.

"Perry's still away." His voice was ragged. Desire bubbled like lava beneath every word.

"I'll meet you there."

"When?"

They spoke quickly, in whispers, like conspirators.

"I'll get away from my aunt as soon as I can."

He pressed a hungry kiss to her lips and stepped back. Straightaway, she missed his touch. "Ashcroft . . ." she began, not sure what she meant to say but unwilling to let him go.

"Oh, topping, here are the mummies." A boy's voice smashed through the searing intensity between them.

Automatically Ashcroft moved to shield Diana. She clutched his shoulders, praying they'd remain unnoticed. It was an echo of the moment she'd clung to him in the alley outside the ballroom. Strange how natural it was to seek shelter in his arms.

"Nasty, smelly things," said a young girl in a superior tone. "Miss MacCallum, I don't want to stay here."

Ashcroft's hand curled around the back of Diana's head and he hid her face in his shoulder. It was such a protective gesture, her heart clenched with guilt. And unwilling warmth.

If he knew the truth, he wouldn't feel protective. He'd feel used and deceived. He'd hate her. As was his right.

"You never even looked at it, Kate," the boy said with justified irritation. "It's shut away in a case. You can't smell it."

"I don't care. It's dead. I hate this place. It's full of dead things."

"Children!" a woman said in a distinctly Scottish accent. "Stop your squabbling."

"Kate's just a silly girl," the boy said.

For all her nervousness, Diana was inclined to agree. She sidled closer to Ashcroft's big, powerful body. Stupid to think he could save her. Stupid to trust him. Nonetheless, she couldn't help herself.

"I am not," the girl said in a sulky voice.

"Are too," the boy predictably responded.

"Children, I promised your mother we'd look at the Roman galleries. If you're good, we'll stop for a cake on the way home."

"I want to see the mummy," the boy whined.

"Next time, Andrew. The wee mummy will be there tomorrow. It's not going anywhere."

The voices faded as they left. Diana released the breath she'd held for what felt like forever and subsided into Ashcroft in blessed relief. Her heart raced so fast, she felt giddy. His arms tightened in what she foolishly read as comfort and security.

Poor, brainless Diana.

"They've gone," Laura said softly from the other side of the sarcophagus.

Ashcroft released Diana with a reluctance she recognized because she shared it. He stepped away from the coffin and bowed to her friend. "Miss Smith."

"You'd better find your aunt," Diana whispered, straightening.

He leaned down to feather a kiss across her lips. Laura's presence didn't seem to bother him at all. "I'll be there at six."

"I'll see you then."

She tried to hide her dazed response to the touch of his mouth. Surely, this overwhelming physical reaction would fade. Surely, it was the result of too many celibate years. She refused to believe her reactions stemmed from the fact that Ashcroft drew her more powerfully than any man she'd ever met.

That same carping voice in her mind scoffed at her sophistries.

He paused before he left and sent her a straight look. "No more games?"

He worried she wouldn't show up, that she teased him. She wished she could blame her behavior on a cause as frivolous as teasing. Instead of something that felt like life or death.

If this afternoon taught her anything, it was that she was helplessly snared in the net of attraction. She wished she'd never started this cruel deception. She wished she was at home helping her father run Cranston Abbey.

It was too late.

Even without Burnley's ultimatum ringing in her ears, she'd go to Ashcroft tonight. For one reason only. Because she couldn't stay away.

"No more games," she said softly and wished to heaven she told the truth.

Chapter Fifteen

I wasn't sure you'd come."

Diana jerked with surprise when Ashcroft spoke from the shadows, and he felt an unworthy pleasure in his fleeting advantage. He flicked away his half-smoked cigar and slid off the marble Roman altar buried in Perry's dark shrubbery. Around him leaves rustled in the erratic night breeze.

"I said I would." She sounded on edge, almost hostile.

The passionate woman who yielded to his kiss behind an Egyptian coffin had regrouped her defenses. No matter. She was as attracted to him as he was to her. That gave him weaponry to demolish any barricades.

He suspected she knew it. Which explained her prickliness.

Odd to think they'd started this affair at her invitation. No question he was now the one in pursuit. Even when she lay in his arms, she was still so damned elusive.

The volatile encounter in the museum had provided him with much food for thought. Her melting surrender. The information she'd provided, however unwillingly. The fact that Miss Smith was undoubtedly the Gypsy companion Diana had mentioned. Perhaps that ramshackle tale about arcane potions might actually have some basis in truth.

He hoped to hell it did.

He prowled toward her, careful to stay under the trees while she remained on the path. Wearing shirt and breeches, he felt wonderfully cool. Or at least he had until Diana arrived to send heat crawling inexorably over his skin.

Moonlight illuminated her face now she'd thrown back the concealing hood of her cape. She looked guarded, and her body was tight with wariness.

Definitely elusive.

For hours, he'd waited in the garden, as sultry afternoon turned to dusk, turned to night. For all his confidence now, he hadn't been sure of her. With each minute, his doubts had grown, devil take her.

His voice remained neutral. "You're later than you said."

She sighed with impatience and peered through the darkness. "Lord above, Ashcroft, you do go on. I may be a bit late. It hardly matters. I'm here now. You're turning into an old woman."

He laughed softly, recognizing her tactic from previous skirmishes. She liked to use offense as a defense. "I'm not accustomed to being uncertain of a lover."

Her tension increased. He wondered what he'd said to perturb her. So many secrets. So many mysteries. What did she hide?

He burned to grab her, continue the afternoon's delightful explorations. He held back. Partly to build anticipation. Although after five days without her, anticipation was nearly killing him. Partly because he knew once he touched her, any chance of discussion vanished.

And he badly wanted to talk to her.

When she'd disappeared so effectively, he'd experienced his first genuine fear in years. His dream lover had deserted him after one explosive encounter. He had no idea how to find her. It was all his fault. When she came to him, he could have delayed and found out about her.

Who was he fooling? From the moment he'd dragged her into the carriage, he couldn't hold back.

He'd promised himself tonight would be different. Tonight, he'd act the civilized man and not the barbarian. Tonight, he'd unravel some of those secrets.

At least he'd damn well try.

"What did your aunt say?"

"She rang a peal over me."

"I'm sorry."

He shrugged, before realizing she couldn't see him. "It doesn't matter."

"I don't want to cause trouble with the people who love you."

He gave a dismissive snort and answered before he thought to stop himself. "Believe me, that's not anyone in my family."

He felt her sudden stillness like a physical blow. Her voice sounded studiedly calm. "Why do you say that?"

What the hell had got into him? He never talked about these things. "It's true," he said curtly.

"Perhaps she doesn't approve of your way of life."

Diana wasn't taking the hint that this subject wasn't welcome. "Oh, that's true too."

"Your aunt brought you up?"

Every muscle tensed in repudiation of her questions. How had this conversation become about him? He wanted to reveal Diana's secrets, not plumb years of painful family background. "Mostly. Now, let's talk about you."

"No, you're much more interesting." Before he mustered a protest, she went on, stepping closer to where he skulked in the shadows. "Where were your parents?"

This strategy was fatally flawed. He should have leaped on her as soon as she arrived, distracted her with pleasure. He abhorred the idea of swapping confidences in the moonlight.

His plans for the evening had been perfectly clear, reasonable. He wanted her to answer his questions, then he wanted to take her to bed.

"Diana, this is ancient history."

God help him, the sweet, low sound of her laugh disarmed him, sapped stirring anger. "Believe me, I want to hear."

"My mother was thrown out in disgrace when I was a child." He spoke stiffly, quickly. "My father died not long after."

"I'm sorry." Did his ears deceive him, or did she genuinely regret his unhappiness?

Feeling like the biggest sapskull in London, he emerged into the revealing moonlight. He wasn't making much of a fist of concealing his reactions while he probed hers. Like so many of his games with her, she still held the advantage. Perhaps because she didn't care, and he, much against his will, did.

"Don't be." He wanted to tell her to mind her own business, but instead he found himself admitting the truth. "It was hardly the happiest of marriages in the first place. By all reports, my mother was a wanton who never spared her husband or her child a thought once she left. My father disliked me intensely. I remember that well enough."

"How old were you when he died?" Her voice was still artificially even.

"Four."

"Old enough to feel the rejection."

"Oh, yes." Talking about his childhood revived all the dark unhappiness. *Damn it, couldn't she leave it alone?*

She drew a shaky breath. His instincts had already told him she wasn't as calm as she tried to appear. "You speak so harshly of your mother. She may have had good reason for what she did."

Her voice vibrated with sincerity. Against his will, he moved closer to that sound. Then realized what she said, and he straightened in resentment. "Good reason to chase after a dozen men in London while her husband cowered at home and bore the humiliation of being a public cuckold?"

"What happened to her?"

The question emerged with such sadness, it made him want to hit something. He thought with fulminating regret of his sensual expectations, drowning now in a sea of maudlin emotion.

How had she done this to him? Diana Carrick was dangerous. She affected him like no other woman.

His voice was harsh with control. "She became some rich man's slut, then sold herself to another after her first keeper tired of her. She died in the gutter, rotten with gin and disease."

"That's terrible." She sounded shocked, devastated.

"She deserved her fate," he said flatly.

"You judgmental bastard." Her voice vibrated with feeling.

He took a moment to register what she'd said. And an extra, crucial moment to realize she'd turned on her heel and headed toward the gate.

"Diana, wait!"

He, who never pursued any woman, lunged after her. The first time he grabbed for her, all he caught was a handful of cape. With a savage movement, she twitched it free and kept going. She'd reached the gate before he gained a decent grip on her arm.

"Let me go," she snarled, straining against his hold. She was a tall, strong woman, and he needed to exert a surprising amount of force to stop her marching off.

"What's the matter?"

"Nothing."

He'd had enough experience to know that when a woman spat "nothing" like an expletive, something was indeed wrong. She trembled under his hand.

Good God, what had he said to send her into such a taking?

"I apologize for upsetting you." He tried for rueful charm. A pity he couldn't quite carry it off. Her questions had veered too close to memories that still rankled. "I usually don't descend into such blatant self-pity. Or at least not publicly."

She whirled around, and moonlight shone bright on her face. When she'd tried to run, he'd wondered whether she was upset or angry. One glance and he immediately knew. She looked like she wanted to kill him.

Such vivid passion in her. No wonder he found her irresistible.

"How can you speak of your mother like that? So smug that she came to grief. You don't know what drove her. Perhaps she was in love. Perhaps your father was cruel. You were a child. You couldn't have known anything about her."

She stopped to drag in a shaky breath, struggling to jerk free. He tightened his grip. He didn't trust her to stay if he released her. Even when she was angry, he'd rather be with her than without her.

What a lowering admission for the heartless rake Ashcroft.

One suspicious corner of his brain wondered why Diana took his mother's fate so personally. Because he couldn't mistake how vehemently his mistress sided with the faithless, flighty Countess of Ashcroft.

Did she worry that he judged Diana as equally flighty because she'd tumbled into a rake's arms? But the situation was completely different. Hester Vale had had a husband and child.

How do you know Diana hasn't?

"I heard all the stories about . . ." he began, but she spoke over him with such heat, his explanation faltered into silence.

"You've already told me your family have no affection for you. Even if they had, they'd hardly take your mother's part." He sustained a blast of furious lightning from her eyes. "What right have you to condemn your mother? You consider an affair that lasts more than a night a major commitment."

He drew himself up, stung by her contempt. And, much as he loathed acknowledging it, hurt. His voice slowed to a coruscating drawl. "Charming. But that's why you're here, isn't it? Because you heard I'll take any female into my bed."

She flinched but didn't retreat. "Well, don't you?"

"No, I do not," he bit out.

Abruptly, the fight ebbed out of her. "I don't believe you," she said dully.

He slid his arm around her waist, feeling her lithe shape, even through the thick woolen folds of the cloak. The anger seeped from his voice. "I haven't touched another woman since I first saw you."

"A few days' fidelity? Should I give you a resounding cheer?" Her sarcasm faded to reveal piercing distress. "How can you speak of your mother with such hate?"

"I don't hate her." Again the truth slipped out before he could stop himself. Unless he knew better, he'd think he was in his cups. Whereas the only intoxication was Diana's tempestuous presence. His hold tightened, and he found himself telling her what he'd told nobody else. "It's the only way I can bear that she left me."

He waited for a dismissive comment, scornful laughter. After all, he was a grown man. What his mother had done thirty years ago shouldn't matter. But the wound was inflicted early, and it had never healed.

Just thinking about his mother made his stomach knot in sick misery. She'd abandoned him. Far easier to hate her than confess he'd yearned for her all his life.

Apart from Diana's ragged breathing, the night fell quiet.

Ashcroft was devastated to realize she wasn't far from tears. He found himself continuing, his heart leaden with humiliation. "It's the only way I can bear my father's hatred and that my family mustered little but contempt for me. If my mother was a worthless harlot, I'm equally worthless. At least the explanation offers a modicum of sense."

He stopped, his heart beating like thunder.

He'd said too much. Far too much.

Diana was a casual lover. Nobody special. Nobody he'd even remember when the short-lived affair was over.

But his lancing anguish at the thought of losing her told him that was pure bravado. Diana touched him in a way nobody else had. And he suspected nobody ever would.

Great Jehovah, he'd had enough of this.

Flinging away from her, he strode a few restless paces up the path. He kept his back to her, afraid of what his face would reveal. His gut cramped with self-disgust as he replayed his mawkish confessions.

He couldn't blame Diana if she left. Hell, he wished she would.

She'd intrigued him from the first, promising passion to lighten boredom and weariness. This affair, like all his others, offered mutual sexual gratification. That was all he asked. So how had it become so much more?

His devastation when she didn't contact him, his happiness on seeing her again, and now the way she bypassed a lifetime's defenses made him realize he risked something deeper. Something that would leave him in tatters when it finished.

Perhaps it finished now.

Perhaps that was a good thing. No more vulnerability. No more uncertainty. No more emotional turmoil.

No more Diana . . .

As a man waited for a death sentence, he waited for her to go. To flounce out that garden gate, never to return.

Even over the furious pounding of his blood, he didn't hear her shift. Clearly the foolish chit meant to stay.

Why? Surely she couldn't want any more vapid revelations from her lover.

Tense as a drawn wire, he prepared to endure some inane remark. Something about knowledge he'd lived with all his life being untrue. Sentimental pap about his family loving him all the same.

She kept silent.

For a long interval, the air between them thickened with everything spoken and unspoken.

Gradually, curiosity stirred, warred with shame. He turned, expecting to read derision or, even worse, pity in her beautiful face.

Diana was so still, he wasn't even sure she was breathing. She stared at him out of eyes mysterious in the darkness. He couldn't mistake her expression.

She looked utterly desolate.

Could she care so much?

She looked as though he'd broken her heart. He stifled the betraying words that welled up, begging for her comfort, begging for her regard. He'd made enough of a fool of himself for one night.

He was an adult, not a sniveling child.

This woman had come to him for sensual experience. That he could give her. So much sensual experience that she'd forget this difficult moment where he felt he'd sliced open his veins and bled out every mortifying secret.

"I want you," he growled, prowling closer.

"Ashcroft . . ." she faltered, sidling back. The desolation lingered.

He couldn't bear to see her so open and defenseless. It made him yearn to be a different man, a better man. The kind of man who could offer her forever and not just a tawdry affair. A man she'd respect instead of just desire.

Although desire offered its own rich bounty.

"Enough," he said in a guttural voice. Without giving her a chance to flee, he swept her up into his arms, turned, and strode toward the open doors facing the fragrant garden.

As he hoisted her high against his chest and climbed the shallow steps, she trembled with need. It had been like this from the first. Ashcroft touched her, and she was lost. But for once hunger wasn't paramount. Anguish was.

His reluctant, excruciating confession had stabbed her to her sinner's soul.

And not just because he proved her instincts right. In spite of his own unruly life, he'd never forgiven his wayward mother for breaking her marriage vows. If he discovered how Diana deceived him, he'd never forgive her either.

But compared to what he'd suffered and overcome, that hardly counted.

"I'm too heavy," Diana protested without force.

"You're a feather." His breathlessness gave the lie to his gallantry. In a commanding motion, he shouldered the door wider and carried her inside.

She smothered a creaky laugh against his shirt. "Hardly."

She recognized he sought to distract her from the fraught conversation. He didn't need to say he'd sealed that confession inside him since his unhappy childhood.

Yet he'd told her.

Guilt tasted like bile on her tongue. After tonight, she couldn't pretend her only importance to him was as a temporary mistress.

Somewhere in the last days, her life had meshed with his. Passion was a bright golden thread in the tapestry, but it wasn't the only color in this rich weave. There was liking and shared humor and mutual, unacknowledged loneliness.

Her pain when he told her about his mother was a terrifying sign of how profoundly she was involved. Pain worsened by proof he trusted very few people, and now he trusted her—and she was as fated to betray him as the sun was to rise on the morrow.

The urge to confess her misdeeds rose like a tide. She dammed the impulse. What did she expect him to do if she told him she used him for her own selfish purposes?

If she delayed the revelation of her perfidy, she had a chance at brief happiness. Except what lurked in her heart didn't feel like happiness. It felt like treason. She hated that she was such a coward.

He carried her up the magnificent staircase, past leering plaster cherubs and smug young men staring out from huge paintings. Her hand tightened around Ashcroft's neck as they approached the room where five days ago she'd sampled paradise. For all her turbulent self-hatred, excitement pounded like a drum with every step closer.

He kicked open the door so it slammed hard against the wall. So swiftly that her surroundings became a blur, he crossed the sitting room into the candlelit bedroom.

The unseen presence of Lord Peregrine's staff was everywhere. In the vases of sweet-scented lilies on each flat surface. In the turned-down sheets, waiting in crisp readiness. In the windows open to the garden, catching any phantom breeze that offered relief from endless heat.

Panting, Ashcroft slid her onto the bed and followed her down. Automatically, she parted her legs so he settled between them, trapping her skirts. He raised himself on his elbows and stared at her as if she were the most beautiful creature he'd ever seen.

Still, he didn't kiss her.

She'd die if he didn't kiss her soon.

Tenderness ran beneath hunger like rich harmony under the melody of a symphony. She smoothed his black hair from his brow. His hair was thick and soft. Softer than William's. He closed his eyes as if savoring her touch.

His revelations burned her mind, stabbed her heart.

She'd known love. Her father. Her mother. Laura. William.

Ashcroft had never known genuine affection.

That made her want to cry. And cherish him forever.

She ached for the ostracized child. A piercing mixture of pity and pain coiled inside her. She tried to stifle her futile yearning to make everything better, cure the ills of his past.

How could she save him when she was so utterly irredeemable?

He opened his green eyes and smiled. Not his usual worldly, cynical smile. Something sweet and dear that made him look ten years younger. Her susceptible heart lurched with agonized longing.

"I told you I was too heavy," she said, her voice cracking.

She wanted him to tell her more of his past, so she could try to heal him. But when he found out the truth, he'd think she pried these confidences from him to forward her deception.

"Desperation lends me strength." Laughter bubbled in his voice like champagne.

"Not the answer I wanted," she retorted without venom. She lifted her other hand and began a gentle exploration of his face. Tracing the arrogant black brows, the blade of his nose, the slashing cheekbones, the hard angles of his jaw. "Mmm, you've shaved since I saw you this afternoon."

He laughed softly, pressing into her touch with a naturalness that sent another jolt to her heart. "I needed to pass the time before you deigned to arrive."

"You could pass the time now by kissing me," she murmured in amused reproof, loving the playful give-and-take.

Every second's delay built delicious expectation. In spite of lies and betrayal, she was happy. And happiness, especially since William's death, was rare enough for her not to dismiss it, however unexpected, however undeserved.

More than anything, she wanted to share that happiness with her lover. She suspected that pure, unfettered happiness was a fleeting visitor in his life too.

"You're a demanding baggage," he said with equal lack of heat.

She stretched, and through the layers of clothing, she felt his body tighten. She loved that he desired her so unstintingly. "Oh, yes, I am at that."

"You're also wearing far too many clothes."

"That's something I can fix."

Her fingers slipped to his mouth. Almost reverently, she traced the sharply cut upper lip, dipping down in the center, lingering at the corners. She gently pressed on the full lower lip.

His mouth hinted at so much. His surprisingly ascetic streak, the intelligence, the perception, the stubbornness, the determination. The rapture of his passion.

He parted his lips and sucked her middle finger into his mouth. She shivered as hot wetness surrounded her flesh. He flicked the tip with his tongue, and voluptuous pleasure flooded her.

"So?" she asked in a shaky voice.

He rolled onto his side, watching her. His glinting eyes made her feel more desirable than any courtesan. He drew her finger from his mouth.

"So?"

"I thought I was to torture you tonight," she said huskily.

"It's more fun if we torture each other." He slid a pin from her hair. With a concentration that made her belly tighten, he smoothed the fallen lock. "You have beautiful hair."

"Flattery will get you everywhere."

"I plan to explore everywhere. That's why I shaved."

She muffled a snort of laughter. "I have a better idea."

His attention shifted from her hair to her face. "Now I'm interested."

She sucked in a nervous breath and summoned her courage. "Why don't I seduce you?"

Chapter Sixteen

hat should take you about five seconds. Including the four seconds I need to shove up your skirts."

Ashcroft stroked Diana's hair with a visible pleasure that made her shake with desire. And something else that cut deeper than desire, something she couldn't let herself acknowledge.

She leaned over him and insinuated one hand behind his strong neck. "You know, I didn't arrive on your doorstep without serious preparation. Before I came to London, I read some interesting books."

"Did you indeed?" A spark of curiosity lit his eyes to jade although the unloved little boy still lurked like a ghost in his gaze. That solitary child made her want to cry.

She'd been so tragically, wickedly wrong about Ashcroft. His life hadn't been easy and shallow, although for the sake of his pride, he strove to give that impression. No wonder he was so ready to defend the defenseless in Parliament.

"Oh, yes. But my knowledge is theoretical. I'd like to develop practical skills, test my researches in the real world."

His expression softened and became alluringly sensual. His beautiful mouth quirked in a way that made her yearning heart slam against her ribs. "Heaven forbid I hinder your education."

"I thought you'd see it that way." Diana struggled to adopt his light tone. It was difficult when she burned to wrap her arms around him, rail at his thoughtless, uncaring family, make up for every slight he'd suffered.

"So you intend to push me around."

"Only in directions you'll enjoy."

She longed to do something just for him, something that didn't advance her ambitions, a gift freely granted to a man who gave her so much and whom she betrayed so egregiously.

He lay back, that smile still teasing his lips, and studied her. She slid off the wide bed and rounded the elaborately carved base. His gaze, brilliant with interest, followed her every movement.

"You're still wearing too many clothes," he pointed out in a prosaic voice that contrasted enticingly with the fire in his eyes.

Her hand rose to the silver clasp fastening her voluminous black cloak. "Who's giving the orders?"

That taunting brow rose again. "I just wasn't sure you knew how to start, your knowledge being purely theoretical and all."

Her lips twitched. "I'm sure I'll muddle through on my own."

"On your own? Surely not!"

Laughter bubbled up like a pure stream. Strangely, when this was over, she'd miss the laughter as much as the passion.

Then she remembered the taste of his mouth. The hot saltiness of his tongue. The deep thrust of his body.

Maybe not quite as much.

Her avid gaze roamed his long, strong form, the alert, intelligent features, the elegant hands lying loosely at his sides on the white sheets.

He groaned and briefly closed his eyes. When he opened them, green shone like emeralds between his thick black lashes. "Whatever you're doing, do it soon, or I won't be responsible for my actions."

"If you get too unruly, I'll tie you down."

The glint became more pronounced. "Informative books indeed. Where does a chit like you find literature like that?"

Fleetingly, the specter of Lord Burnley darkened her world.

No, she wouldn't think of that evil old man now, not when she was about to grant her lover unconditional pleasure. "In the cabbage patch," she said lightly. "Should I tie you up?"

"Only if turnabout is fair play."

Dizzying images of lying splayed and helpless flooded her mind. What a disgrace she was. Only a few weeks in the decadent capital, and she became completely depraved.

The ribald picture didn't disgust. It excited.

"Maybe next time," she murmured, knowing Ashcroft noted her interest and filed it away for later exploration.

"If you don't take that cloak off, I'll rip it away." The words were ragged.

Her breath jammed in her throat.

Under the seductive playfulness, desire surged, dangerous, barely contained. It swirled around her in wild currents. It made her skin prickle under the heavy clothing. It lured her to acts unthinkable a week ago. It turned this room into something outside time. Where only Ashcroft and Diana existed.

Before this affair, she'd blithely underestimated the power of desire. Now she paid a terrible price for that mistake by becoming its slave.

Her fingers teased the clasp. Touching it and moving away, touching it and moving away. "So impatient already?"

His powerful chest heaved as he sucked in a lungful of air. "Already? It's been a damned eon since I touched you."

Nobody had ever wanted her like this. It made her giddy, like drinking too much claret or swinging off the highest branch of a tall tree. "Seconds only."

"Diana . . ." he growled.

She should stop tormenting him. Except she intended to torture him much more before she was finished. He'd taught her the power of making a lover wait.

The question was whether she could wait.

His ardor inflamed her. With unsteady fingers, she released the clasp. She shrugged and the cloak slithered to the floor in a whisper of sound. Underneath was her favorite gown, a dress of surpassing glamour she hadn't imagined she'd ever wear. Red silk that clung to every line of her body. It must have cost Burnley a fortune.

It was raiment fit for a queen. A sultry, wanton queen set to make gibbering fools of her subjects. The bodice, supported by jeweled straps, scooped low, leaving most of her bosom bare.

The dress was gaudy, shocking, spectacular. Completely inappropriate for an audience of one.

Except Ashcroft was the only audience she wanted.

When she put on this dress, she'd felt daring. Now, standing before Ashcroft arrayed like an expensive whore, nerves made her link her fingers at her waist in shaking uncertainty.

She braved a glance in his direction. He was utterly still, and his eyes scorched her. The flutter of a muscle in his cheek indicated his tension. Her gaze darted over his body. His rod pressed eagerly against his breeches. She swallowed to moisten a suddenly dry throat.

"You're superb," he said hoarsely.

Confidence surged, and she straightened. "I wore it for you."

"Thank you. It's beautiful." His smile was ferocious. His hands opened and closed at his sides, revealing his hunger. "Now take it off."

A husky laugh escaped. "You forget who's in charge."

"I'm completely in your power. Now shed that spectacular rag and come to bed."

She read the craving in his face. And decided to torment him a little longer. "Later."

He propped himself on his elbows. Her power was complete illusion. He was large and strong, and he could leap up and grab her anytime. Another of those bone-melting thrills shivered its way through her.

She smiled. "If you get off that bed, I'm going home."

He immediately stilled. "You wouldn't."

No, she wouldn't. "Try me."

"You're a ruthless witch." He stretched back against the mattress and crossed his legs with unconvincing nonchalance. He looked magnificent reclining against the sheets.

"And you're a barbarian, Ashcroft. Lolling around in someone else's bed wearing your boots."

"Then help me get rid of them."

"In this dress?"

"You're welcome to remove it. I remember making that suggestion."

"That wasn't a suggestion, it was a demand."

He arched one expressive eyebrow. "A demand you've had no difficulty ignoring."

He sat on the edge of the bed and began to tug at his boots. She darted forward and knelt before him. "You win."

"You're going to jump on top of me?"

"No. But I'll help you with your boots."

"Pity." However, he readily raised each foot for her attention.

For a charged instant, she held his bare leg, feeling the roughness of hair, the strength of his calf. She pressed a kiss to his shin. He leaned down and plunged his hands into her hair, disturbing the elaborate arrangement.

She looked up and fell captive to deep green eyes. A sigh escaped her, and he took advantage of her parted lips to steal a kiss. As his tongue swept into her mouth in a teasing foray, she melted toward him.

There was only the heated pressure of his lips, the flickering response of her tongue. He made a rough sound of enjoyment and deepened the kiss. She raised her hands to his shoulders, clenching her fingers in the loose white shirt.

She sank into a dark velvet world of the senses. A world where there was nothing but endless pleasure.

He lifted his mouth a fraction. "Come to bed."

The invitation was soft, alluring. Through the fog in her mind, she remembered that if she yielded, she furthered Burnley's plot. And after what she'd learned about Ashcroft tonight, she couldn't bear the idea of cheating him again.

Her heart would crack if she didn't do something for him alone.

"Soon." She rose and lifted her arms to slide the few remaining pins from her hair, loving the way he watched her so intently. Her hair tumbled down about her shoulders. "Take off your shirt."

He obeyed with gratifying swiftness, tugging the shirt over his head and tossing it to the floor. She paused, admiring the hard strength of his chest and arms. He really was a formidable man.

The way he looked at her made her feel omnipotent, commanding, a queen indeed. Worthy of the dress, not just a masquerader in borrowed plumage.

"Now your breeches."

He cast her a suspicious look. "You want me at a complete disadvantage?"

"Oh, yes." She drew the answer out into a long hiss of anticipation.

Hunger flared in his eyes, and he stood. Within seconds, his breeches followed the shirt to the floor.

He was wrong about being at a disadvantage. She cleared her throat and forced out the words. "Lie back."

With surprising alacrity, he obeyed. Her attention glanced

across the birthmark that proved his parentage, then fastened on his penis, rising hard and ready. Moisture welled between her thighs. Curiosity tightened her throat and made her heart pound.

She couldn't remember wanting anything as much as she wanted to taste him. Somewhere in her checkered relationship with Ashcroft, inhibitions had vanished.

Her gaze never shifting from that pulsing length, she knelt on the bed.

Although Diana was yet to voice her intentions, Ashcroft had no trouble reading what she meant to do.

This was far from the first time a mistress had promised to take him into her mouth. He'd discovered that particular path to bliss in his teens. He'd lost count of the women who'd serviced him since.

So why did this feel so ravishingly different?

It was a mystery he didn't particularly want to solve.

Thought exploded to ash as her hand closed around his erect cock. Hot blackness overwhelmed him, and he shut his eyes.

"Oh, yes," he breathed, as she rubbed her fist up and down his length.

He'd been hard all night. Hell, he'd been hard for her for a century. Amazingly, at her touch, he got harder, larger. He ground his teeth and battled for sanity.

The first time she'd touched him like this, she'd been hesitant, uncertain, fumbling. He'd needed to show her what to do. His lessons had clearly taken root. Stroke by tantalizing stroke, she built his blazing need to an inferno.

Feverishly, he caressed her thigh through her skirt. He cracked his eyes open as the silk slid under his hand. She knelt at his side in an uncharacteristically submissive pose. Except if anyone submitted, it was he.

She increased the pressure, and he released a deep groan. A pleased smile curved her lush mouth. Her eyelids lowered so her lashes were dark gold fans on her flushed cheeks. It was the most arousing expression he'd ever seen on a woman's face. The utter concentration. The undisguised enjoyment.

Arousal flared as she licked her lips. The gleaming moisture on her mouth made him think of other ways she could employ that busy, pink tongue.

Would she take him in her mouth? Or would her nerve fail?

Sizzling suspense conspired with pounding need to make him light-headed. His hand tightened on her thigh, crumpling her skirt, as his heart kicked into a headlong gallop.

Under cool silk, he felt warm, supple flesh. He wanted his hands on her skin without the barrier of clothing. He wanted to share the pleasure she inflicted with this slow seduction. And perhaps a modicum of the torment.

"Take off your dress. I'll touch you while you touch me." His voice was harsh with restraint.

Instead of giving him his way, she lifted her hands off him. She looked directly at him, shaking her heavy fall of hair back. That evocative smile still flirted with her lips.

She knew exactly what she did, the darling jade.

His cock throbbed with frustration, his heart slammed to a stop. It was a warm night, but compared to the scorching heat of his skin, the air felt like ice.

Amusement sparked in her face. She didn't replace her hand where he wanted it, blast her. "You promised to lie still."

As he looked into her lovely face, for the first time he wondered if he'd met a woman he wanted to keep for longer than a few weeks. Even more shocking, he wondered whether, in such company, monogamy might have its benefits.

Dear Lord, save him from such madness. He needed to get a grip before he started spouting romantic absurdities. Diana was only in Town for the summer, before she retreated to that confounded mysterious village in Surrey. And a dull life as a respectable widow if he believed the tale she'd spun him.

Perhaps he could convince her to stay. Or visit the capital regularly.

Like every week.

Every day.

Every minute.

"I feel like a specimen at the damned Royal Society," he said, not entirely joking.

She watched his face as if he were the air she breathed. "You'd be the most popular exhibit. Especially displayed as you are. Or perhaps in the British Museum. You have a fondness for the place. After today, I must confess I too have a liking for it, especially the Egyptian rooms."

"I'm neither dead nor dusty, my love."

My love?

Clearly she sent him into such a fever, his normal, well-considered reactions were lacking. He'd return to something approximating sanity once he'd had her.

A hundred times.

Maybe.

She ran her finger down his bare thigh, steering clear of where he wanted her. She raised her finger and inspected it. "You're right. No dust. The housemaids are doing their duty."

He laughed. He couldn't remember the last time anyone teased him. Nobody considered themselves on such relaxed terms with him. No friend. No lover. The realization struck him as a sad reflection on his existence.

"Come here," he said without moving, although he withdrew his hand, most reluctantly, from her leg.

She looked wary. "Why?"

"Because I want to kiss you. Then I promise to endure your torture." He sent her a meaningful glance. "Although don't expect to escape retribution."

Her color intensified. Her skin had the bloom of a ripe peach. In the soft candlelight, she could be a girl with her first lover. He wondered if her husband had had any idea of the treasure he'd won in the young Diana. He could picture her ten years or so ago. Ardent. Generous. Virginal. The idea struck Ashcroft as poignant in a way he couldn't explain.

Although jealousy stirred.

And he was jealous of no lover.

"I think that can be arranged," she murmured, trailing her finger down the center of his chest as if checking for more dust.

Did she mean it? He'd longed to put his mouth on her sex since he'd first seen her. Another blast of excitement crackled through him.

When she pressed her lips to his, she tasted fresh and almost innocent. For a brief, enchanted interval, she kissed him chastely. Just moving in a subtle exploration that nonetheless made his pulses thunder like an avalanche. His fingers twisted in the sheets.

Her hand crept up his shoulder to stroke his face. Poor bedazzled fool he was, the touch felt like tenderness. And that scored his heart deeper than passion.

The chaste kiss couldn't endure, not when desire raged like a forest fire. Her tongue flicked out to test the seam of his lips. He opened his mouth. The kiss changed from a sweet prelude to develop heated momentum. By the time she drew away, they both panted.

He ached to touch her but reined in the impulse. Her face hovered so close, it was a blur, but he felt the brush of her breath and her hand caressed his cheek with what he still read as tenderness.

Idiot, Ashcroft.

He fisted a silky hank of her hair and rubbed it against his cheek. He waited for her to speak, but she remained silent apart from her uneven breathing.

She pulled away until her features came into focus. The tenderness in her touch shone in her face. He wasn't blockhead enough to mistake that.

He tried to stem the tide of warmth that flooded his heart.

Her brows drew together, creating a faint line on her forehead. Swimming in the darkness of her eyes, he saw trouble. He forced his sluggish brain to work. Was something wrong?

"What is it, Diana?" he asked roughly, cursing the delay but unwilling to let her continue if she genuinely didn't want to do this.

As clearly as if she drew the curtains in a house at evening, he watched her conceal her expression. Suspicion tightened his gut, but he was too close to the edge to heed it.

She smiled, but the beautiful honesty was absent. "I'm nervous. I've never done this before."

He told himself that made sense. His assurances rang hollow. He tightened his hold on her hair. "Trust me."

"Ashcroft . . ." she said shakily. Her slender throat moved as she swallowed. The erratic pulse fluttered at the base of her neck.

"What is it?"

For one electric second, he thought she meant to say something momentous. Confess some sin. Reveal some secret. Open her heart.

The second vanished.

The glance she cast him was pure seduction. The tremulous moment of uncertainty might never have existed. He tried to tell himself he'd imagined it. He knew better.

As she placed a hot openmouthed kiss on his chest, he couldn't summon will to pursue his curiosity. Her soft lips moving on his skin, the dampness of her breath, the lick of her tongue threatened to banish any thought but desire.

If only he wasn't sure she worked to achieve that end.

She gently bit his nipple. Sensation crashed through him like a carriage running him down at full tilt. Her tongue soothed the sting. He released her hair to let her pay the same attention to his other nipple. He didn't need to voice the invitation aloud.

She lifted her head, briefly met his gaze, and straddled him. Myriad impressions fed his dazed senses. The warm drift of her hair, a silky tickle across his bare chest. The rustle of her skirts. The slide of silk against his flanks. The waft of scent, hot with arousal. His cock jerked even as his nostrils flared.

His hands clenched in the sheets as he fought the urge to roll her under him and thrust hard. Every second they'd been apart, he'd wanted her. This delay was excruciating.

She trailed her mouth down his stomach. He drew breath so hard, his belly turned to rock. Much more delay, and promises be damned. He'd have her.

A strangled groan escaped. "For God's sake, don't make me wait," he forced past a jaw aching with tension.

"Patience," she said, and his heart lurched at the laughter in her voice.

He ground his teeth with frustration. "You ask the impossible."

Still, she incited him with pleasurable licks and bites across his belly. She slipped down, coiling over his body. Still, she took her time, tasting him, experimenting, testing what set him shivering with need.

He shook like a man with malaria. Sweat sprang onto his skin. His heart raced fit to burst. His lungs ached as he dragged in every breath.

This inexperienced woman drove him to the limit. He hadn't been as wild since he was a randy adolescent slavering after the dairymaids at Vesey Hall.

After what felt like a millennium, she curled her fingers once more around his straining cock. He trembled under her touch, not far from losing himself. Only the last vestiges of rapidly fading masculine pride stopped him spilling into her hand.

"Christ," he whispered, not sure if it was curse or prayer.

For a long time nothing happened. She held him but didn't shift her hand.

He stopped breathing. His heart stopped beating.

Do it. Do it. For God's sake, do it.

Hell, how much more could he bear?

The quiet shadowy room with its distant sounds of traffic receded. All he knew was the clasp of her hand and the throbbing need in his cock.

Dear God, why didn't she . . .

Wet heat closed around the head, and bright red light exploded behind his eyes. He made a sound deep in his throat, afraid to move unless she stopped. Every muscle in his body tensed.

At first, her mouth was hardly less frustrating than her hand. She exerted no suction. Just let him rest in warmth and moisture.

He was taut as a violin string. Waiting for the bow to strike so the music could flow.

She shifted. Her hair slid across his thighs in a whisper of seduction. He bit back a plea to keep going, not to stop, to give him what he wanted.

Her hand tightened and her mouth flexed. Lightning struck. Her tongue flickered.

He wouldn't survive. She'd kill him before she finished. She took him deeper. His hips jerked before he recalled he'd promised not to move.

Her hand closed hard around his shaft and moved up and down. He was in heaven. Angels sang their lungs out. He swore he heard rippling harp glissandos.

His fists clenched as he fought the urge to compel her to more concentrated action. He could show her what to do. Yet something about her determination indicated she wanted to find her own way.

He just hoped he retained enough sanity to celebrate her arrival when she finally got there.

He made another inarticulate sound, and she seemed to take this as a signal. Her mouth started to move, while her hand performed a complex dance of pleasure.

She still didn't have the rhythm.

Heaven help him when she found the right combination. Her amateurish efforts pushed him close to exploding. The hot pull of her lips made it almost impossible to hold back.

Abruptly, she broke through to another realm. Her hand, her mouth, the sounds she made crescendoed into a tumultuous rhapsody. He teetered on the brink of an endless fiery blaze.

He should stop her. He couldn't come in her mouth. Not her first time.

Control, Ashcroft, control.

His shaking hands slid down to her shoulders, felt hot skin under that damnable red silk. He meant to drag her up his chest and kiss her. He meant to settle her over him and plunge into her welcoming depths.

His hands curled, ready to lift her up, to make her stop, to end before it was too late.

Her grip firmed. She drew hard. All good intentions shattered.

Chapter Seventeen

～～～～～～～～～～～～～～～

$\mathscr{H}$ot, salty liquid spurted into Diana's mouth. Automatically, she swallowed. Her hand tightened on Ashcroft's jerking shaft. His long groan of release echoed in her ears.

Her heart swelled with joy, and dazzling triumph streaked through her. What she did held a truth. A truth lacking in everything else between them, no matter how he touched her emotions and made her quake with ecstasy. She'd found something for him alone. Something outside her shabby bargain with Lord Burnley, something outside her own undeserved pleasure.

Although she'd discovered searing pleasure in arousing him until he couldn't hold back.

His hand drifted down to tangle in the hair at her crown. He was shaking. The rhythmic clenching and unclenching of his fingers against her scalp became an ineluctable part of the wild sensations careering through her.

She drank him dry. Only then did she raise her head and stare along his flat belly and hard chest. His eyes were closed, his thick lashes quivering on his cheeks as he gasped. He looked like a man who had measured the outer reaches of sin and hadn't yet returned to the bounds of reality.

She'd expected to be revolted, but when she'd taken Ashcroft in her mouth, she'd felt more a woman than ever before. She'd sensed both the power of his masculinity and the vulnerability of his humanity.

Slowly she rose, wiping her mouth. When she licked her lips, a new taste lingered. *Ashcroft. . .*

She knelt at his side as she had when she'd begun. In an exhausted caress, his hand slid from her hair to lie open at his side. He looked like he couldn't move to save himself from a tidal wave.

"Take off that damned dress." A sliver of green shone between his lashes, and his breathing gradually steadied.

"Clothing gives me the advantage." She found decadent gratification in having this man, omnipotent outside this room, naked and at her mercy.

A reminiscent smile curved his lips. Her heart, which had only just resumed its normal rate, battered her ribs, then set off on another race.

"You don't need special advantages," he said softly. "I'm all yours."

At last he looked directly at her. His eyes were bright jade. They were always that color when he was happy. It was an unwelcome shock to realize how well she'd come to know him. Another twist in the skein of inescapable intimacy.

"If I'd guessed that was how to vanquish you, I'd have done it much earlier," she said lightly, even as her blood pounded fast and hard with excitement.

Sudden concern shadowed his gaze, and he rested one hand on her thigh. It was where he'd touched her before, curling his fist in her skirts, but this contact was soothing, comforting . . . affectionate. After the passion, this gesture emerged from a different world. A world beyond the deception and desire that trapped her.

"Are you all right?" He met her eyes with an expression as deep as the ocean.

She tried to stop her wayward heart melting. It was too late. Her defenses crumbled more quickly than a wafer dipped in hot tea.

"Yes, I'm all right," she said in a choked voice.

Her assurance didn't seem to convince. Given the way she sounded, she couldn't blame him for doubting.

How could she say her regrets focused on why she came to his bed, not on anything she did while here?

"I swear I didn't mean to . . ."

Flood her mouth with his seed? She was surprised he found it difficult to articulate what he'd done. How she wished she didn't find his demurral so charming. "I liked it."

What an understatement. If she told him exactly what she'd felt, she'd leave herself too vulnerable.

His hand tightened on her leg. "You're magnificent."

What did one say in response to that? "Thank you," she muttered.

He laughed. "You're most welcome. You'd be more welcome if you were naked."

"You won't be much use to me even if I'm naked," she said with faint challenge.

The smile teasing his lips broadened, and the green eyes took on a devilish glint. "Oh, I wouldn't say that."

Her attention dropped to his organ. To her astonishment, it twitched as if responding to physical contact. Anticipation seared her. In spite of that titanic release, he'd have no difficulty performing.

She slid off the bed to stand on the richly colored rug. He piled pillows under his head and propped himself up to watch her.

She loved this dress. As the irreproachable Marchioness of Burnley, she'd never wear such a seductive garment again. In this dress, she'd seduced a notorious rake into incoherent pleasure. In this dress, she'd come closer to freedom than ever before. In spite of how lies and self-interest strangled her.

The time for teasing games was over.

She presented her back and stood trembling as Ashcroft unlaced her. Then with shaking hands, she ripped the red gown off and pitched it unheeded into the corner. Beneath she only wore a shift. Undergarments seemed a coy lie.

Within seconds, she stood bare. The heavy air brushed her like heated satin. She'd never presented herself so shamelessly to a man. Although Lord Ashcroft had seen her before, it felt different when she displayed herself like a courtesan.

His eyes fixed unwaveringly upon her. She bore his intense regard for a few seconds before shielding her mound with unsteady hands.

"No," he said softly, his gaze focusing there. Heat spread over her skin as if he touched her.

After a tremulous hesitation, she obeyed.

"Beautiful." Ashcroft's expression was sharp with yearning. He held his hand out.

A night bird called in the garden outside, and the spell shattered. God help her, she ran to Ashcroft as if more existed between them than betrayal. She leaned down toward him as if he held her heart in his keeping.

He surged up and grabbed her. The room became a dizzying whirl as he dragged her under him. She felt the crisp sheets against her naked back, then the hot pressure of his weight.

The sweet familiarity of his body on hers blasted her like honey lightning. New lovers shouldn't fit perfectly with the merest touch. Her body molded to his in a harmony purer than any music. She arched, rubbing her belly against his pulsing hardness.

He hadn't boasted about being ready. Such a wonderfully virile man was the Earl of Ashcroft.

He kissed her on the mouth, where his essence lingered. While tongues still dueled and teased, he lifted one of her legs. He hooked it over his arm, opening her wide.

Delicious tension filled her as she waited for his possession. Instead, he kissed an erratic, spine-tingling path downward. She was so lost in the mists of pleasure, he'd reached her navel before she guessed his intentions.

She tensed. "Ashcroft . . ."

"You promised to let me torture you."

She had. She just hadn't considered how he'd interpret that teasing offer. "But . . ."

He looked up, and his green eyes were so deep, she thought she saw into his soul. "Please, Diana."

Ashcroft knew Diana didn't want his mouth between her legs. From the beginning, the idea had frightened her.

Why was he so eager to push her into this intimacy?

Perhaps because if she let him do this, she ceded herself in a way she never had before. Perhaps because if this barrier against him dropped, others would.

Perhaps because he wanted her in every way a man could want a woman.

Although pleading didn't come easily, he spoke again. "Please, Diana."

He ached to taste her. When she'd taken him in her mouth, she'd shown him the bright light of heaven. He burned to return the favor. He burned to express his gratitude in the purest way he could.

"I can't imagine why you want this," she said in a choked voice.

Her expression was troubled, but her lips were dark red with his kisses and her cheeks flushed with desire. A woman who looked like that shouldn't shy from relishing the full ration of delight.

"Because you're beautiful everywhere," he said softly, placing a kiss on the top of each thigh and feeling her quiver in response. She was so sensitive, he'd take her to paradise if only she'd let him. "Let me prove that."

"It's . . . wicked."

His laugh emerged as a purr. "That sounds incongruous coming from a woman who just drained me to the lees."

He watched the sequence of emotions cross her face. Shame, which he loathed to witness. Then more to his liking, recollected pleasure. Then, finally, a stoic acceptance.

"Yes," she said on a thread of breath.

He placed a kiss on her belly, feeling her trembling. "You sound like a Christian facing the lions."

A spark of spirit revived. "Can you blame me? You're going to eat me."

"Oh, I am indeed."

He knew he gloated. But her surrender, even if not whole-hearted, set him ablaze with excitement. He placed another kiss just above the feathery dark blond curls.

She studied him as if unsure whether he indeed prepared to rend her limb from limb like a lion. Foolish girl. He meant her to come apart, but never so drastically.

He still held her leg over his arm, opening her to his gaze. For a long time, he stared at the succulent pink folds. He drew deep of her scent. He felt more than lust, although lust was certainly part of what rushed through his veins. She reached into what he'd call his soul, if he hadn't long ago lost his soul in dissipation.

Her breath emerged in jagged gasps, and the muscles under his hand were tight. He didn't need to see her expression to know she was terrified.

In consideration of her uncertainty, he released her leg and slid back up her body to press a kiss that conveyed more tenderness than passion to her lips. Passion was present, but he reined it in, wanting to reassure. After a hesitation, she kissed him back. Predictably, passion broke its bonds, and the kiss turned fierce and hungry. By the time he drew away, he was breathing unsteadily, and his heart crashed like a drum.

For a shuddering moment, he buried his head in the smooth, damp skin at her shoulder. What was wrong with him? No other lover turned him so unrestrained and desperate.

"You won't distract me," he said unsteadily.

"You started it," she said, equally breathlessly. Thank the Lord, she didn't sound quite as frightened.

He raised his head and sent her a direct look. "And I'm going to finish it."

He kissed a line across her collarbone and down to her breast. When he took her in his mouth, she cried out and raised her knees. He drew hard, and she trembled in immediate response.

How would she respond to a more intimate kiss? His blood seethed in expectation.

Before she could tense again, he kissed a path down the soft plain of her belly. She exhaled in a long, shuddering sigh.

Taking this as permission to continue, he nudged her legs farther apart and licked her long and luxuriously. Immediately, the heady taste of her, richer, stronger than the taste of her skin, filled his mouth.

Luscious.

She made a sound deep in her throat. Protest or encouragement? He didn't know. But he couldn't stop. He licked again, pausing to draw on the pulsing center. This time he had no trouble interpreting her moan as one of pleasure.

Elation filled him. He used his mouth and teeth and tongue, exploring the cleft, invading her, sipping the hot dew.

"Wicked . . ." she sighed.

Her hands curled in his hair, tugging in time with his depredations. She undulated under his mouth like the sea, and her sighs rose in a sweet crescendo. Tension filled her. Not the tension of fear. The tension of approaching climax.

He concentrated on bringing her to that ultimate peak. He loved the husky sounds she made, the writhing tension of her body. His senses closed in to contain nothing but him and this woman he pleasured.

Then, as he'd promised himself, she screamed with uninhibited release. She convulsed under his mouth, pressing up into him so his tongue stabbed her, possessed her, stole her essence.

He didn't stop. Even while she quivered, he built her response again. He wanted her world to change.

After this, she'd never forget him. His touch would be etched on her body forever.

Forever.

Because even as he sent her spiraling into ecstasy, he knew it was inevitable that she'd leave.

Diana stretched out in absolute exhaustion, her brain thick with languor. Her body throbbed with receding rapture. Ashcroft had battered her with bliss.

What a gift he'd given her. Her heart clenched hard as she struggled to lock him out. But the pleasure had cut too deep. The closeness had been too powerful.

God forgive her, she could no longer deny he moved her emotions more profoundly than anyone she'd ever known.

Ashcroft sprawled over her, his head resting on her belly, his arms loose around her waist, his torso covering her legs. His face turned in profile, but she saw his satisfied smile. He looked remarkably innocent for a man who had just performed such a lascivious act. Unless one noted the sleek dampness of his lips. Damp with her, she recognized with a bone-deep thrill.

He must be proud of himself. He'd certainly been proven right. In spite of her misgivings, she'd adored what he'd done. Difficult to resent his triumph when he'd shown her such unearthly delight. Difficult to resent him at all when they lay like this, the memory of pleasure extending between them like a perfect gold chain.

Her fingers still curled in his thick dark hair. The air was hot and heavy. In the quiet moment, broken only by the soft susurration of their breathing, she felt a contentment she couldn't remember before. Every muscle was as liquid as water. Her heart beat a slow, solemn song of happiness.

They might have slept. She didn't know. She drifted in a world that held only her and Ashcroft and endless pleasure.

Awareness returned, to Ashcroft rising between her legs. When he angled her hips up, her belly cramped with excitement. She was wet and ready. Even so, the power of his thrust rocked her. She gasped sharply as she adjusted to the intrusion.

He raised himself on his elbows to study her face. His skin was tight against his bones, and his eyes were black with arousal. The perspiration on his skin shone in the candlelight.

"Am I hurting you?" The question emerged as a gruff exhalation.

"No," she responded breathlessly. His unambiguous possession wasn't precisely comfortable, but he didn't hurt her.

She stroked his sweat-slicked back, feeling the subtle flexing of muscle. Her random exploration reached his buttocks. She squeezed that firm flesh. He shivered, and the movement tested her interior passage, scorched her with pleasure.

"Don't stop," she urged, tilting to take him deeper although surely he was as deep as he could go.

The sinews under her hands tautened, and he withdrew, then thrust again. Her hands opened and closed, keeping time with the delicious rhythm.

For a long time, she was lost in the wild music. His whispered praise, her incoherent murmurs of encouragement, the soft moans, the broken breathing, the slide of flesh on flesh, the creak of the bed.

Her climax built quickly. All night he'd primed her for this. If she were honest, she'd been primed since she'd last left his bed. The desperate but frustrating kisses in the museum had only fired her impatience. His mouth on her had been wonderful, astonishing. But this now was what she wanted from him. Him pounding into her body, making her his.

Pleasure seized her, spun her, flung her up into the sky

and held her suspended in absolute delight. Like a greedy child at a birthday party, she snatched at the joy, luxuriating in the magic.

Too soon she returned to the real world. To a body quaking with satisfaction. To the warm, luxurious room. To the presence of her magnificent, ardent lover.

She opened her eyes and looked up at Ashcroft. "You didn't . . ."

He shook his head, his sweat-dampened hair flopping over his forehead in utterly beguiling untidiness. "No."

"Are you . . ."

"Yes."

Strange they could communicate in these half sentences. She couldn't remember being so in tune with another person. William certainly hadn't understood her merest thought, for all he'd been a good, kind man.

Diana smiled and stretched, feeling Ashcroft's hardness, reveling in the glide of his skin upon hers. Aftershocks rippled through her. She felt as though he'd combed every single nerve in her body out like silk ready for the weaver. She felt marvelous.

Still staring into her eyes, he began to move. This time it was different, as if he read her aching, hidden emotions and answered them with his body. He was slow, and at the end of every stroke, he paused, savoring how she felt closing tight around him.

In an agony of impatience, she waited for him to intensify the force, the passion. But he just moved in and out, like waves brushing a shore, ebbing, flowing forward again. Eternal. Repetitive. She felt as though she formed part of a huge, restless sea.

She shifted, changing his angle of penetration, but still he kept to that inhumanly constant motion. Still he stared into her face as if her features held the answers to every mystery.

Slowly, her urge to persuade him to a more urgent pace faded. The thrust and withdrawal lulled her into a suspended state of bliss.

For an interval beyond measuring, there were no seconds, no minutes. The deep, luxuriant seduction might have lasted for hours. She wouldn't know. There was only his body claiming hers. Nothing else.

She was almost sorry when the pleasure inevitably altered, and her muscles tightened with the approach of climax.

She couldn't delay the trembling onset. It moved toward her like a distant storm rumbling closer and closer, promising destruction, fury, a burst of new life.

Fierce sensation whipped her, like a violent wind shook the trees before a tempest.

Even as her response inexorably rose, she watched his face. The control finally cracked. His dark brows drew together as he struggled to hold back. Deep lines of strain ran from his nose to his mouth. His eyes glittered down at her although he must hardly see her, he was so far gone in arousal.

"Oh, Tarquin . . ." she whispered, reaching up and smoothing the tension from his face. His skin was hot and taut under her fingers. "Let go."

Her touch broke some last thread of resistance. He sucked in a great shuddering breath, thrust ruthlessly, then on a huge groan, he poured himself into her.

Her climax crashed over her, with the force of thunder, the fire of lightning, the rush of a gale. It surpassed anything she'd felt earlier the way the sun outshone a candle.

For an endless time, she remained floating in the stars. There was no horizon. No limit. She tasted infinity. Ashcroft was with her. Somehow that was more important than the blinding pleasure streaking through her.

When Diana came back to earth, he slumped against her, pressing her into the mattress. The room was still and sweltering. Her arms twined around his back. She clutched him closer than a miser clutched his gold.

His heart pounded against her breast and his breath was a ragged symphony in her ears. She was too exhausted to move. Her body felt like it was made of straw. He remained joined to her, and her legs cradled him.

She sent up a futile prayer to a God who should have nothing to do with her.

Please, Lord, let this moment last forever.

Even as the silent plea trickled through her mind, she felt Ashcroft shift. He was so close, the tiniest movement registered. Automatically her arms tightened.

Don't go. Not yet. Oh, no, not yet. I can't bear it.

It was as if he heard the desperate cry. He buried his head in the crook of her shoulder and didn't move for a long time.

She closed her eyes and let herself drift into a wonderful warm, sunlit space. Where there was no Lord Burnley. Where a rake could become a faithful lover. Where there was endless forgiveness and kindness and laughter.

Where there was no price to pay for sin.

After the pure perfection of what she'd just experienced, she risked a dream or two. She'd have few enough dreams to comfort her in the cold loneliness to come.

Gradually, the glory faded. Her body still glowed with satisfaction. Ashcroft still rested in her arms as though he had no wish to be anywhere else. But a prickling awareness of where she was chafed her contentment.

She became aware of a gentle patter of rain outside. She'd thought the storm totally contained within herself. It seemed the dry, unbearable summer at last offered respite.

The curtains didn't move, and nothing in this extravagant room was in danger of getting wet. The fresh smell of rain on dusty ground wafted in.

Ashcroft's body was hot against hers, but even so, she felt a pleasant coolness in the air, a lessening of the oppressive humidity that had crushed her since she'd come to London.

Other details slowly impinged on her consciousness. The

room smelled of sweat and sex and the sharp, smoky scent of guttering candles. She guessed it was late. She could have been in this extravagant cave of a room for an hour or a night.

This time when Ashcroft moved, she let him go.

He withdrew and rolled onto his back with a deep sigh. A loneliness bitter as aloes rushed through her. He lashed an arm around her and drew her against his side. Her heart began to beat again.

Oh, poor pathetic Diana, needing this man's touch to keep you whole.

She shifted carefully, noting new aches. He'd used her well, and she was still unaccustomed to a lover of his dimensions. She was unaccustomed to a lover at all.

She closed her eyes and rested her head on his chest, listening to the steady beat of his heart. The intimacy was sweeter than sugar, for all that grim reality knocked relentlessly against the barred door of her awareness.

She waited for Ashcroft to speak, but he remained silent. What had just happened left her awed, astonished, moved, and with a heart tremulously, dangerously open.

She told herself she experienced these feelings in isolation. Only a fool would believe a man of Ashcroft's experience found the sex nearly as world-altering. Perhaps all of his women caught that shining glimpse of eternity.

But when she lifted her head to stare into his face, he seemed as thunderstruck as she. He reached out to hold her chin steady so he could kiss her. An undemanding kiss that formed a fitting finale. His lips moved gently, and she read wonder and care in his salute.

"You called me Tarquin." His voice was soft and warm like a fur cloak on a frosty day.

She crowded into his side to get as close as possible to that beautiful baritone. "Do you mind?"

It was odd how at that vivid, transforming moment, she'd spoken his Christian name. She certainly didn't think of him as Tarquin. He was Ashcroft in her mind. From somewhere his given name had surged up, unstoppable, an expression of all she felt and couldn't risk putting into words.

He shook his head, his eyes calm, his mouth relaxed. "No, I like it. I wish you'd always call me Tarquin."

He didn't need to tell her he extended this invitation to few people. Something cold and hard inside her loosened and unfurled like an opening rose. For the first time since she'd started this affair, she didn't feel like a whore. Her conscience gave a yelp of protest, but she'd become accustomed to ignoring its complaints.

She didn't answer his request to use his Christian name, which was answer enough, she supposed. He cast her a perceptive glance as if he knew the battle she waged against her stupid, wayward heart.

She waited for him to persevere, but he merely said. "Will you stay?"

Self-preservation insisted she leave, snap the bond between them, establish some distance to save her sanity. She couldn't pretend she had any excuse to remain. Sleeping in his arms did nothing to forward her scheme.

Everything went too fast. She was trapped in a hurtling avalanche of feeling. Every time she tried to snatch at a branch or a rock to halt her slide to disaster, it cracked under her hand.

The further she fell, the faster she went. Soon, she wouldn't have a hope of saving herself.

Don't lie to yourself, Diana. It's already too late.

But it was raining outside, and she was snug and cozy in this bed. Ashcroft's arms curled tight around her. She loved the lingering scent of their joining and the soft sound of his breathing.

She lowered her head to his hair-roughened chest and shut her eyes, shutting her mind to cruel reality as she did so.

"I'll stay," she whispered.

Chapter Eighteen

$\mathcal{A}$shcroft glanced up from the books he'd piled on the desk to see Diana in the library doorway. She carried a candle, and the flickering light turned her into a gorgeous creature of mystery and shadows.

She was a creature of mystery and shadows even in daylight.

"I thought you'd sleep," he said softly, stepping out of the circle of lamplight around the desk to take her hand.

An hour ago he'd left her curled up in exhausted slumber amidst the rumpled sheets. He was bone weary too, but after the revelations of the day, the evening, the night, he'd been too restless to sleep.

In the hope that sorting through the books would distract him from the woman upstairs, he'd prowled his way into Perry's library. He'd failed to escape his preoccupation with Diana. He'd known he would even before he made the attempt.

Her fingers curled around his with an immediate trust that pierced him to the heart. "I . . . missed you."

Oh, dear God, how was he to resist her? It was impossible.

"I approve of your wardrobe." He drew her toward the

desk, unable to shift his attention from her disheveled beauty.

Her laugh was low and redolent of sin. "Your shirt was the first thing that came to hand."

"You have my permission to wear it anytime."

On such a tall woman, the loose white garment fell softly to midthigh. As she walked, her breasts slid against the fine cambric with a gentle rhythm that made every drop of moisture in his mouth evaporate.

Without great conviction, he reminded himself that only a beast would use her again so soon after that marathon session.

Restraint grew more difficult when she ran an assessing and frankly admiring glance over his bare chest. His skin tightened as if she touched him instead of just looked. "I approve of what you're wearing too."

He'd tugged his breeches on upstairs and come down barefoot. "It would frighten the ladies in Hyde Park into a riot."

"I'm not sure 'frighten' is the word I'd choose, although a riot is a possibility. "

He released her and edged behind the desk, hoping the barrier might impose control over his unruly arousal. "Stop it."

Heavy lids fell over her eyes, turning her expression breathtakingly seductive. Without shifting her gaze from him, she blew out her candle, her lips pursed as if in a kiss. Another jolt of desire shook him.

A knowing smile hovered around her mouth as she placed the candle on the desk. "Don't you like it?"

He grimaced. "I like it too well, as you know."

"Good." Her smile conveyed something of the cat in the cream pot. He loved this new sensual confidence.

"Then show some mercy."

With a gesture that made his heart slam against his chest, she flicked a drift of golden hair behind one shoulder. He only released his breath when her attention shifted to the books he'd removed from the shelves. "Have you found anything interesting?"

Right now, she was the only thing in all the world that he found interesting, and he suspected she knew it. But he seized the chance to discuss a more neutral topic than how she looked wearing nothing but his shirt. With every movement of that beautiful body, he became more aware that all that lay between him and warm, bare skin was a flimsy layer of cambric.

"Not so far. Perry has a standing order for the latest publications, but he's not much of a reader. Since Olivia left, the pages haven't even been cut on the new books. Sad, really."

Casually she picked up a small red volume and opened it to the frontispiece. "Who's Olivia?"

"You really don't keep up with the gossip, do you?"

She sent him a wry smile. "Only when it comes to the notorious Earl of Ashcroft."

Again he felt a twinge of shame that she knew so much about his decadent antics. Although his decadent antics had brought her to his bed in the first place.

But surely they'd moved beyond that shallow bargain since.

He wasn't sure enough of her to lay money on it. And that was the damnable fact.

He settled for the most uncontroversial answer he could manage. "Olivia Raines used to live in this house on an occasional basis. She's now the Countess of Erith."

Diana replaced the book on the pile in front of her and picked up another one. "Aristotle. Lord Peregrine made a show of learning at least."

Ashcroft reached over to take the book. Her fingers brushed his, and awareness sizzled through him. What in blazes was wrong with him? He was too old to go weak at the knees just because a pretty girl shared an innocent touch. "You read Greek?"

"A little."

"And Latin, I'm guessing."

She shrugged. "My father was a Cambridge man, and I was his only child. In the absence of a son to teach, he gave me an unusual education for a girl."

Ashcroft laughed softly and with unmasked self-derision. "Good God, I'm in thrall to a blasted bluestocking."

She stiffened, and the beautiful ease drained from her manner. "In thrall?"

Yet again, he'd said something to trouble her. Her secrets loomed close, although for a few moments, she'd almost been confiding. Pretending he hadn't noticed her abrupt change of mood, he flicked idly through the pages of the beautiful old book. The *Ethics,* clearly something he needed to keep, if only for his own edification. Perhaps he should start by telling his lover the unadorned truth. "Oh, yes."

His confession didn't please, devil take her. "Ashcroft . . ."

"My reputation as a rake will never recover if the gossips discover I'm bedding a bookish female." Avoiding the looming argument, he broke his stare and turned to sift through another pile. "There's nothing much here that takes my fancy."

He was grateful she took the hint about changing the subject. "He likes Walter Scott."

"No, he doesn't. They were just what he thought a man about town should stock in his library. I doubt Perry has read anything except the sporting papers since he left Eton."

"It's a pity he's changing this room. It's the nicest in the house." Ashcroft was glad to notice the reappearance of her smile. "Except for our apartment upstairs. I have a great fondness for our apartment upstairs."

Ashcroft bit back a groan. He was trying to talk to her, to convince her he was more than just a throbbing pillar of unending lust. Then she had to go and mention bedrooms.

Still, he manfully struggled on with his attempts at a civilized conversation. "You'd enjoy going through my library at Ashcroft House."

She cast him a glance under her thick lashes. "This is where you boast of actually having read the books there. I promise to be impressed by the . . . volumes."

Saucy chit. Hell, she made it so difficult to resist leaping on her. His cock was hard as the thick marble columns framing the door. "If I'd known boasting of my reading material would promote seduction, I'd have brought a list with me."

Very slowly, she replaced the book she was holding and strolled around the desk in his direction. In the candlelight, her eyes gleamed with unmistakable interest. Perhaps he wasn't the only one who found this discussion of books surprisingly arousing.

"Perhaps next time."

He ran a hand through his hair. "Diana, I'm trying to talk to you. So you think I'm more than just a rutting animal."

By now, she stood in front of him. Her glance flickered down, then up to meet his. Definitely cat in the cream pot. She reached out and ran a finger down the center of his chest, jamming his breath in his throat. "I'm convinced."

"And after what we did upstairs, you must be tired."

"Not that tired." She trailed her hand up to circle one flat nipple. Reaction shuddered through him.

"I'm trying to be considerate," he said, even as he succumbed to her touch.

She released a short huff of laughter as she raked her nails through the dark curls on his chest. "For heaven's sake, Ashcroft, I'm already in awe at the size of your brain. Now show me something else that's big."

"Diana, you try my patience," he growled, his hands flexing at his sides.

Her smile broadened. "Patience is overrated."

"All right, if you want a beast, you can have one," he rasped.

Her face flushed with excitement, and her pink tongue flickered out to moisten her lips. "A thinking beast."

"Not right now."

He kissed her quickly and gripped her around the waist. She immediately melted into his embrace. He tightened his hold and swung her around to face the desk.

"Ashcroft?" The word emerged on a shocked gasp.

He'd managed to surprise the siren. Good. He still had a trick or two to show her.

"Hold fast," he grunted, bending her over. He drew in a deep draft of her scent, warm sexually aroused female, apples.

He waited for a protest, however token, but she reached out and grabbed the far edge of the desk. The loose white sleeves slipped back to display her graceful wrists and the taut muscles of her forearms. The shirt rode up at the back, revealing white thighs and the lower curves of her bottom.

His heart battered his ribs, and arousal pounded through him like thunder. She drove him to the edge of control. He knew he wouldn't withdraw from her at the ultimate moment. He hadn't upstairs. He wouldn't now.

It was madness. But the sweetest madness in the world.

Quickly, he opened his breeches so he pressed hard and ready against the luscious globes of her buttocks. With a rough movement, he shoved the shirt out of the way and parted her legs.

In spite of his raging desire, the sight before him made him pause. She had a beautiful arse. Hell, she was beautiful everywhere. No wonder he'd never stood a chance.

Almost reverently, he bent and placed a passionate kiss on each cheek. The fragrance of her need made his head swim. Even without touching her between the legs, he knew she was already wet for him.

She was so delicious, he couldn't resist a bite. A soft moan escaped her, and she jerked under his mouth, but didn't move away.

He bit her again and stroked her damp cleft, feeling her hot dew on his fingers. Feverishly, his hands moved up under the shirt. He cupped the pendulous breasts, flicking her nipples until she cried out and arched her back up into his chest.

"Don't wait, Ashcroft," she gasped.

With sudden ruthlessness, he angled her hips up and claimed her with a single thrust. As he slammed into her, her body opened in immediate greeting.

She clenched around him and cried out, pushing back to take him deeper. Sweet heaven, she was a lover sent from paradise. While she still quivered, he started to move. Hard. Fast. Seeking his own pleasure and knowing his pleasure fed hers.

Quickly, too quickly, he felt his climax building. With a shaking hand, he reached down to press against her mound. She cried out again, backed against him, and lost herself just at the moment he spilled into her with glorious abandon.

He slumped down onto her and pressed a fervent kiss to her shoulder. Holding her steady, he looped his arms around her waist. The aftermath of blinding pleasure left him shaking. He buried his forehead in the crook of her shoulder, feeling her ragged breathing and her quivers of receding rapture.

The only sounds were the gentle patter of the rain outside and the ragged inhale and exhale of their breathing. Then he started to laugh, so exhausted that the sound emerged in unsteady bursts.

He felt her shift, then, God help him, soft tenderness as she reached behind her and stroked his damp hair. Did she know how she slashed away his every defense when she touched him like that? For a brief, deceptive moment, he could almost believe she was in thrall to him as he was in thrall to her.

"What is it?" She sounded as awestruck as he felt.

He raised his head so he could suck air into his starving lungs. "I wonder what Perry will say when I tell him I don't want the books, but I'll give him £10,000 for this desk."

* * *

Afternoon faded toward evening when Robert met Diana at the French doors. She was panting and flustered, and all because she was breathlessly eager to see her paramour. For the tenth time in an hour, she cursed herself for being so utterly hopeless. Over the last week, she'd spent hours in Ashcroft's arms. And each hour away from him, thinking about him.

She was like a dreamy-eyed sixteen-year-old with her first love. Every encounter was more passionate than the last. Every encounter threatened what little emotional distance she managed to maintain.

She'd never known a man like Ashcroft. Fatalistically, she knew he was the one lover who would leave a permanent scar on her heart.

As she followed Robert, she surreptitiously laid a hand over her flat belly. Did a child grow there? A child with Ashcroft's beautiful green eyes and gift for joy? And if there was a child, did she have the heart, the gall to conceal its existence from its father?

When she slipped into the library, Ashcroft's dark head was bent over the desk. The desk where he'd taken her so masterfully and completely a week ago.

Hot color swept into her cheeks as he raised his gaze to hers. "Diana."

Knowledge of the direction of her thoughts sparked in the glinting eyes between their thick forest of black lashes. Of course he knew she was remembering that incendiary encounter. He seemed to have a preternatural ability to read her thoughts, except, thank the Lord, when it came to the purposes that led her to seduce him.

Pray God he never discovered the truth behind that. After these days of closeness, she couldn't bear for him to hate her. As hate her he would if he knew what she did.

"I thought you'd be upstairs." They'd established something of a pattern in the last days.

Without shifting his attention from her, he straightened. "I've got something to show you."

"I think I've seen most of what you've got to offer." Automatically, she fell into a flirtatious, sultry tone.

In Ashcroft's company, she became a different person, sensuous, confident, teasing, witty. She'd miss that Diana when she went back to her old life. Or when she became the respectable Marchioness of Burnley.

But not as much as she'd miss her daring and ardent lover.

She suppressed the thought. She was with him now. She refused to ruin the present by contemplating their inevitable parting.

He laughed, and she couldn't stem the warmth that seeped through her when she heard the appreciation in the sound. "Not by a long shot, my love."

His love . . .

Diana spoke quickly before the endearment could take root in her heart so deeply that she could never eradicate it. Although she suspected it had been too late from the first time he called her his love. "That sounds promising."

His eyes narrowed and focused on her with a harder, more concentrated regard. A hot tide of unadulterated lust coursed through her.

"Come here," he said in a low growl.

Poor dazzled fool she was, she didn't hesitate. His arms lashed her to his body, and his mouth pressed hot and hard on hers. He only lifted his head when she was dizzy, and her heart pounded so crazily, it made her deaf to any other sounds.

"Why did you wait so long to come back?"

She closed her eyes in agony and fought to come up with some reasonable answer. She'd left his bed late this morning and spent the remainder of the day in a restive haze, waiting to return to him. The pretense of having a life separate from his grew so thin, it threatened to rip asunder. "It's only . . . it's only been a few hours."

"Years."

Oh, God help me.

She glanced away from his gleaming jade eyes toward the cluttered desk. "Did you find something interesting among Lord Peregrine's books?"

He kissed her briefly before he let her go and wandered across to a side table. "No. He can sell the lot at auction with my blessing."

"Then what is it? Is there something in that box?" She'd noticed a small wooden crate on the desk. The piles of books had hidden it from her when she first came in.

He poured two glasses of claret and passed her one. "There is indeed." He took a sip. "Open it."

His eyes gleamed with pleasure, as if he offered her a special treat. She tried not to find his enthusiasm endearing. It was a losing battle.

She swallowed a mouthful of wine and set it aside. She knew Ashcroft watched her with an unwavering stare, but she kept her gaze on the box. The lid was loose. Beneath it, she found straw.

Carefully, because she'd seen boxes like this at Cranston Abbey, she shifted the straw to reveal something hard and round wrapped in light blue silk.

Ashcroft balanced one hip on the side of the desk with an elegant insouciance that made her heart beat faster. "My dealer sent it over this morning."

Trying to ignore her lover's attractions, she lifted the object from its packing. It was heavy and about the size of her hand. Slowly she drew away the silk.

And gasped in wonder.

"She . . . she's beautiful."

"Yes, she is."

The alabaster head stared back at her with sightless eyes.

The face was perfect, unmarked, although it must have been many centuries since the unknown artist had carved it. Diana had the same feeling of complete rightness she got when she saw Cranston Abbey. The sculpture was a flawless work of art.

"Is she Greek?"

Ashcroft stepped closer and reached out to run a finger across the elaborate pattern of plaits that formed the woman's coiffure. The tenderness of his touch was so familiar, Diana trembled as if he touched her instead of the carving. "A Roman copy, I think. First century, my dealer says."

"She has an extraordinary expression." Diana couldn't take her eyes from the sculpture. The stone lips were parted on a breath. The wide eyes under their defined lids surveyed eternity with unstudied poise.

"It's as if she's about to speak."

"And she speaks the truth," Diana whispered.

Unlike the living woman in this room. The statue's pure beauty was a silent chastisement.

Diana blinked away tears. Stupid to be so moved by a carving. But her emotions were so close to the surface these days. She was trembling, and, for safety's sake, she passed the sculpture to Ashcroft. Something about the way his big, graceful hands closed over the head, holding it safe, stabbed at her heart.

Good Lord, she needed to snatch some control. She drew a shuddering breath, hoping Ashcroft wouldn't notice how on edge she was.

"Thank you for showing her to me." She was grateful that her voice emerged with only a slight wobble.

"The minute I saw her, I had to have her. Whatever the price." His gaze fixed on Diana and seemed to convey a message that went further than his words.

"She's a worthy addition to your collection."

In the still hours of the night, he'd told her about the wondrous objects he'd amassed. He'd tried to coax her into visiting his house to view the artifacts, but she'd resisted, although her heart had ached to see the collection. More, she'd longed to share his pleasure in the beauty. A pleasure she heard in his voice whenever he discussed some ancient artwork.

It always came back to one thing and one thing alone. Her endless fascination with the man she deceived.

A smile she couldn't entirely interpret curved his lips. "She's more than that." He held the head in front of her. "Don't you see it?"

Puzzled, Diana inspected the marble carving. She saw a beautiful young woman with a high forehead and large, wide-spaced eyes, a straight nose, a voluptuous mouth. Her jaw was delicate but firm and her neck long and slender until it ended in a brutally jagged edge. Once she had been complete. She was no longer. But what remained was breathtaking.

"She's a fragment."

"Yes," he said with a hint of impatience. "But look more closely."

"At what?"

He turned the face in his direction, then turned it back towards Diana. "She's you."

"No . . ." Diana stepped back as though a physical distance would erase what he'd just said.

He didn't seem to register that his statement had perturbed her. Which was odd when he was usually so in tune with her reactions. "Look again. I saw it immediately."

"I can't see it," she said sharply, even as she fought to deny the emotion she saw in his striking face.

Laura had told her he was besotted. Ashcroft had told her he was in thrall. Now she couldn't mistake the glowing warmth in his eyes as he glanced from the beautiful ancient head to his mistress, then back again.

She was going to hurt him, and she couldn't bear it. And it was too late to retreat now. Too late for her and too late for him.

She bit her lip and turned away, reaching blindly for her wine. She was frantic to hide her extreme response to what was in reality just a small moment. A small moment that conveyed so much about the unforgivable damage she wreaked.

"Diana?"

Out of the corner of her eye, she saw him place the head on the desk with a care that cut her. She'd seen that expression on his face before, when he touched her with such sweetness that he pierced her to the soul.

She raised her glass and emptied it in one gulp, hoping the wine would dull her anguish. She turned to face him. "Take me to bed, Ashcroft."

He frowned. "What's wrong?"

Her voice was brittle. "Nothing's wrong. You're here. I'm here. I want you."

She didn't lie. She always wanted him. But on this occasion, the shaking urgency stemmed from her need to shatter the rapport he seemed determined to establish.

Except, she admitted, when he made love to her, he inevitably fortified the bond between them. She was doomed whatever she did. Inch by inch, she sank into quicksand.

This time, when he looked at her, his expression was assessing, probing. He knew she was upset. He was even smart enough to work out why if she didn't distract him first.

She waited for him to challenge her, but instead, a devilish smile tilted his lips. "Sometimes I think you only want me for my body."

She forced herself to respond lightly while every instinct urged her to run away and never look back. Her heart wouldn't be whole again. But perhaps if she left now, he had a chance of emerging without lasting damage from this entanglement. "It's a very nice body."

He tilted his head in acknowledgment, although his glance remained sharp. "Thank you."

"Come upstairs and remind me just how nice."

With pleasing alacrity, he abandoned the Roman sculpture, and Diana's heart began to race with genuine excitement. As he stalked toward her, she tried to tell herself she exaggerated the significance of the sculpture, that nothing important had happened in Lord Peregrine Montjoy's elegant library this afternoon.

But however much she lied to Ashcroft, she never lied to herself. With every day, she veered closer to damnation.

Chapter Nineteen

*I*n their rooms in Perry's house, Ashcroft lolled naked amidst the chaotic bedding and watched Diana dress, hating that she left him. Even if only for the evening.

It was almost three weeks since he'd waylaid her at the museum. Weeks packed with surprises, not all welcome.

One of the least welcome was that every time she went away, he had to battle not to insist she stay. No matter how long they were together, whether they made passionate love or argued some intellectual question or talked quietly about inconsequential matters, it was never long enough.

It just seemed . . . wrong when she wasn't with him.

Like the world turned in the opposite direction or a waltz played with four beats to the bar instead of three.

Her back a graceful arch, her full bosom pressing impudently against the sheer white shift, she rested one stockinged foot on a chair and bent to tie her garter. The picture was enchanting, alluring. He crossed his arms behind his head and enjoyed the view. He couldn't remember a woman who captivated him just with her presence the way Diana did.

She turned, catching him. That could hardly discomfit her—he constantly stared at her. Her eyelids lowered, and a smile lengthened her lush lips, reddened from the kisses he'd pressed on her during the eventful afternoon.

He loved all her smiles. The wry twist of her lips when she expressed her characteristically dry humor. The tender, dreaming smile after they made love. The teasing smile she couldn't hide when she used her mouth on him. The wild triumphant smile when she reached her climax.

Oh, yes, he loved that smile.

This one was inquiring. She was sharp, perhaps the sharpest person he'd ever met. He needed to be careful, or she'd guess he was up to something. Today he took matters into his own hands. He couldn't wait any longer for her to capitulate into trusting him.

When he met her curious gaze, he kept his expression blank. He would have tried for innocent, but he knew when he was beaten.

"What?" she asked softly, her hands pausing on her shapely calf. Her shift hiked, revealing her leg to the thigh.

He swallowed and told himself he'd only had her an hour ago. It was uncouth to fall on her again as if she were a juicy sirloin, and he hadn't eaten for a month.

He arched his eyebrows. "Can't a man admire a beautiful woman?"

"Oh." She blushed and looked away.

One of the many things he liked about her was her lack of conceit. She had no idea how spectacular she was. When he mentioned her looks, she always acted as though no man had praised her.

Her husband had obviously been a blundering dunderhead.

Perhaps he still was. That was one mystery he intended to solve today.

He laughed, and even he heard fondness in the sound. "Particularly a beautiful woman several feet away and half-naked."

Her blush deepened. He found her confusion charming. She was an intriguing mixture, his Diana.

Except, damn her, she wasn't his Diana.

That implied a level of intimacy he was yet to achieve. In spite of their wild antics in bed—and out of it, he recalled two hectic sessions on the rug and another explosive occasion against the heavy armoire near the window—she'd kept him at a distance in every way except the physical.

He'd tried several times to get her to confide in him. He'd tried direct questions, he'd tried tricking her into revealing her secrets, he'd tried using the soft intimacy after sex.

All to no avail. He knew little more now than he had when they'd met. Most of that he'd surmised from hints she dropped, not because she trusted him enough to tell him anything, devil take her.

Frustration and curiosity spoiled his sleep, disturbed his waking hours, gnawed at his peace. He was unused to elusiveness in a lover. The other women he knew desperately wanted him to know about their lives. The other women he knew took sharing confidences, or at least forcing them on him, as a sign he was interested. When generally, he wasn't.

Perhaps this torment was the Deity's way of punishing him for a misspent youth. And a far-from-spotless record in his maturity, he regretted to admit.

He tried not to think of another way the Deity could punish him. When it came to protecting his lover against pregnancy, he'd been fatally careless.

Diana tugged a rich green frock over her head. He hardly cared what she wore. The woman could prance about in a sack, and he'd still believe her the most glorious creature in Christendom. He was in real trouble here, and he knew it. Worse, he couldn't see how to resolve that trouble. If he broke with her, he'd feel even more like a starving dog, chained and howling at the moon.

He felt like that now when he had her. Or at least her lissome, responsive body.

The subject of his discomfiting musings sauntered across to the wreck of the bed and presented her back. "Stop loafing and be of some use." She lifted her disheveled blond hair. The gesture was so naturally sensual, a bolt of desire sizzled through him.

Yesterday morning, after she'd stayed all night—she rarely did that—he'd used breathless kisses to persuade her to remain through the day. The idea of doing that again crossed his mind before he reminded himself of his plans. The sooner he put them into action, the sooner he'd be out of his misery.

He hoped.

He sat up and started to lace her gown, pausing only to place an occasional kiss on her shoulder. She'd washed after she crawled out of his bed, but she still smelled deliciously warm and womanly. Sweet like green apples.

Apples had become the scent of paradise.

The urge to lure her back for play strengthened, but he stifled it. He had to break this impasse, or he'd lose his mind.

"If the Ashcroft estates ever fail, you'll have no trouble finding work as a lady's maid." Her voice was warm with amusement.

Because his thoughts were elsewhere, he answered before he remembered he never talked of those dark days. "They almost did fail. Before I reached my majority, my uncle's mismanagement brought me to the brink of bankruptcy. And with me, the rest of the family."

She stiffened and turned to study him. "You're rich now."

Her gaze was troubled. As usual, he wasn't sure what perturbed her. She was such a bundle of mysteries. It drove him insane.

He adjusted her stance so he could finish lacing her up. "Now."

"You're not what I expected," she said softly as if she continued a long conversation with herself. She didn't sound particularly pleased. "You must have worked like a demon to get everything back on an even keel."

"Stand still, or I'll never get this done," he said absently.

Silence fell as he concentrated on getting her into her clothes. Ironic really when all he wanted was to get her out of them.

"Ashcroft?"

He finished and looked up as she turned to face him.

"You did work hard, didn't you? And you still take responsibility for the Vales, although they nearly ruined you."

He frowned, not liking the direction of the conversation. It always niggled that she found it so easy to unveil his secrets while she was so stingy with her own. "That makes me sound rather lily-livered, my love." The endearment tripped easily off his tongue now and felt as familiar as the touch of her silken skin.

She smiled, although shadows lurked in her eyes. "You're a man of surpassing grit. And generosity. Even if you do operate under false pretenses."

She cupped his face. Like calling her his love, the gesture was familiar. It never ceased to stop his heart. She brushed her thumb across the sensitive corner of his lip. "You need a shave."

Undoubtedly he did. He'd shaved before she arrived this morning, but it was now late afternoon. The hours in between had been perfect happiness, which worried him. Usually, he found himself wishing a lover gone once the interesting stuff was over. He'd never felt like that with Diana.

He forced his muzzy mind to follow what she said. "Pretenses how?"

She hesitated as if searching for words. "You pretend not to care about anything. You pretend so well that the world believes it." She bit her lip and looked uncomfortable. "You're far from the heartless, selfish rake I expected to seduce."

This made no sense, the way so much between them made no sense. "Why would you want to seduce a heartless, selfish rake?"

Abruptly she straightened and retreated a shaky step. Her rosy color faded, leaving her ashen. Something that looked like fear flashed in her eyes. "Only a figure of speech."

Every nerve tautened to alertness. She'd revealed something important. He just wished to Hades he knew what it was. "I don't think so."

She shrugged and laughed. Unfortunately for her, he knew the sound of her real laughter. This wouldn't have convinced the biggest fool in England, and nobody had ever called him that.

"You make too much of this." Her voice was pitched higher than normal.

With artificial insouciance, she faced the cheval mirror and began to pile her hair up. Her actions were no different than usual. Except this afternoon, her hands shook, and her reflection revealed lips flattened with distress and eyes shining pewter with emotion.

He settled against the headboard with studied relaxation, even as his contentment evaporated, leaving a sick feeling in his gut. "Do I?"

"Yes." Her hair refused to cooperate. Perhaps because her fingers were so unsteady. "What is wrong with me today?"

He wanted to know that himself but didn't push it. He forced a lightness he didn't feel, not when his belly clenched in suspicion. "You suffer a surfeit of passion."

The tense line of her shoulders eased at his mocking answer. "That must be it," she said with equal lightness, and her laugh didn't sound so unnatural. She turned, having finally tamed her hair into an untidy chignon. "I must go."

Did she indeed? Why?

His imagination ran amok as he rose and approached her. He stopped just behind her. She glanced up quickly, then as quickly looked away, blushing.

He brushed away the strands that escaped her disheveled hair and pressed a kiss to her sweetly scented nape. He breathed deeply. Her essence was strong here. The scent of heaven. The scent of Diana.

As he lifted his head, he caught a flash of guilt in her eyes before dark blond lashes veiled her expression. Occasions like this, his suspicions threatened to overpower his beguilement.

He'd always known she kept secrets. He prayed those secrets didn't promise disaster.

"Don't go yet. I want to talk to you," he murmured.

"You've had my attention all day, and now you want to talk, just as I'm leaving?" Unexpectedly, her voice was sweetly amused. "You're like a cat, Ashcroft. When you're inside, you want to go out. When you're outside, you want to come in."

"You know how to make me purr." He brushed his lips across the crown of her head and wandered back toward the bed. He stretched out on the mattress again, draping a sheet across his legs to save her blushes.

She turned. "I'm not coming back to bed. We've been at it like rabbits all day. Haven't you had your fill?"

He smiled back, liking her description of their activities. "Never."

Her lips twitched. "I see why you've been through so many women in your nefarious life. You wore the poor creatures out."

He laughed, although he hated her talking about his raffish past. Compared to Diana, his previous affairs seemed shallow, base, unimportant. He'd never had a lover like her.

He patted the empty space next to him. "Sit here."

The enchantress again, she flicked him a glance under her lashes. The brief awkwardness might never have existed. "You know what will happen if I come within a foot of you."

He stroked the sheet again with a deliberately sensual gesture. "I only want to talk."

As nervously as a young deer emerged from the forest at dawn, she stepped closer. "What about?"

"Sit," he said softly.

She released a splutter of laughter. "I'm not your spaniel, Ashcroft."

"Pity. I've got a juicy bone for you."

Shock tinged her laugh. He loved how she reacted to ribald humor. He only had to make a suggestive quip to know she was a gorgeous innocent.

His joke coaxed her to cooperate. The mattress dipped, and her hip brushed his flank, but he resisted her nearness. He really did want to talk.

"Thank you, but I've eaten already." Her smile was sly.

He burst out laughing. "Perhaps you'd like to bury it for later."

She cast him an unimpressed look. "And perhaps not."

"Wicked girl." He picked up her hand and kissed her palm, feeling her tremble. "Sure you haven't got room for pudding?"

"You wanted to talk," she said breathlessly, trying without enthusiasm to tug her hand away.

"I do." He folded her fingers over her palm to keep the kiss trapped inside. He nipped at her wrist and felt her start. He soothed the sting with another kiss. If curiosity wasn't a tightening noose around his neck, he'd let this game reach its exultant conclusion.

"Ashcroft . . ." Her low warning was a seduction in itself.

He sighed. It was so delicious to tease her, titillating his desire with words. Whereas he was about to shatter the mood as abruptly as a brick pitched through a shop window.

He firmed his grip, so she couldn't run away. He drew in a breath, surprised at his reluctance to destroy the gentle warmth.

"Diana, why are you really in London?"

Chapter Twenty

As Ashcroft had expected, the lovely fluidity drained from Diana's body. She gasped with shock, and the pink leached from her cheeks.

"I told you why I'm in London." Her voice shook, and she refused to meet his eyes, sure proof, did she but know it, she lied. "I told you the first day."

He'd studied Diana Carrick with an attention he usually devoted to his latest antiquity, not to living, breathing women he lured to his bed.

And wasn't that a bleak reflection on the depth and value of his relationships?

"I know what you told me," he said steadily. He'd long ago reached the conclusion she had lied about why she became his lover.

She tried to pull free. "Well, then."

He tightened his grip, insisting upon her attention. "Not good enough, Diana."

Startled, she stopped struggling and regarded him directly for the first time since he'd asked his unwelcome question. Like sharks in a shallow ocean, familiar shadows swam in her eyes.

"I don't understand." She didn't sound angry. She sounded frightened.

He ignored a kick from his conscience. "Of course you do."

"You make too much of this, find mysteries where there are none." She drew a shaky breath, and he noted to the second when she decided to elaborate on her unconvincing story.

He might believe it of a thousand other women, but this reckless pursuit of pleasure didn't fit the Diana he knew. She was a vitally passionate woman, but she was also strong-willed and no slave to appetite.

At least she hadn't told him he had no right to interrogate her. That in itself was an admission of the intimacy she resisted.

"At home, my behavior is scrutinized. If I want a man in my bed, the only way I'll get him is with the Church's blessing. I want . . ." She paused. For all his confidence in his ability to read her, he wasn't sure whether she lied or told the truth. A tangled mixture of the two, he guessed.

She relaxed into his hold, indicating her willingness to answer to a point. Fatalistically he wondered when they'd reach that point. She sighed. "I've had eight years of chaste widowhood. I wanted an adventure. Something to remember in virtuous old age."

He believed part of this. He didn't believe all of it. "Why now? Why wait eight years? What prompted you to take this risky step?"

She looked at him in genuine shock. "Risky?"

He shot her an impatient glare. "Don't be a damned fool, Diana. Of course it's risky."

His blood turned to ice when he thought of some of the men she could have selected for her fling. If all she wanted in a lover was a worldly reputation, the list included every rapscallion and whoremonger in London.

He studiously avoided admitting that both words described the Earl of Ashcroft.

The smile she sent him brimmed with unconditional trust. "As if you'd hurt me."

He quashed the traitorous warmth her immediate faith evoked. "You know that now, not when you approached me. And there are other hurts, like an unwanted child or damage to your reputation."

"You sound like you regret my choice."

"Never." Let her not discover how fervently he meant that denial. "But why come to London now? Something must have changed. You're by nature a virtuous woman."

She looked cross. "How can you say that after what we've done?"

He gave a surprised laugh. "That wasn't a criticism, my love. You know I find you irresistible." His tone deepened into seriousness. "Tell me, Diana."

After a fraught pause, she began to speak in a low, intense voice. "A man at home wants to marry me."

Ashcroft's gut twisted. He couldn't speak past the great lump of rage that lodged in his throat.

How could she mention another man? Didn't she know she belonged to him? The crazy thought bobbed like flotsam on the surface of his mind, refused to sink into the mud where it belonged. He wasn't a man who offered forever. He was the notorious, inconstant, capricious Earl of Ashcroft who promised a woman only untrammeled pleasure and a summary good-bye once his interest had run its course.

Which didn't make the idea of another man sharing Diana's bed any more palatable.

She seemed to take his silence as encouragement to continue. Or perhaps having launched her confession, she couldn't stop. "He's . . . he's an older man, rich and well respected in the village."

"Naturally," Ashcroft snapped, then was ashamed of his sharp response.

She flushed and glanced toward the window. He had the feeling she didn't see the sky outside, but some other, more personal image. An image that didn't please her. "You don't approve."

"I'm hardly a pattern card of morality," he said stiffly.

She dragged in a shaky breath. He was dismayed to realize she wasn't far from tears. "If I consent, I'll be marrying him for his money. That doesn't mean I won't be a good wife. He needs me. It's not a one-way bargain."

"Does he know you sneaked up to London for some . . . town bronze?"

He chose the innocuous term, although they both knew exactly why she was here. Ashcroft wasn't particularly conceited. He'd always been aware of his failings. But even when she'd tried to treat him as a whore, he'd never before felt like one.

He did now. And he hated the sensation to his bones.

He caught the blossoming shame on her face. "I told you I required discretion."

"Hurrah for you." He bit back the outrage he had no right to fling at her head. She'd offered him her body, not her faith or her heart or her love.

He didn't want those things. He never did from a lover.

The insistence rang hollow.

Another silence crashed down, laden with cruel words that hovered unspoken. He forced himself to ask the question even though he didn't want the answer. "Are you going to marry him?"

She didn't meet his eyes. "I'm not sure."

He could see she'd made her mind up.

Except still this story didn't ring true. He wasn't sure why. Just some finely tuned instinct hinted there was another layer, another set of complications.

A marriage that offered material comfort but no excitement. That perhaps explained a passionate woman's chase after brief freedom before settling to dull respectability. Especially when she'd already suffered eight years of lonely widowhood.

Her story made perfect sense.

But somehow not for Diana.

It was a sign of his woeful state of infatuation that he'd rather she lied than married another man.

Perhaps she didn't plan to marry another man. Perhaps she was already married. Yet again, he couldn't dismiss the possibility of a living, present husband.

The tragedy was he'd convinced himself she contained a core of truth, and he touched it every time he made love to her.

When she lay in his arms, she didn't lie.

While almost twenty years' experience of the female sex taught him that that was when they lied the best.

Not Diana, his idiot heart cried.

"Do you despise me?" she whispered, still looking out the window.

The answer welled up out of the deepest part of him. "I could never despise you. Whatever you did."

Unfortunately for his pride and for his future welfare, it was true. He lifted her hand to his lips and kissed it with a fervor lacking before.

When she turned to him, her eyes were cloudy with distress. "Remember that."

Her slender throat moved as she swallowed. As if she fought back other, more dire confessions. He wanted to beg her to trust him, to insist he'd forgive her anything as long as she told him what troubled her. But the words choked into silence.

He watched her assume a brighter expression. Although her eyes remained glassy with unhappiness. "I need to go."

Why, if no man waited at home? The wall she placed between them became more frustrating. He threw the sheet aside and rose to his feet.

He wanted to harangue her, demand she tell him everything, save him from having to discover the truth through subterfuge. Instead, he grabbed her and drew her up for a hard kiss. Her lips immediately opened, and the kiss became a long, passionate exploration. He tasted her desperation, her turmoil. When finally she pulled away, his heart thudded fit to burst, and his thoughts whirled like drunken sailors dancing the hornpipe.

She was the most delicious woman he'd ever known. God forbid she hid poison under the honey. Although he'd reached such a stage of enchantment he'd probably die happy even if she did.

"Tomorrow night? Nine?" she asked in a husky voice.

"Eight."

Her voluptuous mouth quirked. "Seven."

"Six." He smiled back, in spite of the grim thoughts rocketing through his mind. "That's my last offer."

She nodded. "You drive a hard bargain. Six it is."

He bit back the invitation for her to spend the day with him. He bit back the urge to grab her and keep her. He hated the uncertainty of this affair. But not so much as he hated the idea of her walking away, even for only a few hours.

"Until tomorrow," she said softly. God rot him for a credulous numbskull, he heard similar regret at leaving in her voice.

She hid herself under the thick cloak and the ugly bonnet. One lingering glance from luminous gray eyes before she lowered the veiling. Then she was gone.

The door opened a few minutes later to admit Robert. "Madam has left, my lord."

"Did you have her followed?"

The footman nodded. "Yes, two men are tracking her."

In Chelsea, Diana shut the library door after her and collapsed shaking against it.

She couldn't do this anymore. She couldn't.

Every day, her deception became more impossible. And today, today she'd come so close to betraying herself. Still wasn't sure she hadn't. Ashcroft had hidden his reaction, but she knew that formidable brain worried at her unconvincing answers like a terrier worried at a bone.

The mixture of lies and half-truths she'd fed Ashcroft this afternoon made her belly cramp with disgust. She could hardly bear to live inside her skin, she felt so dirty and fraudulent.

He said he'd never despise her. If he discovered the truth, he would. He should.

She despised herself.

She sucked in a shuddering breath. What should she do? What should she do?

Feeling a thousand years old, Diana pushed away from the door and moved forward to slump into one of the high-backed chairs near the desk.

Like most of the house, this room was on a feminine scale. Not at all like Ashcroft's huge library, where she'd made her outrageous proposal. At the time, she'd regarded that room with contempt, as if the earl claimed an intellectual standing he couldn't justify. Those rows of scholarly books, that imposing mahogany desk, the dizzying array of maps and globes and scientific instruments seemed pretentious, false. She'd since learned better. He was clever and interested in his world in a way she found increasingly attractive.

She desperately needed to find some facet of his character that didn't appeal to her.

It was all such a horrible, tragic mess.

After spending hours in his bed, Ashcroft's scent clung to her hair and skin. Ashcroft's tangy taste lingered in her mouth. It was as if he'd branded her.

Blindly, she stared ahead. She should go upstairs, change out of this crumpled gown, order a bath. She had to write her bulletin, which became terser with each day, to Lord Burnley. She should also write to her father. She'd neglected him lately. Partly because she'd been occupied with her lover. Partly because she hated setting pen to paper with every word a lie.

Wherever she turned, she betrayed someone.

At least here she didn't do active harm. At least here, she didn't look into accusing eyes, even her own.

Although these days, her eyes held secrets beyond her plots with Lord Burnley. These days, she looked into her eyes and saw a woman hopelessly and endlessly in love. She'd battled against admitting the emotion for so long, but her strivings were useless.

She loved Ashcroft.

And still she meant to use and abandon him.

She closed her eyes, knowing she reached the limits of what she could endure. She couldn't lie to Ashcroft anymore. She loved him with all her heart, and she recognized that the best thing she could do for him was to disappear from his life forever.

How would she do this without tarnishing herself in his eyes? Without revealing the plot to bear his child? She didn't know. She only knew she had to break with Ashcroft before she caused more harm than she had already.

She felt like a coward. But she'd reached the limit of her resources. She'd hide for a little while, then armor herself to take up the tangled strands of her life.

"Diana, wake up."

Laura's voice and the gentle shake on her shoulder penetrated Diana's disturbed dreams. Reluctantly, she raised heavy lids to see her friend bending over her.

Laura straightened, hands on her hips, the lamplight revealing a concerned light in her dark eyes. Behind Laura the door angled open to the black-and-white-tiled entrance hall.

Diana stirred in the chair and winced. Her neck was stiff and at an awkward angle. She must have dropped off to sleep. Not surprising. Passion was exhausting. And a guilty conscience kept her awake even when she found the chance to rest.

"What time is it?" Weariness slurred her question. Gingerly, she sat up and pushed back the tumble of hair. During her impromptu nap, her insecure hairstyle had collapsed.

"Eight. James only just told me you came in. I assumed you were still out."

Not as late as she'd thought. "Have you had dinner?"

"No. Will you join me? Or do you have another appointment?"

'Another appointment,' as they were both aware, meant meeting Ashcroft. "No."

Diana was surprised to note that she was hungry. As usual, the suite at Lord Peregrine's had been furnished with an extravagant repast, but she and Ashcroft had been too eager for each other to pay attention to food. Afterward, she could have stayed to share a meal, but she'd been frantic to leave before she gave away the whole squalid scheme.

"I'll inform the staff." Laura turned away, then paused when a sharp rap resounded at the front door.

Consternation brought Diana to her feet. "Are you expecting anyone?"

Laura's lips flattened in displeasure. "I know nobody in London."

Diana tensed in sudden fear, ignoring the unspoken complaint. "Could it be Burnley?"

Dear God. Not now. Not when she was distressed and confused and looked like a slattern. Not when she smelled like a woman who'd spent all day under a man.

Laura met her eyes. "I doubt he'd knock."

The imperious summons sounded again, echoing through the house with unmistakable demand. Where on earth were the servants?

As if he heard her silent question, James the footman dashed up from downstairs. He was chewing and buttoning his coat. Clearly he'd been enjoying his dinner. Why not? This house wasn't exactly inundated with callers. He hardly needed to be on duty every minute.

Diana turned urgently to Laura. "I can't imagine who it is, but if they want to see me, I'm not at home."

Her friend nodded and left, shutting the door after her. Surely their visitor must have the wrong residence. The only people who knew Diana's London address were Burnley and the few servants of unimpeachable reliability he used.

She waited by the mantel, staring blankly into the unlit grate. Voices rumbled outside, but the house was remarkably soundproof.

When Laura opened the door a few seconds later, Diana lifted her head, expecting to hear that their visitor had left.

Diana frowned in puzzlement. Laura was pale, and her features were set. Her hands twisted in her skirts in an uncharacteristic display of nerves.

When Diana peered past her friend's shoulder, her heart staggered to a horrified stop.

Lord Ashcroft had found her.

Chapter Twenty-one

*A*shcroft . . ." Diana's chest constricted with agonized denial.

All her schemes and stratagems closed in and threatened to crush her. Now he was here, he'd inevitably discover what she did.

He'd never forgive her.

Ashcroft surveyed her from unreadable dark green eyes. His face was a magnificent mask. She had no idea what he felt or thought. Was he furious? Puzzled? Impatient? Triumphant?

"What are you doing here?" With an unsteady hand, she clutched the back of a chair.

Ashcroft sent her an insouciant smile that made her hackles rise. He looked reckless and arrogant and more handsome than any man had a right to be.

With a nonchalance she both envied and resented, he prowled past Laura and set gloves and hat upon a table. "I was passing."

"Liar."

His attention dropped to the head of the cane he carried, and his voice emerged quietly but implacably. "I've shot men for saying less."

She straightened, suddenly not needing the chair's support. Damn Ashcroft. Damn him to hell. He'd broken their agreement. He knew she didn't want him to invade her life outside what they did in bed.

"So shoot me," she said flatly.

"Diana!" Laura gasped.

She darted a glance at her friend. "Why did you let him in?"

Ashcroft had rattled the usually imperturbable woman. "He wouldn't . . ."

Diana was stirred up enough to speak over Laura. "He barged in without permission? What was James doing while Ashcroft stood on the front step? Picking his teeth?"

"Your footman recognized a hopeless battle," Ashcroft said grimly. He turned to Laura. "Miss Smith, I suspect this is turning ugly. Perhaps you should retire."

"Perhaps *you* should—right back to Mayfair," Diana sniped.

Ashcroft gestured toward the door. "Miss Smith?"

"Laura, don't you dare go!" Diana leaped forward.

Laura dodged her and backed toward the door. "I'm sure you want privacy."

"I'm sure we don't!"

It was too late. Laura had rushed down the hallway and was halfway up the stairs.

Diana couldn't bear to stay and face Ashcroft. She set off after Laura at a determined march, only to come to a trembling halt as he lifted his stick and swung the door shut in front of her.

Seething, she whirled on him. "Let me pass. I have no wish to speak to you."

Keeping the cane pressed to the door, he leaned back against the delicate desk. "You know, I find your temper exciting." His low drawl scraped across her nerves. "But then I'm sure you've guessed I find everything about you exciting."

She sucked in a breath, fighting to come up with something to make him realize how he'd betrayed her. He seemed to consider what he did a lark, a joke, just another game they played.

For Diana, Ashcroft's arrival was unmitigated disaster. If he'd found his way to Chelsea, surely he'd trace her back to Burnley. Then it wouldn't take him long to unravel the whole sorry plot.

He'd hate her. He'd despise her. He'd believe she'd lied to him with every word, every caress, every sigh.

Why hadn't she taken precautions to keep her location secret? In the early days, she'd been careful, but she'd grown lax. She'd trusted him, confound the man.

The elaborate system of defenses she'd constructed to keep her lover and her real life apart now seemed fragile as paper. Beneath her anger, sour fear churned. Fear fed her temper.

"You had no right," she said in a shaking voice.

He arched his eyebrows in that damnably familiar expression. "You'll let me into your bed but not your front parlor?"

"Don't pretend to misunderstand." His innocent act didn't gull her. He was aware what a crime he'd committed. "You know I wanted our liaison kept secret. I didn't go to your house. I definitely didn't want you to come here. I made all that clear at our first meeting."

His smile, like his tone, was dry as dust. "You labor under the misapprehension you'll get everything your own way just for the asking."

She took a trembling step toward him. "And what have you proven? Apart from that I can't rely on your word."

A severe light entered his eyes. "I needed to know if you have a husband."

Bafflement stole her breath. "Why would I lie? I told you from the beginning what I wanted. Whether I was married or not was of no importance."

Displeasure compressed his mouth. "It seemed a rather

one-way bargain. In my favor. I needed to know what you got from the arrangement."

"You accepted readily enough," she said acidly. "You got a willing woman in your bed. I would have thought you'd appreciate my lack of demands."

His jaw hardened into a stubborn line. He looked like a man who could conquer empires. He looked like a man who knew what he wanted and intended to make sure he got it. "That may have been true, but my requirements have changed." His tone was inflexible, matching the diamond-hard purpose in his face.

He clearly meant to daunt her, but he'd chosen the wrong target. She glared back, wishing he hadn't done this mad thing, wishing everything remained as it was this afternoon.

No, even that was too complicated, too riddled with future unhappiness. She wished instead that this affair was the sordid, shabby, unemotional mating she'd planned.

Instead of . . .

Her mind shied away from describing how she felt in Ashcroft's bed. It brought her too close to heartbreak.

She met his uncompromising green stare with an uncompromising stare of her own. She forced out a stark answer. "My requirements haven't changed."

"Too bad."

"Did you follow me home? You must have dressed faster than lightning."

He shook his head. Curse him, he didn't look remotely regretful or guilty. "Perry's people followed you. They reported back, and here I am."

"Yes, here you are." She shot him a scowl and flounced away in a rustle of skirts to stand by the window. Even as she strove for control, genuine distress seeped into her tone. "What got into you, Ashcroft? What did you imagine would happen when you arrived? A warm welcome and a glass of wine for your refreshment?"

He settled more comfortably upon the desk. Devil take him, he had no cause to look so at home. "Now there's a capital idea."

She ignored his answer. He couldn't charm his way out of this. She spread her hands in helpless incomprehension. "What if I were married after all? What if my husband had answered the door? Would you have tipped your hat, wished him good evening, then asked for your mistress?"

He gave a short laugh. "Your staff assured Perry's men that two ladies live here alone, without the benefit of masculine supervision. You and Miss Smith."

"Why, why did you think I'd lied?" Then even more pertinent, "Why would you care? You've had married women in your bed. What does it matter if I'm another?"

He lowered the stick from the door and set it on the floor, twirling it absently in his long-fingered hand. No need to bar the door. They both recognized she wasn't going anywhere anytime soon. "You know you're more than that."

She stared at him with utter dislike. At this moment, she sincerely wished she'd never met him. "Why would I know that?"

He shrugged as if he didn't say anything unusual or unexpected. "Because you're a frighteningly intelligent woman, and you don't miss much with those glorious gray eyes."

She couldn't bear him to say it. If he said the words aloud, they could never pretend this affair was a passing fancy. For either of them.

She swallowed hard and wondered if this was the end. Where could they go from here?

Not long ago, she'd sat in this room and told herself she couldn't continue to deceive him. Now the time arrived, she couldn't endure the idea of never seeing him again.

Turning away so she couldn't watch his face, she summoned the lie she must speak. "Do you know why I selected you, Lord Ashcroft, out of all the men in the kingdom?"

He didn't reply, but she knew by his taut silence that he'd noted both her frosty tone and the way she'd called him Lord Ashcroft. She hadn't done that since their earliest days.

She stared out the window at the quiet square. Her voice was brittle with control. "I chose you because I'd heard you were a man who never mixed sentiment and sex. You've disappointed me."

It hurt to force the words out, but to her surprise, they emerged clearly and evenly and coldly. She sounded like she meant what she said. She curled her hands in her green skirts before she realized the gesture betrayed her turmoil. She straightened her fingers out of their fists.

Still he didn't speak.

When it became apparent he intended to make neither protest nor denial, she struggled to go on. "As you can't . . ." In spite of her best efforts, she stopped. The prospect of sending him away forever slashed like a knife. The blade pierced her heart and twisted. She braced as though she faced an enemy. "As you can't promise you'll make no emotional demands, we must reconsider our association."

With every word, blood dripped from her split heart. What had she done? How was she to live without him? Even her glittering future at Cranston Abbey couldn't compensate for how she felt right now.

His lack of response made her speak more firmly. "Your presence here is the last straw. We must end our affair. Now."

He made a stifled sound.

She frowned out into the dark, empty square. Surely she misinterpreted what she'd heard. Angry, puzzled, distraught, she turned.

She hadn't mistaken the sound. The cur had laughed at her. His face was still alight with amusement. "What a load of rot, my love."

"You . . ." Speech failed.

"Diana, stop all this nonsense. You don't want to leave

me. You don't want to stop what we do. As to whether there's more between us than bed sport, we both know it's far too late to worry about that."

She did know it. And she hated herself for bringing him to this pass. More than his pride would suffer when he discovered the truth. And with every second, she realized the chance became less and less likely of her escaping with her despicable secrets intact.

Damn her for a foolish, thoughtless, cruel witch.

Still she tried to make him see reason. "I want you to go," she said stubbornly, clenching her fists and glowering into his striking face.

His smile flashed, strong, white teeth, lines of humor radiating from his eyes and bracketing his mouth. "No, you don't," he said implacably.

He strode across the room. Grabbing the back of her head, he held her captive for a hard kiss. A host of familiar impressions overwhelmed her. The fresh scent. The spicy taste. The warmth of his skin. The way he loomed above her, so tall and lean and powerful.

She was on the verge of sinking into the kiss. Then she remembered how inevitably she'd hurt him if she continued the affair. She squirmed and made a muffled sound of protest.

He lifted his head and sent her a knowing look under his sweep of black lashes. Despite her anger, her uncertainty, her sadness, she shivered with sensual awareness.

Contradictory impulses vied inside her. She should send him away. She should beg him to stay. She should resist him. If only to prove he didn't have the upper hand.

Even if he did.

"Stop it," she said stiffly.

Her lack of enthusiasm didn't discourage him. "If you're set on going, the least you can do is kiss me good-bye."

Her mouth turned down in disapproval. "You don't think I mean to say good-bye."

He laughed softly, his breath brushing her face like a caress. "So convince me you do."

He looked remarkably happy for a man losing a mistress he claimed to value. Damn his overweening self-confidence.

Damn her for confirming his confidence by staring up at him in misty bemusement.

"I'll convince you when you reach for me, and I'm no longer there."

"I hope that day never comes."

That statement sounded uncomfortably like commitment. Even while her aching heart opened to his words, her conscience shrieked. He tilted her chin with his other hand. His eyes conveyed a message she didn't want to acknowledge.

"You don't mean that," she challenged. "You'd say anything to win."

He arched his sleek black eyebrows. "What do I win?"

"Your own way," she snapped, jerking her chin without managing to break free. His hold was gentle but unbreakable.

"More than that, surely. You underestimate yourself, my love."

How she wished he'd stop calling her that. Warmth trickled through her veins every time she heard those two evocative words in that velvety baritone. She told herself he'd whispered that sweet endearment to a thousand women and never meant it.

Hard to believe that when he looked at her as though she was more precious than gold.

Because she was so close to weakening, she made herself scowl. "Let me go."

He laughed, and his hold didn't shift. They were both aware if she really wanted to escape, she'd struggle a bit harder. She doubted he'd hold her against her will. But her will was as pliable as a willow twig.

He knew it, the cocky scoundrel.

"You promised to kiss me good-bye."

"I promised to show you the door."

"Temper," he whispered, and his mouth touched hers with a soft tenderness lacking in his earlier kiss. That had been all command, meant to demonstrate who was in the ascendant.

She kept her lips closed, even as the heat of that fleeting contact seeped into her bones, oozing like honey all the way down to her toes. He thought she'd collapse in panting desire after the merest encouragement. He wasn't far wrong, but she meant to fight all the way.

Then collapse into his arms . . .

Oh, Diana, what happened to sending him away forever for his own good? How did that determination turn into this silly, arousing game?

The hand on her chin shifted to stroke her jaw, trailed down her neck to rest against her collarbone. Her frantic pulse leaped as his fingers drifted across the base of her throat. Her breasts tightened and swelled against her bodice, yearning for the touch of his hand, the benison of his lips.

She'd wanted him from the first instant she'd seen him, but unaccountably what they'd done over the last days fed that desire instead of satisfied it. It was as though, having got what she wanted, all she wanted was more.

God save her, he was like opium.

He kissed her again, tiny busses to the corners of her lips, in the philtrum, on her chin, across her nose. She knew this was war. He sought surrender, and he intended to get it. To that end, she'd expected him to employ the passionate arts he wielded to such devastating effect. Instead, he seemed set to tickle her into willingness.

Except every kiss knocked a chip off her defiance.

He kissed her fluttering eyelids, between her brows, her temples. Her lips tingled for the touch of his, but he avoided anything deeper than these playful kisses.

Could one die of sheer frustration? If so, her days were numbered.

She growled softly. Her fists tightened so hard that her nails dug into her palms. The sting helped maintain a shred of resistance. "I won't change my mind," she said in a husky voice, spoiling the impression by tilting her head to prolong his lips' contact with one cheekbone.

"I see you're an unshakable rock of determination," he whispered against her face, resting one hand on her nape. He wasn't even pretending to compel her to accept his kisses anymore. More galling, she wasn't pretending she didn't enjoy his attentions.

He continued in a wry voice. "Nothing will make you relent. Not wind. Not rain. Not ice. You're like a great monolith of the ages. People will come from miles around to admire you. Like Stonehenge."

He was impossible. She couldn't contain a muffled giggle at the idea of Diana Carrick rising in solitary glory from Salisbury Plain to the amazement of onlookers.

"Stop it." She wished she sounded firm and determined, like the monolith he'd just called her. But even in her own ears, she sounded breathless and close to yielding.

"Stop what?" He nipped at her earlobe. Response jolted her.

"You know." The urge to grab him and force him to kiss her was a swelling torrent. She managed to control it. Just.

She reminded herself she was angry. He'd betrayed her. But nowhere near as badly as she'd betrayed him. Best to end everything before bitterness and recriminations. Before she hurt him.

The imperative came from a long way off. A soft echo of voices she'd heard long ago. Much more immediate was the tall, gorgeous man teasing her with the possibility of pleasure and in the process giving more pleasure than flesh could withstand.

"No." He blew gently in her ear and continued his nuzzling exploration down her neck.

His lips brushed a particularly sensitive nerve near her

shoulder, and she released a breathy moan. She waited for him to concentrate on that place, but he hovered close without making contact.

He really was punishing her.

"Tell me," he said softly, his words brushing her skin. She trembled and her heart raced at a dizzying pace.

She swayed toward him. She strove to bolster her pride, but the lure of his touch was too strong.

"Tell you what?" she asked dazedly, not following the conversation. She hardly remembered what the fight was about. All that mattered was he stopped toying with her and kissed her properly.

"What I'm doing."

"You're seducing me." She wasn't sure whether it was accusation or request.

"See? I said you were clever." Amusement lurked in his deep voice. Her lonely heart yearned toward that warmth, beckoning as a snug bed on a cold night.

"Too clever to fall for a rogue's tricks," she said with complete lack of conviction.

He laughed softly and pressed his mouth to that throbbing nerve in her neck. She'd reached such a pitch of desire, her body clenched in immediate response.

"So I'm not succeeding?" he asked against her shoulder. His voice was thicker than usual.

"What do you think?" Close as she was to giving in, she wasn't yet there.

"I think I need to work a bit harder," he murmured.

One hand slid up her rib cage, trailing fire even through the rich silk of her gown. He stopped just short of her breast. Her nipples tightened to the point of pain, and she bit her lip to stifle her excited moan. Her legs wobbled, and she reached out to grab his shoulder. Just for support, she assured herself.

"Ashcroft . . ." The word was an undisguised plea.

"Yes?"

Diana knew what he wanted. Her so lost in enchantment, she forgot about ending the affair. She summoned her last scraps of resistance. Not enough to make her move away but enough to defy him. "You won't win, you know."

"I've still got a few weapons in store."

At last, at last, he curled his hand around her breast, his palm pressing the pebbled nipple. She shuddered, and the moan finally escaped in a long, low keen. Against her will, she pushed into his hand.

"You don't play fair." The frantic beat of her heart made speech almost impossible.

"Nobody said I did, my love."

"You shouldn't call me that." She only just kept contact with reason.

Heat radiated from him like a great forest fire. His hand dropped to her bottom, urged her forward. Under his teasing, he was all desire. Against her belly, he was hard and ready. She drew a shaky breath full of musky male arousal. This seduction seduced him too.

"Don't you like it?"

"No." She twined her arms around his neck.

"I can see that."

She gave a protesting wriggle and heard his breath catch. Her helplessness receded. He was hungry for her. More than hungry. He was famished.

"Why don't you kiss me?"

He didn't cooperate, blast him. "Patience."

She slid one hand up his strong neck in a gesture even she recognized was a caress. She tugged sharply on a lock of hair. "Stop teasing me."

Still he resisted. The laughter drained from his eyes, and he moved away slightly to study her. She was such a fool, but the distance between them felt like absence.

"Are you leaving me?" he asked in a raw voice.

"Yes."

Immediately, she saw he didn't believe her, although she spoke the truth. "Then I'd better kiss you before it's too late."

Her lips stretched in a triumphant smile. "My thoughts exactly."

"Close your eyes."

"Ashcroft," she said warningly. "Charming as your conversation is, I've had a surfeit this evening."

It wasn't true. His words enchanted almost as effectively as his touch. But if he didn't place that beguiling mouth on hers in the next second, she'd scream like a banshee.

"Close your eyes," he said again and with such rich persuasion in his voice, she couldn't help but obey.

Without her sight, she felt vulnerable. She expected him to continue teasing. He knew it drove her to the edge of madness, and he was in a mood to toy with her like a cat toyed with a sparrow.

She'd fluttered against his claws until exhausted. Now she waited in fatalistic stillness.

His hands glided up to her shoulders and tightened. His mouth opened over hers with unconcealed need. Her lips parted to give him access. He kissed her rapaciously.

For a few seconds, she was quiescent, then she kissed him back, stroking his tongue, returning for a longer foray. Tasting the deep, rich flavor of Ashcroft.

He was like manna. Would she starve without him?

He curled his arms around her waist, dragging her against his body. He was shaking, as much victim to this storm as she.

Soon, kissing wasn't enough, although she continued to press her mouth to his in desperate craving. He pulled away, panting, and she opened dazed eyes.

He was pale and drawn, vibrating with urgency. Without releasing her, he swiftly glanced around the room.

"Ah," he said in satisfaction.

The world rocked as he swung her around and lowered her onto the delicate pink sofa. She felt the thin padding beneath her back and against her side, then the impetuous weight of Ashcroft's body.

He grunted against her lips, shifted, and tensed, bumping the back of the sofa. "Damn it, this couch is made for midgets."

She laughed. Like the rest of the library, the sofa was constructed on the small side. Certainly far too small for what Lord Ashcroft had in mind.

"It doesn't matter. You can't make love to me here. Laura might come in." She tried to squirm into a sitting position, but his body trapped her.

He wriggled to find a more comfortable place kneeling over her. Without success, she noticed with the beginnings of genuine amusement. The great lover's sudden gaucheness touched her heart in a way his self-confidence couldn't.

The best he could manage was resting on one knee between her and the back of the couch and supporting himself with his other leg on the floor. The position looked uncomfortable, unwieldy.

"You're naïve if you imagine Miss Smith isn't aware what we're doing," he said dryly. "She's no fool, that lady."

"Nonetheless you're not . . . having me on the sofa."

He smiled down at her. "Care to place a wager?"

"You're so sure of yourself, aren't you?"

"I'm sure of you," he retorted, and nuzzled her shoulder, pushing aside her bodice.

She trembled, and moisture bloomed between her legs. Her body recognized and welcomed the pressure of his. Her body didn't care about pride or principle. Her body wanted him to shove up her skirts and take her.

He raised his head, his nostrils flaring. His smile turned deeply sensual, and heavy lids lowered over his eyes. She knew that expression. He meant to take her without delay.

"Ashcroft," she protested, flattening one hand on his shoulder and pushing.

He didn't budge. Of course he didn't. He had no intention of going anywhere. He had every intention of satisfying the lust that lit his face.

How had they come to this? She'd thought to throw him out with a flea in his ear. Instead, she was flat on her back, her body preparing itself in wanton swiftness for his.

"You know you want to." He settled himself more securely and threw one leanly muscled leg over her skirts.

Somehow, he made himself at ease on the minuscule piece of furniture. She had no idea how. She'd have thought it mathematically impossible.

"You're such an arrogant ass," she said with a lamentable lack of force.

"Aren't I indeed?" he agreed amiably enough.

His new position leaning on one elbow left the other hand free. He brushed her hair back from her face with a gesture whose tenderness made her heart ache.

His hand dipped across her face, down her throat, across the bare skin above her bodice. She knew exactly where he headed. Her skin tightened in anticipation.

His fingers insinuated their way under the gold braid, slipped lower to brush her nipple. The crest tightened. Her hand curled in the soft blue wool of his coat. Her breath came so hard, it emerged in shaky sobs. With her other hand, she grabbed his wrist.

"Should I stop?" he asked with an idleness contradicted by the simmering light in his eyes, hot jade between the thick lashes. He stared at her bosom with a concentration that made gooseflesh break out all over her.

She bit her lip, knowing if she agreed to his touching her breast, she agreed to this encounter reaching its conclusion.

It was impossible to fight him and herself at the same time.

She should tell him to go. If she insisted, he'd relent. If she insisted as though she really meant it, unlike her pathetic attempts so far. She couldn't blame him for dismissing those as coy prevarications.

She drew breath, ready to reject him.

Instead, two unsteady words emerged as she released him. "Don't stop."

Oh, she was hopeless.

He sighed with satisfaction and plucked at her nipple, shooting vivid sensation through her veins. She shifted restlessly, seeking relief, but nothing quenched the flood of desire.

Still tormenting her breast, he bent his head and kissed her. She responded with all the unspoken, disastrous longing in her heart. She loved him, and she was grimly aware she was running out of time for his kisses.

After a long interval of delight, he wrenched his mouth from hers and rained kisses across her neck. He slid her dress out of the way. The air was cool on her naked skin.

She cried out softly when his lips closed on her nipple, then cried out again when he drew hard. She thrust her fingers into his hair and pressed his head closer.

The sensation was purest torment, purest pleasure. Feverishly, she cupped him. He groaned against her skin and tilted his hips, pressing into her hand. Even through his breeches, he felt like a furnace.

"Oh, yes," she sighed as he turned his attentions to her other breast. She surrendered with a wholehearted enthusiasm she should regret but couldn't.

Suddenly the tiny sofa offered ample room. He bunched her skirts, lifting them so the evening air chilled her thighs above her stockings.

His face was buried in her neck, and her dress was up around her waist. One hand trailed teasingly across the top of her leg. She ached for him to touch where she burned, then for the more profound invasion.

He knew that, the devil, and taunted her with delay.

She arched to encourage him to shift his fingers those last few inches. Her hand tugged at his breeches.

Suddenly he went still.

"What is it, Ashcroft?" she asked in a choked voice.

Surely he didn't mean to deny her. That would be cruel, and everything she knew insisted he wasn't a deliberately cruel man. Teasing and infuriating, certainly, but not cruel.

He raised his head, his face drawn with tension. "Don't you hear that?" he asked sharply.

She frowned. What on earth was wrong?

Then she heard the knocking. Someone was at the front door. Someone insistent on entering if the peremptory banging was any indication.

Don't let it be Burnley. Anyone but he.

Horror flooded her, turned her heart to stone. Hurriedly, she pushed Ashcroft away.

This time he didn't resist. She scrambled up against the arm of the sofa, tugging at her dress. She needed a maid. She needed a fresh gown. She needed time to present an appearance of composure she didn't feel.

How debasing for the marquess to discover her tousled and half-naked and smelling of her lover. She felt sick at the prospect.

"Are you expecting someone?" Ashcroft rose to his feet and watched her with a shuttered expression in his beautiful eyes.

"N . . . no," she stammered, knowing fear was clear in her voice and her face. She acted as if she had something to be guilty about.

The problem was, she had.

Nervously she glanced at the closed door. The knocking had ceased, so she guessed whoever it was had been admitted.

She pulled at her bodice in another futile attempt to appear as if she hadn't made love most of the day. Ashcroft extended a hand to help her as she staggered to her feet, but she ignored him.

A grim knell of foreboding tolled in her heart. She felt like a whore awaiting her pimp.

How could she face Lord Burnley like this?

But when the door soundlessly opened, the man who walked through on Laura's arm wasn't Lord Burnley.

It was her father.

Chapter Twenty-two

$\mathcal{S}$truggling to dampen his rampant arousal, Ashcroft watched Diana. Her face was white as parchment and filled with acrid shame. Miss Smith's eyes settled on her friend with visible concern.

He stepped forward to speak, but Diana stopped him with an emphatic gesture he couldn't misunderstand. "Papa," she said in a strangled voice.

Shock held Ashcroft motionless. The suspicions that had always lurked beneath his endless desire reared up like venomous snakes ready to strike.

His expression severe, the old man turned in his daughter's direction. He still wore his hat and coat, and he leaned heavily on a cane. He was tall and gaunt, neatly but inexpensively dressed. Ashcroft guessed he was a lawyer's clerk or small-scale merchant. An incongruous parent for Ashcroft's gorgeous, modish mistress. This man couldn't have funded Diana's house, clothes, servants.

So who in Hades had?

Diana ventured forward to press a kiss to the old man's cheek. He stiffened in rebuff. Ashcroft caught the lancing hurt that darkened her eyes as she turned in his direction. He had a feeling she didn't see him at all. She looked sick with fear and humiliation.

Ashcroft remained silent because clearly that was what she wished, but questions multiplied. He was grateful the old man didn't glance at him. He still trembled with frustrated desire. Nor had Diana's hurried attempt at a toilette achieved much. Her bright hair tumbled down her back like a lascivious milkmaid's.

"Papa, what . . . what are you doing here?" She sounded uncertain, afraid, unhappy.

He hated to see her proud spirit brought low. His Diana always met the world with her head high.

His Diana?

Hell, what was wrong with him?

He felt disoriented, disconnected, as though a perfectly solid floor had suddenly collapsed beneath his feet. He'd long ago recognized that Diana kept secrets. But the passion always seemed real. Tonight, he couldn't help wondering if the woman who had shared his bed with such enthusiasm comprised nothing but falsehood.

Anger tightened her father's features, forcing Diana to retreat a few steps. "That's a question I should ask, daughter." The man's voice resonated with perplexed rage. "You've told me for weeks you and Laura are staying with Lady Kelso, yet when I call on her, I'm informed you're not there. In fact, they've never heard of Mrs. Carrick, supposed companion to the countess."

Diana winced. Her hands twined at her waist, and her distress was a tangible presence. "I'm . . . I'm sorry, Papa," she said almost soundlessly.

Her father continued as if she hadn't spoken. His cultured accent made Ashcroft place him slightly higher in society than his plain appearance indicated. But no way was this man aristocracy or even gentry.

"I prevailed upon George Coachman to bring me from

Surrey. The fool should have come straight here. He must have known the Kelsos would turn me away. Apparently everybody in my vicinity is party to this conspiracy."

"Is there trouble at home?" Diana shook like a reed in a gale.

Her father looked more austere. Ashcroft noted little resemblance between them, apart from perhaps the height and the stubborn line of the old man's jaw.

"I think any trouble is in London, don't you, Diana?" her father said in a frigid tone.

With every cold word her father spoke, each as pointed and deadly as a dart, Diana looked more devastated. Ashcroft shifted restlessly, burning to defend her but knowing his championship was the last thing she wanted. After that first begging, terrified glance, she hadn't looked at him. It was as if he didn't exist.

"Papa, I . . ." She faltered into silence and bit her lip.

"Well should you stammer and blush, daughter," he snapped. He leaned more heavily on his stick, but his expression remained accusing. "Who pays for this house?"

"I . . ." Diana shot a helpless, begging glance at Miss Smith. Miss Smith remained silent.

"Don't pretend you do. William left you some money, but not enough to fund an extravagant visit to London. I can't help but feel Lord Burnley is behind this."

Burnley?

Appalled disbelief paralyzed every muscle in Ashcroft's body. The sensation of falling through plain air intensified.

That unmitigated blackguard, the Marquess of Burnley, knew Diana?

Burnley was the sort of aristocrat he despised. A brute who believed his rank gave him the right to transport children for minor crimes or hang them if he could get away with it. A man who fitted perfectly among those other fools and powermongers whose overweening arrogance and blind conservatism consigned most of the nation to poverty and ignorance.

Ashcroft and Burnley clashed frequently and bitterly in Parliament. Thanks to the draconian politics of most of the ruling class, the contests usually ended in Burnley's favor.

So why should Lord Burnley's protégée, if that's what Diana was, seek out the dissipated Earl of Ashcroft? Burnley must have described Ashcroft to her as the devil incarnate. Yet she'd brazenly offered herself with some humbug about wanting sexual experience.

Bewilderment, suspicion, wild surmise juggled for a place in Ashcroft's mind. Nothing made sense.

Was this a plot? He couldn't see what she or Burnley hoped to gain. If the affair became public, Diana would suffer, not Ashcroft. His reputation with women was so tainted, the world hardly expected him to act the knight in shining armor. If word got out he'd debauched a virtuous country widow, the ton wouldn't raise a hand to hide a yawn of boredom.

Nonetheless, Ashcroft's skin itched with wariness.

While his brain winnowed contradictory facts, he watched Diana. She looked stricken, lost.

She looked guilty.

Ashcroft didn't understand. Mysteries piled on mysteries, and every time he thought he'd solved one puzzle, a hundred more sprang up in its place. Unraveling Diana's secrets was like trying to kill the damned Hydra.

Her hands curled in her skirts, and her tiny pants of distress punctuated the discussion. "It's not what you think."

Her father scowled at her. "No more lies. You've told me enough to last a lifetime. I'm ashamed of you, Diana. Ashamed."

"I can tell you . . ."

"I don't want to know. Come home now and leave whatever sins you've committed behind. You have work to do in Marsham."

"Yes, Papa," she said in the most subdued voice Ashcroft had ever heard her use.

Yes, Papa?

What the hell was this? Was she really submitting to her parent's will and returning to the country? What about him? Ashcroft shifted, every sinew resisting what she said.

At her ready obedience, her father's voice lost its edge. "George is outside. We can be home and safe tonight. Laura will . . ." He stopped abruptly and turned in an odd, unfocused way in Ashcroft's direction. "Who's there?"

Diana's horrified gaze bored into Ashcroft, silently begging him to be still. "N . . . nobody, Papa," she said shakily.

What was the woman wittering about? Ashcroft stood next to her, large as life. Unless she meant her denial as an insult. His belly knotted in angry dismay.

"Heaven forgive your deceit, girl," the old man said with returning anger. For the first time, he stared right at Ashcroft.

Diana's father's face was alight with angry curiosity. His eyes were blank and milky.

The old man was blind.

When Ashcroft turned up at her house, Diana's tower of lies had tottered. Now with her father's arrival, it collapsed into rubble.

A ghostly cracking filled the air around her. The sound of her entire world crumbling to dust.

Or perhaps it was just the sound of her heart breaking.

"Who's there?" her father said in a sharper voice, banging his stick on the floor. "Make yourself known."

"My name is Tarquin Vale." Ashcroft stepped forward.

His beautiful baritone was neutral, and Diana couldn't read his expression. By now he must know she'd lied to him from the start. He'd guess she was involved in some conspiracy with Burnley. He must loathe her for the deceit she practiced, even if he didn't yet know how that deceit revolved around him.

Her heart thundered out an anguished protest. She wanted to beg him not to hate her although she knew it was far too late to redeem herself in his eyes. Far too late to save him from devastation.

"Vale?" her father asked in astonishment and with audible displeasure. He reached out as if to test for the reality of this man. Her father would assume Ashcroft was her lover. His eyes might fail, but his brain was frighteningly acute.

Her voice was unsteady. "Papa, this is the Earl of Ashcroft. Lord Ashcroft, may I present my father, John Dean of Marsham in Surrey?"

"Your servant." Her father's face set with disapproval, and his tone made it clear he considered himself anything but subservient. "I've heard of you, sir."

Diana fought back the urge to defend her paramour to her father. What was the use? After today, her father would never believe a word she said.

"Mr. Dean. I called on Miss Smith and Mrs. Carrick to discuss antiquities. I was introduced to the ladies at the British Museum, and we discovered a mutual interest in Egypt," Ashcroft said smoothly. An urbane shell had descended on that handsome face, and try as she might, she couldn't penetrate it.

Not even the stupidest clodpole in the kingdom would believe that story. Why did Ashcroft try to shield her? He should be furiously angry.

"Lord Ashcroft is just leaving," she interjected quickly.

Ashcroft leaned back against the flimsy desk and folded his arms. He surveyed her with raised eyebrows and a mouth that twisted in sardonic amusement. The stance was heartbreakingly familiar. It generally indicated he'd made his mind up about something and had no intention of budging but didn't plan to make an issue of it. No, he just meant to sail through, his will prevailing.

"I'm at leisure this evening, Mrs. Carrick. I distinctly remember saying that when you invited me to supper with you and the charming Miss Smith."

The charming Miss Smith cast him a quelling glance. Diana gritted her teeth and only just stifled a growl of aggravation. Apparently Ashcroft meant to be difficult.

"Well, I'm no longer at leisure," she said crisply. "I return to the country with my father."

"I believe it's time you left, my lord," her father said in the same tone he used to quell dissension among the farm laborers.

She found it in her to admire his courage. He was a humble bailiff, and the Earl of Ashcroft was a powerful nobleman.

Her father always stood up for principle whatever the cost. Which meant he'd utterly despise what she'd done if he ever found out the full story. Dear God, he'd despise her anyway after tonight. He never believed the end justified the means. Harsh experience had taught her he was right.

"I hoped for some conversation with Mrs. Carrick," Ashcroft said with the suave address he used when he wanted his way.

"My daughter isn't staying in London," her father said. "And what conversation with you could reflect to her credit?"

Ashcroft's lips tightened at the slight. Although they all knew it was justified. What wasn't justified was for Ashcroft to take blame for her wickedness.

"Mrs. Carrick?" Ashcroft inquired, as if he believed she'd change her mind just for the asking.

For one tremulous second, the idea of flinging herself into Ashcroft's arms and defying Burnley, confessing all, begging him to take her somewhere this couldn't touch them, rose like a mirage. So tempting. So impossible.

If she threw herself upon Ashcroft's mercy, what guarantee he'd want her into tomorrow? Even if he forgave her, he had a reputation for inconstancy. She'd captivated him briefly. Nothing indicated she captivated him further than that.

She bent her head, closing her eyes in a silent prayer to a God who by rights shouldn't listen to such a miserable sinner. She wouldn't cry. She wouldn't cry.

Her father hated her. She abandoned Ashcroft. Her future was a bleak wilderness.

Tears wouldn't help.

Nothing would help. Even becoming mistress of the house she'd always coveted, the house that had exacted a greater price than she'd ever thought to pay.

"I'll fetch my cloak and bonnet, Papa," she said in a dull voice.

Without sparing a glance for Ashcroft, she slipped through the door, closed it behind her, and rushed across the tiles toward the staircase. Mercifully, none of their small staff were present.

She felt strangely numb although howling pain lurked just outside the glass wall separating her from the world. Some functioning corner of her mind told her she was wise to get out now. She'd broken with Ashcroft and would never have to see him again. A swift, final separation was best, like wrenching an arrow from a wound.

Let the blood flow and cleanse the poison. Then they could both start to heal.

Except she had a grim premonition she'd never heal. She should have listened when Laura insisted she risked more with this scheme than giving her body to a man she disliked, then forgetting him. A transaction as simple and unremarkable as handing over a penny for a cake in a bakery.

Becoming Ashcroft's lover had cost her soul.

Through her clamoring misery, she heard the door behind her open, then close. Her headlong flight didn't slow.

"Diana, wait."

Oh, heaven save me.

She lowered her head and walked more quickly, hardly seeing where she went. She had a superstitious certainty if she reached the stairs, she was safe. Ashcroft wouldn't pursue her into her bedroom. Surely not with her father so close and a band of servants on call. Not even the libertine earl was so blind to convention.

She set foot on the first step, placed a foot on the next, and released the breath she hadn't realized she held. Her hand automatically reached for the banister.

A tanned male hand closed over hers. Hard and ruthless, it pressed her palm into the polished wood.

So warm. His hand was the only warm thing in her frozen universe.

Her eyes focused on the stairs ahead. She couldn't face Ashcroft. If he looked into her eyes, he'd know how she'd betrayed him.

And she'd know he knew, which was worse.

"Please let me go," she said tonelessly.

"Diana, what's all this about?" He sounded kind, concerned . . . *loving*.

Although obviously that last was a product of her overactive, tortured imagination.

"Please let me go," she said again, tugging at her hand. He held her against the smooth wood.

"Not until you talk to me."

She wished he didn't sound so calm. She wished he didn't sound like the lover she'd cherished. Why didn't he rage? Why didn't he curse her to Hades as a faithless, lying slut?

Couldn't he see it was over? Couldn't he see they had nowhere to go? Not together. Not with the wonderful open sensuality that was the most precious gift they'd shared.

With a pang, she remembered the joy of laughter and intense conversations in the dark of night and, most of all, knowledge she was no longer alone.

Perhaps the sensuality wasn't the only gift.

Her body would ache for his for a long time. The crevasse in her heart would never knit. She knew that already.

"There's nothing to say," she mumbled.

"Look at me, Diana."

Fear held her still. "I have to go. My father is taking me back to . . ."

"Diana."

Reluctantly, she met his eyes. The green was flat, like malachite. He was pale, and a muscle flickered in his cheek.

Guilt clenched her stomach so tight, it hurt. She knew she injured him. Only the knowledge that staying would injure him further kept her resolute.

"I told you I was leaving," she said, feeling like she scraped her skin away with a razor.

His lips lengthened in displeasure. "You didn't mean it."

"Yes, I did." She cast a nervous glance at the library door, but her father didn't appear. Perhaps Laura kept him back to give Diana a last private moment with her lover. "I came to you for worldly experience. You've given that to me. Goodbye, Ashcroft."

He jerked back as if she'd struck him, although he didn't release her. "That's all the explanation you offer?"

For the first time, she heard a trace of anger.

That's right. Shout at me. Insult me. It's what I deserve. If you do, perhaps I'll stop feeling like vermin. Perhaps I'll stop wanting to beg you to keep me, love me, forgive me.

His voice hardened. "What's going on, Diana? What's Lord Burnley to you and your father?"

That was easy to answer, at least in part. "My father is his bailiff."

Ashcroft frowned. "Your father is . . ."

"Blind, yes. I help him. That's partly why he wants me to return. He needs me on the estate."

Ashcroft's eyes were assessing in a way she hadn't seen since the earliest days. "There's so much you're not telling me. Who sponsored your visit to London? Why did you come to me in the first place? What is Burnley's part in all this?"

Her heart slammed against her ribs, and she fought the urge to confess. At least then there would be honesty, even if honesty left him abhorring the very sound of her name.

Except what good was a confession? If she was pregnant, she still needed to keep the baby secret so Ashcroft didn't interfere when she married Burnley.

She steeled herself to do what was best for Ashcroft. Her voice was surprisingly firm. "The only thing I'm telling you is good-bye." Then the ultimate heresy. "Our affair was enjoyable while it lasted, but with my father's arrival and your unwillingness to follow my rules, it's become complicated."

She expected him to storm off in disgust, but he studied her carefully, thoroughly. Under that speculative regard, she shifted in discomfort.

He spoke as though tracking her was perfectly reasonable. "I knew you hid something. I had to find out."

"Now you've found out," she snapped back. Although they were both aware that wasn't true. "You must know when you went against my express wishes, I'd finish the affair. It's run its course."

"You don't believe that." He sounded as if what she said was unimportant, mildly amusing.

Her smile felt like a rictus grin. "I've dabbled in decadence, Ashcroft. I've satisfied any curiosity. I'm ready to resume my real life. And I'm sure you're eager for your next conquest. After all, you must grow bored with your country widow and pine for something more exotic."

A crease appeared between his dark brows as if he considered what she said and still couldn't make sense of it. "You harp upon my reputation. Yet I'm not the one leaving, you are."

She hated that he was perceptive enough to see her defensive maneuver for exactly what it was. She tugged again, and this time, he let her go. It seemed tragically symbolic of their looming parting.

"Our arrangement was only for a week or two." With every second, she found it harder to keep her voice even.

"Fuck our arrangement," he said on a sudden explosion of temper.

She flinched at his language. "I don't owe you anything," she said shakily, as her stomach lurched with excruciating misery at how unjust she was.

She braced against her screeching conscience. She took another step up, although she couldn't summon will to run upstairs and leave him for the last time.

Poor weak Diana. Poor lovesick Diana.

His regard remained unwavering, and he didn't move. His upturned face was tight with emotion, and she couldn't mistake the longing in his dark green eyes. How could she? It mirrored the longing in her breaking heart. She swallowed, trying to convince herself it was best if she left now.

"Kiss me," he said hoarsely, stretching a hand out in a pleading gesture. "Forget all this nonsense and kiss me. Then come home. I don't understand what you're doing, I don't understand why you're here or what bloody Burnley has to do with anything, but you must know it doesn't matter compared to what we share."

"Lord Ashcroft . . ."

"You call me Tarquin when you lie in my arms."

Oh, what sweet memories his words evoked. But she must stay strong. Not just because she was a coward but for his sake. For the sake of the child she prayed she carried.

"It doesn't mean anything." The words emerged as a whisper.

"Like hell it doesn't."

Before she could protest, he rounded the newel post in a single stride and mounted the first step. He filled her vision, made every sense leap to life. He was so tall, their eyes were level even though she hovered two steps above him.

The unconcealed yearning in his face held her motionless.

She spoke on a burst of anguish. "Why are you doing this? I told you it's over. That should be enough. Go."

His jaw set in adamantine lines, and his eyes sparked. "No."

He snatched for her arm, but she jerked out of reach, losing her balance. Before he caught her, she grabbed the banister. If he touched her, she'd shatter. As it was, her control was brittle as Venetian glass. "Shall I tell the footmen to throw you out?"

He laughed dismissively. "London doesn't contain footmen big enough to expel me from this house."

He was right. James would last about twenty seconds against Ashcroft if it came to a contest of strength. Not just strength. Determination vibrated from Ashcroft's impressive form.

Anyway, she didn't want to throw him out. She didn't want these glorious days to finish in vitriol and pain.

What she wanted didn't count.

Her voice throbbed with sincerity and sadness. "Ashcroft, this achieves nothing. Let's not part in rancor. You have more experience of ending affairs than I . . ."

A savage expression crossed his face, and he made a slashing gesture with his right hand. "Stop talking about other women. They don't matter. In your heart, you know that."

"I don't matter either," she said softly and with a bitterness that came from knowing she spoke the truth.

"Of course you do." His eyes sharpened as they did when he suddenly hit upon the winning argument in a discussion. "You don't want to matter. I wonder why."

Fear iced her blood. This time she did back up a step. She'd turn and flee if she wasn't sure he'd come after her, propriety be damned. "I can't believe you expect a lifetime commitment from your other bits of muslin."

She saw him disregard her comment as the inflammatory remark it was intended to be. How had he become so familiar with her thoughts and feelings? It wasn't fair. He was the only man she could imagine spending the rest of her days with, and by insinuating herself into his arms, she had put him forever out of reach.

He just wants you back in his bed until he tires of you. His pride smarts that you leave him. His feelings aren't engaged. You're deluded if you imagine they are.

Except that when she observed his bewildered anguish, those cynical, knowing words seemed the delusion. "There's something else happening." He frowned thoughtfully. "You're not a woman who dives into bed with the first man who takes her fancy."

"How do you know?" she asked sharply.

He shrugged. "I know you."

She recognized that too, but she rushed to deny his claim. "After less than a month? Don't make me laugh."

His eyes darkened. She hated to hurt him, but better to do it like this than deal him the killing blow of learning he'd been little better than a breeding animal.

"Diana . . ."

"Diana!"

The word seemed to echo. She was so lost in Ashcroft's gaze, she barely registered the different voice. She blinked and returned to bleak reality.

Her father stood in the doorway, Laura behind him.

With crazy relief, she stared at Ashcroft. She didn't have to lie again. Her father saved her from damning herself forever in Ashcroft's eyes.

"I'm coming, Papa." She saw Ashcroft register her eagerness.

Hostility steamed off her father's spare frame. "We're for Marsham."

"Diana, don't go." Ashcroft's voice played wild melodies up and down her spine.

He grabbed her arm, and this time, she couldn't evade

him. The urgency of his touch only underlined the cruel fact of her betrayal.

She folded her lips together and shook her head helplessly. Trapped between the two men she loved and knowing she wronged both of them, she couldn't maintain her control.

There was only one thing she could say. It emerged as a tear-thickened whisper. "Good-bye, Tarquin."

She wrenched free, turned, and stumbled upstairs, grateful beyond words that Ashcroft didn't pursue her.

Chapter Twenty-three

～～～～～～～～～～～～～～～

$\mathcal{A}$shcroft hammered on John Dean's door. He'd left London in the dark and arrived in time to hear the church bells ringing out, summoning the faithful to Sunday service.

Although a dog barked inside, nobody answered his insistent knocking. Were they all at church? He was reluctant to barge his way into a public place and make a fool of Diana. Although she'd had little compunction about making a fool of him.

His seething anger surged, but he battened it down. He'd stewed about her and her mysterious purposes all night. Only one thing made sense. That bastard Burnley must have paid for her sojourn in London.

What Ashcroft needed to know was why. And he wanted to know why she'd set out to seduce Burnley's enemy.

Diana had a lot of explaining to do. And this time, he wasn't going to let desire distract him, damn it.

He banged again on the stout door. He was tired, he was furious, and he was sick of not getting answers. Last night, he'd left Chelsea in a raging temper, telling himself Diana Carrick could go to hell. Then curiosity and resentment got the better of him, and he'd ridden down here like a man pursued by devils.

Finally, he heard the sound of a bolt shifting. When the door opened, he braced to confront his perfidious mistress.

Instead, he found himself staring into John Dean's blind eyes. Beside the old man, a decrepit spaniel bared yellow teeth and growled.

"Lord Ashcroft," the man said in a cold voice.

With difficulty, Ashcroft muzzled his impatience. "How did you . . ."

Dean didn't stand back to invite him in. "I can't imagine any other man would try to demolish my door on a Sunday morning."

Ashcroft drew a shuddering breath and struggled for composure. His sudden chivalry was devilish inconvenient, but he couldn't shame Diana in front of her father, however accurate the old man's suspicions about his daughter's fall from grace might be. "Mr. Dean. I have urgent business with Mrs. Carrick. May I speak to you inside?"

"No." Dean gripped his cane as though he intended to beat Ashcroft off if he had to.

Ashcroft kept his tone even. "Is Mrs. Carrick at home?"

"My daughter will never be at home to you, sir."

Ashcroft stiffened. "Surely that's her decision."

"No, it's mine." The man faced him without flinching. It was as though those blank eyes read the stains on Ashcroft's soul, knew what he and Diana had done in London. "I'm her father, and my will prevails under this roof. Go back to your whores, Lord Ashcroft."

"Mr. Dean . . ."

"Good-bye, my lord." Dean started to shut the door. Astonished, Ashcroft realized he'd received an unequivocal dismissal.

"Wait." He spread one hand against the closing door.

Dean's eyes narrowed, and his chin jutted in a way Ashcroft found piercingly familiar. "I have no doubt you can force your way in here. I am, after all, old and blind while you are young and strong. The servants as well as Diana and

Laura are at church so I'm alone and defenseless. But this is my house, and you aren't welcome."

Shame twisted in Ashcroft's gut. What was he doing here, bullying a man who only shielded his daughter's honor? Nonetheless, he tried again. "Your pardon, Mr. Dean. My actions must seem precipitate. But all I want to do is talk to your daughter."

"My daughter doesn't want to talk to you. And if you had a shred of principle, you'd realize she's better off never seeing you again. Good day, my lord."

The door shut in Ashcroft's face, and he heard the bolt slam home.

For one mad second, he contemplated bashing the barrier down, shoving his way in, ignoring Dean's refusal. But that would just confirm the old man's poor opinion of his character. Ashcroft cursed his vile reputation even as he recognized that he reaped what he'd sown. And that any punishment for his multifarious sins was long overdue.

None of which eased his fuming frustration.

His fists curled against the door as he strove to control the restless demons of anger and humiliation. After a few seconds, he slowly straightened on a shuddering breath.

He wasn't finished with Diana Carrick yet. Not by a long shot. But this wasn't the way to get her to listen to him.

Ashcroft waited in the woodland at the edge of Cranston Abbey's magnificent park, landscaped by Capability Brown, owned by a man he despised to the bone, maintained by an army of gardeners he struggled to avoid. Fortunately, thick summer growth made skulking in the bushes reasonably easy, however it chafed his pride.

What pride?

Since Diana's departure, his pride had disintegrated to dust. Lurking like a homeless vagabond in Burnley's shrubbery for three days was the least of it.

And he was yet to speak to her, damn it all to hell.

After his previous failure to see her, he'd relied on a more usual form of communication, letters insisting on explanation, demanding her return. After a week of no reply, he'd recognized that his first impulse had been correct. He must confront her physically. She'd find him harder to ignore when he stood before her, reminding her of their transcendent passion.

He'd left London for Marsham nine days after his first visit. How the mighty had fallen. Once he'd have sworn he wouldn't pursue a woman into the next street, and this was twice he'd invaded this peaceful little village in search of his errant mistress.

He still didn't understand what had happened to him since he'd met Diana Carrick.

By all that was holy, they'd been lovers a matter of weeks. In that time, she couldn't change him and everything he believed in. She'd have to be a miracle worker to do that.

He'd forget her soon enough.

Once he discovered why she'd left.

Once he talked her into coming back, and he took his fill.

Which would probably require the next thirty years.

At least.

He insisted he only wanted to talk to her. Too much remained unsaid, unexplained. Unfortunately, he, the cool man about town, didn't trust himself not to steal her away if he got within reach of her. Every minute without her increased that risk. He hoped a trace of civilization remained under the barbaric savage.

He wouldn't bet on it.

Whenever he'd watched men make fools of themselves over women, he'd wondered how in Hades the poor saps reached such a pass. Now, to his everlasting regret, he knew.

By the time he arrived in Marsham, he'd reined in his anger long enough to establish a strategy. He couldn't risk Diana's father or Burnley discovering him. Nor could he be sure Diana wouldn't run off if she guessed he pursued her.

He registered under a false name at an inn in the nearest town. While he set up vigil in the bushes, he sent his valet into Marsham to buy drinks in the tavern and learn all he could about Burnley, his bailiff, and, most important of all, Mrs. Carrick.

Unfortunately, so far, his valet discovered little to contradict Diana's tales. Although he hadn't managed to identify her prospective bridegroom. The only rich man locally was the Marquess of Burnley.

Diana indeed ran the estate, if nominally as her father's assistant. Ashcroft's valet related copious anecdotes about young Mrs. Carrick's cleverness and diligence.

The glowing reports had been unwelcome. Ashcroft wanted an excuse to hate her, something to shatter this damnable fascination, which persisted no matter how she'd deceived him. But it seemed she was exactly what she claimed. A country widow of respectable but not spectacular standing. Which made those fashionable clothes and the opulent little nest in Chelsea a complete puzzle.

Questions never ceased to torment him. Had Lord Burnley funded her visit to London? Had her mysterious betrothed? In either case, why?

In spite of everything, Ashcroft couldn't believe she'd accept money from one man and immediately jump into another man's bed. He'd always been a complete cynic where women were concerned. Early and extensive sexual experience ensured that. But something about Diana made him doubt she was so venal or so wanton.

And didn't that make him a credulous numbskull?

Other facts, like her husband's untimely death, turned out to be true. The impression in the village was she'd worn the trousers in that union, although William Carrick had been a good man, and the couple had been close. Tidings which made Ashcroft's teeth gnash, God forgive him. After all, the poor sod died too young and with a loving wife left to mourn. He deserved compassion rather than jealous resentment.

Ashcroft leaned against a beech tree and folded his arms across his chest. He directed a disgruntled glare through the leaves at the house where Cranston Abbey's bailiff lived with his beautiful daughter. The place was on the edge of the estate in its own grounds. A tidy, unpretentious building from last century. Just behind it, the village church's square tower rose into the sky.

Of course, he'd caught glimpses of Diana since he'd arrived. Never alone. And he needed her alone. Despite his anger and confusion, he didn't want to ruin her reputation in this village. Another sign of how she undermined his will, devil take her. He should let the hellcat suffer the consequences of lying. Although for the life of him, he still couldn't work out exactly what her game had been in London.

He wanted to know what she'd been up to. He *needed* to know.

As if to mock his dark humor, the summer day was perfect. He wasn't surprised when Diana and her father emerged from the house, and she settled him in a chair in the sun. Ashcroft's pulse surged at the sight of her. Even at this distance, the stiffness in their interactions indicated John Dean hadn't forgiven his daughter.

The old spaniel, now familiar, ambled out and flopped at John Dean's side. The scene was so classically bucolic, it could be a sentimental painting. Not for the first time, Ashcroft felt out of place in this rural idyll. Over the last days, he'd realized Diana Carrick had a life, a family, duties, and purpose. None of which had anything to do with her London lover.

Had she meant it when she called him a passing amusement?

He quashed the thought. He'd never believe that. He wouldn't let doubt eat away his determination.

Miss Smith appeared at the door and beckoned Diana inside. With a heavy sigh, Ashcroft slid down against the beech. He stretched his booted legs across the leaf-strewn grass and drew a small morocco leather volume from his pocket.

As so often recently, he found himself unable to concentrate on the printed word. Trapped in the leafy woodland overlooking Diana's home, his troubled mind pricked at him. Undistracted by anything except his angry misery, he confronted a life as barren as a desert.

How lowering to fall into self-pity.

It was all Diana's blasted fault. He'd been content before she barged into his library with her wanton demands.

Except that wasn't true. He'd been restless before she arrived, and their affair had lent his existence untold depth and richness. Good God, he couldn't imagine himself prowling after any other woman like this.

In an attempt to divert himself from his brooding, he opened his book. The beginning of *The Aeneid* stared up in its neat lines of Latin verse. With a disgusted gesture, he closed the volume. Somehow, reading about a genuine hero made him feel even more like a starving mongrel dog.

At a distance, he heard a door snick shut.

With no great optimism, he lifted his head. Diana would be off to her work on the estate, and as usual, she'd have company.

Yes, it was Diana. For once on her own.

His ridiculous, yearning heart performed a crazy dance. No matter how he told himself he couldn't trust the wench, nothing cured him of this immediate, primitive reaction. She bent briefly to speak to her father and clicked her fingers to the dog, who staggered to his feet and shook himself.

Sudden, preternatural excitement tightened Ashcroft's every muscle. Perhaps at last, at last, he'd get her to himself. He refused to acknowledge the bursting elation as the joy it was. Just as since she'd left, he refused to acknowledge the echoing emptiness in his life as a symptom of how he missed her.

Expectation throbbing in his gut, he watched her with

unwavering attention. She'd go back inside. She waited for someone. She'd stand talking to her father and never leave her garden, tormenting Ashcroft with her impossible nearness.

For all his anger, he burned to touch her.

The book slipped disregarded to the grass. His hands shifted against his thighs as if they cupped her breasts, stroked her satiny skin, tangled in her hair.

It was wrong that she wasn't with him. A sin against nature like the sun setting in the east or two moons in the sky.

She didn't retreat into the house or look up to greet one of the endless stream of tenants. Instead, she clicked her fingers again to the dog and set out across the lawn, the old hound tottering after her on arthritic legs. As if she knew Ashcroft waited, she headed directly for his hiding place.

He loved her free, hip-swinging walk. She ate up the ground with a countrywoman's long paces, so foreign to the mincing prance most of the women he knew affected. She wore a dark blue pinafore over a brown dress. The sleeves were rolled up in silent declaration that here was a woman who worked, not one who lounged around eating bonbons and entertaining callers. Her luxuriant hair was confined in a crown of braids, plainer than the elaborate styles she'd sported in London. In the sunlight, the gold shone rich as ripe wheat.

Shock that his ramshackle plan might actually succeed pulsed through him. Waiting like a thief had never seemed a satisfactory tactic. Had proven less than satisfactory. If he'd the vaguest notion of an alternative method of ambushing Diana, he'd leap upon it.

Still she strode toward him. His heart missed a beat, set off on a wild gallop. Now she was close enough for him to see her expression. In spite of her confident progress, she looked pale and troubled.

She looked beautiful.

The dog paused to nose without enthusiasm at a clump of

weeds. Then he lifted his head with a sudden tensing of his body. He whined softly and padded toward Ashcroft.

"Rex!" Diana called. "Rex, come back!"

She hitched up her skirts to chase the dog, providing a breathtaking flash of stocking-clad calves. She wore sensible half boots, and as she rushed ahead, her dark blue skirts swishing across the thick summer grass, he caught a flash of crisp white cotton petticoat. A demure sight to tantalize a rake, but it set desire raging like flames through a dry woodpile.

"Rex!"

The spaniel whined again, then barked sharply. He ran toward Ashcroft with surprising speed, given the rickety way he'd trailed his mistress.

Diana swore under her breath. With salty relish. No missish oaths for his woman, he was pleased to note. He'd always liked her earthiness. Especially when she devoted it to pleasuring him. She swerved off the path and pushed through the thick green growth.

Ashcroft lurched to his feet. He hadn't been nervous with a woman since he was a lad, but he was nervous now. He sought the rage that had fortified him through the last days. It was absent. Instead, a blazing tide of anticipation overwhelmed him.

The dog appeared first, rustling through the bushes to growl and glower at him with rheumy brown eyes. Just behind the dog, Diana burst into the small clearing, frowning, her concentration on her runaway pet, her hair starting to tumble. She was no better at securing her coiffure here than she'd been in Perry's gorgeous seraglio of a bedroom.

A thousand memories hit, hard as a hammer, soft as swan's down. Diana arching under him, crying out her pleasure. Diana naked and languid after love. Diana laughing. Diana arguing. Diana challenging him as no woman had.

Diana . . .

Words fled. A lump the size of Mount Snowdon lodged in his throat. His hands curled at his sides, and he thought his heart must burst, it thumped so crazily.

"Rex . . ." Then she looked up and saw Ashcroft.

She stopped on an audible breath, the pink seeping from her cheeks. A shaking hand rose to clench between her breasts.

Still trapped in silent stasis, he observed the expressions flash through her gray eyes. He read a radiant happiness that made his blood sing. Then dismay, then fear and unmistakable guilt. Finally, some complex, dark emotion he didn't understand.

"Ashcroft," she whispered, as if the word were a curse.

Diana was trapped in a nightmare. Identical to the cruel dreams where Ashcroft appeared in Marsham and accused her of betrayal. Although the nightmares weren't as painful as her other dreams. Where she shuddered awake trembling, sweating, verging on climax, wondering why the phantom arms holding her didn't hold her in reality.

She'd missed Ashcroft so much. He'd latched such hooks into her heart, she'd never shake him free. Since returning home, she felt like she'd had a limb amputated.

She hadn't expected him to accept dismissal without a fight. It wasn't in his nature to give up on something he wanted. And she'd deceived him into wanting her, heaven forgive her.

A neighbor had mentioned a stranger asked after her the first Sunday morning she was back. She'd known immediately it was Ashcroft. What surprised her was that her father had managed to turn him away. Her father, who had barely spoken to her since her return, never alluded to the encounter.

The letters that arrived in handfuls last week hadn't surprised her either. She'd insisted she wouldn't read them. Of course she had. Over and over.

She'd insisted she wouldn't keep them. They currently resided under her pillow, creased and stained with tears she shed in the privacy of her chamber.

How stupid. How pointless. How adolescent.

Every night she pored over his increasingly agitated requests for her to come back. She knew the words by heart. No wonder Ashcroft haunted her. She was like a dedicated drunkard. Knowing liquor gave her a headache but unable to stop reaching for the sherry bottle.

Even so, she knew better than to answer his letters. When the correspondence ceased, she told herself it was inevitable. He'd found another woman to share his breathtaking passion. Diana was safe. He'd never trouble her again. In a few months, he probably wouldn't remember her name.

How she wished the idea made her a scrap happier.

Dreams still came at night to shatter her rest. She felt as if something essential to her existence was missing, and she must find it quickly before she stopped functioning altogether.

Which didn't prevent sick terror coiling in her belly when she caught him so close to Marsham, so close to Cranston Abbey, so close to Lord Burnley.

Curse him. She'd left him. Why couldn't he stay left?

"What are you doing here?" The question vibrated with anger. Anger and distress, although she hoped he didn't guess how upset she was to see him. Rex whined.

Ashcroft's eyebrows arched in the familiar expression. "Surely that's obvious. You need to answer some questions. Let's start with what you were doing in London. Who paid for your house and clothes? Why did you seduce me?"

As if he hadn't spoken, she continued in that same quaking voice. "I don't want to see you."

Even as her eyes devoured him as though he offered the only light in a long, dark winter.

Since they'd parted, she'd relived every hour they spent together. Yet now he was here, details pierced her like jagged shards of glass. The precise angle of his jaw. The lazy glint in his green eyes. His height. He was still the only man who made her feel delicate and feminine. That alluring curl of his lip when he smiled, as if they shared a joke the rest of the world never quite got.

"That's unfortunate." In contrast to hers, his voice was firm and decisive. "Because I want to see you."

His stare reminded her of his focused attention when he wanted sex. She licked dry lips at the idea of his touching her. She wanted it so much, yet only disaster loomed. She must stay strong. And she had to get rid of him before he was discovered.

"Come on, Rex," she said flatly. She turned on her heel and stalked away, the dog shuffling behind her.

"No, you don't," Ashcroft said softly, lunging forward and hooking his hand around her upper arm. The contact stopped her in her tracks.

Rex growled. "Quiet, Rex," she said. Then to Ashcroft, "Let me go."

He ignored her. "Did you get my letters?"

She faced him down with stubborn defiance, even as her blood rushed with excitement at his nearness. "Yes."

His hand tightened. "And?"

She tried to sound implacable. Instead, her response just emerged as sulky childishness. "And nothing. I tore them up and threw them in the fire."

His beautifully shaped mouth quirked in wry amusement. "Harsh fate. Didn't you want to see what I said?"

Who could blame him for disbelieving her? The pile of letters stashed in her bedroom proved she lied. "No. How did you know I'd be here today?"

In a less-self-assured man, the expression that crossed his saturnine, intense face might be embarrassment. "I've waited for three days."

She stared at him in shock. "I don't . . ."

He shrugged, still with that discomfited air. "You didn't answer my letters."

Oh, Ashcroft . . .

She felt so sick with guilt and love, her heart cracked. She bit her lip, glanced away, and fought tears. This notorious rake had endured days braving the elements to talk to her. Without his saying so, she knew he'd never done such a thing for a woman before.

And she was achingly aware she wasn't worth a single moment of his time.

She had a sudden memory of the supercilious rakehell she'd encountered in his beautiful library. So far removed from this devastated, suffering man. Bile filled her mouth, and roiling self-disgust made her wish she'd never forced her way into his life.

Logic told her the anguish wouldn't always be this sharp. Her heart insisted otherwise.

She ignored her heart. She had a bleak premonition ignoring her heart would become a habit in the future. Rex whimpered and nudged her skirts, seeking reassurance. He'd been jumpy for days, sensing the discord in her father's house.

Abruptly, she drooped in Ashcroft's hold, the fight leaching from her. Her voice emerged as a low, choked murmur. "There's nothing for you here."

"There's *everything* for me here." He stepped closer, towering above her. If he took her in his arms, she'd shatter. His tone deepened into velvet seduction. She felt as much as heard it. Every hair on her skin rose in longing. "I don't care what you've done. Come back, Diana."

She knew what it must cost him to say those words. How she wished she could obey the soft entreaty. It hurt to speak. "It's over."

He released her and stepped back. Immediately, she missed his touch the way she'd missed him for ten miserable days. She lifted her hands to rub her arms, although it was a warm morning. The coldness lived inside and had nothing to do with the season. Rex crowded her in silent sympathy.

Ashcroft's jaw hardened. "Tell me why."

If only she could. She braced herself to lie once more. With all this lying, it should become easier. She reached a stage where she'd gag if she had to force out another falsehood.

Just one more, she promised herself. Send Ashcroft away, then you'll never have to lie to him again.

But when she read the burning emotion in his face, she couldn't say the lacerating, insulting words. Instead, she shook her head with dull obstinacy and turned away. "I'm sorry, Ashcroft."

She managed two steps, Rex sticking so close to her heels, he tangled in her skirts.

"Wait, Diana!" Ashcroft leaped after her.

Wildly, she swerved to evade him. "No, Tarquin." His Christian name slipped out before she could stop it.

Rex yelped when she stepped on him, and she twisted to avoid trampling the spaniel. Ashcroft dived to catch her as she teetered.

She plastered both hands across her belly in an automatic gesture of protection.

Chapter Twenty-four

$\mathcal{A}$shcroft froze as if struck by lightning.

He tried to speak. Nothing emerged. He cleared his throat. Tried again.

Gently but remorselessly, he shifted his hold on Diana's waist and turned her to face him. After brief resistance, she capitulated. Her mouth turned down in misery. She was ashen and trembling.

This time he managed to say the impossible words. "You're pregnant."

He thought she was pale before, but the color bleached so drastically from her skin, even her lips turned white. He saw her consider denying the charge and recognized the moment she decided on honesty.

Odd he could read her so accurately, yet she managed to keep such a quantity of secrets.

"It's too early to say," she said, even as that betraying hand cradled her belly where he already knew his child grew. The dog gave another soft whine and pressed against her as if to offer comfort.

"When did you last have your courses?" Ashcroft asked relentlessly, more to convince her than himself.

"That's none of your business," she said sullenly, without meeting his eyes. All her vinegar had drained away.

He was every kind of lunatic. He should have known her Gypsy remedies were absolute nonsense. She was less experienced than a kitten, for all she'd been married. Now the two of them were stuck in this mess.

Hell, after all these years, he was snared. With a respectable woman at that.

It was a damned disaster.

He waited for horror to overtake him. For anger and denial and recriminations and suffocation.

He waited . . .

And felt a slow, shimmering joy.

Diana carried his child. She'd grow round and glowing, nurturing his son or daughter inside her glorious body. She'd give birth to a baby who, he prayed, would be the image of her.

"Say something, Ashcroft," she said in a stark voice. She stared at him as if she beheld a volcano or a flooding river. Some unpredictable force of nature.

He tried to tell his heart that his joy was futile. That he wasn't fit to be a father. That he'd find some solution to this dilemma that left him free to resume his life of debauchery.

The fountain of happiness refused to be quenched.

He cleared his throat again. His voice kept deserting him. He had so much to say, sentences swarmed into his mouth, but only two words emerged. Two words he'd already spoken.

"You're pregnant." He sounded like he'd been caught in a hurricane.

Diana looked wretched. Ashamed.

Foolish girl. Surely she'd soon feel the happiness he did.

She rushed to fill the silence. "Even if I am, don't worry. I promised I'd take care of any repercussions. I don't expect you to do the honorable thing. I'd never expect that."

He brushed aside the insult. The wild song in his heart

rang too loudly for him to worry about her opinion of his old self.

Just as he'd waited for horror to descend at the discovery of her pregnancy, he waited for every nerve to protest at linking himself to one woman for life. He'd always avoided the parson's mousetrap the way a cat avoided water. For the same reason. It was a totally inappropriate environment for a louche roué like him.

Except marrying Diana promised paradise. With the full approval of Church and state, he'd have her in his bed. She'd never sneak away again. His days would be full of looking at Diana and talking to Diana and arguing with Diana and sleeping with Diana. Even at this euphoric instant, he recognized marriage was no heaven, but right now, it beckoned like heaven.

For the first time in his life, the universe was absolutely right. Whatever Diana's secrets, at this moment, he knew they didn't matter. What mattered was that he wanted her, and she carried his child.

He drew himself to his full height. He clasped her more firmly around the waist, a waist that would expand as his child thrived.

"Marry me, Diana." To his surprise, he sounded utterly sure.

She stared at him aghast, her pupils dilating with the force of her feelings.

Fighting back the hurt that pricked his bubble of happiness, he hurried into persuasion. "I know you think I won't make an acceptable husband. I swear I've changed. It sounds asinine to say a good woman's been the saving of me, but these last weeks with you, I've . . ."

She placed a trembling hand over his mouth, and he fell silent. He stared into her gray eyes, flat and lightless as the sea under cloud, and this time, he read her emotions with complete accuracy.

She looked as though her best friend had just died.

He frowned. Of all the responses he'd expected to his impulsive proposal, and in truth he had no idea what he expected, this turbulent sorrow seemed out of place. He was inexperienced offering marriage, but other men survived the deed. A speedy acceptance of the fellow's hand or, in fewer circumstances, a polite refusal were usual.

This biting, unspeaking grief was singular.

"Diana . . ." he began in bewilderment, but she slid her hand over his mouth. How strange to read tenderness in her touch when she was so appalled by his proposal.

To his shock, tears sparkled in her eyes. Since they'd first made love, he'd never seen her cry. Not even when her father caught her with her lover. Not even when she sent that lover away.

Although he wasn't sure what she wanted, he couldn't help lifting one hand to cup her face. She was so distressed. What had he said? The sight of her weeping made him want to cut his throat. Her pain was his.

She tried to pull away, but he didn't let her. "No . . ." she forced out in a strangled voice.

His heart plummeted to his gut. "No?"

He wanted to sound uncaring, but his voice cracked and betrayed his pain with mortifying clarity.

She tried again to escape before settling in his hold, panting like a frightened bird. He'd never viewed her in such a fragile light—to him, she'd always been a Valkyrie—but something about her now struck him as vulnerable and broken.

"Ashcroft, it's impossible," she said, still in that constricted voice, as though she contained a storm of tears. "I'm sorry. Your proposal is kind and flattering."

Kind and flattering? What bloody rubbish was this? It didn't even sound like her. His Diana didn't rely on polite platitudes.

Dull-bladed anger mashed his heart. Every time he asked her for something, she said it was impossible.

He released her waist and grabbed the hand still pressed against his lips, drawing it away. Not before he brushed a phantom kiss across her fingertips. He'd gone over a week without touching her. Even through the turmoil, the contact of skin on skin quieted the devils howling in his soul.

"Diana, think before you reject me." He went on before she phrased further objection. "I'll do my best to make you happy."

She swallowed and forced out an answer that was no answer. "You don't understand, Tarquin."

Pathetic creature that he was, he found solace in her use of his Christian name. "Then help me understand."

All his life, he'd battered his head against doors that were perpetually closed. Not this time. She wasn't going to keep him out. No matter how she tried. He wasn't a helpless child anymore. She owed him more than this. She mightn't love him, but she cared. He wasn't stupid enough to think she didn't. He'd seen her eyes when he was so deep inside her, he'd touched her heart.

Diana stared at him with complete devastation. However she reacted to his proposal, he couldn't accuse her of taking his offer lightly.

He spoke urgently. "Why is it impossible? I'm free. You're free. We're both of age and in possession of our wits. Well, at least I used to think I was. We'll establish a family, a life together. Doesn't that tempt you?"

"Tarquin, it's not you . . ."

The line women always used to pacify a rejected suitor. Not that he'd heard it himself before now. He abandoned any pretense at pride. "I'm a man of good fortune, Diana. Houses. Gold. Land. You'll live in comfort. The child will want for nothing."

Some unreadable emotion crossed her face, made her appear tired and drawn. He had a glimpse of how she'd look as an old woman if life presented only bitterness and disappointment.

Her voice vibrated with anguish. "Ashcroft, I beg you, say no more."

"I will speak. What's to stop our marrying? I'll look after your father. Is that what worries you? Good God, I'm taking on a wife and a baby. I'm sure I'll find room in the mausoleum I live in for a grandfather."

This time she managed to break away. He let her go, failure setting up a grim knell in his heart. Tears poured down her pale cheeks. She dashed at them with unsteady hands. "Don't ask me again. I can't marry you."

"Why?"

Again that word. *Why.* It would be engraved on his tombstone. He drew in a shuddering breath and fought for a control that had moved out of reach long ago.

"Why, Diana? You're carrying my child. Surely that's reason to favor my suit. What's to become of you once the baby's existence becomes known? You can't hope to hide such news in a village the size of Marsham. At least let me give you the protection of my name." Acid edged his voice. "You liked me well enough to crawl into my bed. Surely you like me well enough to allow me to offer honorable recompense."

"There is no honor," she said brokenly, swinging away and burying her face in her hands.

Although he'd never lied to himself about his lack of virtue, her response cut him to the quick. "I know I'm the world's greatest rogue, but I swear there's honor in this proposal."

"I'm not talking about you," she said in a muffled moan.

He frowned. This didn't make sense. She was a respectable widow whose only sins, as far as he knew, related to her affair with the rakehell Earl of Ashcroft.

As so often when he pushed for answers, he had the feeling he missed pieces of the picture. Big, important pieces. Every time he thought he made sense of what happened, the picture changed.

A fence rose between him and what he wanted. He could see his goal across the barrier, but he couldn't reach it.

"Tell me, Diana," he said sharply, snatching her arm. He expected her to recoil, but she remained trembling in his grasp. "Why won't you marry me?"

He watched her expression change, harden, become purposeful. She straightened like a soldier about to face a firing squad. "I can't lie to you anymore, Tarquin," she said in a low voice. "You'll hate me, but I have to tell you the truth."

Grim premonition struck him that after pushing for answers for so long, he wouldn't like what he was about to hear. "The truth about what? Why won't you let me give our child my name?"

"Because Mrs. Carrick is going to marry me. Her child will carry the proud name of Fanshawe, not the degraded label of Vale."

At Lord Burnley's intervention, Diana's heart crashed to a halt, and her faltering confession died on her lips. Her belly clenched with the painful realization that she was sinfully late offering to tell Ashcroft everything. Instead, he'd now discover the worst, and in the cruelest possible light.

Curse her for all the evil she'd done him.

Slowly, she turned, and through a glaze of tears saw the marquess watching from the edge of the glade. Burnley's face set in triumphant lines. Rex made a soft sound of distress and butted her leg.

Her desperate gaze switched to Ashcroft. Fleetingly, she saw the ardent lover. Then he became once again the man she'd first met in Mayfair. In charge of himself and his world. Proud. Superior. Impervious to feeling.

After the last weeks, she knew better, but she couldn't criticize his need to present a strong façade to his enemy. She was shocked to the bone to realize Burnley and Ashcroft were indeed enemies. Not just rivals in politics. Not just men with nothing in common apart from the incendiary secret of Ashcroft's parentage.

What quivered between these two powerful noblemen was hatred. Naked and dangerous as a drawn sword.

Ashcroft was the first to break the fraught silence. He let Diana go and straightened, his eyes never shifting from the older man. "Lord Burnley."

Burnley's thin lips twisted in a contemptuous smile that chilled Diana's heart. He'd never expressed any warmth for his bastard son. In the years she'd known him, she'd never seen him express warmth toward anything. But his disgusted expression said he nurtured no fatherly feelings at all.

"Lord Ashcroft. As usual, you intrude where you're not wanted," he drawled.

Ashcroft's curt bow was pure insolence. Diana's hands formed claws in her skirts. How she wished she'd never started this greedy, vicious scheme.

She was going to be hurt. She'd recognized that long ago. What terrified her to the point of screaming was that Lord Ashcroft, who didn't deserve to pay for her unjustified ambition, would suffer a killing blow in this verdant glade.

She didn't mistake the gloating relish brightening Lord Burnley's green eyes. He meant to use Diana as his weapon to crush Ashcroft to dust beneath his heel.

"Lord Ashcroft, please go," she said in a thready voice, but both men ignored her.

Ashcroft shrugged with a nonchalance that would have fooled anyone who didn't love him—or didn't hate him with a virulence that poisoned the very air. He sounded casual, uncaring, in control. "Surely setting foot on your land to speak to a lady of my acquaintance doesn't constitute trespass."

"It does if the lady has no wish to speak to you," Burnley returned smoothly.

Now she saw them face-to-face, Diana unwillingly found a stronger resemblance between the two men than she'd expected. She hadn't seen it when Ashcroft was her lover, kind, witty, perceptive, generous. Here he acted the grand seigneur, and he looked startlingly like his father.

The likeness didn't flatter him. He looked remote, his handsomeness glittering cold as a diamond. Hard to remember she'd held this man in her arms while he gasped his release. Hard to remember he'd been so frantic to see her, he'd pursued her into his enemy's territory and begged her to marry him.

Once he discovered the truth, he wouldn't want to marry her. That sweet leap her heart had given at his proposal would never recur.

She closed her eyes and summoned a prayer for Ashcroft. Her soul was too weighted with sin to form the words. She wasn't such a hypocrite, she imagined God would pardon her and listen to her entreaties.

Not even the promise of Cranston Abbey compensated for the damage she'd done to herself, her father, and, most of all, Ashcroft.

"The lady can speak for herself," Ashcroft snapped, as she opened her eyes.

"As her betrothed, I speak for her. Perhaps you didn't hear me. Mrs. Carrick is the next Marchioness of Burnley, and she bears my heir."

In spite of Ashcroft's efforts to appear unmoved, Diana saw the color drain from his face. She couldn't mistake his pain. And she inflicted it. She deserved to suffer the torments of the damned for this.

The eyes he turned on her flared with accusation. "What's this about, Diana?"

She felt utterly sick. "Ashcroft, I told you I couldn't marry you. I told you to leave. You don't . . ."

Burnley stepped forward, leaning on his stick but looking heartier than he had for months. Clearly trouncing the earl so thoroughly improved his health. That and the news that she was pregnant.

She wasn't sure yet, but her cycle was regular, and she was a week overdue. Her deepest instincts insisted the breathtaking passion she'd shared with Ashcroft bore fruit.

"No need to spare the fellow's feelings, sweeting."

Diana shuddered at the endearment. Burnley had never called her anything remotely affectionate in all their long acquaintance. She didn't like it.

She cast a pleading glance at Ashcroft. "For the love of heaven, go, Ashcroft."

"I agree with Mrs. Carrick." Satisfaction dripped from Burnley's words. "You've made your ridiculous marriage proposal. She's refused. Any man with a modicum of backbone would remove himself to lick his wounds. You're just like your mother, victim to sickly sentiment when everything indicates your attentions are unwelcome."

Burnley must have eavesdropped for a while. Diana's soul cringed at how Ashcroft would feel knowing such a private, vulnerable moment had a witness. A witness who felt only contempt for him.

"Ashcroft, you don't need to hear this." She reached out, but he shook her off as though she didn't exist. She deserved the dismissal, but it still stung.

"What's that about my mother?" Ashcroft asked sharply, stepping toward Burnley. His eyes were the same pale green as the famous celadon porcelain at Cranston Abbey. The inhuman coldness made her shiver.

Burnley's mouth flattened. "Your mother was a brainless slut."

Diana gasped even as Ashcroft stiffened. "You knew her?"

"Of course I did." Burnley's voice vibrated with derision. "All prim propriety and virtue until I tumbled her into bed. Stupid little jade. She gulled herself into thinking she was in love, and that excused anything she did. God knows why her husband took her back."

"My father didn't take her back." Ashcroft's voice retained that unearthly calm.

His gaze didn't waver from the old man who visibly relished his rival's humiliation. Because, Diana realized with nausea, that's what Burnley had always considered Ashcroft. A younger, more virile version of himself over whom he must prove his superiority.

"He did the first time she kicked over the traces. Your mother was such a martyr to love, she didn't stay. Not once she'd pupped you. Moronic bitch imagined I'd find a way to marry her."

"Ashcroft, go, please," Diana said brokenly, grabbing his hand.

He didn't glance at her although his hand curled around hers so hard it hurt. All his attention fixed on the marquess. His expression was tight with abhorrence. And dawning understanding.

Burnley hardly needed to speak the next words. "Because of course I'm your father."

Chapter Twenty-five

*A*shcroft stared at this smug, evil old man, waiting for disbelief to overwhelm him. It didn't. Burnley's statement had a grim, inevitable air of truth.

He wasn't a fool. He'd always suspected he might be a bastard. It explained so much about how his family treated him, as if he had no right to his place as head of the Vales. As if he was responsible for his father's early death. As if his mother's sins were visited on his head. He doubted details of his parentage were familiar to the wider family, but his aunts and uncles must know, and their dislike carried into the next generation.

"Tarquin, what does it matter?" Diana's voice lowered to broken pleading. "You've lived your whole life without knowing he's your father. It doesn't make any difference to the man you are. He's just out to score points against you. If you leave, you'll deprive him of the pleasure."

She clutched his hand as though she sought to bolster his courage. He hadn't noticed until now. Briefly, he turned and looked into her beautiful, troubled face. She looked agitated. She looked frightened. One thing she didn't look was surprised.

He ignored Burnley, who was incandescent with triumph. "You knew."

She flinched as if he hit her, although he'd spoken calmly. She bit her lip, a sure sign of nervousness, and nodded reluctantly. "Yes, I knew."

She sounded bitterly ashamed, and her shoulders slumped in misery. She wasn't crying anymore, although the sticky trails on her cheeks testified to her distress. His brain stirred from its shock and sluggishly pieced together clues, hints that had kept his suspicions alive no matter how she lulled him into a sensual daze.

"This should prove entertaining," Burnley said with relish.

The old man shuffled across to lean against a tree. He looked like he settled in for an evening at the theater. Ashcroft supposed for someone of his twisted tastes, this counted as rich diversion indeed.

"Lord Burnley, please leave us alone," Diana said with a sudden show of defiance.

Briefly, she was the bold, adventurous woman who'd insisted she belonged in Ashcroft's bed. The woman he'd trusted. The woman he'd liked and respected.

That woman was illusion.

"I wouldn't dream of it, my dear."

Ashcroft noticed the frozen expression that crossed her face at the endearment. She clearly knew exactly what Burnley was like, which made her betrayal even more heinous. The bitch deserved her fate, marrying this monster. She'd find no joy in her nuptials. Burnley would freeze her into solid ice within weeks of the wedding, wring all the spirit from her.

She'd pay for what she'd done.

He wished the knowledge made him feel one iota less like she'd dug out his guts with a rusty spoon. The powerful mixture of rage and anguish threatened to strangle him. Desperately, he beat it back.

Think, man, think.

More connections set up in Ashcroft's mind. Once he knew about his parentage and the collusion between Diana and Burnley, the essentials of the vile plot unraveled like a ball of wool.

Burnley lost his family in the fire, then . . .

He stiffened with horror. Burnley's heirs had been his half brothers, his nieces and nephews. He'd only known them at a distance—political allegiance made friendship with anyone called Fanshawe untenable—now he'd never know them as people who shared his blood.

"It was all about the baby, wasn't it?" he asked Diana in a cold voice, as if the old man hadn't spoken, as if she hadn't begged Burnley to leave them alone.

How bizarre, how humiliating to admit this poorly dressed, inexperienced widow had made a fool of him. He who had kept his head with London's greatest courtesans and the wildest members of the ton.

He fought back his pain. His scientific curiosity was like a lid on top of a volcano, but at least it let him retain a shred of pride. Revelation had piled on revelation today. If he surrendered to his emotions, he'd drown.

"No, it wasn't all about the baby." When she met his eyes, she appeared sincere. What an actress. "Not all of it. Whatever else you believe, I beg you to believe that."

"I wouldn't believe you if you told me the sky was blue." He'd have a confession from her before he left. He deserved that much. "At least let us have honesty. Tell me about the plan. You may as well. I've worked most of it out."

She tugged free. He waited for her to weep and beg forgiveness and pretend innocence, but she straightened her shoulders and sent him an unwavering stare. He admired her courage, much as he wished he didn't. That at least wasn't false, even if everything else was.

How unfair that she still struck him as breathtakingly beautiful. The most beautiful woman he'd ever seen. His new knowledge of her should turn her into a foul hag in his eyes.

As he studied Diana's exquisite features, he tried desperately to hate her. Instead he hated that he couldn't find it in himself to despise her.

Perhaps he would in time. He prayed he would. The agony of knowing what she'd done without the anodyne of detesting her was like being skinned alive.

"Oh, for God's sake, this becomes tiresome," Burnley snapped. "Yes, the wench tricked you into making her pregnant. I'm delighted a child of my blood will carry on the name. Now all I need is a boy."

"What a pity I couldn't ensure that outcome," Ashcroft said sarcastically, his attention not shifting from Diana's stricken face.

He had a sudden urge to injure her the way she'd injured him. Although even here she had the upper hand. His feelings were engaged, and all she wanted was to become a bloody marchioness.

His voice lowered into silky derision. "Perhaps we can arrange a repeat performance. The lady is impressively enthusiastic. She's to be commended for her devotion to your causes."

Diana looked devastated. What a pity he couldn't trust that her pain was real. He tried to find refuge in cynicism, but her betrayal cut too deep.

"Your offer is noted." Burnley sounded as uninvolved as if he decided whether to repair a tenant's house with thatch or slate.

"Always glad to be of service. I find myself asking why you didn't fuck her yourself," Ashcroft demanded with sudden heat, battling the urge to smash his fist into Burnley's face.

Diana gasped as though he wounded her physically. He shouldn't care. He should consign the slut to hell.

Burnley gave a soft chuckle. Ashcroft hated that this man

lorded it over him. His father? He'd prefer to think pond scum had spawned him.

"You had the advantage of youth and vigor."

Aha, that didn't sound like Burnley. Burnley never surrendered the smallest quotient of power. Siring his heir definitely counted as power.

Ashcroft surveyed his father. The man seemed twenty years older than when he'd last appeared in Parliament. Right now, triumph lent Burnley energy, but long illness and exhaustion marked that sharp-boned face.

Only one explanation made sense. It was harsh but fitting. *Papa must be impotent.*

Satisfaction surged. How it must smart to know the marquess's only chance of continuing his line was via the bastard he scorned.

For the first time since Burnley had interrupted his embarrassing marriage proposal, Ashcroft felt a smile curve his lips. "I should thank you for the pleasure you've given me in the last weeks. How sad that you'll never find out just what pleasure, Papa." He injected a world of derision into the last word. "The trull's a fine ride. One of the best I've had."

The best he'd ever had, but he denied Diana the reward of knowing she was unforgettable, and not just because she'd led him down the garden path.

Great Jehovah, he was a dolt. Even now, after all he'd discovered, the misery in her expression made him want to reassure her, to take her in his arms and protect her.

What from? She got just what she wanted, the faithless jade.

He had to forget those transcendent hours at Perry's mansion. They'd been lies, with no more substance than soap bubbles blown from a child's pipe.

Lies, lies, lies. Every single instant she'd spent with him.

The repetition didn't convince his heart.

Damn his heart. His heart had led him disastrously wrong, and he intended to treat it as a stranger from now on.

Diana shifted closer. For a forbidden instant, he closed his eyes as the sweet, fresh scent of apples flooded his senses. She didn't smell like evil and betrayal. He wished to Hades she did.

She curled her hand around his arm and bent her head after casting a surreptitious glance at Burnley. Her voice shook with remorse. False remorse, of course. "I'm sorry you had to find out this way. I'm sorry you had to learn such a man is your father."

"I'll survive," he said dryly. "I've lived till now without dear Papa's loving care. I'm sure I'll continue to thrive. You're the one marrying the toad."

"What are you talking about?" Burnley called rudely.

Diana ignored him, which said a great deal for her bravery. Once she married Burnley, she'd be at his mercy, and he was a man who didn't know the meaning of the word. Ashcroft bit back sick fury at all her lush, passionate femininity allied to this dry, vicious old man.

Oh, let me hate her. Dear God, let me hate her.

"You can't despise me more than I despise myself." She sounded like regret scalded her. If only he believed her. "When you hear why I cheated you, you'll hate me even more."

"Highly unlikely." He wished she wouldn't sound as if his bad opinion was a tragedy. She must know he was awake to her machinations. He drew her farther away from Burnley and kept his voice down, although she didn't warrant such consideration.

She spoke in a muffled whisper. "I'm marrying him for the house."

"The house?" He frowned in confusion. Did Burnley threaten to turn her and her father out of their home? Then he realized what she meant, and he sucked in a shocked breath. "You want Cranston Abbey."

His voice was rough with contempt. Briefly, stupidly, he'd imagined she offered a valid excuse for inflicting this excruciating punishment.

"Yes." She raised her chin and stared directly at him, owning her sins without prevarication.

He bared his teeth in a sardonic smile although he didn't feel remotely amused. "Three weeks in my bed in return for the richest acres in England? You're one pricey whore."

She recoiled before a proud mask fell over her pale face. "I've loved the estate since I was a child. I've run it for years. I'm chatelaine in all but name."

"Bravo," he said ironically. "It's still not yours."

Her lips flattened at his jibe. "It will be."

"He's sick, dying, isn't he?"

She cast another glance at Burnley, who looked increasingly irritated. "Yes. And he's . . ."

"Impotent. I'm his only chance of a child in the direct line. Because of the fire at Deshayes."

She looked like he tortured her. Ridiculous, really, when all her dreams came true, and he was the one on the rack. "I'm sorry, Ashcroft. You'll never know how sorry. I was wrong to involve you. By the time I realized how wrong I was, it was too late."

"Yes, clearly you couldn't tell me," he said scathingly. "In all those hours we spent together, you found no opportunity for confession."

"Don't . . ." She drew a shuddering breath. "By then I'd lost my honor. I couldn't go back to what I was. And you'd have tossed me out on my ear if you had known the truth."

Would he? He didn't know. What he did know was that finding out this way was worse than having his flesh sliced away inch by inch.

"I'd probably have fucked you one last time," he said snidely because he was just so damned angry with her. Even as he ached to sweep her into his arms and carry her far away and pretend she was the woman he wanted her to be.

Her lips thinned as if she held back pain. "Stop saying that . . . that word."

"Why? It's something short and sharp and animal to match what we did. I can't conjure a more suitable term."

"It wasn't like that for me." She flushed but stared at him squarely. "Naturally, none of that matters. You hate me, and you never want to see me again. I understand that. It's how anyone would feel. I tried to save you from finding out, but it was cowardly. I should have told you when you came to Chelsea."

"You should have told me long before that."

"No, I should never have started this."

He gathered courage to ask the question burning on his tongue since his world had fractured. "Are you pregnant?"

She released him. He tried not to miss her touch. Her touch lied. It always had. "I don't know. It's too early."

A nice, sensible answer, except he could see she believed she was. The wave of possessiveness was an unwelcome revelation. He summoned rage as his only defense. When it was already far too late to raise bulwarks against this ruthless, beautiful invader.

"How do you know the child is a Fanshawe? Was I your only lover?"

Her eyes darkened with what he could only read as hurt. Oh, cruel and clever jade to make him feel the villain. "I didn't lie about everything, Ashcroft. Although I can't blame you for thinking I did. You are my only lover since my husband's death eight years ago. Trust me or not, but it's the truth."

He almost believed her, even if that made him the biggest numbskull in Creation. "You're not Burnley's mistress?"

"I told you . . ."

"He hasn't always been impotent."

She spoke through stiff lips. "No, I've never shared Lord Burnley's bed."

"How can you be sure I'm his son?" He'd already accepted his heritage. It was like a part of him had known before Burnley told him.

"Your birthmark," she said reluctantly.

"So once you saw my brand, I was ready for breeding." His tone was abrasive.

"Don't." Her voice cracked, and she tensed brittle as dried grass. She seemed to have reached a state of anguish beyond mere tears.

"Mrs. Carrick, I believe it's time for Lord Ashcroft to leave." Burnley sounded as though he owned everything in sight. He did. This was his estate, and clearly he'd bought Diana long ago.

She drew herself up and fought for composure. She didn't shift her gaze from Ashcroft's face. Her voice grated with despair. "I did you wrong, and I sincerely beg your pardon. Even though I know you'll never grant it. I don't deserve your forgiveness."

Ashcroft wondered how they'd come to this. Hell, he shouldn't care. After all, he'd had a right rollicking time with her. He usually asked no more of his affairs.

From the start, Diana was different.

Yes, the cunning strumpet duped you, his cynical side said snidely.

She said the words he'd already heard, but this time, the parting was final. "Good-bye, Tarquin. God keep you."

She sounded genuine. But she'd sounded genuine when she quivered with pleasure in his arms. He now knew that wasn't true.

Well, the pleasure was true. It was the friendship and the affection and the laughter that were lies. And those were the greatest betrayals. She could have used his body without doing this mortal harm. She'd touched his soul, and he'd never forgive her for that.

Even so, he couldn't let her go like this. Not carrying his baby. Not when he still wanted her, curse her enduring allure.

He caught her wrist, feeling the wild race of her pulse.

"No, Diana. Wait. You can't mean to hand my child over to that cur."

Burnley straightened and stepped toward them. "Have you no pride, man? She's made an utter fool of you. Cut your losses and scuttle back to London."

Ashcroft ignored him. "Diana?"

"I promised," she said in a toneless voice. She refused to look at him.

"Break the promise."

"I can't."

"Why? You don't love him."

Her head jerked up, and she stared at Ashcroft with wide, astonished eyes. For one explosive second, the unspoken question lay between them as to whether she loved Ashcroft.

She'd never said so. She was a lying trollop, but if she told him right now she loved him, he'd accept that was true.

The moment evaporated, and dull misery returned to her face. "Love isn't the issue. If I marry Lord Burnley, I'll have control of the estate until my child reaches his majority."

How strange to realize that Ashcroft had always had an invincible rival for her. This house. Not the living husband he'd conjured up in his imagination. Not her beloved William. Not Burnley. "Only if it's a boy."

"It's a boy."

How could she be so certain? It was lunatic. Although he believed her. And damned her for her ambition and her cupidity. And for not throwing everything she wanted over the windmill to come back to him.

"In that case, I wish you joy, Mrs. Carrick," he said with such coldness, she flinched.

He turned on his heel and bowed to Burnley with a sarcastic depth he knew the older man didn't miss. "My felicitations, Papa."

Without a backward glance, he stalked toward the gates.

His heart brimmed with a foul brew of hatred and anger and pain. And longing. In spite of everything, the longing was paramount, so stabbing it almost crippled him.

He heard a sharp whistle behind him but scarcely paid attention. Until four brawny men in livery surrounded him.

"Ah, my audience grows," he said dryly, lifting his stick with a show of bravado. "Perhaps Lord Burnley should consider selling tickets."

He might be in turmoil, but not to such an extent he couldn't read the threat these big, powerful brutes posed. Burnley must put a height requirement on his footmen. These fellows looked him straight in the eye, and very few men, even of his own class, did that.

Part of him, the part that itched to tear down the world and fling it into space just because Diana didn't want him, welcomed the looming fight. Physical pain might distract him from the lancing emotional agony.

One heavily muscled fellow stepped forward. "His lordship wants us to escort you off the estate, Lord Ashcroft. Come quietly, and there won't be any trouble."

Ashcroft knew better. These men were tuned for violence. He could smell it in the air as sharp as smoke from a fire.

"Mrs. Carrick, let us return to the house." Burnley's voice, smooth, confident, powerful, flowed over Ashcroft like acid. "I want to discuss the drainage of the west marsh."

That put Ashcroft in his place. Less important than an acre of soggy pasture.

He didn't turn to look at Burnley and his future marchioness. He couldn't bear to see Diana again. It hurt too much. "Don't wait on my account," he called over his shoulder.

"Lord Ashcroft," Diana said softly but clearly. "I did you wrong, and I deeply regret it."

"Too late for that, my dear," Burnley said imperiously. "Coming?"

"Yes, my lord," she said, subdued.

"Ashcroft, don't let us detain you," Burnley said.

The dog whimpered. Ashcroft guessed the animal wasn't particularly fond of the lord of the manor. Clever beast. He wasn't too fond of the wretch either. Odd to think all his life he'd missed his father, yet now he'd found his real father, and he felt less emotional connection than he did to his scullery maid.

"Shh, Rex, it's all right." Diana's voice sounded thick as if she cried.

I will not care. I will not care.

"If you'll follow us, my lord." The burly footman gestured with spurious politeness toward the exit.

"I'm at your disposal, gentlemen," Ashcroft drawled and stepped between them, every nerve on alert. Burnley had no reason to rough him up, except that a beating scored a final point over his defeated rival.

Such was the reality of his dear, fond Papa.

Ashcroft strode ahead of Burnley's henchmen along the faint path under the overarching trees. Then, like a shout, he felt the change in the air.

He whirled, raising his fists. It was inevitable he'd go down. When he did, he intended to take a few of these thugs with him.

Chapter Twenty-six

~~~~~~

*L*ord Ashcroft! Lord Ashcroft, can you hear me?"

The strident voice that made Ashcroft's ears ring emerged from a distant world. Ashcroft struggled to escape it, but he couldn't move.

Vaguely, he wondered why that was. Then pain struck like a thousand red-hot hammers. He'd been split into jagged pieces and nailed together again without much care.

"Lord Ashcroft?" The voice persisted, making his skull vibrate in agony.

Rough hands on his head provoked another clanging blast. Like cymbals with gunpowder. When he groaned, only a weak, mewling sound escaped. He battled to open his eyes, but the lids weighed more than bricks.

"Let's get him inside." The disembodied voice came in and out of focus in a bewildering fashion.

He wanted to protest the order. Tell the grating voice he was perfectly capable of walking. That he resented the implication he couldn't make his own way.

Hell, he must have had a skinful last night. His head pounded fit to explode. When he tried to point out he needed no help, he couldn't force the words out.

The voice droned on. It was damnably familiar although

right now, he couldn't place it. Thoughts flitted through his mind, but before he caught them, they darted away like moths fluttering around a lamp.

Nor did he know where he was. Some vague recollection insisted he should be lying on grass, and it should be morning. Even behind closed eyes, he knew it was dark, and something hard and cold and solid under his aching ribs jabbed him.

Steps?

"Careful with his lordship, boys. Heaven knows what's happened."

The voice briefly made sense again. It continued while Ashcroft faded away into a nightmare world crammed with fiery agony. What the devil had he been drinking?

"Charles, grab his shoulders. I'll take his legs."

Ashcroft mustered an objection but only managed another pathetic whimper before he drifted off again.

He endured a painful earthquake as his torturers picked him up. Good God, did they think he was a sack of potatoes? He tried to summon a demand to be gentle, but no sound emerged.

Merciful blackness descended.

When he surfaced, he managed to unglue his eyelids. At least he knew where he was now. He lay on his library sofa in London. Apart from a fire and one lamp, the room was dark.

How had he got here? He'd been . . .

Memory crashed over him like a huge wave of cold, filthy water. He recalled everything in exact detail. He'd been in Surrey discovering just what a fool Diana had made of him. He'd learned his parentage and heartily wished he hadn't. He'd fought off an army of Samson-like domestics.

Which explained his current agony. If not his current location.

A face swam toward him out of the gloom. "My lord, can you speak? What happened? We thought you were in the country."

His brain sluggishly sifted the words, slowly made sense of them. Identified the speaker. His butler bent over him with a troubled frown on his distinguished face. Behind him hovered two footmen.

Burnley must have given his brutal minions orders to dump Ashcroft on his own doorstep. A message in itself. Clearly he wanted his son well away from Cranston Abbey.

And Diana Carrick.

Ashcroft winced and closed his eyes again. Against all logic, losing Diana hurt worse than his physical injuries. Deliberately, he concentrated on his aches instead of his disastrous amours. He dreaded to think what a mess he was in. The violent pain when the men had lifted him indicated it was more than bruising. He guessed something was broken. Perhaps several somethings.

His recollection of the brawl was painfully vivid. For a while, he'd been angry and heartsick enough to give as good as he got. But eventually numbers had prevailed. Dear Papa's henchmen packed a hell of a punch. Nor had rules of gentlemanly conduct restrained them.

He recalled brief flashes of consciousness through the ensuing hours. He remembered Burnley's thugs slinging him into a cart. He'd surfaced in snatches to indescribable agony as the cart trundled to its destination.

Ashcroft House in London, hours away from Cranston Abbey. He must have been out of it for a considerable period of time. Was it even the same day?

"My lord? Can you hear me?"

Devil take his butler, there was no need to shout. He tried to speak but only managed an inarticulate grunt. He was alert enough to hear the consternation in the man's voice when he turned to the footmen.

"Hurry. Fetch the doctor. His lordship's been set upon by footpads and looks likely to die."

Likely to die?

Hell's bells, he refused to turn up his toes. His demise

would make things far too convenient for his papa and that treacherous jade.

In spite of the pain, in spite of the beckoning blackness, he cracked open his eyes. This time, he squeezed out something approximating a sentence.

"Won't . . . die."

Damn Diana Carrick and Edgar Fanshawe. Damn them to hell. They thought they'd vanquished Tarquin Vale. He'd show them how wrong they were.

He was going to live. He was going to make their lives a misery. Dying was too easy. He meant to trouble that vile duo for years yet.

Diana stood in Burnley's rose garden, surrounded by the flush of late blooms. The south façade of Cranston Abbey stretched before her, golden and glowing in the sunset. Ostensibly, she was here to decide when the roses were due to be prepared for winter. But as usual these days, her mind wasn't on the task.

Two months had passed since that horrific day when Ashcroft discovered her perfidy and marched away, his green eyes glazed with hurt and anger. She thought her heart had broken then.

In the endless days since, she'd learned a heart could break over and over.

He hadn't contacted her. How could she expect he would? He must hate the mere sound of her name.

For her sanity's sake, she tried not to dwell on those weeks in London. But she couldn't help remembering the touch of Ashcroft's hand and the sound of his voice. The expression in his eyes when he looked at her, as though she were the most glorious creature he'd ever beheld. The desperation in his body when he'd thundered into her. The naked emotion on his face when he lost himself to passion.

She was strong, she didn't think of him often.

Only at sunset.

Sunrise. Morning. Noon. Afternoon. Evening . . .

She bit her lip and battled futile tears. Lately, she'd been ridiculously weepy. These days it took little to turn her into a complete watering pot. And something about the house's elaborate, symmetrical façade as the sun sank and the last roses released their heady perfume struck her as unbearably poignant.

Perhaps because since London, the fragrance of roses was a piercing reminder of those days and nights at Lord Peregrine Montjoy's improbable mishmash of a house. She fumbled in her pocket for a handkerchief.

"Here you are. I've searched the estate for you."

She turned slowly, blinking the moisture from her eyes. Lord Burnley stood at the end of the path. These days he leaned more heavily on his stick. The last months hadn't been kind. The disease eroding his remaining hours bit deep. It was as if he'd expended his final vitality vanquishing Ashcroft.

He'd lost so much weight, his clothes hung loose. Once he'd stood ramrod straight. Now he stooped, and his shoulders hunched against pain. Skin stretched tight against the bones of his face, and his eyes were sunken and dull.

Even without knowing of his illness, she'd guess he hadn't long to live.

Always the opportunist, he'd arrived at her father's house the day after Ashcroft's departure to press his suit. He'd been shocked when she refused him.

Shocked, but strangely not angry.

Which was unlike the marquess when his will was thwarted. He was like an overindulged child, and the sound of "no" drove him to distraction. Vengeful distraction. She remembered how he'd badgered a farmer who'd opposed his right of way over a property into bankruptcy just to prove nobody gainsaid Lord Burnley.

Nonetheless, she couldn't regret her decision to reject his offer. After what she'd shared with Ashcroft, she couldn't marry Burnley. More, she couldn't benefit from the evil she'd done.

The Abbey was lost to her. And that was how it should be.

Her dream had hovered within reach. She only had to say one word of agreement, and Cranston Abbey came into her care. But the dream was irredeemably tarnished by the wickedness she'd perpetrated in striving to attain it.

After Burnley's proposal, days passed, on the surface each like every other day. She continued to work. Making decisions about the estate. Assigning tasks. Answering questions from the tenants. The thousand duties that tied her to Cranston Abbey as closely as roots bound an oak tree to the soil.

All the time she felt like a watch with a broken spring. The numbers remained on the dial, but the mechanism no longer worked.

Now, with the marquess's appearance, a distant warning clanged in her mind.

Perhaps Burnley had finally decided to throw the Deans off his estate. After all, he'd sought Diana out, and he hadn't done that since she refused his hand. She tried to summon fear, resentment, anxiety. The pall of bleakness that had settled over her like thick fog since London didn't shift.

She dipped into a curtsy. "My lord."

"Are you well?"

Burnley was the most self-involved man she knew. He never inquired after anyone's health. Tightness at the back of her neck alerted her he was up to something. She summoned a conventional answer. "Yes, thank you."

"Would you like to sit down?"

She guessed he wanted to rest. He might be a sorry excuse for a human being, but only a monster would expect a dying man to remain on his feet. This was turning into a very strange interview. Curiosity stirred but not strongly enough to pierce the perpetual throb of loss.

"Yes, thank you, my lord." She waited for him to settle in an arbor massed with climbing white roses before she reluctantly joined him. Usually she wouldn't risk such *lèse-majesté*, but he'd suggested sitting, and unless she plopped herself down on the grass like a farmhand, she had nowhere else to perch herself.

A silence fell. Again, not like him.

Usually he went straight to what he wanted—invariably he wanted something—then moved on to his next target. It struck Diana she knew Lord Burnley as well as she knew her father.

She wished familiarity meant esteem.

He was a spider sitting in his web, waiting for the hapless fly to collide with his sticky trap. Inevitably, when dealing with Burnley, Diana played the fly.

In a proprietary gesture, his hand curved over the top of his stick. "Have you heard from Lord Ashcroft?"

Diana gave a start. Ashcroft's name crashed through her haze, shattering it. Before she reminded herself it revealed her vulnerability, she bit her lip to stifle a whimper of misery.

Blindly, she stared at the beautiful house. The house that had brought her to this pass. Although she recognized the fault lay with her greed and arrogance. Cranston Abbey was bricks and mortar. She was flesh and blood. She possessed a heart and soul, and her sins had crushed both.

"I don't mean to cause distress," Lord Burnley said in the kindest voice she'd ever heard him use.

Diana was tensed tighter than a thread on a bobbin. She strove to speak evenly. "No, Lord Ashcroft hasn't contacted me."

"What about your future, Diana?" Burnley still sounded concerned.

She didn't trust this new version of her employer, but his question was fair. She stared down at where her hands twined in her lap. Her wedding ring hung loose on her left hand. She'd lost weight since she'd returned to Marsham.

"I haven't decided," she said softly.

Burnley released an impatient sigh. That was much more like the man she knew. "You have more than yourself to think of," he said in a critical tone.

Was that a threat? She was surprised he hadn't already used her family against her to gain her compliance. "There's my father and Laura, I know."

"And the child."

Chapter Twenty-seven

Burnley's words struck Diana silent as if he produced an ax and brandished it before her.

The child. The child who made her sick every morning. The child who grew relentlessly in her womb. The child resulting from lies and treachery. And breathtaking joy.

Without thinking, she stroked her belly with one hand as if she communicated with the baby. Her father didn't know about her pregnancy. Laura must—the signs were unmistakable if you lived as closely as she did with the other woman—but she hadn't said anything.

Diana hadn't spoken a word about her pregnancy since Ashcroft made that preternatural leap of intuition in the woods. Burnley had avoided the subject when he'd asked her to set a date for the wedding.

Stupid. Stupid. Stupid. She thought if she didn't talk about the baby, the baby wasn't real. When of course the baby was.

Wake up, Diana.

The baby's existence meant she couldn't continue to drift in this dumb, suffering trance, as passive to her future as a steer on its way to slaughter. Soon her future would batter on her door and scream for decisions. Lord Burnley's presence now meant she had to act, had to decide, had to choose some path.

"Yes, there's the child," she said tonelessly, the admission a defeat.

The old man appeared relaxed, approachable, in a way she'd never seen. Her gaze fastened on the hand that held his stick. He might sound at ease, but his grip was painfully tight. His hand was thin and clawlike, nearly transparent. Like something that already belonged to death, not life.

"You believe I did you a great wrong," he said heavily, when she didn't continue.

Questions of good and evil weren't the usual topic between her and the marquess. She cast him a startled glance, but he stared at the magnificent house, just as she had.

Whatever the state of his soul, hers was too black to endure another lie. "No, I did the wrong myself."

Through the sleepless nights, she'd had ample opportunity to assign blame. Some essential honesty made her recognize that her own weakness had brought her to this pass. Lord Burnley could never have coaxed her into bartering her virtue if she hadn't been flawed to begin with.

"You imagine yourself in love with that worthless blackguard." Burnley sounded irritated, as if she'd let him down by falling prey to emotion. She supposed she had. "I should have considered the possibility, but you've always been a woman of remarkable good sense."

"Good sense hasn't marked my actions recently, my lord," she said dryly. She had no intention of acknowledging her feelings to Burnley.

"He's an eminently forgettable fellow."

Oh, how wrong he was to dismiss Tarquin Vale. The awful irony was Burnley couldn't see he'd produced a son to be proud of. Handsome, strong, intelligent, and with a surprisingly firm grasp on principle for someone universally touted as a conscienceless rake. Ashcroft had always been so much more than she bargained for.

Not that she deluded herself that Ashcroft was any plaster saint. He was used to getting his own way, he was spoiled, he was stubborn, and he certainly hadn't stinted his sensual explorations.

Faults certainly. Not irredeemable ones.

He was still far too good for her. That was tragically apparent. Had been apparent from the first if she'd used her eyes and not let her own ambition and Burnley's prejudice against his only remaining child blind her.

"Hard to forget him when I carry his baby," she said with a bite.

She waited for Burnley to protest, at her rudeness if at nothing else. He remained silent.

When he did speak, he surprised her. Although she should have guessed where this conversation headed. Her slowness in realizing what he was up to was just another symptom of her abiding misery. She wasn't usually so dozy when it came to Burnley's manipulations.

"I want you to think of the child as mine. I already do."

Dismay held her motionless. He couldn't mean to renew his suit. She'd refused him. Categorically.

"Lord Burnley . . ." she stammered when she summoned breath to speak.

The hand on the stick clenched until the knuckles rose hard and round against the skin. "Listen to what I have to say, Diana."

"I can't marry you," she said flatly.

She turned to face him. His eyes burned in his worn face. Green eyes. Like his son's. The blazing glare made it impossible to look away.

"Consider the facts. You've achieved exactly what you set out to do. You seduced the scoundrel, you bring Cranston Abbey an heir of the direct line. All this because you love the house."

Once she had, but she'd changed. Now she'd gladly consign every stone in the Abbey to Hades in return for one glimpse of the man she loved. "I . . ."

He gestured with his free hand to silence her. "You're the perfect guardian of this heritage. A heritage your child can hold, completely, legally, without question. Your blood will walk these halls, your blood will own this land, your blood will join the glorious line of Fanshawes. Doesn't that make your heart leap? I thought you the only woman in the world who could focus on the end rather than fretting over the means. What's happened to your ambition?"

"Lies and deception smothered it," she said, still in that flinty voice.

Burnley made a contemptuous sound. "Sheer rot, woman. You're not thinking clearly. You haven't thought clearly since you met that damned degenerate."

She lurched to her feet. This was torture. Although she should have been prepared. Burnley never gave up on what he wanted, and he wanted an heir for the Abbey. Which meant he wanted her for his wife.

"Stop it," she said sharply. "I won't listen. You're like the devil, twisting facts until I can't tell right from wrong."

Anger glinted in his eyes. "You dare to speak to me with such insolence?"

"I dare."

Surprisingly, his thin lips stretched in a smile. His eyes sparked with admiration. "What a marchioness you'll make. That's the spirit I've always seen in you. Not this moping coward."

His compliments gave her no pleasure. "I won't be your marchioness."

She waited for an explosion, but he sent her a serious look. "You're still not thinking straight, Diana."

"Aren't I?" she asked with a hint of challenge.

What right did he have to prod and pick? She wanted to be left alone to seek perdition her own way. Floating without complaint toward oblivion. She didn't like the way Lord Burnley awoke her temper. It meant she felt. And feeling hurt like an amputation without opium.

"It's absurd. You've endured the worst." He straightened, and briefly he was the man who had ruled the estate like a despotic king. "Now you won't accept the reward you've worked so hard to attain. Ashcroft won't give a fig what you do. Believe me, you humiliated him. He won't come for you. Even if he did, even if he was weakling enough to forgive you, he'd offer you nothing better than a role as his temporary mistress. When he's had his fill, degraded you completely, he'll pass you on to some other rogue. It's not a fate you'll relish, my dear. The heat of Ashcroft's passion is fleeting as a candle's. It won't warm you for long."

"I know there's no future with Ashcroft," she said dully, wishing she could argue. Burnley only reiterated what she'd told herself in the lonely watches of so many tear-drenched nights.

"If you reject me, what future do you have, apart from disgrace and ruin? You're going to bear a child. Don't you think that child would rather be brought up as the Marquess of Burnley than as a pauper drab's bastard?"

His questions smarted. Because much as she hated him, she had to acknowledge he was right. She had more than herself to consider. There was a baby.

Burnley must have scented his advantage because he went on more emphatically. "And what about your father and Miss Smith? Do you think they'll appreciate losing the roof over their heads because of your fine sense of ethical imperatives?"

"Would you . . ." She couldn't bear to finish the question.

The smile developed an edge of superiority, became more what she was used to. "I can't offer employment to a woman who bears a child out of wedlock. And her family shares the scandal. I have my tenants' moral welfare to consider."

The foul mongrel. He'd tried the velvet gloves, now it was the iron fist.

Helplessly, she cast around for something to counter what he said. There was nothing. He was cruel, but he spoke the truth.

Even if Burnley meant to keep her father on, how could she bear growing round with Ashcroft's offspring under the judgmental gaze of the villagers? The thought was too crushing to bear. She was such a hypocrite, but being publicly labeled a slut was more than she could countenance.

"You're blackmailing me."

"I'm merely pointing out the realities."

"And the realities fall right into your lap," she responded acidly.

"I offer the protection of my name. I offer my fortune and home. I offer your unborn child a secure future. You'll have a generous allowance and more freedom than most married women dream of. Soon you'll be a rich widow. It's clear to both of us I'm not going to last much longer." He spoke carelessly, although the hand tightened on his stick, indicative of the private battles he'd fought with his mortality.

"It's wrong to marry you." Her hands curled into fists at her sides. Even as his ruthless logic lashed at her like a whip.

She had a child to worry about. She was responsible for her father and Laura. Reconciliation with Ashcroft was impossible. For herself, she'd send Burnley to the devil. She was young and healthy and could surely make her way. But this decision wasn't for her alone.

Burnley continued in that same adamant, utterly certain voice. "Will your child agree when he learns he could have been a master of the kingdom, rich, respected, powerful, and instead he's a nameless guttersnipe without two pennies to rub together?"

It was unquestionably true.

The awful tragedy was Lord Burnley offered her everything she'd once thought she wanted. Now she didn't want any of it.

My son may.

The voice came from deep inside. She couldn't deny its brutal veracity.

Her child deserved a future. Undoubtedly a future as Burnley's heir was a better bet than anything she'd supply in the harsh, unforgiving world. She waited for Burnley to harangue, to persuade, to overplay his hand so she could summon her temper and refuse him.

Canny weasel he was, he remained silent.

His green eyes studied her. As if he tracked each thought trudging through her mind and lodging, unwelcome, in her grieving heart.

Still, she resisted inevitable surrender. It was wrong to give herself into this man's keeping when another man possessed her soul.

That other man could never be hers.

Only now did she acknowledge that despite the dictates of reason, a tiny, stubborn trace of hope had lingered that Ashcroft would forgive her. That he'd return to Marsham and beg her once more to marry him. Gallop up on a white charger like a knight of old and sweep her into his arms and tell her everything would be well.

She almost smiled at the fatuous image, even while her heart split finally in two. Drawing in a deep breath, she glanced toward the empty horizon as if checking one last time whether her knight rode to her rescue.

She stared straight at Lord Burnley. "I'll marry you, my lord."

Shaking, Ashcroft collapsed into the chair behind his desk. He gasped like a landed trout and sweat covered his skin.

"Hell . . ." he breathed as dizzying pain racked his body.

It was late. Around midnight. Autumn chill tinged the air

and a fire burned in the grate. His butler, bloody old woman, had looked askance when Ashcroft had ordered the library set up for work tonight.

Perhaps his butler had a point. Just getting downstairs had tested Ashcroft to the limits of endurance. He battled the craven impulse to ring for someone to carry him straight back to his bed. He'd been trapped in this house for two months now. Unless he took his convalescence into his own hands, he feared he'd be trapped here forever.

He'd thought his fitness returned. He'd thought he was ready to tackle the stairs. And after the stairs, perhaps to-morrow a stroll in the square.

He was wrong.

With an unsteady hand, he poured a glass of brandy, spill-ing a few drops on the desk and clinking the decanter against the crystal glass. He swallowed the spirits in one gulp, feel-ing it sear a path to his belly.

His cracked ribs had healed, as had his broken arm. But his leg had been badly smashed in the savage beating at Marsham and clearly still wasn't strong enough to carry him far. Disappointment dug deep. He couldn't bear much more lying around on his back, with nothing to do but stew about Diana Carrick and how she'd played him for a complete clodpate.

His doctors were astonished that he'd survived at all. But then his doctors didn't know what a tonic incendiary rage offered. Some days, he swore if he as much as saw the trai-torous witch, he'd wring her neck.

Other days, his yearning for her was so strong, he'd take her to bed. Then he'd wring her neck.

He preferred the anger. The anger was powerful, ener-gizing, righteous. The yearning left him feeling like a dog starving in a gutter.

Tonight, before he'd come downstairs, he'd dreamed of her. That was nothing new. She'd haunted his delirium from the moment Burnley's bullies had tossed him across his own doorstep like a handful of rubbish. Through his slow recovery, her mocking, deceitful shade had been a constant presence.

He'd give up his hope of becoming a whole man if only he could banish her beautiful, lying ghost forever.

The desk was piled high with bundles of post. More were stacked on the tables against the walls. On doctors' orders, his correspondence and newspapers had been kept from him. But it was more than time he took charge of his responsibilities. Surely once he occupied his mind, Diana's memory would fade. He'd no longer spend every waking hour, and most of his sleeping ones, hating her almost as much as he hungered for her.

The woman might have verged close to destroying him, but he was damned if he'd let her succeed.

With a determined gesture, he grabbed the first packet of letters. His leg still objected to the exercise, and he stretched it out beneath the desk to ease the stiffness. Agony sliced through him, clenching every muscle. When his vision cleared, he started to sift through the mail.

After an hour, he was starting to see double. His leg ached like the very devil, and his head felt like it was full of pea soup. Knowing he'd have to give up soon but unwilling to return to the cage of his bedroom just yet, he lifted one last pile of papers.

A letter dropped to lie on the blotter.

A letter in an unknown feminine hand. Completely against his will, his heart began to pound wildly. Hell, what was the matter with him? He refused to get excited at the possibility that Diana had written. He despised the trull. Anyway, surely she'd long ago married Burnley and currently suffered the torments of the damned as the bastard's wife. Just as she deserved.

Still, his hand trembled when he picked up the flimsy missive.

From its plinth on the bookshelf, the wide alabaster eyes of the Roman head mocked him. He smothered the urge to smash the beautiful little sculpture to dust and returned his attention to the letter.

It could be from anyone. It could be from one of his cousins. Or a former mistress. Or someone requesting his assistance for a charity or in support of some reform in Parliament.

Even as he fed himself those sensible caveats, his heart lodged in his throat. And curse him, he fumbled as he broke the seal.

It took a moment to focus. His eyes went automatically to the signature.

Reality slammed down. The letter wasn't from Diana. Even if it was, what could she say that could possibly compensate for all she'd done?

He drew a deep breath and concentrated on the message. To his astonishment, Miss Smith had written. Two lines only. Informing him Diana was to marry Lord Burnley at St. Mark's in Marsham on Wednesday, 24 October 1827 at ten o'clock in the morning. Then a signature.

He checked the date. The letter was four days old. Tomorrow was the twenty-fourth. Or today, as it was past midnight.

For a moment, he squeezed his eyes shut. The pain in his leg ebbed under the searing memory of Diana's betrayal, the anguish as powerful as it had been in that sweet summer glade two months ago.

Why did you do it, Diana, why?

The question tormented him as it had tormented him since then. Except he knew exactly why she'd deceived him. Because the mercenary trull wanted to be a marchioness. Because she wanted to hold Cranston Abbey in trust for her child.

His child . . .

From hard-won habit, he struggled to close his mind to the thought of his baby. As he closed his mind to memories of that baby's mother.

His efforts were never very effective.

His reluctant attention returned to the note. Miss Smith must believe he cared that his former mistress married her coconspirator.

Miss Smith was fatally wrong. Diana Carrick could rot in hell. He never wanted to see the mendacious bitch again as long as he lived.

With a savage growl that came from the depths of his being, he crushed the letter into a ball and flung it into the fire.

Chapter Twenty-eight

~~~~~~~~~~~~~~~~~~~~~~~~~~~~

*D*iana's wedding day dawned sunny and bright, perfect October weather. Strange to see the world *en fête* when everything should be gray and stormy to match the misery in her heart.

As she trudged downstairs to go to the church, she looked without optimism for her father. Still, her belly cramped with hurt to notice he wasn't in the hall to give her his blessing, however reluctant.

Such a different occasion to her wedding to William. She'd left laughing on her father's arm to walk the short distance to St. Mark's, and her heart had caroled hallelujahs at the prospect of becoming Mrs. Carrick. Her whole life had stretched before her like a richly patterned carpet, a life of companionship and love and fulfillment.

Today, she knew her heart would never sing again. She felt a thousand years old. Soiled to the bone.

Three months ago, this wedding would have proved her crowning achievement.

Three months ago, she'd been a different woman.

Nervously, Diana smoothed the skirts of her yellow silk gown. The dress was part of her London wardrobe, and when she'd put it on this morning, it hung with unbecoming looseness. It would have to suffice. Even if she'd had the heart to get a new dress made, she hadn't had time. After obtaining her agreement, Burnley had quickly organized the wedding.

When she expressed doubts about the rush, he'd told her he wanted no questions about his child's legitimacy. She supposed that made sense, although if she went to full term, the baby would be born six or seven months after the ceremony.

She suspected Burnley was afraid she'd bolt. But she resigned herself to her fate. Where could she go to escape unhappiness? Nowhere. At least marriage provided for her child and gave it a name.

She paused when she reached the base of the staircase and met Laura's compassionate gaze in the shadowy light. "Has he said anything?"

Laura shook her head, automatically identifying the "he" Diana referred to as John Dean. "No."

She looked straight at Laura. "Where is he?"

"In his study. With Mr. Brown."

Pain shafted through her. When she'd told her father five days ago she was marrying Burnley, he'd turned away and he hadn't spoken to her since. If he encountered her in a corridor, and in such a small, cluttered house, avoiding each other was impossible, he treated her like a stranger. She'd tried several times to breach the wall between them, to explain her good fortune would be his as well. He just kept walking as if he were deaf as well as blind.

Fleetingly, Diana contemplated throwing open the study door and insisting her father acknowledge her wedding day. The impulse died as soon as it was born. What was the point? Her father would never forgive her for whoring herself to Ashcroft, for lying, and now for giving herself in a loveless marriage to Burnley.

"You think I'm wrong, don't you?" she asked, although Laura had made no secret that she considered Diana's choices destructive.

"I can't judge you. I don't have the right." Laura touched her arm in a fleeting gesture of comfort. "You're doing this for the baby."

It was the first time Laura had mentioned the pregnancy. "I wanted the house. It was madness." Diana realized she spoke in the past tense, and Laura would notice the telltale slip.

"Yes. Now you know better."

"Now it's too late to change anything," she said bitterly.

Laura's eyes flashed, although her response was calm. "No, it's not."

"Yes, it is," she said finally.

To her relief, Laura didn't argue. Instead, she bent her head as if acknowledging the grim inevitability.

Diana paused to check her appearance in the mirror near the door. When she woke up, she'd been sick. Most days started like that now, but her stomach had since settled. She looked pale and composed. Hardly bridelike but not nearly the apparition of doom she'd imagined. She collected her worn prayer book from the hall table and glanced at Laura. "I'm ready."

It was a lie. She knew that she'd tell thousands of similar lies in the future.

The familiar stone church with its square Saxon tower waited ahead as Diana stepped down from Lord Burnley's carriage. She'd suggested walking, but his lordship had been appalled that his new marchioness planned to arrive at her wedding on foot, like a peasant.

A sign of how protocol would crowd her in future, she supposed. If she ever started to feel again, she guessed she'd find the rules and regulations tiresome.

Right now, like everything else except the life growing under her heart, it didn't matter.

To her relief, the ceremony was to be a quiet one. Lord Burnley had promised a general celebration when the baby was born. Even so, someone, the vicar and his wife she assumed, had decked the doorway with garlands, and Fredericks, who waited outside, appeared incongruously carnivalesque, with bright posies on his hat and in his buttonhole.

She paused in the doorway and swayed as the sickly smell of hothouse flowers hit her. Her vision faded, and nausea, thick and sour, rose in her throat.

Laura grabbed her arm, holding her upright. "Diana, are you well? Do you want to sit down?"

And delay this awful encounter? No, if she did this, she did it now.

"It's just the flowers," she said, panting through her mouth and fighting dizziness.

She pulled away from Laura and took a shaky step inside. Another. Into the cold gloom of the parish church. A deep breath. The haze receded, and her eyes adjusted. Down at the far end of the aisle, Lord Burnley stood before the vicar. Next to Burnley was a soberly dressed older man she didn't know. Some parliamentary acquaintance, she supposed.

The overwhelming perfume still cloyed, but her stomach subsided to a mild rocking rather than a violent heave. The prospect of bringing up her meager breakfast in the nave was too humiliating.

As so often before, pride came to her rescue.

She'd arrived at this pass through her own actions. She refused to faint or cry or cower. She'd confront her bleak destiny with head held high and steadfast heart.

"Are you sure you're up to this?" Laura asked at her side. "Lord Burnley won't mind waiting while you gather yourself."

"I'm ready," she said, just as she'd said at the house.

It was still a lie.

She raised her chin, straightened her spine, and took a pace of spurious confidence. Behind her, Laura and Fredericks fell into line. They formed a de facto train as she walked down the uneven flagstones toward the altar. And her bridegroom.

What happened held a terrible inexorability. As if forces she couldn't control moved her. Once she'd set these events in motion by offering herself to Ashcroft, she'd put herself on the path to this moment.

Around her, the church was hushed and nearly empty. She felt the weight of a thousand watching ghosts in the still air. Not hostile ghosts, but ghosts who whispered that good could never come from a union forged in misery and deceit.

No music accompanied her procession. She was glad. This ceremony was perjury enough without adding the trappings of joy.

Burnley turned to watch. He was beautifully dressed in a black coat she hadn't seen before. He must have had it made for the wedding. The finery only emphasized the exhaustion in his face. In spite of his best efforts, he looked ill and infirm. Although the sharp green eyes were alight. He knew he'd won, against her, against Lord Ashcroft, against his unknown distant cousin, against the whole world.

And he wasn't a man to wear victory lightly.

A gloating smile, the image of the one he'd worn when he told Ashcroft about his parentage, twisted his thin lips. It was clear he basked in unalloyed joy as all his plans came to fruition.

The world was ordered on his terms and would stay that way.

Diana bit back the acrid reflections. She was as guilty as Burnley. More so.

Laura took her prayer book from her and sat in the front pew. Gossip would spread when it became known Diana's father hadn't attended her wedding. A scattering of people formed the congregation. Long-serving staff from the house, mainly. All of them as familiar to Diana as family.

Their expressions indicated the range of responses she'd already received to her betrothal. Shock. Jealousy. Resentment. Sentimental pleasure. Curiosity. Bewilderment. Neither Marsham nor the wider world would ever accept her as the marchioness. Her humble birth would always be held against her.

Her child would triumph. Her child would hold the title unchallenged and receive all respect and duty owed to the marquess. Surely she'd learn to find satisfaction in that knowledge.

Raising her bonneted head, she stared blankly at the man she was about to marry. One of his hands rested on his stick. The other stretched out to take hers as she mounted the short flight of steps to the altar.

Neither of them wore gloves. Burnley's skin was dry, scaly. She was reminded of a lizard or some other cold and reptilian creature.

She bit back a shudder and turned with Burnley toward the vicar. The kindly old face was lined with concern as he surveyed Diana and her incongruous bridegroom. Like everyone at Cranston Abbey, he relied on the marquess for his livelihood. He wouldn't speak against the match, whatever he might think privately.

The service started. She didn't listen. Instead, she let herself drift in a dark sea of chaos. The only reality was that what she did secured her child's future.

Odd to think that until she'd fallen pregnant, she hadn't considered that she and Ashcroft created a new individual. What a foolish, shallow creature she'd been when she entered into this scheme. How she deserved to pay in years of misery.

She realized both the vicar and her bridegroom looked at her expectantly. They must have reached the part where she indicated her willingness to become the Marchioness of Burnley.

The vicar cleared his throat and asked again whether she consented to become Edgar Fanshawe's wife.

She opened her mouth, feeling as though she flung herself off a high mountain. Foreboding shivered through her.

Another voice spoke before she could squeeze the words from her tight throat.

"This marriage will not proceed."

Ashcroft.

For an incredulous moment, she stood stiffly, staring straight ahead. Had she dreamed that beloved voice? She must have. He hated her. He never wanted to see her again.

Burnley didn't move either, although he tensed. "Go on, Vicar."

The vicar, to his credit, looked perturbed and glanced past Burnley down the aisle. "I'm sorry, my lord, but if this man knows of some impediment to the match, I must hear him."

"He doesn't know of any damned impediment, he's just here to cause trouble. Go on, I say, or find yourself another living."

The vicar whitened, either at the language or the furious tone. "My lord, I protest."

Their contending voices faded to a background buzz as Diana snatched her hand from Burnley's and slowly pivoted to peer into the body of the church. Someone stood silhouetted against the light in the doorway. The contrast between the dimness inside and the sunlight outside prevented her seeing him clearly.

Only one man she knew stood so tall and straight, conveyed such leanly muscled power.

"Tarquin?" she asked on a frayed whisper. Her legs trembled, threatened to collapse as she realized he truly was here, not a phantom conjured up by her lonely heart.

"Continue with the service," Burnley snapped, snatching her hand in a grip that hurt for all his physical weakness. He breathed noisily through his mouth as though mustering every ounce of strength.

"This is most irregular." The vicar sounded worried and unhappy.

Diana stood puppetlike in Burnley's grasp. She wanted to run to Ashcroft, fling her arms around him, but some force rooted her to the floor.

"Stop this travesty." Ashcroft's deep voice echoed off stone walls like a command from on high. He shifted from the archway and made his way toward her.

Immediately, Diana realized something was seriously wrong. He'd always moved with a crackling vigor that set her heart racing. Now he walked with a cane, slowly, awkwardly, as if every step pained him.

"What's the matter?" She wrenched herself free and darted out of Burnley's reach down the aisle.

"The result of a slight altercation." Ashcroft's wry amusement was so familiar it made her heart clench with longing.

She blinked away the burning tears distorting her vision. Her breath escaped in a shocked sob.

"Tarquin, what happened?"

She lifted her hands toward him, then lowered them to her sides. She still wasn't sure why he was here, although surely if he hated her, he wouldn't stop the wedding.

Or did he intend some warped revenge? Was he here to discredit her in the eyes of her neighbors and destroy her chance of marrying Burnley?

How could he do that? A scandal wouldn't stop her wedding. Nothing could, apart from her anguished yearning for this man and not the man she promised herself to.

"Tarquin?" she repeated on a rising note.

"Ask your betrothed," Ashcroft said savagely, and the look he sent Lord Burnley scorched.

"Shut your damned mouth, you mongrel," Burnley snarled, and she heard the tap of his stick as he limped down the shallow steps.

"You've been hurt," Diana said brokenly, losing her battle to keep her distance. She ventured a pace closer.

Her horrified gaze drank in the signs of suffering on his handsome face. A long scar, red and angry, marked one lean cheek.

A vivid memory of his leaving the estate in the company of Burnley's burliest footmen assailed her. How could she have missed that the marquess intended Ashcroft physical harm?

In a surge of hatred, she whirled on the man she'd been about to marry. "It's you. You did this to him."

Burnley stared her down with a supercilious expression. "Don't be ridiculous, girl."

"No, it was you." Her voice vibrated with outrage. "It wasn't enough to try to crush him with what you told him. You wanted to kill him in truth."

Burnley dismissed her anger with a scornful huff. "Don't be so dramatic, woman. Come back and finish the service. This fool's interruption is futile. There's no reason you can't marry me."

"Yes, there is," she said steadily. "You tried to kill the man I love."

She heard Ashcroft's soft hiss of surprise behind her.

Burnley clearly wasn't aware that once she found out he'd hurt Ashcroft, he lost all chance of marrying her. "Oh, for God's sake, cease this nonsense and say your vows," he said impatiently.

"Diana, don't."

Ashcroft's voice made her turn. His face was dark and intense and serious as she'd never seen it, even when he'd proposed marriage in the glade. Before Burnley's louts attacked him.

"He hurt you."

"It doesn't matter."

"Yes, it does." Her voice thickened with tears.

"Don't be a ninny, Diana," Burnley burst out behind her. "He's here because taking you away is the only revenge he can wreak."

Ashcroft ignored him. "Come with me."

Burnley's strident voice became a distant clamor. She felt like she drowned in Ashcroft's green eyes. For a moment, nobody else existed.

She drew in a deep breath. Her frozen heart began to beat hard and fast. She took another step, although she didn't yet touch him.

They would have time for touching later, when they left the shadow of this place. Now was time for one word and one word only.

"Yes."

Chapter Twenty-nine

Yes.

The word was a pure note that chimed through Ashcroft's soul. Praise God and all his angels. Let bells ring out. Let fireworks fill the skies.

For a moment, the dark church faded away, and all he saw was light. He looked at Diana, at the joy shining in her face, and wondered how he'd reached this pinnacle.

He was going to marry this wonderful woman. He'd live with her until they were old. She was going to bear his children and turn his chilly barn of a house into a home. The world would never be cold again.

Astonishment paralyzed him. He could hardly believe that his final, reckless throw of the dice had gained the prize. He hadn't arrived with any conviction that his last desperate effort would meet with success. On the excruciating journey down from London, he'd been grimly sure he'd fail.

Yet Diana capitulated as sweetly as the sun rose on a bright new day.

More than capitulated. She offered him her heart with a generous openness that made his own heart slam against his ribs.

He still reeled from hearing her say she loved him. He'd

never expected that. Yet she owned what she felt proudly and without hesitation.

What a woman his Diana was.

He could never condone her actions, but he understood why she'd done what she had. She'd devoted a lifetime to Cranston Abbey, and after her husband's death, he guessed she'd filled the wintry landscape of her widowhood with love for the house.

Burnley, pox on him, had used that dedication to further his rotten schemes.

Which had left Ashcroft with a stark choice. To scotch her from his life because she'd lied, even if she'd suffered as she'd lied. Through all the weeks of cursing her for a deceitful witch, he'd never mistaken that.

Or to forgive her unconditionally.

The choice was no choice at all. He took what he wanted and didn't look back, or he allowed old evil to poison his only hope of happiness.

"I'll take you back to London," he said gruffly, extending a trembling hand. He wasn't ashamed of his unsteadiness. The sea of emotion was too titanic for a mortal man to contain.

"Diana, don't be a fool," Burnley blustered behind him, limping nearer.

"This is most irregular," the vicar fussed.

The small congregation was agog. Every eye fixed on the drama in the aisle. Ashcroft felt their burning attention like a physical force.

Diana smiled at Ashcroft as if he encompassed her whole world. Even the lingering pain of his injuries subsided under that smile. She accepted his hand with a steady grip. "Let's go."

"Burnley, what's all this?" Lord Derwent, Burnley's toady from a hundred parliamentary debates, followed the marquess, as usual without initiating effectual action. "Ashcroft, what the devil are these antics?"

"Fredericks, stop them!" Burnley demanded, ignoring Derwent.

A man loomed up behind Diana in unmistakable threat. Ashcroft recognized the ringleader in his thrashing. The fellow was incongruously and ridiculously bedecked with flowers.

Ashcroft's hand clenched hard on his cane. He'd dearly love to horsewhip the brute, but he was in a church. Nor did he want to risk a riot with Diana here.

Diana didn't spare the thug a glance. Instead, she released Ashcroft and wheeled to confront her jilted bridegroom.

"I will not marry you, my lord. Ever." Her voice was low and laced with hatred. Then in a softer tone, "Let us go. You failed. As you should have failed. For your own vanity and greed, you set out to steal something that wasn't rightfully yours. To my shame, I helped. Let justice be done at last."

Burnley glowered around the church in furious consternation. Enough people were present to start a rumor campaign.

"Shut your mouth, you fool jade," he hissed, raising his hand. "Or I'll make you shut up."

"Touch her, and you're a dead man." Ashcroft knocked the old man's arm aside. Burnley staggered back, almost losing his balance.

It reminded Ashcroft that Burnley was more than twice his age and sick. But the urge to do violence was so strong, he could taste the bloodlust on his tongue. He wanted to crunch the marquess under his heel like a cockroach.

"You'll pay for that," Burnley growled, tottering upright. "Fredericks."

"My lord." The man bowed as a wolfish smile curved his lips. He was bigger than Ashcroft and more heavily muscled. He also had the advantage of a whole body, not one crippled by injury.

Good intentions be damned. Drawing a gasp from the

congregation, Ashcroft slid a small pearl-handled pistol from his coat pocket.

His dear papa's feral rage didn't surprise him. The marquess hated to lose. By stealing away his bride at the last minute, Ashcroft shattered his greatest triumph.

"My lord! This is outrageous! Recollect where you are," the vicar cried in horror, wringing his hands. Nobody spared him a glance. Fredericks halted in fulminating silence when he noted the gun pointed at him.

Ashcroft gestured for Diana to join him. She darted to his side with gratifying eagerness. Her arm snaked around his waist, her softness pressed into his flank. When she'd given him her consent, she'd looked as powerful as the goddess, her namesake. But now he felt her trembling. He rested his arm across her shoulders, partly for support, partly because he couldn't bear not to touch her.

"We'll make it," he murmured for her alone. "I haven't come this far to fail now."

She tilted her bonneted head to look up into his face. Her eyes were as brilliant as a thousand candles. His heart somersaulted as he realized she did indeed love him.

Ashcroft suddenly felt invincible. Burnley and his self-serving plots couldn't defeat them if Diana truly loved him.

His voice was calm and sure as he addressed the contemptible cur who had given him life. "I've got what I want. I mean to leave without causing harm. However, if it's a choice of Mrs. Carrick or the well-being of you and your lackeys, Burnley, you know my decision."

"Don't make this more difficult than it must be, my lord," Diana said quietly.

Burnley sneered even as he shook with chagrin. "You brainless slut. I offer you greatness, and you choose this whoremonger in my stead. May you rue your decision forever." He drew himself to his full height, and his glare sparked with spite. "If you imagine your useless lump of a father will keep his house after this, you're mistaken, madam. And that harlot of a Gypsy can go to hell too."

Laura rose and curtsied with visible irony to the old man. "I'm much obliged, my lord." As if she didn't have a care, she sauntered toward Diana and Ashcroft.

Well said, Miss Smith.

Ashcroft had always liked the girl, right from the first meeting. He now had reason to be eternally grateful to her. "Neither Miss Smith nor Mr. Dean will suffer, Lord Burnley. You forget you deal with a man of equal standing to yourself. There are grave matters outstanding between us, and should I seek legal redress, your name and reputation won't survive unscathed."

"You puling puppy!" Temper contorted the old man's face, and he took a step closer to Ashcroft and Diana although he couldn't hope to prevail. "You think to threaten me?"

"I think to keep what is mine," Ashcroft said in a hard voice.

Burnley growled low in his throat. "Take the drab. You're welcome to her."

"With pleasure," Ashcroft said sardonically, although he didn't lower the pistol. The prospect of revenge still beckoned, but he stifled the impulse.

What was the point? He glanced down at the woman by his side and realized winning was revenge enough.

After this, his enemy had neither family nor wife nor heir of his direct line. His enemy would spend his few remaining days contemplating his abject failure. A fitting end.

"God rot you, whoreson," the old man snarled, vibrating with rage.

Ashcroft supposed that proved as suitable an epitaph to his relationship with his father as any.

He had a golden future to look forward to. Lord Burnley belonged in the past. Perhaps he should even be grateful—without Burnley's machinations, Diana would never have come into his life. He bit back an unworthy urge to thank the marquess for presenting him with such a priceless gift.

"Let's go," he said softly to Diana.

"There's nothing more for us here," she said equally softly, and the smile she sent him conveyed all the things she wanted to say but couldn't while they had an audience.

Cursing his injuries, he limped toward the church door. Diana walked at his side, one arm around his waist, her head held high and a glow in her expression he'd never seen before. Laura followed them, her pleasure unconcealed.

Outside, his carriage waited. Tobias held the door open as Ashcroft released Diana and pocketed his pistol. "We need to collect your father and take him to London, where he'll be safe. I've got servants waiting outside your house. I don't trust Burnley not to take revenge beyond evicting him."

"My father won't want to leave his home. He's stubborn," Diana said, meeting his eyes.

He realized that reaction set in. Diana looked dazed, worried, overwhelmed. When he'd seen her at the altar, he'd been shocked. She'd been pale and drawn, a shadow of the vibrant, spirited woman he recalled. Anyone looking less like a bride was hard to imagine. Briefly, when she'd faced down Burnley, she'd returned to the woman he remembered. But with every moment now, she looked closer to tears.

He wanted to comfort her. He wanted to tell her everything would be fine. But something about her made him keep his distance while they had observers.

And he had an obligation to fulfill. Ashcroft reached to take Miss Smith's hand. He bowed over it as he would to a great lady. "I owe you more than I can say. Thank you."

"It was nothing. I knew you and Diana belonged together the first moment I saw you. I can't explain it."

"If I hadn't received your letter, I'd never have known about the marriage. I would have come for her, but it would have been too late."

Diana frowned in confusion. "Letter?"

Miss Smith straightened and sent her friend a defiant look. "I wrote to Ashcroft the minute you agreed to marry Burnley."

Shocked, Diana stared at him. "She begged you to come and save me?"

He shook his head. "She just told me the date."

Laura smiled. "I knew he wouldn't let you marry that devil."

The sparse congregation surged out of the church, buzzing with avid curiosity. Ashcroft was thoroughly sick of conducting his private affairs under a public gaze. "Let's go."

He handed Diana and Miss Smith into the carriage and leaped in after them, then grimaced as his leg reminded him he wasn't ready to bound anywhere yet. He settled on the seat opposite the two women, his back to the horses. He would give his right arm to sit next to Diana, to touch her. Especially as with every second, she seemed to withdraw further from him.

His injuries must shock her. Was that the only thing that perturbed her?

For one glorious instant inside the church, he'd thought all their difficulties were behind them. Clearly, his joy had been precipitate.

Patience, he reminded himself. He'd waited months for this. He could wait another hour or so.

Diana's gaze glittered with troubled emotion as it settled on him. She took stock of his physical state, he guessed. He loathed that he didn't come to her a whole man.

The carriage rolled into motion. "You don't look like you should have left your bed." Diana's voice was husky. "Will you be all right?"

He shrugged. "The doctors say I'll recover. My leg's the worst of it, and, of course, the scar. But with time, I'll be good as new."

"I'm glad," Miss Smith said.

"But still you've suffered because of me," Diana said almost soundlessly. "It's my fault."

He reached forward and took her hand. It trembled in his, and for one tense moment, he wondered if she meant to pull away. With every second, he felt the chasm between them widening, and, damn it all, he didn't know what to do about it.

He itched to sweep her into his arms, to share everything in his heart, but he needed privacy and time to resolve what still lay unspoken between them. And right now, he had neither.

"It doesn't matter, Diana." He meant it.

"Yes, it does."

He couldn't mistake the flash of guilty devastation in her expression before she turned and stared fixedly out the window. His hand tightened on hers in silent confirmation that the only thing that mattered was that they were now together. He just hoped to hell he could make her believe that too.

Ashcroft had brought an army of servants and a cavalcade of vehicles from London. When he'd made his plans for evacuating John Dean, he hadn't been sure Diana would reject Burnley. If she did, they'd need to get out of Marsham quickly and completely.

To his surprise, Mr. Dean unhesitatingly agreed to abandon his home. Ashcroft realized that after a lifetime in Burnley's employ, John Dean held no illusions about how the marquess was likely to react now his plans were curtailed. Diana's father looked less than overjoyed to have the notorious Earl of Ashcroft in his house, but he was cooperative about his departure.

Right now, Ashcroft didn't care about the reception the old man gave him. He cared about making sure everyone Diana loved was safe. He cared about getting Diana away from this accursed place that had nearly destroyed her.

It was only after a bustling hour, when the house was empty and Miss Smith, Mr. Dean and a bewildered Rex were safely tucked into the carriage, that Ashcroft realized he hadn't seen Diana. She'd supervised the start of the packing, but he couldn't recall catching a glimpse of her since.

Fear carved an icy trail down his backbone. Surely Burnley couldn't snatch her without someone raising the alarm. The place swarmed with Ashcroft's servants.

She must be somewhere finishing up a last task before she left. Still, he set off at a broken run through every room, then the back garden. No sign of Diana. He damned his imperfect body, which moved so slowly when he needed to be in fighting condition.

His heart thumping in panic, he dashed up to the carriage. "Diana's missing."

Miss Smith started to rise, her face tight with concern. "She went inside when we got back from the church."

"Have you seen her since?"

"No."

"Mr. Dean?"

The blind man curled his hands over his stick and frowned thoughtfully. "Have you tried the churchyard?"

"Why would she . . ." Ashcroft stopped, knowing he wasted time, and turned back.

If her father thought Diana might be in the churchyard, that was where he'd look. He had to find her before Burnley did. Grotesque images of the marquess making her pay for her defiance danced through his mind.

"There's a gate through the back garden," Miss Smith called after him.

He paused and turned back briefly. "Go to London. I'll follow." He looked at Tobias, who stood holding the carriage door. "Leave me the gig, the two strongest footmen, and mounts for both of them."

Drawing his pistol, preparing for the worst, he set off at an uneven gallop, ignoring the agony from his injured leg. His pain didn't matter. He had to find Diana. Behind him, carriage doors slammed, and the vehicles rattled away.

His imagination bursting with gruesome possibilities, he barged his way through the gate and into the small graveyard behind the church. Only to find himself in a haven of peace.

No mayhem. No violence. Just late roses, moss-encrusted gravestones, and birdsong.

Ashcroft drew in a deep breath as relief quieted the wild pounding of his blood. Feeling mildly sheepish, he pocketed his pistol.

Diana stood close by. She concentrated so hard on the markers in front of her, she didn't raise her head at his arrival. She'd taken off her bonnet, and her gold hair was lustrous in the sunlight.

Ashcroft limped over to stand behind her. Traversing the rough ground was hell on his leg. He'd left his stick in the house when he'd set out on his frantic chase after Diana.

He immediately guessed why she was here, in spite of the looming danger. The moment her father mentioned the churchyard, he'd known. So he felt no surprise when he found her before two graves, one much newer than the other.

He remained silent as she bent to lay roses on the graves. One for Maria Caroline Dean, beloved wife of John Dean, the other for William Addison Carrick, beloved husband of Diana Charlotte Carrick.

Once Ashcroft had been petty enough to resent William Carrick. No longer. The man had loved Diana, and he'd died far too young. All Ashcroft felt was a piercing compassion for what William had missed.

I'll keep her safe, William. I swear it on my life.

"You're saying good-bye," he said quietly, reaching up to cling to an overhanging tree branch.

His heart clenched when she turned around. She dashed tears from her cheeks, and her voice was raw with regret. "And asking forgiveness. Neither of them would be proud of me."

Chapter Thirty

*A*shcroft abhorred seeing his strong, vivid Diana so hurt and despairing. From the depths of his heart, he vowed to revive the glowing, confident girl who had promised herself to him in the church.

"Diana . . ."

She spoke before he could go on. "You make me so ashamed." Her eyes were the color of slate as they focused on him. "What you did in that church was the bravest thing I've ever seen in my life. It took my breath away. You risked such humiliation, you risked further injury, yet you still did it."

He shifted to ease the strain on his leg. Her unstinting praise was undeserved. He hadn't felt brave. He'd only felt desperate. "I had to try."

"But you should hate me." Her voice cracked with distress. "You *must* hate me."

What purpose lying? She'd immediately see through any comforting falsehood. And there had already been too many lies between them. "Believe me, I did."

She flinched so quickly if he hadn't been watching, he'd have missed it. Her chin rose to its familiar angle but without her usual spirit. He knew her conscience tortured her. She'd set out to deceive, but deceit had never come easily.

"You should still hate me." She swallowed, her slender throat working, and the next words emerged with difficulty. "Your injuries are my fault. Every moment of pain you've endured during the last two months occurred because I wanted something I had no right to possess. Burnley might have given the order for his men to attack you, but the responsibility is mine."

"It takes more than a few beef-witted thugs to kill me, my love."

She chopped the air in an emphatic gesture of negation. "Don't make light of what you went through. I look at you and . . . and I despise myself."

"Burnley used you."

He extended his hand in her direction, but she backed away across the grass as though he threatened her with violence. Cynicism tightened her features. "And I was so eager to be used. Don't blame Burnley for my transgressions. You must know I lied to you from the beginning."

He frowned, lowering his hand to his side. Awareness of danger lurked at the back of his mind. But right now, Burnley and his minions seemed a minor risk to his happiness compared to the corrosive self-hatred he read in Diana's face. "Diana, for the love of heaven, let's put this behind us."

Straightening, he gingerly tested his weight on his injured leg. Red-hot pain lanced through him as he released the bough. He gritted his teeth and rode out the agony. At this moment, he couldn't countenance any possibility of appearing weak.

He had a question of his own, although he already knew the answer. He was surprised to realize he'd always known it, even when his misery made him curse Diana as a traitorous witch.

"Was it really all lies, what happened between us in London?"

"Why should you believe anything I say?" she said unhappily, refusing to meet his eyes and folding her arms in front of her in a defensive stance.

He fell back on the unadorned truth. "Because I believe in you."

"You shouldn't," she said in a thick voice, still not looking at him. Her quivering tension made him resist the urge to fold her in his arms and insist he didn't care about her sins.

He understood why she wanted his anger. Although he could tell that the turmoil she'd suffered in the last months had already punished her to the point of destruction.

For a moment, a taut silence extended. A silence broken by her ragged breathing. Then she chanced a glance in his direction. A frown darkened her face, and she stepped closer, although not close enough to touch him. Again, he had to battle the impulse to drag her into his arms.

"Ashcroft, you shouldn't be standing."

His jaw hardened in stubbornness. "Bugger my injuries. Answer me."

"Please . . ." She drew a shaking breath. "Please sit down, and I'll tell you everything you want."

For the thousandth time, he consigned his physical infirmities to the deepest realms of Hades. "Very well," he said unwillingly.

He limped the few steps to a weathered oak bench not far from the graves. He imagined it was a place Diana had often sat during the quiet, lonely years of her widowhood. Carefully, he lowered himself. While he hated to admit she was right, he couldn't remain upright much longer.

Biting her lips, she laced trembling hands at her waist. Her tone turned low and intense. "Of course it wasn't all lies. The desire was always real."

"Just the desire?" He tensed as he awaited her answer.

"And the love," she said in a choked voice, turning away and staring into the distance as if she made a shameful confession. "I fought against loving you, but how could I stop myself? You're the man I've waited for my whole life."

His hands fisted on his knees even as her admission made

his heart lurch with raw joy. The craving to touch her was like a scream, but he beat it back. "You still love me. Or at least you told Burnley you did."

"Yes, I do love you," she said huskily. She went on as if she hadn't said anything extraordinary. "That only makes what I did worse. I could have stopped. I should have stopped. Once I realized what you were like, once I recognized how I wronged you."

"You were afraid of Burnley."

"No." She looked directly at Ashcroft, and the stark honesty in her face stabbed him to the soul. "Well, of course I was afraid of him. I'm not a fool—he's a frightening man. But the truth is once we became lovers, I couldn't bear to leave you. I knew if I confessed what I did, you'd hate me and send me away."

He derived some consolation from learning that during those tumultuous weeks in London, when he'd felt so helpless against his hunger for her, she'd felt equally helpless.

"When I started this, I wanted the Abbey." Her voice was subdued. "It was a kind of sickness. I'd do anything to get what I wanted, even turn thief and liar and whore."

"I'm sorry I can't give you the house." He'd bring the moon down from the sky if it would make her happy.

He supposed that as Burnley's last surviving offspring, he should summon some interest in Cranston Abbey. He couldn't. He'd seized Burnley's greatest treasure when he stole Diana from his father. Anything else, including the impressive baroque pile that was the Fanshawe seat, came tainted with the old man's evil.

Diana shook her head. "Don't be sorry. Justice has been served. Lord Burnley deserved to fail, and so did I."

No. No, no, no.

His heart slammed against his chest in burning denial. "Do you feel like you failed?" he asked sharply. "Really? Even now?"

Her eyes were stormy with anguish. "I don't care about the

Abbey. I haven't cared for a long time. I only care about you. And I feel like I failed you."

Oh, dear God, he couldn't bear it. Yes, she'd hurt him. Yes, she'd acted against her deepest principles. But he couldn't endure hearing her denigrating herself like this.

Not his Diana. His Diana was proud and beautiful and brave.

With a clumsiness he resented, he jerked to his feet. As his weight came down on his stiff leg, he stumbled.

"Damnation!"

Now was his chance to play the hero, and he proved weak as a kitten. He needed to be strong. He needed to be powerful. In spite of how far they'd come, they weren't free yet. He still hadn't won the lady.

With a choked gasp of distress, she swiftly swung forward to catch him. As her arms closed tight around him, her voice broke with remorse. "Oh, Ashcroft, how can you even bear to look at me?"

"How can I bear not to?" At last he touched her. Her warmth seeped into him like balm, filled every cold, empty corner. For one blessed moment, he stood silent in her embrace, his cheek resting on her hair. She felt like heaven. She smelled like fresh green apples.

With a long, jagged sigh, she buried her face in his neck. Her voice was hoarse and muffled against his skin. "I don't know how you've mustered the generosity to forgive me, but I can only be thankful that you have. I'm yours. I'll stay as long as you want me."

As long as he wanted her?

What the hell was this? He drew away just far enough to look down at her. "What in blazes do you mean?"

"Oh, devil take these tears." She lifted shaking hands to her face, but nothing dammed the endless flow. "Do you have a handkerchief?"

"Of course." He fumbled in his coat and handed her his handkerchief, still puzzling over what she'd said.

"Thank you." Roughly, she wiped her face. "I never cry."

This sounded more like the woman who had seduced him against his better judgment. And to his endless delight.

"I can see that." Still, he couldn't let her strange statement go unchallenged. "Diana?"

Her gaze was unflinching as she crumpled the white square of material in her hand. "I mean I'll be your mistress."

He frowned. She wasn't making a scrap of sense. "I don't want you to be my mistress."

She paled, and he caught a flash of piercing hurt in her eyes. She stepped back, and he felt the distance between him like a blow. Her voice shook. "But in the church, you asked me to come with you."

Ashcroft growled deep in his throat and grabbed her arms with adamant hands. "As my wife."

Under his grasp, she trembled like a leaf in a high wind. "You never said."

"I asked you to marry me after you left London."

Her mouth parted in astonishment. "That was two months ago. When you didn't know what I'd done."

"I know now. I still want to marry you," he said impatiently. He struggled against kissing her. If he kissed her, he wouldn't stop, and he reluctantly acknowledged that they needed to put the past behind them. "It's taken me thirty-two years to propose to the woman I want. It will take more than two months to change my mind."

Her gray eyes widened with stunned disbelief. "But you can't want to marry me. You . . . shouldn't."

He dragged her against him, curling his arms hard around her as if he feared she might try to escape. "I can and I should," he said firmly.

"Tarquin . . ."

For a moment, she stood unyielding in his hold. He braced for protest, argument. Then it was as if something snapped inside her. With a strangled cry, she subsided onto his chest and began to sob with a heartbroken fierceness that made him want to smash something.

"Diana, don't cry. Please, for God's sake, don't cry."

Automatically, his arms tightened around her. She'd been hovering on the edge of control since he'd found her near the graves. But the fury of her breakdown filled him with savage anguish. Feeling completely at a loss, he stood speechless under the torrent of weeping and incoherent apologies.

All the time his brain worked feverishly at what she'd just revealed.

When he'd claimed her in the church, she'd believed he offered her only a temporary liaison. Yet still she'd unhesitatingly chosen an uncertain future with him over a life of luxury and security as the Marchioness of Burnley.

For months he'd wrestled with what she'd done. He hadn't lied when he told her he'd come to terms with the past. He'd thought his forgiveness was complete. He'd thought he trusted her unconditionally.

But somewhere in the murky depths, a drop of doubt must have lingered. Now that last doubt vanished like dew under a hot sun.

Diana loved him unequivocally. She loved him more than Cranston Abbey or her pride or her self-interest. He longed to shout his triumph to the skies.

His arms firmed around her heaving shoulders and she melted against him with a naturalness that made his heart surge. His injured leg protested with standing so long, but this moment was too precious to sacrifice, whatever his pain.

Cry, darling, cry. Then cry no more.

Eventually, the tempest of weeping eased. "You're very reckless with our child's future," he said softly.

"How do you know I'm pregnant?" She spoke into his chest, her voice clogged. "It was far too early to be sure when you came to Marsham."

"Because that's why you were marrying Burnley."

She raised her head and stared up, her face sticky with tears. Her nose was red, and her eyes were awash. He'd never seen her look so beautiful.

"I could have married him for the house." Even now, she resisted any attempt to let her off the full measure of guilt.

He smiled down at her. "Diana, I'm not a fool. I know what the delay in your nuptials meant. If the house was all you wanted, you'd have married him the instant you returned from London. Why wait to reap your reward? I can only guess that without the pregnancy, you'd never have agreed to marry him at all."

She raised a trembling hand to his cheek as if afraid he'd rebuff her. Didn't she know by now that she was everything he wanted in the world?

"I told him no at first. How could I marry him when I was so utterly in love with you? It was sinfully wrong to promise myself to another man. But everything was . . ."

Perhaps one day, he'd accept her declaration of love as his due. But not yet. Perhaps never. "You needed to give the baby a name and a home. I'm sure he threatened your father and Miss Smith too. I know him too well to imagine anything else. Alone and unmarried, what choice did you have?"

The ache in Ashcroft's chest eased as he watched the desperate misery drain from her face. He lifted one hand to press her palm against his cheek.

"I don't deserve your faith," she whispered, scrubbing at her damp cheeks with the soggy handkerchief.

"Yes, you do."

Perhaps over the next fifty years he'd convince her of that. It gradually dawned on him that he needed time and an ocean of love to heal the wounds of the past.

Well, he was certainly man for the task. And today, they'd made a good beginning. But the need to whisk her away to safety became urgent.

"Diana, we should go." He drew her hand away from his

face but kept sure hold of it. He turned and led her into her father's garden. "I don't trust Burnley."

She nodded and pocketed his handkerchief. He noticed she seemed calmer, less poisoned by regret. Even her voice was no longer laced with guilt. "He can't hurt us, Tarquin. Not when we love one another."

Joy welled, threatened to overflow. He stopped and lifted the hand he held to his lips. "I'm so happy about the baby. I've never had a real family."

"We'll make a real family together."

The certainty in her tone ignited imperishable hope in his heart. He and Diana would prevail. They'd struggled through the fires of hell to reach this moment, but now the future extended before them like a broad, sunlit plateau.

His hand tightened on hers. "I'm set on becoming the dullest of fellows. The reformed rake. The faithful husband. The doting father. I hope you won't rue the change, my love."

"Am I, Tarquin?"

He didn't immediately hear the quiet question. Most of his attention focused on whether Burnley's minions skulked ready to ambush them. "Are you what?"

"Your love."

He halted as if he smacked into a pane of glass and released her, Burnley completely forgotten.

Foolish woman. Of course she was his love.

Good God, he'd loved her from the first, although it took him an absurdly long time to recognize it.

Surely she knew. Surely he'd told . . .

He'd never said the words.

Not in the heights of ecstasy. Not when he'd proposed. Not when he'd snatched her away from his despicable father.

What a blundering dunderhead he was.

"Diana, you're my reason for living." He caught her arm and waited for her eyes to meet his. The doubt he saw there made his gut clench. His voice deepened with sincerity. "After the beating, the memory of you kept me alive. The doctors were convinced I'd die. But I had to live to find you. You're my shining star in the darkest night. You're the music that makes my soul sing. You're the air I breathe. You're everything to me."

A faint troubled line appeared between her delicate brows. She studied his face as if what he said made no sense. "But do you love me?"

"What do you . . ." Devil take him, he realized he still hadn't said the words.

He paused and sucked in a deep breath. Strangely what he said next emerged from a deeper part of his soul than his earlier declaration, heartfelt as it was.

"I love you, Diana."

For a moment, she was so still, he thought she hadn't heard him. Then the tension rippled out of her, and her eyes sparkled dazzling silver. "And I love you, Tarquin."

He smiled at her. She was his beloved and his life. "Anything else is a mere afterthought."

She cast him a glittering glance under her eyelashes. His soul expanded with delight as she became again the alluring siren he remembered from all those decadent hours in London. Apart from the tearstains on her cheeks, little trace remained of the distraught woman who had sobbed in his arms.

"Don't you think you should kiss me?"

"Already I become a henpecked husband."

Her lips twitched. "A mere shadow of your former self."

"Indubitably."

"A disgrace to the fraternity of rakes."

"A complete disaster as a rake."

She tilted her head up in unmistakable invitation. "Shall we proceed, my lord Ashcroft?"

He swept one arm around her waist and drew her unresisting body close. "With all my heart, my dear Mrs. Carrick."

For all the lightness between them, his heart gave a premonitory thud. He couldn't mistake the significance of this moment. From here, his existence started anew.

Very gently, he placed his mouth on hers. Passion was never absent when he was with her, but right now, reverence emerged paramount. He loved her more than he'd ever imagined he could love anyone. And against all logic, against all justice, against all common sense, even, she loved him back.

She trembled with swift response and parted her lips, kissing him with a fervor that told him more clearly than words how she'd missed him.

From now on, she'd never miss him again. His Diana indeed.

Forever.

Epilogue

~~~~~~~~~~~~~~~~~~~~~~~~~~~~~~

Vesey Hall, Buckinghamshire
October 1829

$\mathcal{D}$iana, Countess of Ashcroft, rose from the satinwood desk in her sitting room. She placed her hands behind her back for a long and satisfying stretch. All afternoon she'd been poring over the estate accounts.

A child's laugh outside attracted her attention, and she wandered to the open window. In the garden below, Laura presented the young Lady Hester Maria Catherine Vale to her grandfather.

Her heart brimming with poignant joy, Diana watched her father settle the usually rambunctious eighteen-month-old child on his lap. Hester was, without question, a hellion, and she caused endless chaos and trouble. But strangely when she was with John Dean, she transformed into a perfect angel. Now she sat with completely uncharacteristic still-ness while her grandfather traced her face.

Diana heard the door open behind her but didn't turn. The sudden charge in the air told her exactly who it was.

Strong arms circled her waist and drew her against a hard male body. "They're kindred spirits, aren't they?" Tarquin's voice was a baritone rumble in her ear.

She relaxed back against him, glorying in the warm security of his embrace. When she'd married him, she'd loved him to distraction, but two years together had deepened and strengthened the bond between them until she felt they shared the same heartbeat.

"How I wish I had his magic with her."

"You have plenty of magic for me." Tarquin nuzzled her neck and desire sizzled through her. She'd wondered if time would temper her physical response to him. But she wanted him more with each passing day.

She placed her hands over his where they laced at her waist. "I should hope so."

Not that it had been unalloyed tranquillity and joy since her wedding. Her father hadn't immediately reconciled himself to her union with a man of Lord Ashcroft's reputation. At first, his hostility and disappointment had been marked, for all that he'd accepted Tarquin's offer to live with them. Lately, to her relief, she'd noticed a thawing in John Dean's attitude, but a distance still extended between the men she loved. Perhaps it always would.

Her father had needed time to forgive her too, although these days, they regained much of their former ease. Hester helped. It was hard to be on one's dignity in her vivid presence.

The sticklers in society treated the earl and his lowborn wife with disdain. Tongues still wagged about the Ashcrofts' quick marriage and the untimely arrival of their first child. Wild stories about Tarquin's dramatic appearance in the church at Marsham had circulated, and a large segment of the ton was convinced Burnley must be Hester's father.

Diana hardly cared. A little ostracism was small price to pay for happiness. And she couldn't help but be thankful that none of the gossip, however vicious, verged near what had actually happened between her and Tarquin and Burnley. That would ignite a scandal indeed.

"I just went through the post," Tarquin murmured against her skin.

"Oh?" He found the spot on her neck that always drove her wild, and she couldn't summon much interest in letters.

To her regret, he lifted his lips and rested his chin on her shoulder. "The new Marquess of Burnley is setting the ton on its ear. He chews tobacco, he wears moccasins to assemblies, and he refuses to allow people to address him by his title. He's a backwoods democrat through and through."

She laughed softly. "Oh, poor Burnley. He'll be rolling in his grave."

Or burning in hell. Tarquin didn't need to say the words.

Burnley had died at Cranston Abbey a few months after Diana deserted him at the altar. He hadn't lived to learn that his longed-for male heir was in fact a girl.

In her white-hot outrage after discovering how Burnley had ordered Tarquin beaten, she'd wanted him to atone painfully and publicly for what he'd done. But her husband, whose judgment she'd come increasingly to admire, had reminded her that people other than Burnley would suffer if details of their tangled past emerged.

She'd had to find satisfaction in the knowledge that Tarquin's enemy spent his last days stewing on the collapse of all his wicked plots. For a man as addicted to power as Burnley, his impotence in every sense would sting worse than acid.

Tarquin's arms tightened around her, drawing her closer into his big, powerful body. "I'm considering asking for the American's support in Parliament."

"He's your cousin, I suppose."

"He'll never know."

She and Tarquin had discussed ways to straighten the snarled threads of family history. In the end, it seemed best to leave well enough alone. He was Earl of Ashcroft for good or ill. Too late to go back on that, even if he could. But in an attempt at recompense, he'd gifted the eldest sons of the various branches of the Vale family with estates. Most of which the spendthrift fribbles were quickly driving into bankruptcy.

The best of it was that in the process, Tarquin finally made peace with his past. He'd even called Hester after his mother. Yet again, Diana marveled at his generous heart.

"Are you busy?"

A slow smile curved her lips. She knew where this was leading. "Not right now."

"I think Laura and your father will be occupied for a while. Don't you?"

Her smile broadened as she looked out on the sunlit landscape. "It's likely. But I don't want to take you away from anything important."

She still loved to tease him. That hadn't changed.

His hands tautened on her arms, and she felt the impatient nudge of his erection against her buttocks. "Believe me, this is important."

"A large matter indeed."

"Definitely."

As he turned her to face him, she didn't resist. She responded to his kiss with joyous abandon. When he lifted his head, she was breathless.

"You still drive me mad," he groaned.

"I'm glad." She traced the thin white scar down his cheek, the only relic from his savage beating. She rather liked it. It made him look dangerous, a pirate. Her pirate. He no longer walked with a limp, and his body had regained all its former strength and vigor. "But you should be gentle with me today."

He frowned in quick concern. "Aren't you feeling well, Diana?"

Her laughter bubbled with joy. "I'm feeling marvelous. Although that may not last. With Hester, I cast up my accounts with revolting regularity the first few months."

Pleasure illuminated his intense features, and he kissed her quickly. "I'd hoped. When?"

"If I'm correct, next spring."

His stare was purest jade. "Diana, you make me so happy."

The sweet sincerity of his words brought tears to her eyes. "I was horribly weepy in the first weeks too."

The devil's smile appeared on his face, more devilish these days because of his rakish scar. "You just need distracting."

Excitement made her heart race. "Here?"

He arched his eyebrows in the familiar expression. "It wouldn't be the first time."

She twined her arms around his neck and yielded to bone-melting anticipation. "You're insatiable."

His smile was all libertine. His smile was all for her.

"For you, my darling, always."

Have you missed any of these
unforgettable romances by
Anna Campbell?
Turn the page for a glimpse at more
of her sizzling romances with
Avon Books!

✒ *Captive of Sin* ✑

Returning home to Cornwall after unspeakable tragedy, Sir Gideon Trevithick stumbles upon a defiant beauty in danger and vows to protect her—whatever the cost. Little does he know the waif is Lady Charis Weston, England's wealthiest heiress, and that to save her he must marry her himself! But can Charis accept a marriage of convenience, especially to a man who ignites her heart with a single touch?

$\mathcal{T}$here is one alternative." Gideon's tone was neutral, artificially so, Charis thought. His eyes didn't waver from her face. "We could get married."

For one radiant moment, joy flared inside her.

Married . . .

She rose and took an unsteady step toward him. "Gideon . . ." she began as wild happiness exploded in her breast.

His troubled expression halted her in her tracks and reminded her of his pain when she'd told him she loved him. She sucked in a tremulous breath and looked at him properly.

Her glittering palace of hope disintegrated. The hands that had risen toward him fell back to her sides and formed fists of anguish.

"What's this about?" she asked in a flinty voice.

He shifted away from the windows, back toward the fire. He stopped before her, still too far away to touch. Of course.

"It's the obvious solution, Charis." An unexpected moment to realize he'd started to use her real name naturally. He spread his gloved hands as if appealing to her to see things his way. "If we're wed, I have a husband's legal rights."

Since she'd met him, becoming his wife had been a hopeless dream. Now he proposed, and she wanted to run away and cry her eyes out. Because he married her to save her, not because he wanted her as his life companion, the woman in his bed, the mother of his children.

"You said you'd never marry. Never have a family." Her lips felt as if they were made of wood. "That's changed?"

"No." He held himself rigid as a soldier on parade. His voice was implacable. "It will be a marriage in name only."

**ON SALE NOW
FROM AVON BOOKS!**

Tempt the Devil

Olivia Raines has ruled London's demimonde with an iron will and a fiery spirit. Sought after by London's most eligible men, she has never had cause to question her power until she meets the notorious Julian Southwood, Earl of Erith. From the moment he saw her, Julian knew he must possess her. So when he discovers a secret that could destroy her livelihood, Olivia has no choice but to bargain with the devil.

*E*ven as Olivia spoke the words to place her in Lord Erith's bed, her instincts screamed to deny him. Her mind told her she risked no more than she'd risked with any other keeper. Her deepest self insisted the earl threatened everything she'd created since she'd accepted harlotry as her inevitable fate.

Unreasoning fear tightened every muscle.

Fear was her oldest, most insidious enemy. More powerful than any man.

I will not surrender to fear.

And why should she be frightened? Since reaching womanhood, she'd never met a male she couldn't dominate. Lord Erith was nothing special. She'd have great pleasure proving that. To the world. To him. To herself. Her reluctance now was just part of the odd humor that had gripped her since she'd ended her last affair, months ago.

A sharp ache in her wrists made her realize how hard she clutched her hands together. Deliberately, she relaxed her grip, although she already knew he'd noted the betraying gesture.

Something—satisfaction, triumph, possession?—gleamed from under his heavy eyelids.

"Good." He stood and stared down at her. She'd never been so conscious of his impressive height or the latent power in his body. "I'll see you tonight, Olivia."

It was the first time he'd used her Christian name. Given what they'd soon do to each other, the small intimacy shouldn't matter. Somehow it did. That deep voice saying Olivia shredded her protective formality and laid her bare as if she already stood naked before him.

I will not surrender to fear.

She tilted her chin and glared. "I don't entertain my lovers in this house," she said icily.

"I didn't imagine you would." His narrow, sensual mouth curled into a sardonic smile. "I want every man in London to know you're mine. I want to see you. It builds the . . . anticipation."

How could he make such a harmless word sound more decadent than all the profanities she'd heard in a lifetime of whoring? The temperature of her voice sank another couple of degrees. "I belong to no man, Lord Erith."

"You'll belong to me," he said steadily.

**ON SALE NOW
FROM AVON BOOKS!**

☞ *Untouched* ☜

When Grace Paget is kidnapped and spirited away to a remote manor and told she is to grant the inhabitant his every desire, she risks everything to save her virtue . . . Lord Sheene knew nothing of the plan to bring him this woman, and wants nothing to do with the scheme. But as the unlikely pair find themselves ensnared in a deadly web, they also discover freedom and breathtaking passion in each other's arms.

*L*ord Sheene kept his back to Grace as he looked out into the twilight. Yet again, his isolation struck her. His physical isolation. And also his spiritual isolation. Perhaps that alone constituted his madness. So far, she'd seen little other sign of his affliction.

He spoke without turning. "Stay away from Monks and Filey. They don't make idle threats."

Again, that instinctive animal awareness of what happened around him. Were all madmen so attuned to their surroundings?

She wouldn't have thought so.

A sudden memory pierced her of his intense concentration on the spindly rosebush that morning. His hands had been so deft, their very sureness breathtakingly beautiful. Her wayward heart dipped into an unsteady dance at the thought of those hands on her skin.

Grace, stop it! You're in enough trouble as it is.

Heavens, she must regain self-control and quickly. The last thing she needed was an infatuation with her fellow captive.

She hadn't thought about a man touching her for pleasure in years. Certainly not since her marriage and the collapse of her girlish fantasies.

She stepped up to stand beside him. The window faced the darkening woods. The day had been clear. Now the first stars shone in the cloudless sky. It could have been a landscape by Claude. If one didn't know an unscalable wall circled the trees or two homicidal devils guarded the gate to this perilous Eden.

The silence allowed her to say something she was guiltily aware she should have said earlier. "Thank you, my lord. If you hadn't come . . ."

"Don't think about it." He focused those uncanny eyes on her. Except that after a day and a half, she noticed their strangeness less and their beauty more.

"I can't help it." She'd been frightened and wretched for so long, even before her abduction. But nothing matched the horror that had gripped her when Monks stared into her face and promised rape and death. Compared to that, the mad marquess was a bastion of security. The clinging ghost of today's panic made her speak more freely than usual. "You were magnificent."

**ON SALE NOW FROM
AVON BOOKS!**

ℰ Claiming the Courtesan ℳ

The Duke of Kylemore knows her as Soraya, London's most celebrated courtesan. Men fight duels to spend an hour in her company, and only he comes close to taming her . . . Dire circumstances have forced Verity Ashton to barter her innocence and change her name for the sake of her family. All she wants is her freedom, but with a notorious rogue determined to possess her in every way possible, can Verity ever escape the man who claims her both body and soul?

I thank Your Grace for your continuing kindness." Soraya stepped toward Kylemore and kissed him on the mouth.

They rarely kissed, and a kiss as a gesture of affection was an unprecedented event.

But that was what this felt like to Kylemore. She wasn't trying to seduce him. After a year, he would recognize seduction. And he'd already given her the extravagant pendant. Even greedy as she was, she couldn't hope to coax another maharajah's bauble from his pocket.

No, he could only assume she kissed him because she wanted to.

That revolutionary idea had just taken hold when she drew away. The soft pink lips that had clung so sweetly to his, and sweetly was the only word he could bring to mind, curled into a faint smile. "Good day to you, Your Grace."

He snatched at her hand and, still lost in the memory of her kiss—which was absurd given the debaucheries they had indulged in all afternoon—raised her slender fingers to his lips with the reverence due a princess.

When he lifted his head, he caught a bewilderment that matched his own in her silver eyes. "Good day to you too, madam."

He released her and strode from the room, down the stairs, and out of the villa he'd bought her a year ago. But no matter how far he went, he couldn't quite banish the memory of her mouth on his in a kiss that was almost . . . innocent.

His infamous, dangerous, enigmatic Soraya. And he was no closer to understanding her now than he'd been six years ago.

**ON SALE NOW
FROM AVON BOOKS!**

If you love Anna Campbell
and are looking
for more scintillating passion
in a contemporary setting,
you won't want to miss rising star
Toni Blake!
Turn the page for a sneak peek
at the latest installment
in Blake's Destiny series . . .

Sugar Creek

*When Rachel Farris ran from Destiny, Ohio, fifteen years ago,
she had no intention of returning. But with her grandmother in
danger of losing her apple orchard to a family enemy, Rachel
decides to head back long enough to save the day . . . and then
leave just as quickly. Gruff, by-the-book police officer, Mike
Romo, wanted the land stolen from his family decades ago, but
he wasn't prepared to contend with shapely trouble in tight de-
signer jeans. And neither sexy cop nor prodigal hometown girl
anticipated the snapping electricity that threatens their most
carefully laid plans.*

$\mathcal{T}$he first thing Rachel noticed was the way he scowled at
her from behind typical mirrored cop sunglasses.

And the second was . . . oh dear. Oh *my*. Her throat went
dry.

He was no Deputy Dawg—and a far cry from Barney Fife. In
fact, he was . . . a cop *god*. With thick, dark hair and olive
skin, a day's growth of stubble covering his strong jaw, and
shoulders that filled out his beige uniform quite nicely, he
was . . . shockingly hot. Even behind mirrored sunglasses.
And in Destiny, of all places! How was that possible?

But then she recalled her friend Amy—who still lived
here—mentioning some sexy-as-sin Romo being a town po-
liceman. Her heart beat faster than before, and she suddenly
had to work to control her breathing.

Even while he snarled at her.

But wait—stop. Get hold of yourself.

Sure, he's hot—but he's a Romo. And a mean, growly one at that.

He proved her point by glancing back down to grouse, "Out-of-state license."

"That would be because I live out of state," she heard herself reply dryly. She didn't normally talk back to cops, but apparently she just couldn't take this attitude from a Romo lying down.

Not that she would *mind* lying down with him. If he were a little nicer. And not a Romo, of course. But he *was*—and her unwitting attraction to him was making her all the more irate.

Her remark earned another handsome scowl, to which he added, "Edna's not frail or ailing, by the way. So your excuse doesn't fly."

Oops. Clearly, he knew the town well enough to know Edna was the only Farris left who might have a granddaughter coming to see her. "Well, that's not how *she* tells it," she argued. "All I know is that she summoned me to help with the apple harvest, so that's what I'm doing—if you'll kindly let me go on my way."

To her surprise, he lowered his chin, appearing suspicious. "You don't look like much of an orchard worker."

Who asked you? She bit her tongue for once, though, and tried to regain her composure. In fact, it suddenly hit her that all her powers of persuasion had pretty much gone out the window somewhere along the way. So she gave her head a confident tilt, and in her smoothest voice replied, "My skill set might surprise you." And . . . hmm, was that being confident—or flirting?

"And no way I'm letting you off that easy," he added.

Okay, didn't matter whether it was confidence or flirtation since, either way, it hadn't worked. So now *she* scowled at *him*. "Come on, Romo, cut me a break."

When his dark eyebrows rose behind those sunglasses, she realized what she'd just said—but again, she couldn't let him . . . *win*. Since, that quickly, that's what it felt like with this guy—a matter of winning or losing. Farris *vs.* Romo. She couldn't let him get the best of her without at least fighting back.

"I've got news for you, *Farris*," he practically growled. "Maybe you can argue your way out of tickets up in Chicago, but not in Destiny. You were going twenty over the limit."

Whoops. Twenty? Really? Still . . . "Can I be honest with you?" It was time for a new tactic.

"All right," he said dryly, sounding doubtful already.

But that didn't stop her from gazing up into that sexy cop-god face, and saying, with true sincerity, "When such a low speed limit is posted on such a wide-open stretch of highway, I don't actually know how a person can be expected to *go* so slow. I'm sure you know what I mean—it's nearly impossible."

And when he peered down on her, his expression softening a bit, she suspected he was beginning to understand her point—and she found herself wishing she could see his eyes. Were they as gorgeous as the rest of him? What color were they? Brown, maybe? That was when he said to her in a completely patronizing tone, "Let me explain it to you, Farris. You *ease. Off. The gas.*"

Okay, he was hot as hell—but still a jerk. So she forgot all about his eyes and said, "Romos always *were* smart-asses."

"Farrises," he announced, "*set the bar* for being smart-asses. Not to mention the fact that they have a long history of not abiding by the law."

All right, that might be true, but she still rolled her eyes in an exaggerated manner and tried to look deeply insulted. "Can you just give me my ticket now so I can get to Edna's before she has a heart attack or something?"

Mike Romo seldom stood around arguing with traffic offenders, but something about this woman had gotten under his skin, quick. Maybe the fact that she was a city girl to the bone, made obvious not only by her arrogant attitude but by the stylish haircut that didn't quite reach her shoulders, the trendy dark jeans she wore, and the sleek-looking scarf hanging loose around her neck. Or maybe it was because she was extremely attractive—blond, slender, the works—and had probably thought that would get her off the hook. Or . . . maybe it was just because most people didn't have the nerve to backtalk him when openly breaking the law.

"I *could* arrest you, you know," he informed her—mainly because her lack of regard for authority pissed him off. Yet as he heard his own words, something low in his gut warmed, and he realized he could think of a plenty of things to do to her that would be a lot more pleasant than arrest.

SUGAR CREEK: A Destiny Novel

By Toni Blake

**ON SALE NOW
FROM AVON BOOKS!**

At Avon Books, we know your passion for romance—once you finish one of our novels, you find yourself wanting more.

May we tempt you with . . .

- **Excerpts** from our upcoming releases.

- Entertaining **extras**, including authors' personal photo albums and book lists.

- Behind-the-scenes **scoop** on your favorite characters and series.

- **Sweepstakes** for the chance to win free books, romantic getaways, and other fun prizes.

- Writing **tips** from our authors and editors.

- **Blog** with our authors and find out why they love to write romance.

- **Exclusive content** that's not contained within the pages of our novels.

Join us at
www.avonbooks.com

AVON

An Imprint of HarperCollins*Publishers*
www.avonromance.com

FTH 0708